A GREAT BIG SHINING STAR

Niall Griffiths was born in Liverpool in 1966 and now lives in Wales. He has published seven novels: *Grits*, *Sheepshagge*r, *Kelly + Victor*, *Stump*, *Wreckage*, *Runt*, and *A Great Big Shining Star*. The film of *Kelly + Victor* was released in 2013.

NIALL GRIFFITHS

A Great Big
Shining Star

VINTAGE BOOKS
London

Published by Vintage 2014

2 4 6 8 10 9 7 5 3 1

Copyright © Niall Griffiths 2013

is available from the British Library
ISBN 9780099507680

The Random House Group Limited supports the Forest Stewardship Council® (FSC®), the leading international forest-certification organisation. Our books carrying the FSC label are printed on FSC®-certified paper. FSC is the only forest-certification scheme supported by the leading environmental organisations, including Greenpeace. Our paper procurement policy can be found at: www.randomhouse.co.uk/environment

MIX
Paper from
responsible sources
FSC
www.fsc.org   FSC® C016897

Printed and bound in Great Britain by Clays Ltd, St Ives Plc

To Deborah
once more
a light
alight
in endless
night

FIRST

Celebrity is the acceptance of any man or of any group of men as in some way valuable to mankind. To investigate the problem, we shall have to define celebrity. We shall also have to define mankind.

Fernando Pessoa

SOME WORDS, STILL, or some sounds like words, howling from her holes and wrapped around the blundering blade:

FAAAAAAAAYYYYYAAAAAAMMMMMMMM

NEEEEEEEEEEEEEEEDDDDDDD

LIIIIIIIIIIVVEEEE FURRRRRRVVVRRRRRRRR

FFFFFFFFFAAAAAAYYYYYYYAAAAAMMMMM

YOU SEE MEEEEEEEEE

NOW YOU SEE MEEEEEEEEEEEEEEEEEEEEEEEE

And the screaming and the spurting and the red red fog around these sounds like words:

GIIIIIIIIIVVVVVVVVEEEE MEEEEEEEE

GIIIIIIIIIVVVVVVVVVEEEEE

MEEEEEEEEEEE

And the little children thrashing below, the little red-streaked children, the spattered children shrieking, floundering, chased by the sounds like words riding on the wild and unleashed shapes of blood:

GRRRRRRRAAAAAAYYYYYYTTTTT

BIIIIIIIIIGGGGGGGGGGGG

SHEEEEEEEENNNNNAAAAAANNNNNN

STAAAAAAAARRRRRRRRR

And then water. No pain. Then nothing of this earth.

AND

I beseech you, therefore . . . by the mercies of God, that ye present your bodies as living sacrifices, holy, acceptable unto God, which is your reasonable service.

Romans 12:1

WINTER

—It hurts, mum.

The weight of the dressing, as if there is another face on Grace's face. Or the swelling of her own, as if another face inside her face is ripping its way through to be seen, with talons, scalpel-talons.

The car leaves the carriageway and moves down a slip road and through a village which suggests a world removed from that one in the mechanical thunder on the overpass above which keeps the beamed pub in almost permanent shadow below. Here, red-brick cottages abut fields, all traffic is stilled, two hunched smokers huddle in the doorway of the Farmer's Arms and the branches of trees still bear traces of off-white snow like a growth, like mould. They pass horses, Grace and her mother in the car, two big brown horses standing at a fence, their breath fogging their faces as if they burn inside. Grace takes them in at a glance. Says it again:

—It really, really hurts, Mum.

—I know it does, love. But end of the day it's gonna be worth it, yeah? You'll see. When them bandages come off, you'll see.

—When's that?

—What?

—When the bandages come off.

—They can come off soon but the splint's got to stay on for a couple of weeks, yeah? Them plugs as well, the surgeon said.

—These plugs? A couple of *weeks*?

—What they said.

Grace moans.

—Grace, you wanted this, love. And I paid good money for it, yeah? Take some more codeine if it's hurting. In the glovebox, there. Water in there as well.

Grace pops two pills from the blister pack and swills them

down with water, winces as she swallows, coughs and whimpers with the pain. She wants to look at herself in the vanity mirror on the sun visor but she's already seen herself and she knows, and loathes, what she looks like: the blue-bruised eyes in the swollen red sockets, the straight H-shaped lines of the splint like an insult to the curvature of her face, the bandages already manky with leakage. Yesterday, in a big brown building in the big city just over the border to the east, masked men had, in an overlit room behind the room with the stack of magazines and the fishtank in which the bog-eyed fish swam aimlessly saying 'oops', knocked her comatose with drugs as she lay supine on a table under a burning white light and then they drew on her face, on the clear skin of her face, and then put a nail-like implement, a chisel-like thing, up her nostril and hit it three times with something that looked like a hammer, *was* a hammer, a small hammer. Blood leapt and ran, it did, shocking red under the bright white light. Steel tools were laid out, clean and gleaming and sharp as razors. Blades, hooks, grapples, vices. The men forced tubes into Grace's throat, pushing insistent against the resistance of muscle. The xylocaine in Grace's system, before it turned her face into a mask, caused skin and muscle to twitch and jitter, jump, and the girl in her catatonia turned her head a little to the left and whimpered and moaned. The men clamped her head still, twinned that clamp with a smaller one on her nose. Used the hammer and chisel-thing, hit and hit until the bone at the bridge broke and the entire nose when it was wiggled between latex-gloved finger and thumb crunched and gave and sank like a rotted plum. Each nostril was then prised open giving out blood, another large gout, and a scalpel-thing was wormed in and sickle-shapes of cartilage sliced away, sawn away, and deposited on white cloth on a gleaming silver tray where they lay, earthworms in the sun, once-living things desiccated, dead, under the always-burning overhead light. Bits of flesh, matter, tweezered out of the bloody-black runnels the nostrils had become. Curls and twists, maroon and purple and scarlet. Bruises began to bloom. *OK*, said one of the men in the masks. *Now we can really go to work. Now we can make good.* The spike

8

was removed and replaced with a spatula-thing which was held in place while another masked man took up a 3 lb hammer. *Precision is everything*, the man mumbled behind his mask, below his eyes lit with a flashing spark of what? Creation? Endeavour? *Now we must break the nasal bones*. Four ungentle strikes with the hammer, nose bone cracked with a sound that bounced off the shining walls of the room and more blood gushed. *Let's see what comes out*. Then the earthworms. The purple worms and red rice-grains. Then stitches and a splint and plugs for the nostrils. Grace lying there unconscious with a face turning black and her mouth slack around tubes, yesterday, in the big brown building in the big city to the east.

A hedged lane, outside the car. Barely wide enough for the vehicle; unleafed branches, frosted bluey-white, scratch at the wings. Grace moans again.

—Alright, love, don't go on, yeah? Pills'll start working soon.

And an hour after the shredding, in that big brown building in the big city, Grace had been awake, hardly alert, in bed, next to flowers in a vase, her eyes just slits in a pink and swollen head. Her mouth hanging open to breathe around her plugged and pummelled nose and the plasters and bandages wedding-caking her face. She said something, some vague entreaty, in a weak and small and laboured voice and one of the masked men now without his mask leaned over her and said: *Your nose came out really really nice*. Bruised and blooded Grace. Battered Grace. The bleeping of a machine. Receptacle to vomit in next to the bed. Her eyes looked up at the leaning man, her eyes deep in dressing and flesh outraged. Exhausted and terribly unwell she looked yet she said something about *Christmas* and *something good at the end of it* and the leaning man now without his mask looked pleased.

The car crests a hill. Below is a town and behind that town is the sea, grey and lagging under a same-coloured sky. Only a straight horizontal of dark distant cloud to separate water from air.

—I need a pee.

—We're nearly home, Mum. Can't it wait?

—I know we are love but I've got this weak bladder. You know what it's like. I'll stop off at the Nag's Head.

She turns the car into the car park of a pub but the pub has wood instead of glass for windows and a FOR SALE sign above the door. Already the paint in the frames is beginning to scale and flake.

—Shite. When did *this* one close down? I'll have to go behind a tree.

—A tree? Can you not just wait until we get home? We're nearly there, yeah?

Grace's mother doesn't respond. Parks the car at the bottom of the car park, where trees and undergrowth encroach. She takes some tissues from the box on the dash and tells her daughter she won't be long and leaves the car and vanishes into the bushes.

The engine begins to cool and tick. Grace hears birdsong and shivers in the bit of winter that had pounced into the car when her mother opened the door. She feels the empty building behind her, the wrestling greenless vegetation in front of her, the flat macadam beneath the car. She gently touches the bandages on her face. Fingers her hair bundled up on to the top of her head, matted slightly and needing a wash. This new nose on her. This new face on her. The dusting of snow on the branches around and mottling the car park and on the peaks of the old pub's roof. All these still and silent things being nothing but what they are. Tick, tick. Faint moan of wind. A grumble from Grace's midriff beneath the padded jacket because she had to fast before they smashed and then rebuilt her nose. The drugs. The numbing drugs. Rearranged the rubble on an empty stomach. Soup. Or cheese on toast. The birds twitter and chirrup and for what? An internal bubbling begins, somewhere in her breast. The left side of her brain begins to tug at the other, as if in an attempt at escape, at unmooring. Her skin begins to tingle. It is like panic. Grace presses the radio on but there is no reception here and the abrupt roar of static makes her brain tug tighter and her heart trip harder. Still those things – the naked trees, the empty pub – remain outside the car. Trees and the building and the bushes and the car park and behind her there is a road and along that road is a housing estate and beyond that is the town by the sea where Grace lives and has always lived but here in this abandoned car park next to the abandoned pub and pressing up against the misting windows of the car all other things are older than Grace, older than her mother, older than man. Not just those big bare trees which will soon bloom green again but the hill on which the car rests and on which her mother urinates and the seething soil beneath the tarmac and the boiling lives that thrash in that soil or, once-lives, rot. No fence no walls only that dirt beneath the potted tarmac and the tiny creatures beneath the bark of the trees and the earth too in which they are rooted, these all out-age Grace with the wounded face and her mother squatting unseen. They are just what they are, these things, and their existence is a stillness. It is a gigantic quiet. An immense stillness set against the frantic fluttering in Grace's chest and head and on her skin and she is about to wind the window down and scream for her mother when she sees her mother reappear from the bushes and come towards the car.

—That's better. Bloody bladder drives me mad. What's wrong, love?

Grace sinks down into her seat and shakes her head. —Let's just get home. I'm hungry and I'm tired, yeah?

—Course you are, love. You've been in the wars. And you've been dead brave.

They reverse out on to the road and head down the hill towards the town and the sea.

—I'll make you a nice big bowl of tomato soup and you can have a sleep. Like that? And then I'll run you a nice hot bath. End of the day, love, you've got to pamper yourself, after what you've been through, yeah?

Grace sits quiet, swallowing something down, feeling it rock to a settling with the movement of the car. Her town begins with some neat pebble-dashed bungalows, square small gardens speckled with frost. She passes the signpost for the town, the name of it up there, and she remembers the time when Robbie Rossiter who she last heard had become a fireman spray-painted a giant knob and balls on it with teardrops squirting out of the end. Long removed now but the memory usually makes her smile. The outrage in the local paper. What is the world coming to. In my day. When I was a lad. She passes her old school which she left a couple of years ago on one of the happiest days of her life and she'd give it a sneer were it not for the fact that that small movement of her face muscles would hurt even underneath the codeine. Look what I'm becoming *now*. Call me a waste of space *now*. One day you'll see, you'll see, you'll see, and that day is coming. She's heading towards it. There is no commotion inside her any more, she left that writhing on the cold car park of the useless and gutted Nag's Head pub on the top of the hill which is nothing now but a route out of the town in the same way that she left bits of the old Grace in that big brown building in the big city to the east over the border, behind her now.

At home, her mother sits her in front of the TV, wrapped in a fleece, and makes her soup and bread. Not toast; soft bread so as not to scrape her sore and swollen throat. Grace eats, just bird-like nips and nibbles, from a tray on her knee while she watches *The Xtra Factor* and then she sleeps for a while on the sofa and when she awakes she has a hot and frothy bath and is pleased that the mirror on the bathroom wall has misted over so she cannot see herself but in her bedroom, smelling nice, and comfortable in her Silly Moo PJs and Ugg boots, she sits at her dressing table and looks at her face and cries and her mother sits by her and comforts her and tells her that it's all going to be worth it, the pain, the discolouration, it'll all be worth it when the bandages come off, you'll see, end of the day. Grace releases some tears for the bits of her left behind, over the border, the bits of her labelled Hazardous Material and incinerated in that big brown building. Her lost nose. Her old nose gone and burnt, never thought she'd miss that ugly horrible thing with the bump at the bridge and the nostrils too flared, fine nose, really, but imperfect is not good enough. She's always known that. Her mother leaves her and goes downstairs to make food and night has fallen now and Grace turns her computer on and as it boots she takes her mobile and holds it at arm's length and photographs her own face and studies the images then sends them to her Facebook page and sits down at her desk, the desk scattered with gonks and cosmetics and dirty cups and glasses and copies of *Heat* and *OK!* and *Grazia* and scribbled-on Post-it notes, luminous pink, most of which baffle her. What are they meant to say? To tell her? What cryptic messages did she expect herself to recollect how to decode? A cut-out picture of Jennifer Aniston with her nose circled in black biro. Angelina Jolie, the same, Pixie Lott too. Grace fingertips her newly washed and still-wet hair back over her ears and skims her home page, which tells her again that thousands of miles out in space a vast ball of fire and ice is hurtling towards her at a speed unimaginable and that fires in foreign countries have taken hundreds of lives as have droughts in other countries far away and floods in still others. Tells her again that life on Earth is due to shrivel and die and that Katie Price has been photographed in a nightclub with a cross-dressing cage-fighter and here's that photograph, click for more, Grace does, closes her eyes and has unwanted and unsummoned memories of a wave of water one Boxing Day a few years ago, the bloated floating bodies drifting past like aubergines, and here's a turmeric-skinned woman with huge and invented tits holding hands with a man in make-up. Here's ten more photographs of that same woman with that same man. Not in fire and not in ice but in an ever-spreading wetness.

Grace examines the pictures of the woman and the man in the nightclub for a while then accesses her Facebook page and already she has two messages:

signet to a swan, babes

and

butterflies from caterpillars
end of the day Grace it'll be worth it
thinking of getting it done myself
take the plunge girl!!!!!!!!

She reads these several times and studies the pictures of herself. Glad she washed her hair. Is that me? That's me. Behind these bandages there's a new me. The me I always should've been.

Her mother calls her down for food and over shepherd's pie they watch *I'm A Celebrity . . . Get Me Out Of Here!* Men eat worms. Women swim in shit. Both men and women eat insects and when they spew Grace and her mother laugh. The regurgitated legs, jointed, and wing cases and antennae. A wonder turned to puke. Animal's eyeballs pop between bleached and capped teeth and ichor shoots and sight goes to shite and Grace and her mother as one go: —Eeeeeewwwww!, and eat their shepherd's pie.

Her mother washes the dishes as Grace watches *Big Brother.* Then they both eat Ben & Jerry's Chunky Monkey ice cream and watch *Big Brother's Big Mouth* and then they watch a couple of soaps that Grace's mother had recorded for her last night while Grace was knocked out in the big brown building to the east. Grace's belly begins to bloik and gurgle and she groans and does a stomach-clutchy thing and leans forwards in her chair dry-retching and her mother asks her what's wrong and Grace runs to the toilet followed by her mother and bends herself over the bowl and vomits as her mother stands over her holding her hair back out of the way of her face. Half-digested potato and mince in a thick maroon gruel clotted black.

—It's alright, love, her mother says. —You've been swallowing blood all day. Doctor said this would probably happen.

Another lurch and heave, more matted blood-clumps. Grace's back buckles and flounders and her mother makes croony, soothing noises and then helps Grace to wash her face and stands there watching as she brushes her teeth wincing and 'ow'-ing and gargles with mouthwash. The nasal dressing damp with sweat and tears. Grace fans her own face with her fingertips and blows air out through her mouth and her mother leads her to her bedroom and puts her gently underneath the duvet and then fetches her some hot chocolate and a couple of small white pills.

—Codeine. And a temazepam, just a small dose, yeah? Help you sleep.

She props her daughter up on pillows, tells her that she mustn't lie flat in case pressure is put on the shattered nose. Grace tells her that her face is hurting and she answers that she knows it is but it'll feel better in the morning and it'll all be worth it in the end. Tells her that the doctor said that the bleeding will continue for some days and the cotton-wool plugs will need to be in for a fortnight but that there's plenty of painkillers in the house and that she's proud of her, so proud, her Grace, her dad would be proud, too. And her grandad. She has brought in a washing-up bowl and placed it at the side of the bed and she points this out to Grace in case she needs to be sick again and she tells her that if she needs anything, doesn't matter what the time is, just call for her mum and she'll come. She sits on the edge of the bed until her daughter is asleep and then she leaves the room and returns downstairs and watches more telly, *The Only Way is Essex*, then takes a temazepam herself and goes to bed. The lights off in the house except for the weak beam of the nightlight on the landing at shin level. For the weak bladder, the small-hours toilet treks. Faint bumps and creaks as the house cools, settles into itself in the winter town at the edge of the sea.

A few hours later, in the half-dawn, Grace half-wakes to the pain returned to her face. Propped up in a sitting position against the headboard she opens her eyes and regards the objects in her room, their shapes returning as the world spins back to light, a grey half-light as yet. The idling computer on the desk, the screen black but ready to leap to life and colour at a touch. Willy Roberts leaning over it from the wall. The mounds of shoes, the hanging clothes, the posters, the piles of *OK!* and *Heat* and *Hello!*. She feels a sneeze building and a fear with it, images of her nose flying off in all directions like red and wet streamers, but the urge passes. Once her nose contained forty million receptor cells in the epithelium, but many of those were cut off and burnt and replaced, it seems, with mere pain. She sits half-awake in the silence and the half-dawn. Scratches her leg with a fingernail. Pruritus; an irritation of nerve endings evolved as a way for the body to fend off tiny attackers. Mites and parasites. Scratch scratch. Sandpaper sound. Skin surface receptors pick up the minuscule movement in the nerves and issue a warning signal to the cerebral cortex, which sends an order to scratch. Grace's fingernails dislodge the irritant, whatever it is. Too small to see. Scratch scratch. Insect bite or reaction to cloth or the residual detergent in that cloth or the dye. Half-upright and half-awake in the half-light Grace sits and scratches her leg and then touches delicately the H-shaped dressings on her face and yawns and winces, sucks air in over clenched teeth. Breath of especial depth triggered by an automatic reflex that fills the lungs to capacity and expels carbon dioxide, other toxic exhaust. Breath rate falling with tiredness thereby taking in less oxygen so the yawn a rebalancing or a restabilisation of pressure around the eardrums or as a way even of cooling the brain since a cold brain is more alert than a hot one and is there a skull adrift on the earth that does not swell with temperatures hectic and fervid? Such small wonder, though, on the rumpled bed, here in the half-light.

There's a noise outside, in the small garden beneath the window of Grace's bedroom. Something falling over, not a clatter, a slide and a soft thump; plant pot, perhaps, a bin bag full of rubbish, something. Grace gets out of bed unsteady and moves to the window, the bare soles of her feet whispering in rhythm on the carpet. Pulls the curtains aside and looks out and down. Feels the generated coldness of the glass against her injured face. Sees the garden beginning to shadow in the grey half-light, the patches of ice and snow on the small square of grass and mantling the wheelie bin and the frame of the bicycle propped up against the back brick wall. By that bike's rear wheel is a toppled bin bag which ripples a little as if in a wind yet there is no wind and Grace looks and sees a shape detach itself from the shadows and become a cat, a black and white tom with a KFC bone in its mouth, one of the group gone feral that haunts the ginnels and alleys behind the Chinese takeaway on the promenade. They wail, sometimes, these cats. At night-time they stand on garden walls and car roofs and make noises like abandoned souls. Growls and yowlings, an ugly music that can make the skin creep on Grace's forearms. She watches the tomcat, now, watches him strut lordly on the wall, stepping delicately through the shards of glass half-buried in the cement, stepping with a grace exquisite and sure, never once nicking his paws.

The bone in his mouth. How he walks, down there, a blue-blood, without urgency but possessed of a certain knowledge of, and complete comfort in, himself. What he is is what he is, a tomcat on a wall in the half-light with a scavenged chicken bone in his jaws and he needs nothing other, ever, than this. Just his catness: a body that shows no sharp angles to the wind of the world. Something shudders through Grace as she watches the cat leap from the wall down into the cobbled ginnel on the other side and go from her view and all she's left with now is the cast phantom of herself in the cold glass, half-seen and half-formed, a floating smudge of bluey white where her face is. She looks at the place where she last saw the cat and shakes her head, incomprehension in the gesture, and then she returns to her bed and waits on sleep. Her mother has left a codeine pill on her desk and a glass of water and she swallows the pill and settles back, pillow-propped, and waits in the half-light for the no-time of sleep to coax her back.

Sometimes it bothers her, as it does now, skin scabbing over, swallowing blood and the dawn sky studied, that the planet has no brakes to arrest its spin, no stay to its eternal turn and the lives, the billions of lives, it draws into its empty centre. Sometimes such thinking, unformed even as it is, knocks this Grace sideways. Sometimes such thinking unformed and unacknowledged and never to be articulated shrinks the girl's scalp to the bone. She turns her face away from the window and closes her eyes. Waits for the pain to be killed, for sleep to come. Sees the graveyard at the end of the promenade abutting the beach, sees it as it must look now, in the half-dawn, with the stones and the marble crosses and the bushes skeleton'd by winter. Knows it is there and how it looks. She touches tenderly the wrappings on her face and thinks of the magic occurring beneath them, the glittering wings waiting to unfold. Coming to her are the flashes of cameras and the flashes of recognition in the eyes of strangers. Coming to her is as much of the world as she wants or needs. Her face feels as if it is bulging outwards, like the prow of a boat on a river unknown, pointing her to a favoured future.

Grace is moving towards what she knows she should be, here in the half-light, half-asleep.

Her eyes blink once and then close and then she is being nudged gently awake by her mother.

★

Hrrrrrrrrrrrrrrrrrrrrrrrrrrrrrrrrrrrrrrrrrrrrrrrrrrrrrrrrrrrrrrrrrrrrrrrrrrrrrrrrrrrrrrrrrrr

★

The season's snow has been and gone. No recent falls, and the snow which stuck has thawed now somewhat and then in places refrozen and turned the pavements into glassine rinks. Gritter-trucks have salt-sprayed the main roads to grey and brown slush. *Treacherous* is the word on the weather forecasts. As if solid surfaces have any duty of trust to us, or faith. As if anything is betrayed by them other than our own sense of centrality. The crusted snow on the roofs of the houses on the promenade and the floating ice crystals in the air outside and the concentric fern-shapes that have, overnight, frosted the outside of Grace's bedroom window refract the beams of the slow-climbing sun to throw a faint mandala of light and shadow on Grace's bedroom wall, above the humming PC, across the famous faces flat and pinned up there.

The radio is on, in the empty bedroom. That, and the home page on the screen, both tell of new fears that an enormous glacier in Greenland is due to crack and split and re-enter the sea and send a tsunami south-east across the arc of the planet. An echo of 2004, the various voices say. No earth-tremor this time but the melting and weakening of the ice and also a hurricane imminent in the winds building off Bermuda made ferocious, even more ferocious, by the heating of the sea. Catastrophe, the talk is of, in this empty bedroom. Cataclysm, and no ears here to hear. Stoked heat brings fever. Delirium. Frenzy. A cold and icy world outside that clamps frigid fingers around each burning face. The news on the radio finishes and a chirpy voice introduces JLS.

18

Door opens, and Grace is brought in, crying. Her mother's arm around her. Around the H-shaped dressing Grace's skin is bruised all dark colours and there is bilious drool on her underlip and chin. She is saying in a strangled voice that she just wants it to stop, the being sick, she's sick of being sick and sick of the pain in her face and she's wishing now that she'd never had it done and her nose feels like it's falling off and what if she ends up looking like Jodie Marsh? With a kind of tiny bum on the tip of her nose? Her mother tells her that Jodie Marsh is a rich woman and a sexy one too. Apart from the nose like but she's made a hell of a lot of money, that woman has, one *hell* of a lot of money. She sits her daughter at the desk of the humming machine and accesses her Facebook page for her and there are new comments on there which say things like **looking better already!!!!** and Grace's mother says *See??* and strokes her hair and soothes her and tells her that Jezza will be on in a minute and then she goes downstairs. She's got things to do. Grace's mobile trills twice, incoming text. She opens her phone and reads the wee screen. From her boyfriend. Asking her if she's okay and tells her to check her emails. She does. One from him:

nice photos watch the copper chopper don't land on your face ha ha. looks sore is it? listen good news i know an agent in london wants to meet you i found him online. starting to happen!!!!! i'll be round later xxx

An agent. In London. Grace getting out of a limo outside Chinawhite and the paps there on their knees scrabbling for that precious up-skirt shot. On their knees in the gutter and Grace's Blahnik'd ankles kept tight together or maybe just one quick flash for the appetite. But her face is bruised and battered and bandaged and she replies to the email that he's not allowed to see her yet and then her mobile cries and the text says **i'll b round 2nite** and she texts back just the one word **NO** then turns her phone off and her computer too and goes downstairs where her mother sits her at the kitchen sink and cleans her face, tugs the plugs gently from her new nostrils and scabs rip and blood comes broken, maroon, to pool in her frenulum and Grace cries and her mother makes soothing noises and inserts two new cotton-wool plugs and Grace says that she can't eat so her mother pours her a glass of orange juice to wash down more painkillers and makes her a cup of sugary tea and tells her that soon she'll be even more beautiful than she was before. They go into the front room and sit down side by side on the sofa in front of *The Jeremy Kyle Show*.

—Is the pain any better at all, love?

Grace shakes her head. A tiny and careful movement. —Had a dream my nose had fallen off. Just lying there in the sink and loads of blood.

—You should've woken me up.

Grace says nothing.

—It'll all get better, love. You'll see. It's started to heal already.

—How can you tell?

—I just can, yeah?

And this is a new day. A new day for a new Grace, Grace with a new nose and a new day begun. The sharp winter sun hangs above the still sea near to the house and across, many miles across, a black crack appears in ice, a layer of ice miles thick, one black and jagged zigzag crack which slowly very slowly starts to widen and move across the ice layer's surface. A black and sawtoothed causeway Z-ing across and sullying the pure whiteness of the ice, widening and deepening, becoming bigger, blacker, all those many miles across the sea, far, far from here, this sofa on which the two women sit, the house around them, the town, the country. Many miles away. And a wind begins to blow.

—It'll all get better, Grace's mother says. —Nothing to worry about. When them bandages come off and them bruises all go. You'll see.

Grace shushes her mother as the show starts and tucks her legs beneath her. Sniffs and winces, blows on her tea and winces, sips. Sniffles again and swallows blood, more blood, like rust behind her tongue it is, a dull and brown and heavy taste. A clot slides down her gullet like a slug. And a wind begins to blow. Somewhere up near where the earth curves, and where all is white and blue and black and castles of ice drift on water, a wind begins to blow.

And strut and preen for the camera's eye. It's only the gaze that counts. Well well well. My baby, not my baby. I'm not the father. Those all-important lie-detector results. Horrendous dentition releasing screams. A scuffle, and Grace and her mother laugh. Remark on the fineness of Kyle's shirt. He introduces *the genius* who tells a man with a bloodhound's face that he needs to tackle his drinking problem before anything else because that's the root of all his other problems. Howls from the audience. A cloud passes over the sharp winter sun and spatters thin sleet against the windows and Grace pulls the cuffs of her towelling gown down over her knuckles and wipes her face, the exposed bits of it, the cuff there discoloured with sweat and oozing and blood gone sepia. Sun reappears. Sleet dies away. Wee squall just. A crack widens, a wind builds. A gaze which takes in everything. The last guest is introduced and the audience whoop and clap and a thin young woman comes grinning on stage, shorts, heels, boob tube. Like an open cutlery drawer she is. Prominent ribcage and kneecaps knobbly under suet skin. She speaks in the accent of the city to the east in which Grace got her new nose. What she wants: *the glamour the lifestyle the celebs.* These words. Needs to raise £3,500 for a boobjob to 34DD because that's what's needed to *bag a footballer* and then her older sister comes on stage laughing and shaking her head and calls her younger sibling *a material girl. We've got your mother on the phone. You there? What's your take on this? End of the day you've gorrer go with your dream, haven't you?* Claps and whoops. The girls onstage grin. The younger one says: *I'll do full modelling but I'd need something to hide yunno cos I wouldn't get THAT out.* Claps and whoops. Kyle smiles, says: *The world is crammed with people who never go for their dreams and end up bitter and twisted so go for it, achieve it.* Claps and whoops. The eye blinks. End of show.

—Oh no you don't, Grace.

—What?

—I saw you, then, looking down at your chest. It's not gunner happen, love.

—They'd look better on me than her.

—Yes, but I won't be paying for them. Not after the nose. Your dad didn't leave me *that* much money.

Oh but how the eyes would stare. How the gaze would swing at Grace, look on her, keep her there. How this world would be marked.

—You hungry, love? Think you could manage to eat something now, yeah?

—Bit of toast maybe.

—With a bit of jam on it, yeah?

Grace smiles at her mum. Her mum leaves for the kitchen. *This Morning* comes on. Holly Willoughby, look at her hair. Lovely hair. A tight red sweater and what are her breasts they are perfect. In size and shape. Lucky cow. She must be happy. Must be happy behind those perfect bumps. If only there was a button to press or a handle to turn to make them grow. If it was that easy. To draw the eye, capture the gaze, displace more air and *bulge* into the world. That's it, isn't it, *bulge* into the world. *Force* it to notice. Yes, but Alison Hammond is only a big minger and *she's* on telly and famous. How—

Grace's mother comes in, puts tea and a plate of toast on the coffee table. Grace bites, tastes not jam and burnt bread but something coiny. Blood, still. She forces herself to swallow and her stomach mutters in skirmish.

—That reminds me, love.

—What does?

—Rachel called the other night. Asking how you were. How the op went.

—What did you tell her?

—You're gunner have to see her soon, Grace.

—No.

—She's your sister.

—She's stupid.

—Maybe she is but she's your older sister.

—She's stupid. Grace makes a yapping mouth with her right hand. —She'll be giving me all this about God n stuff. You

22

know what she's like. Her and that bloody what is he? Doctor or something.

—Still n all. You've got to see her sometime, love. She worries about you. Doesn't matter what you think about her and her opinions and everything, at the end of the day she's your sister.

Grace shrugs. —Whatever.

—I'll tell her to pop round, shall I?

Grace shrugs again. They both watch the TV. Grace can't eat any more toast and she tosses the crust paring on to the plate. Holly Willoughby's face.

—Beautiful girl, that, says Grace's mum. Grace goes upstairs. Fancies she can *hear* her mother's shrug from behind her.

Heart thumping, skin going tighter. What is this it is like panic. Something a bit like panic. In her a need arises to escape, the house, the town, her own skin. Run and run until her essence outruns her skin and bursts free, leaves it standing and deflated in the road like a doll. She sits at her desk and accesses her home page and there's Ronan Keating looking sad and she clicks on that image which offers links which she clicks on too and after a few more clicks she's on the Stephen Gately memorial page. Don't think. Don't think. Poor man, early thirties. It surrounds us. Don't think. Ronan's already got himself a memorial tattoo. Such devotion. Must've loved him like a brother. A fathomless darkness on which Grace surfs. Friendsatrest.com, gonetoosoon.com, Lasting Tribute. Patrick Swayze; on his memorial wall, Grace contributes the words **I hope you have found peace.** And look, a girl two towns away last week committed suicide. Hung herself in her parents' garage. Dad found her. Seventeen years old. Belinda was her name. **Having a party up there, Bel!!!** and **keep the Breezers cold for me, hun! See u soon! Love Kit xxx**. Grace stares, clicks, reads. Stares and clicks and reads. Heartbeat normal, now. Skin just a covering for who she is. A modifiable one, at that. There's nothing to worry about. Always in control, remain always in control. Yet it surrounds us. And what insulates us from it, keeps us at a distance from its bottomless grief, is very, very thin. Like ice. Like cracking ice.

Stomach gurgling. As if there are two entities in there, in disagreement, at odds. An argument getting heated.

Footsteps up the stairs. Grace clicks back to her home page, holds her stomach, groans. Her mother's head appears around the bedroom door.

—You okay, love? I've got to go shopping. Wanna come with? Do you good, get out of the house. Bit of fresh air, yeah?

Grace groans again, leans over the waste-paper basket. And this is a new day for the new Grace, Grace and her new nose.

★

Huuuuuuuuuuuuurrrrrrrrrrrrrrrrrrrrrrrrrrrr

★

The days pass. The days pass with Grace in them, around her they pass, Grace and her new nose. Nights, too, in which she often dreams that her nose comes loose with a wet crunch and slides down her face to plop off her chin or that she coughs or sneezes and it explodes, disintegrates, leaves her face in sudden wet smithereens. Eating is difficult, as is the vomiting – purple pancakes in the toilet pan. She's less groggy and nauseous after a week but her face remains swollen, pink and proud around the dressings. Food stays inside her, now. Converted into energy, and growth. Her boyfriend texts her, emails her, tells her he wants to see her but she tells him that he can't and that he'll just have to wait. The last patches of snow melt away but the frost forms sastrugi on the roofs and walls and a kind of healing happens. The sea's colour brightens, becomes a less heavier grey. The planet turns. A wind builds, a continent away, over a huge water. After two weeks, Grace returns to the hospital in the big city to the east and a man examines her face and declares himself pleased and a nurse gently cleans that face and tugs the cotton-wool plugs from the nose around which scabs have formed and these scabs break and blood seeps then trickles then sprints through the cracked crust and to Grace it feels like her entire face is leaking out of her nose, there is a sort of terrible outward suction, and the pain is great and she cries and her mother and the nurse comfort her and shush her and the nurse removes all dressings except for the splint, but that can come off she says in a week's time, after the septum stitches have dissolved. **I'm comin round**, her boyfriend says. **Not yet yr not** says Grace. They talk on the telephone and in cyberspace but she will not yet let him see her face anywhere except her Facebook page and she stays at home and watches TV and cooks with her mother and reads *Hello!* and *OK!* and *Heat* and watches the TV and tries to sleep and stares out of her bedroom window and one minute she holds everything in hate, the world and herself, and the next she feels like she's standing on the roof of her house looking out over the town that has shaped her and which she'll soon leave and out, too, over the sea, to places agleam just beyond the horizon that await her all lit up. A blueness comes back to the sky and falls out of it into the sea. Stains the sea. Birds can be heard singing of a morning. Grace and her mother return to the hospital in the big city to the east and the splint comes off. At last the splint comes off and there's the new nose. See it, world, Grace's new nose which means Grace's new face. Everyone look at Grace's new face which means Grace's new life. The faces of her mother and the kindly nurse looking at her. They smile. Grace's mother puts her hands across her face, over her mouth and chin, and regards her daughter. *Oh my God, Grace*, she says. *Oh my God*. The nurse holds up a mirror. First thing Grace sees is the yellowness, the staining of the skin, yellow on the cheeks shading to orange at the nostrils and then greyblue up each side of the nose that now has no bump or slight downward curve. That is now a perfect nose. That is straight and smooth and draws the eye up it to the bumpless bridge and on to the fine high forehead and of course the eyes, the big and dark and pretty eyes, the gazer cannot help now but notice the eyes, now that that magnetic bump on the bridge of the nose has been sheared away the looker cannot help but see the eyes.

—Oh my God, says Grace. —Look at me. Look at me, Mum.

There is no pain. The pain has gone along with the bump,

the ugly bump at the bridge. Sheared away, sliced away and burnt.

—My nose, Mum. Look at my nose.

—It's gorgeous love. Absolutely gorgeous. Worth every penny. Why are you crying?

—Cos I'm happy Mum. I'm so happy.

—Oh love.

The nurse looks on and smiles as mother hugs daughter. Wants to hug them too. This is why she does the job. These happy hugs here.

The YouTube footage shows the face of a young woman very close to the camera. Eighteen, maybe. No older than twenty. Even with the bruising it is a pretty face, and the bruising in the low-definition resolution appears as colourless smudges on the cheeks and faint shadows on either side of the nose. The eyes are big and dark. The lips are full and a smile plays across them in little dimple brackets. The hair is headbanded back from a high and white forehead and the cheekbones can be seen as small smooth bulges softly curving down to a narrow, rounded chin bisected by a shallow cleft. It is a pretty face. *I'm Grace Allcock*, the young woman says, *and this is my new nose.* She turns to the left, turns to the right, then faces front again. *See? No bump, now. It used to look like a beak or something but I had it operated on. My mum paid for it. She's the best mum in the world. Did it hurt? God yeah. And I was sick and everything for days. Couldn't eat, couldn't sleep. It was horrible. But see?* She turns to the left, turns to the right. Faces front again. *See it now? No bump, nothing. It's a perfect nose. I love my new nose. That's it. Bye!*

Comments come in. **Well done hun** and **brave girl** and **what are you doing tonight grace** and **wish I had your guts** and **go for it babes** and **very good grace now show us your tits**. Comments from America, France, Australia, all over the world. Singapore and Ireland and Chile. India. The world over.

In a few months' time this promenade will be packed. On the beach, on the benches, in the caffs and pubs, in the amusement arcades, eating chips and ice creams, all going pink in the sun which, the weather forecasters are already saying, will be high and hot. There'll be cars with music coming out of the open windows and adults shouting and children screaming in their playful panic and lots of skin going pink and red. In a few months' time. Now, though, there's a feller and his dog and a brewery wagon delivering barrels and crates to a pub which isn't open yet and lots of gulls either flying and squealing or scavenging for scraps at the bins and Grace and Damien, their breath fogging their faces, wearing veils of vapour, standing at the railings with their backs to the sea, the lagging and leaden sea. The exposed skin on their hands and faces has been teased pink by the cold air as if slapped. Grace's fading facial bruises push out at the pink of the undamaged skin on her cheeks and forehead and eyelids and nothing can stop this, the ways in which the body behaves. Reacts and ages and rots. Real time never ceases to simmer. Behind Grace and Damien, at their backs, a wave breaks and hisses on the shingle, and another, and another. Behind those breakers, on top of a rotting piling periscoping from the oily water, sits a cormorant unnoticed, his wet wings spread to the weak winter sun, his head tilted back. No movement in him. Black-cloaked bird. Akimbo wings which leak light like the sun.

—Can't believe it, Damien is saying. —Just can't fucking believe it man, yeah?

—Told you it looked good, didn't I?

—Yeah, but.

—*Told* you so.

—Yeah but you made a right fucking fuss. All that whinging on the phone.

—What did you expect? I'd just, like, had half my nose sliced off? In the hospital? Put to sleep while they sliced of half my fucking nose? Think that's going to *tickle* or something? Duh!

Damien pulls his cap down lower on his forehead. —Do you have to, like, turn everything you say into a question? Cos you always do it? And it, like, really gets on me fuckin nerves?

Grace glowers. Damien softens. —Still looks dead good, though. Sorry. Just messing.

He leans his face towards hers and Grace flinches away.
—No!

—I was only gonna kiss your new nose.

—That's what I'm scared of. It'd hurt.

—Would it?

—Course it would, duh. Not healed yet properly. Be a couple of weeks before you can touch it, even? I mean *even*.

He hugs her instead. Feels the stored winter coming out of the top of her head on to the underside of his chin, his throat. Can smell her scalp, the shampoo. Feels her body, little as it is, lithe, in his arms. —I'm dead proud of you, end of the day.

—Are you?

—Course I am. You're dead brave. And you're gonna be famous. Want me to tell you about this agent feller? D'you wanna know? You haven't asked.

They walk, westerly along the promenade, towards the old church at the end of it and the graveyard there with its stones all smudged and scoured and soft-edged by the salt wind off the sea, centuries of briny abrasion off the sea. Damien found the guy online. Based in London, he is. Did some surfing, snooping around, got some names, emailed the geezer and told him about Grace and he checked out her Facebook page and all that stuff and he reckons he can get her some modelling – *modelling*, he said.

—But he wants to see you when the bandages come off. Wants to see what you look like with your new nose, yeah? But he's interested.

—Modelling? Tits out and that?

—Well, yeah. *Nuts* and that, y'know.

—They're not big enough.

—Don't get much bigger than *Nuts* and *Loaded*. What do you want, the *Sunday Times*?

—My tits, duh. They're not big enough.

—That's what *you* think. But it's up to them, innit?

—Who?

—The magazine editors and that. It's a start, Grace. Get in *Loaded* or something and who knows where it'll lead? Plus they pay top dollar, those mags. *Top* dollar. This agent feller, I checked him out, he's got loads of famous people on his books. Lucy Pinder, I think. People like that. Michelle Marsh too. Foot in the door, yeah?

Grace looks down at her chest. —I still don't think they're big enough.

—God, Grace. Moody cow you. Piss on a bonfire. I've spent fucking hours online for you. It's a break. Foot in the door. This is what you've always wanted, yeah? And you're not happy?

—No, I am. I mean of course I am.

Yet she does not look it. Damien studies her face, the new nose, the new and unbumped nose. The fading contusions around it. The big eyes and the naturally long lashes and the full lips and that face is *perfect* for modelling. He knows it is. See that face in gloss. Under bright lights. Put it in make-up, full and expert, see it in gloss, atop a naked or at least topless torso or maybe the lacy lingerie. Nothing wrong with her tits. Could be bigger maybe but the *shape*, the *shape*.

—What?

—Why don't you look it, then?

—Look what?

—Happy.

—Just thinking, that's all. And me nose still hurts, yeah? She puts her arms around his waist. —I'm dead pleased that you did all that stuff for me. Honest I am.

A wave breaks on the shingle and is sucked back into the sea with a slurpy hiss. They turn up, away from the water, to walk through the graveyard. The stone of the church darkened and blurred by the erosion of centuries, and the gravestones around it too; some old and unreadable obelisks, some new marble crosses, each alike exposed to the salty wind's sculpting. On a bench in this graveyard, some years ago, Grace as a little girl sat with her grandfather one hot summer's day and ate ice creams. Too quickly, she ate hers; it put aches in her stomach and head. *You've cooled your insides down*, her grandad told her. *You need to warm them up again.* So he showed her how to eat the sunshine; close your eyes, tilt your head back, open your mouth for a count of ten then swallow. Simple. And Grace felt her tummy settle, warm and settle, as if a cat was curled up in there, a sleepy cat, soft, purring. *Better now?* her grandfather asked, and little Grace smiled up at him, and when she did that the sunlight inside her shone out through her mouth in several beams between the gaps in her teeth.

And the lichen on these standing stones around her looks to Grace like scabs, ulceration. Cankers, growths, like something seen on the 'disease' page of nowthatsfuckedup.com, that site that Damien so loves. And the carved names, weathered as they are, sanded and almost erased, some of them. These people, these dissolving bones, they've left nothing behind but a carved name and even that is disappearing. Nothing on the planet to say that they lived, that they were here, that they moved across it with their own peculiar gait. Unremembered and uncelebrated, just gone. GERALD LEWIS, b.1945, d.2007, what did you do while you were here? Who did you love, if anyone, and who loved you, if anyone? Unremarked now, fertiliser man, did you honour the miracle of your life? And even if you did, what matters that when now a raindrop ploughs down across your chipped and fading name?

—They pay a lot, them mags, Damien is saying. —Top dollar. Just one sesh, like, is a month's money for most people. Not kidding. And that's just a start. Jodie Marsh? That girl is minted. No lie, *minted*. Started off getting her baps out for the mags like and *now* look where she is.

—Don't want her nose, though.

—No but you'd like some of her money, wouldn't you? And anyway you don't *have* her nose. You've got your own, now, yeah?

They leave the graveyard, and the promenade, and circle back into the town, in the centre of which Grace looks up and smiles at the CCTV boxes mounted on lamp posts and traffic lights and on walls above the entrances to bars and the one nightclub. Imagines the gaze, the eyeless gaze. Somewhere people watch. In offices somewhere and surrounded by screens the strangers see her smile. See her face with the new nose.

They stop for chips at a place by the roundabout around which cars ceaselessly turn, the people inside them either yawning or screaming. They eat the food in, too cold as it is to sit outside. Grace has baked beans with hers. Then they return to Grace's house and have some tea with her mother who Damien tells about the agent. She's excited for her daughter. They drink tea and talk then she leaves the house to visit a friend telling Grace that she's bought that week's mags, a pile of which Grace takes up to her room – *Heat, Reveal, Love It!, OK!, Hello!*. Jodie Marsh's face on a couple of covers. That nose. Upstairs, Damien goes straight to the PC and Grace uses the toilet and then the sink and when she returns to the bedroom Damien's face is flushed and he's accessed a bukkake site. Faces like wedding cakes, ice creams, left out in the sun. Heavy eye make-up just visible beneath the sticky thick sheen like plums trapped in glue. Somewhere in that morass are women. Get celebs get real life get *Reveal*.

—Oh no, Grace says. —Not today. Face still hurts, yeah?

—Not as if it weighs much, yeah?

—Don't care. I'll have to wipe it off, won't I? You're not doing *that* today so you can just forget it.

—On your tits, then. Then we can email that agent.

Grace strips and lies back on the bed and Damien strips and straddles her. Soon to be seen by thousands, those breasts. Soon to be leered over and wanted, desired, and look now what he's doing to them, *on* them, watch him now and see what he does you thousands upon thousands of jealous eyes. Aim for the nipples. Grey syrup rain. Grace wipes herself off with a tissue and then they dress and return to the PC to email the agent the short film that Grace made of herself proudly displaying her new nose. I'm Grace Allcock and this is my new nose.

—Will we get a reply quick?

—Probably not, no. He's a busy man, end of the day. I'm gonna have a bit of a ziz.

Damien lies on his belly on the bed and Grace sits on the floor with the stack of magazines. Jodie Marsh, look at the nose on her. She's everywhere with that nose, like a tiny bum it is, and those boobs. Always getting them out. Damien's breathing becomes deeper and slower as he slips into sleep and Grace reads about Jodie Marsh. The life of Jodie Marsh. What she reveals of it. What she chooses to reveal of it. Grace touches with a fingertip her new nose, very gently, and studies the glossy covers and turns the pages. Looks at the pictures. Look at these pictures. Looks at the pictures and reads about Jodie Marsh, who's everywhere, at the moment, with *that* nose and *those* boobs because she's promoting a new show called *Totally Jodie Marsh: Who'll Take Her Up the Aisle?*, the publicity still for which shows Jodie dressed in three white belts and a pair of white and furry boots. Yeti feet. What's this, it's a programme about Jodie holding auditions for a husband, is it? But she married Matt Peacock in the Sugar Hut club. Yes but they got divorced. Fame? *I hate it*, Jodie says. The press? *Vile.* Men? *I hate men. Men have evil inside of them.* So who's gonna take her up the aisle. And why does she want to be taken up the aisle and be filmed and photographed doing it. Grace is glad that her nose didn't come out looking like Jodie's but her boobs, though, her boobs . . . *Zoo* magazine paid for Jodie's boobjob, the operation, the augmentation. Get them out, now, get them out. Did she pay for her own tattoos? One of them on her arm reads 'only God can judge me'. Those white teeth, those bioluminescent teeth, were paid for by Channel 5's *Cosmetic Surgery Live*. Those veneers. And fat = failure. Yes, fat = failure. Grace ate chips and beans a couple of hours ago. Fat = failure. In 2005 Jodie's best friend Kim was murdered by her boyfriend aged twenty-three. And then Pixie, Jodie's chihuahua, died, so Jodie had the two names tattooed on her neck in the shape of a cross and there it is, there, the tattoo on the neck. Grace is touched by this commemoration, this gesture. The permanent entwining and enscribing of those names, chihuahua and murdered girl. Never will *they* fade away to nothing like the names on the gravestones exposed to the wind and the rain and too the people that bore them. Gerald what was your surname? Forgotten already. Rot man alive only in the hearts that if any cared for you and who may still be breathing but what does the world care about that. Fat = failure. And now here's Jodie declaring that she got the boobjob reversed and what she has now is real unlike that plastic tart Jordan which is why her, Jodie's, autobiography is called *Keeping It Real*. She's *allowed* to call it that. *Entitled*, she is. She's written a book? She reads them too, not a stupid girl, she's got eleven GCSEs all at grades A and A★, and three A levels. She's an educated woman. She reads books: *For me it's really nice escapism just to lay back and read about a beach house in America, it's hot and they've got butlers serving their drinks. That's what a book is: escaping the dull, boring monotony of everyday life.* Not a stupid woman. And her life has had its tragedies, oh yes it's had troubles and pain, her attempts to bring colour into it just make other people jealous and that's what the belts are, the three white belts, it's fun and colour, fun and colour. *The dull, boring monotony of everyday life.* Rain rattles on the bedroom window, thrown down from a grey sky. The planet is turning, again, away from the sun. And in doing so is turning back towards it. Grace looks at Damien. His right arm hanging limply over the side of the bed. The left side of his face lost in the floral pillowcase, the breath leaving his sleep-slack mouth slowly and deeply, a thick rhythm. His underlip shining with dribble. *I don't do it for attention*, Jodie says. *I've always dressed outrageously. It's fun, and men look at me and think, 'I'd shag her.' I do get upset by the stick I receive but I think, 'You're just slagging me off because you're fucking jealous and need a shag.'* Yes, yes. Jealousy destroys so many people. Boring life. Green eyes will gaze at Grace and go glassy with envy. Those green eyes. Jealousy moves in people like blood and breath and everyone will look at Grace and think *I want to be her.* People on the street, in clubs, people who she'll never meet in the flesh, those real losers who'll sit at home and see her on TV or on their computer screens or in the shining pages of the glossy mags, gazing at her, wanting her, to fuck her, to be her. Everyday life. The dullness and the boredom and the monotony. Grace sees Jodie smile with those shocking white teeth and *that* nose and *those* tits and then she looks at the slumbering Damien and behind her, above her head, the last flung beams of the sinking sun trace orange paisley on the window.

A door closes downstairs. Grace hears her mother: —Grace! Want to eat something?

Damien grumbles and mutters in his slumber. Grace goes downstairs, into the kitchen, where her mother is unloading a bag of shopping on the worktop next to the vase of flowers and the small TV. Bags from Sayers bakery, in parts translucent with grease.

—Iya love. Were you asleep?

—Not me. Day is. What've you got?

—Pasties. Corned beef for me and you, ham and cheese for Damien when he wakes up. What's that look for? You *like* pasties, yeah?

Grace's nose, her new nose, has wrinkled. For the first time in some weeks her nose has wrinkled without pain and nor, now, does the expressive wrinkling stop at the ugly bulge at the bridge and gather there like ripples of tiny fat because now there is no bulge. Now there is no bulge.

—What's the face for? her mother asks again.

—I had chips and beans earlier.

—So what?

—Well, so now pasties. Fat equals failure, Mum, yeah?

Her mother laughs. —What?

—Fat equals failure.

—Where'd you get that from?

Grace shrugs. —It's just what I think.

—Fat equals failure?

—Yes.

—It does, love, yeah. Just eat half a one, well. Got to have something for your tea, haven't you?

Grace shrugs. Her nose wrinkles again but this time at the smells arising from the pasties in their bags on the worktop and her mother can tell the difference.

—Go and get Day. I'll put some peas on.

Grace goes back upstairs. Damien is awake, sitting up on the bed, scratching his head, his eyelids puffy. He smiles at Grace. —Teatime, yeah?

—Pasties.

—Good.

—I told her that fat equals failure but she wouldn't listen.

—What?

—Fat equals failure. I told her.

—Maybe you shouldn't've pigged out on the chips and beans then should yeh? And put the light on. Can't see a thing, yeah?

Grace flicks a switch. Lights up the room. Closes the bedroom curtains against the deepening darkness.

Damien pulls his hoodie over his head. —I want beans with my pastie.

—She's making peas.

—That'll do. Some oven chips as well.

—Again? Fat equals failure for fellers as well.

—I'm not the one who's wanting to be a model, am I? End of the day I can eat whatever I want. He cools his brain down with a yawn. —Anyway. You checked your emails yet?

Grace sits at her desk, stabs at the keyboard and accesses her home page. Winds building. Clouds swirling in a spiral off Greenland and beginning to look like an eye. Giant white eye. Ice cracking. The wave will travel between Iceland and Ireland but will maybe break up on the Isle of Man. We don't know yet. Grace's inbox is empty.

—Nothing yet?

—No.

—He's a busy man, end of the day. Give him a chance, yeah?

Exit email. Back to home page. Hurricane Gwen they're calling it. Like a giant eye. Log off.

—I'm hungry. We'll check again later, yeah?

They go downstairs. Sit in the living room and eat pasties and peas off plates on their knees and watch people in an Australian jungle eat insects and eyeballs. A kangaroo's penis. A kangaroo's testicles. Teeth bite down and liquid spurts, thick liquid and jellyish. Bit like sperm. Probably *is* sperm, a testicle as it is. Grey syrup rain. The three of them go: —Eeeeewwww!, and laugh.

★

Huuuuuuuuuuurrrrrrrrttttttttttt

★

Days pass. Weeks pass. Christmas comes and Christmas goes and Grace gets only some smellies from her mother because

35

the nose was her main gift. Damien buys her underwear. She buys him aftershave with money borrowed from her mother. The straggling patches of ice thaw and vanish and the planet tilts, grinds, turns like a millstone towards the sun. Mornings become more musical. Grace looks at herself in the bathroom mirror, her fingers laced together at her nape, elbows squeezed towards each other. That nose. Her nose. She returns to the hospital in the big city to the east where a man without a mask declares himself very pleased with his work and Grace says *Yeah, but* and he tells her that the swelling won't subside fully for about four months. Not completely. Nor the bruising. *I'm a better version of me*, she murmurs, as she looks in the bathroom mirror. *Better version of me*. With her fingers laced at her nape like that one evening she feels a lump under the skin, tender, just below her hairline, slightly painful, and when her mother returns from the shops she asks her to take a look and she does and tells Grace that it looks like she's developing a boil so Grace scrubs it and scrubs it and when it comes to a head she goes to the doctor in the town who lances it and drains it and dresses it and calls it a furuncle which might return and might start to exude a liquid, a pus, when squeezed which might give off an unpleasant smell. How the body will do this. React and rot and age. On the way home from the doctor's a panic builds in Grace. All that money, all that pain for a new nose and look. Smelly lumps on her neck. What's the point? Bet Jodie doesn't get boils. Running free from everything the progress of the body towards powder, the life of it an essence separate from the mind both individual and collective and what can be done about that? Slice it, excise it, chip it and sculpt it and pattern it and mould it and still it continues to do what it does, rot and react and age. A monster it is. Alien to itself. Back home her mother tells her to keep her neck clean and eat less fatty foods and Grace tells her to stop bringing pasties home, then. Fat = failure. And she doesn't eat much fatty stuff anyway. *But* says her mother.

Grace's friends come to visit. She has a New Nose Party and some friends come for a sleepover and they drink Breezers and cider and watch TV in Grace's bedroom. Eat crisps and pizzas. Laugh a lot. Two of the friends have wonky noses but the other two are perfect in both face and figure thinks Grace. They're pretty. They have boobs. One of them mentions that she'd heard that Willy Roberts is soon to release a comeback single so they go online and Google him and there he is, after a year or so away from the screens and out of the pages, Willy Roberts, looking lush from behind as he smiles over his tribal-tattooed shoulder above his naked arse. Is he in the shower? Yes, he's having a shower. Clean for his comeback. Preened for his public. A new tribal tattoo on his back, another one, below the crucifix and between the angel's wings and the Sanskrit words and the Latin words and there are some Chinese characters too. Or Japanese. Something. What's he been doing while he's been away? Exploring himself and the world. He's been in the Himalayas looking for the yeti. In the Rockies looking for Bigfoot. Camping out on the banks of Loch Ness. Wants, next, to go to Mexico to look for the chupacabras. *I just think that there are so many things in this world that we don't know about, that we're scared to go looking for.* He's fought his addictions to vodka and caffeine and nicotine and he wants to put all that behind him now and explore himself and the world. His new song's downloadable already. So Grace downloads it. She and her friends shriek about it, the Breezers and White Lightning bottles pyramiding on the windowsill.

The man with the mask in the big brown building to the east had told Grace that fresh sea air would be helpful in the healing process so she takes walks along the pebble beach, with her mother, with Damien, with her oldest friend Shelly. With Damien she has a contest to see who can hit with pebbles the protruding old paling on which the seabirds sometimes sit to dry their wings and so they bend and choose and throw fine grain, banded schist, rocks formed from small particles of mud aeons ago after being annealed in colossal heat and compressed, then, with immeasurable force. Painted egg, arrowhead, the creamy veins like tentacles through the smooth black body. They bend and choose and throw mica schist, which bounces sparks back from the weak sunlight when in the raised fist. A flint pebble, smoothed by the waves, cored by a tapering hole that formed, once, around a sponge. Bi-coloured chert. Limey mudstone, they bend and pick and throw. A Devil's toenail, oyster Gryphaea, shellfish fossil, red sedimentary chunks bearing little round O's of sea-lily segments, crinoid, and bryozoa sea mat, marks made many millennia ago when the world was not as it is now but what it is now was forming in these small vegetables. Waiting to be born in their sap. A piece of chalk they pick and throw, holed by a boring bivalve mollusc. So the world is what it is and can never be other since all worlds it contains. Small cones of water erupt from the sea around the old wood paling. The mussels on it and the barnacles on it exposed and then covered again by each rolling swell and loll of ocean. Damien picks up a chunk of brick. There's a faint thunk. He's won.

It's a Thursday when Grace checks her emails and scans her inbox and shouts *Ohmygod!* She's on her own so she calls her mother and then calls Damien. *I'll forward it to you*, she says, a wobble and flex in her voice. *He wants to meet me. He wants to meet me. Ohmygod it's happening. Oh. My. God.*

★

Huuuuuuuurrrrrrrrrrttttttttttttttttt

★

Chlorite schist in small greenish slabs. Good for skipping across the even water anterior to the breaking waves. Liassic limestone, cross-hatched by veins of white calcite crystals. Like a sweet. A kind of humbug with a chewy centre. In the sandy bank at the tideline, between the pebble bed and the water, infinitesimal life abounds; life so small that, in the film of moisture that glues one sand-grain to another, it moves in shoals, flickers like mackerel, the pinhead smear of brine for such life an ocean entire. Has predators, in that full-stop pond. Is hunted.

On Grace's desk the machine goes on humming. In its screen can be seen her mother's face, Damien's face, her face too as he sits before it in the hours after midnight, sleep at a distance, in her Silly Moo PJs and her hair tied back and her new nose painted a browny-yellow that fades back to flesh with each passing day. It hums, the machine. Hums and hums. Images and knowledge are called up on it and to its left, on the desk, sits a pile of magazines, Willy Roberts's smirk on one, Katie Price's pout on the other. Moving clockwise around the machine there is a dirty mug in a flower pattern, old coffee crust inside it, an empty bag of Doritos, a desk tidy containing one biro and a scrunchie scribbled with blonde hairs, some coppers in a jam jar, a pair of balled-up socks, white, ankle, a lipstick like a tiny toppled tower, and a mound of CDs. On the machine's right is the tangle of wires that power it. Behind the machine, the humming machine, the Anaglypta wallpaper, painted eggshell blue, is hidden by a large poster of Willy Roberts leaning towards the camera with his top lip curled in a sneer against a microphone, clutched in both hands. Four Post-it notes are stuck to it, vivid pink Post-it notes, but the writing on them is indecipherable. Behind the poster, a tiny spider has made its home between wall and paper, in the thin world there; a money spider, wee predator, the male of the species, head modified with four eyes atop a protuberant slender stalk and four more eyes midway on that stalk. A memo himself he is, this tiny spider, a reminder from the offices of nightmare. He waits there, in his web, in his slim world, waits for the wind of Grace's breath to send tiny winged things into his web. A feast he has, when Grace gets excited, which is often, there, at the screen of the humming machine. When she exhales the spider eats. To the right of the poster is a dark brown spatter-shape where cola once sprayed from an agitated bottle. This is what surrounds the always humming machine and the eyes that gaze at it.

They meet him in the bar of his hotel on the outskirts of a big city to the east, not the one in which Grace was given her new nose although she is driven through that one, or rather around it on the ringroad, the signs for HOSPITAL causing a lurch, both pleasant and not, in Grace's chest. She's wearing Zandra Rhodes Carmenz high-heeled sandals, the *shit* they are, sexy as all fuck, and a knee-length Clockhouse floral print dress, grey roses on a navy blue background, that she saw Daisy Lowe modelling once in a catalogue. Damien has had two new nicks shaved into his eyebrow for the occasion and is wearing a white T-shirt under a leather jacket over baggy jeans, the waistband of his boxers peeping above. During the journey Grace has sought approval from her mother and from Damien many times: Do I look okay? This dress, the shoes? How's my nose looking? Each time the response has been reassuring and positive but Grace seems to require this every minute and her mother feels some relief when she pulls the car into the dropping-off area at the big brown building with flags hanging from it all lit up from below.

—This it?

—Yes.

—Size of it.

—It's posh. Dead posh. You're sure you're okay?

Grace nods.

—Certain?

Grace nods.

—Just get in there and be yourself, yeah? You'll knock him off his feet. And I'm only a phone call away if you need me, yeah?

—Yes Mum.

—You'll look after her for me, Damien, won't you?

—Course I will Missus A. She's in good hands, yeah? Don't worry about anything.

Kisses and hugs and more reassurances, compliments, and Grace and Damien leave the car. Wave as it pulls away. Inside the bar there is a huge plasma TV screen on the wall tuned to Sky Sports with no sound from it audible above the piano music piped in from somewhere. The lights are low. There are men and women dressed in black trouser suits with white aprons. The agent is sitting beneath a fern on a banquette and flicking through a menu and drinking a glass of white wine and Damien is the first to spot him. Nudges Grace with his elbow, nods at the biggish man with the grey crew cut studying the menu beneath the fern's frondy curls. Exactly as he looks on a screen. Different in no way except size. And dimension. He looks up and sees them and grins and beckons them enthusiastically over and locks his eyes on Grace as she approaches him and takes a shoulder of hers in each hand and regards her face at arm's length.

—Just as gorgeous in the flesh. Nose healing well I see. He tips his head slightly to the left and then the right to examine her nose from different angles. —Looks good on you. Suits you. As does the dress. Sit down, sit. What'll you have to drink? No, I'll choose. Champagne.

He waves a waiter over and orders and looks at Damien.

—And you must be the fellow who initiated contact, right? Damien nods. —Yes.

—Smart boy. What's your name again?

—Damien.

—Damien. Like in *The Omen*.

He limply jerks Damien's hand twice and turns back to Grace. —And you, of course, are Gracie Allcock.

—Grace.

—Gracie's better. Gracie Allcock, more of a ring. Graaaacie Allcock. It's the most exquisite name I've ever heard. I can work with a name like Gracie Allcock. I can work with *you*. What you have, Gracie, is something we call marketability. Which means that—

—I know what it means, Damien says.

—That *you*. The man outlines Grace's shape with his hands in the air above the table. —The whole package of *you*, well, people will be prepared to pay just to have a tiny piece of it. The teensiest piece. To hear you speak, see you walk. No, don't blush. Although it does become you. They'll buy a magazine if your face is on the cover. A newspaper, even. They'll get a glimpse of you online and then they'll tap in their credit-card details just to see a little bit more of you. You understand?

This is all abrupt and this is all so fast. The presence of this man seen so many times flattened on a screen and now he has lines in the skin of his face and a colour and sheen to his eyes and individual hairs on his head. Rings on his fingers and manicured nails and a little gold hoop in the lobe of his left ear. So fast, this, like that roller coaster at Alton Towers that made Grace sick that time when she was very young after her dad disappeared. Making her dizzy. A spinning top in her head. She's aware of Damien as a coloured blob at her side but the man's lips are moving and what is coming from them is like the constantly rising and bursting golden bubbles in the liquid that has appeared in a glass on the tablecloth under Grace's nose. Her new nose that was sliced and hacked out for this, so that she could be here, opposite this man in this hotel bar. Just the beginning but the beginning was when Grace looked at herself in the mirror one morning and thought *ugly*. Or even when she looked at an often-seen face on glossy paper one time and thought, yet again, *pretty*.

—I'm going too fast, am I?

—Yes, Damien says.

—Gracie? I'm rushing you into things, am I? Just tell me if I am.

Grace shrugs.

—Okay. I'll slow down. It's just that I'm excited. Star quality, you know? Gets me all of a dither. I can only apologise. Let's eat.

Again he beckons a waiter with a sweep of an arm and orders the Chinese banquet. Tsingtao beer and more champagne. Asks Grace to tell him about herself; not the nuts-and-bolts stuff, no, the where and when she was born etc., she told him all that in her emails, rather about what she wants from life, what she wants to be, who she admires, who she dislikes, all the stuff that makes Gracie Gracie. The stuff that constitutes her marketability. He makes frequent references to Max Clifford's *vision*. To a nonplussed Grace. Who's Max Clifford? Only a marketing genius. Dim sum and dumplings. Damien asks for a fork. The agent shows Grace how to use chopsticks, taking her hand in his, folding her long and painted fingers around the rods. See? Max long ago understood the way the world was going. The direction it was taking. He saw it all before any of us and now we share his vision.

—And my vision for you, Gracie, is . . .

The bubbles go on popping. Rising and popping and golden-coloured and they never seem to exhaust themselves in the glass, they never seem to run out. Grace leans over her bowl of food, her face over it, her mouth, so that she does not stain her dress. Damien leans and jabs his fork into the platter at the centre of the table, shoves food into his mouth. *Nuts* magazine, *Zoo*, *Loaded*. Just the start. The agent talks about Lucy, Michelle, Chantelle, Jodie, even Katie. About hunger and need and everything else. About the bottomless thirst of the public. About Max Clifford, again:

—I mean, just look at what he did for poor Jade, may she rest in peace. He crosses himself and kisses the knuckle of his thumb. —Even as she was dying, as the poor girl was leaving this world, Max saw an opportunity. Man's an absolute genius. He licks soy sauce from around his lips, dabs his mouth and chin with a napkin. —More champagne? More beer?

He raises a hand and clicks his fingers. Grace is surprised to see that people actually do that, in restaurants, in real life.

Anne Robinson says that women who won't have surgery *lack self-belief*. They say *my husband likes me as I am but of course he bloody does. Safe in your box, unthreatening. As near to his mother as he can hope.*

Grace's mother gives a nod. This is true. Not to go under the knife is, what, it is surrendering. It is giving in. Look what it's done for Grace, so soon. Still some bruising around her nose, very faint but still some, and she's breaking bread with a powerful man who's going to make her famous. Rich and famous.

She puts the magazine on the coffee table to the left of the empty foil carton that contains only a few worms of noodles still. She's okay. Grace is okay. Knew there was something special about that one. She flicks through the channels and there's Anne herself, presenting some programme about, who, Madonna, Brangelina. She touches her face, the forehead, the nose, the cheeks, the softening of the neck where it joins the jawbone. That Madonna – she's in her fifties. So's Michelle Pfeiffer. Cher! She's drawing her pension, that one. Had so many facelifts she's got a cleft chin and a beard. Jackie Stallone, nearly ninety. Ninety! Yes but she looks it. Hideous old witch. From a bad dream, her. But fair play to her because she won't give in or surrender and at least she's not dead.

About eight grand for a facelift. A deep lift that tightens muscles down to the bone, after which the fat under the neck is sucked away. Or incisions are made behind the ears and skin is removed and the entire face is lifted through those incisions, those slices, those cuts, the whole face hoiked up towards the crown of the head. Three weeks to heal. Is that all? Apparently so, yes. The whole face is basically lifted away from the bone but it's miraculous the way the body heals itself although there are of course risks: blood clots numbness tightness asymmetry infection scars and injury to nerves. But worth the risk. Fuck age and what it does.

Anne's talking but she doesn't know what about. Is that Jennifer Aniston? Or just someone who looks like her or who wants very much to look like her. She's okay, Grace, she's okay. Out there getting famous. A nice lad that Damien he'll look after her and keep her safe. She'll be okay. She had her dad's nose but not any more, oh no. Every time she saw that bump she thought of that man. Didn't come out right, Grace didn't come out right, but that's been rectified now and great is the world in which that can be done. The child is the flaw made flesh. But no more, no more. All that Grace's face echoes now is her mother's, with the big dark eyes and the straight nose. The face blurring at the edges and kind of melting into itself as it ages. Late forties, that's still young. Younger than Madonna. *Much* younger than Cher. But the body and the flesh contains chaos within it and all age is is a losing of control, a surrendering of control, fuck ageing and what it does.

Leslie Ash and her exploding lips. Once so beautiful she was and now look. A fish that slurps up mud off the ocean floor and Grace's mother, ho, she doesn't look like *that*, ho, no.

Grace is okay. She flicks channels. *What Katie Did Next*. She watches.

Eyelid rejuvenation. The upper lids drop, droop, and bags, puffy bags, develop on the face below the eyes and the operation to remove them is called blepharoplasty. Excess fat and skin trimmed away, loosening muscles are tautened. Cuts made in the crease of the upper eyelid and below the lash line and sometimes flabby bags are removed from inside the lower lid so that there is no visible scar. Laser resurfacing, skin peels, fine-line reduction. Removal of discolouration. Two weeks to heal. Tightness numbness excessive lachrymosity a drooping of the lower lid scarring and difficulty closing eyes. Cat-eyed appearance. A new, unusual expression, a new face yes but God not *that* new. Permanent results. About four grand.

Flick. *I'm A Celebrity . . . Get Me Out Of Here!*

Look at them eating worms. Big spiders crawling on their faces. Rats on their bodies. Leeches. Snakes. Cockroaches and centipedes. Christ what people will do. She wishes Grace was here to watch this with her and laugh with her like she usually does, like *they* usually do, laughing together, mother and daughter, the telly on loud and the night held back behind the window-glass. But she's getting famous. She's out there getting famous. With a man who's going to make her rich and famous and her mother in here alone with pandemonium being built beneath the skin of her face. Rich and famous and envied.

The mobile phone on the coffee table cries. A text from Grace: **GOING GR8!**

That'll do. Her mother smiles and sits back and watches people writhe in slime. *She's* had work done, that one there. And *her*, and *her*. Gemma Atkinson's tits; they're too *good* to be natural. And don't pretend he got to be that shape without some lipo, no, some haven from decay.

Grace presses Send and puts the phone back in her bag and considers herself in the mirror. The new nose. Bruising barely noticeable but she tops up the concealer anyway. Without the champagne her heart would be beating fast, her mouth would be dry and her eyes would be wide as she watches the huge door swing open to let her into the gleaming world beyond it because that's what's happening, here, in this hotel bar, a gateway is opening and she's walking into the land of her dreams and it is pretty much perfect, pretty much as she always hoped it would be except for one thing; Damien is getting drunk and is acting like a cock.

She can hear him from the other side of the room, as she exits the toilet. He's shouting something in an *EastEnders* accent and gesticulating wildly with his arms. *Cor blimey!* He notices her approaching and is energised further, pulling invisible braces away from his chest.

—Apples and pears, jellied eels! Oi lahv the Queen and the Kray twins!

The agent looks nothing but bemused. —I'm not from London. I'm from Essex.

—Diamond fahkin geezah!

—Damien, shut up. Grace sits down beside him and tries to burn him with her eyes. —You're making a fool of yourself.

His eyes on her are wet and sloppy. —Me, is it? *I'm* making a fool of myself, am I?

The agent looks at a point over their heads and smiles. —Ah. Here comes security.

—Oh yeah? And that makes you grin like a wanking Jap cos of why?

—Damien!

—Are we all okay here?

The agent holds his palm out. —Fine, fine. Too much to drink, that's all. I'll call if we need you.

The waiter glares down at the top of Damien's head and then leaves. Grace glares too. Damien goes to refill his glass but the agent removes the champagne bottle from his hand.

—You've had enough, young man. You're going to despise yourself in the morning.

—Am I?

—Yes, you are.

—Give me that bottle, yeah?

—No.

—Fuck yeh then. Fuck yeh both.

Damien stands and staggers. The waiter appears and takes his arm but Damien jerks it away and lurches through the restaurant towards the exit doors on to the street. The waiter looks at the agent.

—Don't let him back in. Call him a taxi, see he gets home safely. Charge it to my room. Where does he live, Gracie?

She tells him. The waiter says: —That's a long way away Mr Wellin. It won't be cheap, sir.

—No matter. The agent shrugs. —Just see that he gets there safely and in one piece. And have another bottle sent up to my room.

—Yes sir. No problem.

And then Grace is walking towards the lift. The agent is beside her, telling her that this often happens, he's seen it a hundred times before; the boyfriends or husbands get jealous and start behaving badly. It's a possession thing. They think that they want their partners to chase and fulfil their dreams and they encourage them in that, they support them all the way, until it actually starts to happen. They just don't know how to handle it.

Chase and fulfil their dreams, Grace thinks in the lift. Rolls those words around her mouth, tastes them. All four walls of the lift are mirrored and Grace can see herself reflected into infinity, her nice new dress and her new nose going on forever and the tall man with the grey crew-cut hair next to her too. Forever they go on. They never end. Sucked up in the lift towards the night sky.

—What do you see, Gracie? he asks, smiling down at her.

—What do I see?

—Yes. He gestures at the walls. —Tell me what you see.

—I see me. And my new nose.

He smiles. —I see a beautiful young girl who's going to go on and make a biiiiig splash. And whose boobs could be just a teensy bit bigger. Just a *teensy* bit. The merest smidgen.

The lift stops and the doors slide open. Grace is walking down a low-lit corridor and then she's in a room that is dominated by a huge bed and a huge flat-screen TV stuck on the wall opposite the bed and there is a big mirror and some wooden pieces of furniture and a deep sofa and a glass-topped coffee table and the light comes from a standing flexible lamp in a corner with its glowing head bent like a flamingo's or a crane's.

—Just a *tiny* bit, the agent says, and holds his thumb and forefinger about an inch apart. —Make yourself at home, Gracie Allcock.

47

—Can I use the toilet?

—Of course you can. *Me casa tu casa* or however it goes.

Grace locks herself in the bathroom. Sits on the toilet and urinates. The champagne is continuing to bubble, inside her head, pressing on her bladder and she can see, in the bright light that falls from the wall-mounted spots, each crack between the tiles, the tiny bottles of shampoo and conditioner and body wash, the matchbox soaps, the toilet roll folded into a V. A door has opened. Into the white fire of a great and massive mystery? No. That happened perhaps when Grace was supine in the operating theatre and a man in a mask advanced on her with a blade. Overhead light winking in a glint off the sterilised steel.

She looks down at her chest. A teensy bit bigger. She regards the bumps her breasts make against her nice new dress. The little bulges they make. She stands and wipes and flushes and looks at those breasts. This face. The things happening to this tingling skin and the person it, crackling, surrounds.

The champagne has arrived. The agent is holding a flute of it and is sitting on the bed propped up against the headboard and he's taken his trousers off. He's wearing his shirt and socks and underpants and is pointing with his glass at the TV screen on which Katie Price is doing some pouty and swimsuity thing on a beach.

—Now there's one that got away, he says with a sigh. —I'll always regret that one. Curse myself every day for not seeing her potential when she was just a gawky teenager. I've poured you a drink.

—Thank you Mr Wellin.

—Mr Wellin? I'm Jerry. We're friends now. No need for the formal. I'm Jerry and you're Gracie. Sit down and have a drink with me.

He pats the bed at his side and Grace sits and drinks. Sees the long hairs on his white legs. Curl of a vein like a purple worm on one shin. The white sports socks tight to the ankle, the left one rolled down a little to reveal crenellated vertical lines on the skin from the elastication.

—I like your shoes, Gracie.

—Thank you. Grace waggles one foot in the air.

—Your dress, too. There's a certain style to you, Gracie Allcock.

—Thank you, Jerry.

—That's better. How's the champagne?

—Fine.

—You ever drunk it before?

—No.

—Thought as much. Well, get used to it. There's rivers of the stuff coming your way, rivers. He looks at the TV. Katie is holding a baby. —Every day I kick myself, he says, and flicks through the channels. Rolling news. A serious man is pointing at a map of the northern hemisphere. There's the white splash of Greenland. Arrows emanate from it across the sea and between Ireland and Iceland to a crook of Britain, a recess in the country not far from where they are now, on this bed, in this hotel room, in this city. Not far from where the wave will hit, or so they're saying. Flick. Willy Roberts singing on stage somewhere. Flick. Some faces eating insects. Flick. Football. Flick. Back to Katie, on a horse.

—There are some papers you need to sign, Jerry says. —But let's wait until morning.

Jerry puts his glass on the bedside table and slaps his bare thighs with both hands and Grace doesn't know why he does this. Maybe the image of the horse on the screen has set up in him some desire to somehow mimic its gallop, because that's what it sounds like, the rhythmic slapping, an approximation of the sound of a galloping horse. And there must be some events, some small instances of movement and speech, between Jerry Wellin doing this and then putting his dick in Grace's mouth, but if there are, she'll never recollect what they were; it's simply three steps: storm warning – slap slap – suck. That's all. The movement is seamless and organic and puzzling, even in its logic, it is puzzling. The arrows pointing at a part of Britain that Grace knows and then the horse thing and then her new nose is touching Jerry Wellin's belly and he has his hands pressing down on the back of her head and small flares of pain go off in the remodelled bridge of her nose every time it bangs against his belly which is rapid and often. Not like watching a door open but kicking that door down. A battering ram. A violent storming of a place of shamelessness so welcomed and extreme as to demolish the very notion of shame, all of it, all of it, the arrows from Greenland then Katie holding the baby and then on her horse then the rhythmic slapping and then the choking and the spurting, the grey syrup rain, and then the spitting in the bathroom sink under the burning bright lights and the rinsing of the mouth with water and the groggy return to the bed next to the snoring agent, all of it, all those things, stages on a journey that once started – and it has – can never end. Ice cracks. Light hums and burns. Somewhere a wind begins to build up there on the turning globe at the outer curve of it where all is white and blue, in a perennial half-light. Begins to build.

*

Huuuuuuuuurrrrrrrrrrrrtttttttttttttt
Huuuuuuuuuuuuurrrrrrrrrrrrtttttttttttttttt
HUUUUUUUUUURRRRRRRRRRRRRRTTTTTTTT

SPRING

Turns the world again. Towards the sun again. The bruising disappears from around Grace's nose and some sort of healing happens. The boil reappears on her neck and must be lanced again and drained and Grace returns from the doctor's, back to her mother's house, past the primary school she went to behind whose chain-link fence at the lower end of the field the yellow brontosaur of a digger cranes next to a hole. Along the promenade next to the glittering sea and beach on which several dogs run and people stroll and out of the deep pebbly pockets in which gusts of salty breath bloom. The beach, at its tideline, bears a scurf of thousands of dead starfish, washed up a few mornings ago, once orange now flabby white, a mushy and rotting rim. Many seagulls stab and scavenge, some crows, too. Thousands of starfish, dead on the foreshore. As Grace watches, a golden retriever bounds into the mess, snaffles up a few huge mouthfuls as its owner bawls at it then drags it away by the collar and chases it back up the beach with a swipe of a leash. All those starfish. Grace has never seen such a thing before. Or if she has then she has long forgotten it.

At home she sits on the sofa and flicks the TV on. Jeremy Kyle. Her mother's out somewhere, drinking coffee and eating cake with a friend in one of the prom caffs that have just reopened after the winter, or shopping, or having her hair done, or sunbedding. Something like that. Grace touches the sticking plaster on her neck that hides the drained boil. Might be a nice new nose but the body will not be tamed. Cannot be tamed. This, this. Pus inside her. Her toes are too long, calves too thin, thighs too heavy, hips too wide. Her fanny is ugly; she examined it once with a hand mirror and was reminded of a bacon sandwich. There is a roll of fat around her middle. Her navel is okay, an inny rather than an outy, but it remains unpierced and that's no good cos everyone has a pretty little chain through their belly button these days. Her ribs are prominent, her tits far too small. Weedy shoulders. Noticeable collarbones. No definition to her neck. Lips not pouty enough, not full enough. Chin too dimpled. Forehead too high. Hair limp and lifeless. Nape, well, she can't see her nape. But it is leaking pus. Back flabby, and how can that be, if her ribs stick out too much, how can she have a flabby back? Doesn't make sense. Christ but nature has been cruel to Grace. Arse too flat as well. Not rounded, unattractive. Back to the fat thighs and the thin calves and the feet with the too-long toes. Work is needed. A lot of work.

Let's have those all-important lie-detector results. Time for the truth.

Such an ugly body, such an unbecoming face. Such an ugly body that leaks smelly pus. That shits and pisses and sweats and bleeds. Bleeds into the tampon that Grace is now bearing, that she has plugged herself with. She scratches at her forearm until ruby beads appear on the skin. How it goes on. How it will not be tamed. The ice has melted and the winter has gone and the world has turned towards the sun and things are greening again and the body, this body, will not be tamed. Like an arrow in the heart. Rot and react, rot and react. Like those starfish. Flee from it all. Escape.

Well well well.

IS the biological father.

Betrayal. That's what it is. Grace punches herself in the belly. Says *oof*, although it doesn't really hurt. Punches herself again, harder, which seems to set up some process in her bladder so that she has to visit the toilet. Sitting on the cold seat she takes a magazine from a stack at the side of the bath on the ottoman. *Steal Her Look*, says the magazine's cover. Above a picture of Megan Fox. Grace sits and seethes and pisses and reads.

Some early holidaymakers populate the prom. So soon after the winter and already it is warm and they have come for the seaside and the caravans and the jet skis and the casino on the pier and the seafront bars. Yesterday the council sent a digger and a truck to clear the beach of the rotting starfish and the smell of their decay has gone now, replaced by frying onions and the sea's usual ozone and brine. Not what could be called 'busy' as yet, but the town is reanimated, after the abandonment that winter imposes. Not what could be called 'warm' as yet, but the skin still is bared, white, pale blue in parts, raw turkey'd with gooseflesh. The promenade full of parked cars. A bouncy castle. Some music from the arcades and sports bars.

Grace and Damien sit in the tattooist's. Reconciliation, this. Or an attempt at such. Together getting marked. Damien is wanting her to apologise but she tells him that she's already done so, several times over.

—And you got home okay didn't you?

—Yeah. But.

—So what are you going on about? Doing my head in, yeah? And he paid for the taxi, didn't he? Must've cost a fortune. So be grateful, yeah?

—For what, mate? For what you and that twat got up to after I'd gone?

—I've already told you. Nothing happened, yeah? We finished the food and I got pissed and Jerry paid for a taxi home. Another one. He's a generous man, in case you didn't notice.

—Jerry, now, is it?

—Cos, like, that's his name? What else am I supposed to call him?

Damien sits quiet. Then says: —See that boil on your neck's come back.

Grace turns sharp eyes on him. —Oh shut up. You are so vile, you.

—I'm just saying. Did you have it drained again?

Grace ignores him. Flicks through the magazine she's been holding rolled up into a tight cylinder on her lap. Turns to the page on which the recognisable person in the backless ballgown is printed.

Damien leans. —Which one is it again?

—That one. Grace puts her fingertip on the tattoo in the small of the recognisable person's back.

—It'll look good on you.

Grace accepts the apology but tastes semen at the back of her throat. The banging belly.

—Who's going first?

—You are, Grace says.

—Why me?

—Cos I want to know if it hurts.

—Hurts? What, after the nose op you're worrying if it hurts? Grace shrugs.

—It won't hurt. Just a needle, end of the day. Just a little prick, like. And you've had loads of those, yeah?

The tattooist calls Damien into his studio where Damien takes his fleece off and has drilled into his upper arm a series of tiger stripes, vertical wavy parallel lines with pointed ends in black ink. The fourth such design this week, for the artist. Like a law; every male below thirty must have such markings, in this country. Damien saw a footballer once with such a tattoo and it looked cool as fuck, dead individual, so he thought he'd get it done too. He's noticed other guys with similar designs but that's all he's done, just noticed them, nothing else. They simply registered on his retina as trees do, as rocks do. There's another one of them tattoos. It doesn't hurt, really. Bad burning sensation at first but then it just becomes a constant yet mild throb which is over surprisingly quickly.

—There ye go, lad. The tattooist speaks in the accent of the big city to the east as he dresses Damien's weeping arm. —Keep this on for a couple of weeks, then rub it with Vaseline or moisturiser every day for a couple of months. Don't fucken pick it.

Damien pays, returns to the waiting area. Gives Grace a smile, all teeth. —Piece of piss. Dead easy. Nothing to worry about, yeah?

Grace goes into the studio, shows the tattooist the page in the magazine. That one, there. That's what I want. The slag-antler. The tramp-stamp. Fifth one of these he's done this week. Like a law etc. He's a big, bearded man but he's gentle with Grace as he sits her down in the chair, facing backwards, so that her forearms are folded on top of the backrest and her chin is resting on them. He rolls her top up, tucks the hem of

54

it behind her bra strap against slippage. Grace's skin jumps a little at the touch of his fingers. The banging belly, the banging belly. She hears a drill start up. The tattooist consults the picture and rolls his eyes. Another one. Like asking a top chef for beans on toast. Could do this with his eyes closed. Put the pumping needle in the skin.

They buy tea at the kiosk on the promenade, in styrofoam cups, and sit on a bench to drink it. Damien asks her if it hurt and she shrugs. Blows on and sips the tea. A group of young men and women walk past and despite the memory of frost in the air some of the men have their tops off and tucked into the back pockets of their jeans to hang like tails and some of the women are wearing crop tops that show their bellies and backs. So much skin so goosebumped. All of the men have the tiger stripes on their arms. All of the women have the antlers on their backs, just above the buttocks, in the small. Grace and Damien watch them loudly pass. One of them is carrying a football and they're headed no doubt for the beach. Look at their tattoos. The tattooist had told Damien that now he was marked from today until nine days after his death and he seemed happy about that. Said it with a grin in his beard. Grace and Damien stare as the people mostly marked alike pass.

—Let's have a look at it then.

Grace's mother is leaning against the fridge. The sunbed session earlier that day has re-tangerined her and the lines in her face are pronounced as a result; the hidden skin that the AV cannot reach. She's eating a Crunchie and Grace and Damien are at the table sharing a pizza.

—Can't Mum. It's got a dressing on it.

—For how long?

—Couple of weeks.

—Yours as well, Day?

—Yeah. Can't show it for at least two weeks, yeah?

—Did it hurt?

—Not really, say Grace and Damien in unison, but her mother senses some fracture between them, a distance, a wobbling of the air. Mother's intuition. She knows something is wrong.

—You heard from Jerry yet?

Grace shakes her head. Cheese threads on her lips like impatient worms. —Haven't checked my messages today.

Grace's mother nods. —Better go and do it then. Got to push yourself out there, love, yeah? Be, what's the word, proactive, yeah? No one's gonna do it for you, end of the day.

—I know. Finishing this first. Starving.

—Always hungry, you. Fat equals failure, yeah?

—I know, but starving equals weak and dead.

Grace's mother laughs.

Tomorrow night, the email says. **Alma de Cuba. Short notice I know but you simply MUST be there. MUST MUST MUST. It's harvest time.**

'Harvest time'? He wants her to work on a farm? Picking vegetables and that? Only the Poles do that these days. What's he talking about?

I've got you on the guest list and booked you a double room in 'our' hotel. You can take a female friend. FEMALE. Any problems call me Jxxx

She sends an email back: **fine but whats harvest time?** A minute later the reply comes back from a BlackBerry:

Google it. Google 'harvest + footballers'. And good luck!!xxx

Grace Googles. Damien's downstairs with her mother, eating Ben & Jerry's in the kitchen, *Celebrity Weakest Link* on the portable. That Anne Robinson. Grace can hear her screeching through the floorboards. The sinking sun is sending red rays into her bedroom, casting Klieg lights on to the pictures on her walls. Grace clicks on the top hit and reads about harvesting and footballers and her breath, quickened, sends a midge, barely perceptible speck of life, bred in the standing pools of brackish water anterior to the dunes, against the wall and then sideways left behind the big poster and into the web of the tiny spider behind Willy Roberts's right eye, forever frozen in a listing wink. Feeds the spider, the hurrying breath of newly inked Grace.

'Harvesting + footballers'. How Grace's heart does pound. This is what it's about, here, this is how the world begins.

She chooses Shelly to accompany her because she's known her the longest, since they were at primary school in fact, the school behind the chain-link fence set back a bit from the eastern end of the promenade. She chooses Shelly because she's her best friend. Because she's good company. She chooses Shelly because she's slightly overweight and not as pretty as Grace. They catch a train to the big city and check into the hotel in mid-afternoon and drink WKD that they'd smuggled into the room in a backpack although there was no need to do that, the receptionist telling them that the room bill and all other expenses were being picked up by Mr Wellin. They call for sandwiches from room service and sit at the table in the window bay eating them. Prawn on one, chicken sub. Two hearts busy. Jerry calls to check that everything's okay and to tell her to be at the club at 7:30 and that she's on the guest list plus one and to go straight to the front of the queue and speak to the door staff and if there are any problems at all to call him and he'll sort it out. Have fun, he says. This is your moment, he says. Gracie. The twenty-first-century Gracie. She and Shell look out at the city some storeys below and they prink and they preen for some hours, drinking, the telly on in the background. MTV. Nails filed and polished. Bikini lines plucked. Vajazzling discussed and decided against. Legs shaved, armpits too. Long baths taken. Hair styled seven ways before a satisfactory way is found and make-up applied then removed then reapplied. This shade? No, that. Prune and mulberry. Glittery around the eyes. Which earrings? I've brought ten pairs. Busy, busy hearts. At 7 p.m. Grace is looking at herself in the mirror all made up and she's wearing a tight and small black dress, Warehouse, drape sleeve, that hems at the knee and a pair of black and white cowboy boots because she saw Sienna Miller wearing a similar outfit once and it looked dead sexy and cool and individual. Shell is, well, Shell is wearing some dress with a floral pattern on it and some sort of high heels and her hair's all piled up on top of her head and Grace tells her that she looks gorgeous, proper special. Lush. They go downstairs, laughing in the lift. Grace, not for the first time that day, recalls a hairy belly, a bulging and banging hairy belly. Their heels click on the marble floor of the lobby. They ask the receptionist to call them a cab. He does. *On Mr Wellin's account,* he tells them. *You don't have to pay a penny.* The taxi arrives and the Sikh driver conveys them for some time between big brown buildings and over a stretch of motorway to the club. Look at the size of that queue. Even from inside the cab Grace and Shell can hear the music from inside, 'Poker Face' by Lady Gaga. Poker face, Grace thinks. Poke her face. Gag her.

They get out. All the eyes on them. Straight to the doorman, the clack and knock of their shoes on the flagstones, the doorman in the black jacket behind the red rope. Feel the eyes on them. This is what it's about. The gaze. Assessing or envious or simply a-seethe, the gaze is the goal, the gaze, those eyes, the people looking. Grace's heart thumps. Her mouth is dry. She is dizzy, slightly spinning. She is holding on to Shelly's arm. Shelly is holding on to hers.

—Help you, ladies?

—We're on the guest list.

—Names?

—Grace, *Gracie* Allcock. Plus one.

—Allcock. The man smiles and consults a clipboard. —Guests of Mr Wellin, he says, and there's something in his voice. He's not just stating a fact, as he reads it. There's something else there, in his tone, as there is in his eyes when he looks Grace up and down, again, something new and different. Respect? Not quite. Curiosity? Grace doesn't know. But it makes her tighten her grip on Shelly's arm.

—Right, he says. —Good. He turns to look inside the club foyer and beckons over a slim blonde woman in a white trouser suit, halter neck. Bling. Hair like gold fibres. Skin proper brown not sunbed satsuma. —Jessica? Look after these two, will you? They're guests of Mr Wellin.

—It'll be my pleasure. She has a voice like a cat's purring. —Follow me, girls.

—Jess'll look after you, ladies. Have a great night.

Grace releases Shell's arm and Shell releases hers. They follow Jessica's exposed back and Grace, again, curses the tattoo dressing that has prevented her own dress from being backless and as she steps over the threshold, through the red rope that has been unclipped for her, she cannot resist a direct look at the people at the head of the queue, all of whom have been watching her for the past couple of minutes and all of whom saw it all: the consultation of the guest list, the welcoming smile, Jess and her bling and care. Grace in her cowboy boots. Grace with her new nose. All of this they saw, they've seen, they've been watching. And the faces whether male or female are to Grace just blobs, floating blobs, but the eyes in them are clearly defined and big and taking Grace in, the details, absorbing every inch of her, and in that one quick glimpse as she steps lightly into the club Grace can see her future. Sees what awaits. The staring eyes, the many eyes, the staring and starving eyes. Either gulped in the gaze of a thousand wide eyes or registered on just one world-sized, this is how the world began and begins for Grace. Black pool of a pupil that she's plunging happily into. Leaping. The splash she will make. Is making. With her new nose. Leaping and laughing. Poke her face. Gag.

She and Shell follow Jessica's brown and muscular back around the dance floor and through the lights that pump and throb and through the music and around the bar and up some steps and into a roped-off area. More red ropes which Jessica unclips and grants access. She shows the two girls to a table and asks them what they'd like to drink.

—Vodka, says Shell and Grace nods.

—Finlandia, says Jessica.

—No. Vodka.

—Yes. She nods. —Just straight?

—And Coke.

—Vodka and Coke. Two of them.

She waves a waiter over and whispers in his ear. He leaves. She stands, the tight shape of her, the coolly contrasting colours of her, and looks down at Grace and Shelly.

—He'll bring the drinks over. Anything else you need, just ask him. Now I've got to go and mingle but I'll be over to check on you two later, okay? The teeth in the smile are impossibly white. Chalk, milk, a hint almost of the lightest blue. —Relax. Enjoy yourselves.

She waves goodbye by raising her left hand palm down and rubbing her middle and ring fingers together three times. The waiter brings drinks: two tall glasses containing vodka, a bowl of crushed ice, another of lemon and lime slices, two small bottles of cola. Gaga ends, becomes La Roux.

—There you go, ladies. Courtesy of Mr Wellin. Anything else you need just holler. He smiles. Again with the teeth and the dazzling. Ultraviolet, agleam. He goes.

—Phwoar, says Shell. —Lush.

Grace laughs. —What are you like? He's a waiter!

—Still but. He's lush.

—We're not after waiters here, Shell.

—What are we after, then?

—Dunno yet. But we'll find out, yeah? Cheers.

They clink glasses and drink, gasp, put cola and ice and lemon in the raw vodka then drink again. They're dancing in their seats. Their bodies and their minds are racing, reacting. They are surrounded by flesh, flanks and midriffs, nearly all of it female and all of it coloured tan or tawny or tangerine. Nails long, picturesquely painted. All belly buttons pierced. Rings and bracelets and necklaces and anklets catch the lights and bounce them back. Hair blonde, almost uniformly so; the odd brunette or redhead swamped by the yellow and the golden and the nearly white. The smalls of many bared backs bear the tattoo, *the* stamp, *the* mark, and Grace wishes again that she'd been inked some weeks ago so that she could show here and now that she too is marked, cool, individual also, like them. The teeth around are whiter than the whites of the eyes above them, even caged as they are within long black spikes of eyelash, in faces that seem not, really or much, to move, that are untouched by any line or crease, lips that oddly bulge and swell and eyelids that rise at the corners into folds with which no Caucasian has ever been born. Grace and Shell gaze, and gaze, swivel in their seats. So much skin moving past them. Basketballs bouncing over their turning heads.

—There's Alicia Duvall, Grace says. —I'm sure that's Alicia
Duvall.

—Who's Alicia Duvall?

—Her over there. In the purple dress showing her fat arse.

—Yeah but who *is* she?

—Some slapper. Famous for shagging footballers.

A face that doesn't look right, in the throbbing lights. That
sags and warps beneath the garish rind of what once was skin.

—How'd you know it's her?

—Recognise her. Seen her face before, in the papers and
that?

—Yeah but how can you tell it's her? I mean she looks the
same as everyone else here, doesn't she?

Grace looks around. —Sept us.

—Apart from us, yeah.

—And d'you know why?

—Why?

—Cos we're young, Shell. End of the day we don't need to
hide wrinkles and stuff do we? Know what a mean?

—What wrinkles? Only wrinkle I've got is between me legs.

They laugh loudly and slap their palms together and raise
their glasses to their faces and drink. Eyes are on them. They
feel the eyes on them like the welcome breath of someone
wanted.

—And d'you know where we are? Grace leans over the table
towards her friend. —VIP area! Alma de Cuba! We're fuckin
VIPs Shell!

Laugh again, drink again.

—Your nose looks gorgeous, Grace. Proper, *proper* special.
Thinking of getting it done meself. Now that I've seen yours.

—Why? Nothing wrong with your nose, yeah? You've got
a perfect nose. Mine had that horrible bump.

—Yeah but look at this. Shell points to her right nostril
—See how it's a bit bigger than the other one?

Grace narrows her eyes. —No. Can't see any difference, yeah?
You've got a perfect nose.

—No, it is. The right one's a bit bigger than the left one.

—D'you think so?

—I know so. Every time I look in the mirror.

—Fuck it, then. Get it done. Save up and get it done. Or borrow the money, yeah? End of the day you've got to be happy with yourself, yeah?

—Does it hurt?

Grace nods. —But it's worth it. Best thing I ever did. I mean look. She gives Shell her profile, her right profile.

—It's perfect. Angelina.

Grace grins. Angelina. She looks like Angelina. Her grin grows.

—More vodka yeah? Where's that feller?

She waves to the waiter and orders more drinks. Big ones this time. The waiter smiles and tells them that he might as well bring the bottle, yeah? Seeing that it's paid for and everything.

—Might as well mate.

He goes to fetch it.

—Isn't this good? Isn't this just the best fuckin thing ever?

—Too right it is. Look where we are.

—Alma de Cuba!

—Vee Aye fucking Pee!

—Talking of pee.

They go to the toilet. The roped-off area has its own lavatories so there is no need to traverse the dance floor. They link arms and feel eyes on them as they cross the VIP area and Grace wiggles her arse in the tight black dress and looks straight ahead giggling, will not meet any of the eyes that look at her, gaze at her, gulp her up. There's a woman in the toilet dressed in black, standing at the sinks, and Shell and Grace pee in adjacent cubicles and as they preen at the mirrors after washing their hands the woman sprays something from an atomiser on their necks.

—What's that for?

—Make you smell nice.

—I already smell nice, yeah? Grace says.

—This is just to keep you topped up.

—Ta very much.

They leave the toilets.

—What was all that about? Her with the spray?

Shell shakes her head. —They have them people in these posh places.

—Think we should've given her some money?

—Dunno. Maybe.

—Don't see what for. Got me own bloody perfume on yeah?

—I'll give her a quid later. Got some money from me mum before I came out.

They return to their table. A bottle of Finlandia awaits, a dent in it but three-quarters full still. Pearls of moisture on its sides.

—God I'm gunner be pissed.

—Aren't you already?

—Nearly.

—Drink up then.

Grace pours the vodka. They add cola, lemon, ice. Drink.

—Fancy a dance?

—I'm having one, says Grace, and she is, in her seat, her shoulders going, her waist, her head lolling in loose rhythm on her neck. If she stands to dance they'll see her boobs. Or her lack of them. Amongst these women with the brownish beach-balls, spherical and swollen, bursting out of low-hung tops or barely contained by spaghetti straps, horse chestnuts newly torn from the shell. There is a gaze yes and there is appraisal in that gaze but Grace does not wish or want to stand straight-backed and uncontoured amid all these oiled hillocks.

—On the dance floor, I mean.

—Not yet. Let's wait for a *good* song and get a bit more drunker, yeah?

Willy Roberts's new track begins. The opening strings. Grace and Shell say *Yessss* and look at each other as they weave and bob in their seats.

—Awesome.

—The *shit*.

A man appears at their table. He has slicked-back hair greying at the temples and lined mahogany skin and is wearing a white waistcoat.

—Mind if I join you two girls? I want to join in the fun.

Grace and Shelly, seated, look up at him. They can see the underneath of his chin. There is a small cicatrice there

63

that evidently will not tan, like a cooked prawn glued to his skin.

—I mean, you two are irresistible. I told myself to keep away, I did, young things like yourselves, but. What are you drinking?

And then Jessica in her whiteness and bare-backedness is at his side, long fingers of one hand on his shoulder, the nails white like her trouser suit, her red lips whispering in his ear, her sleek ponytail halfway down her back, wisping across the tattoo in the small. She hisses a few words into the man's ear and he smiles and backs away, showing the palms of his hands.

—My mistake. I apologise. Guys better than me . . . or richer than me, anyway.

He smiles and winks at Grace and then gives Jessica a look and is gone. Jessica also winks at Grace and then is gone too.

—What was all that about?

—Just some oldie fancying his chances, yeah?

—Yeah but Jessica.

Grace shrugs. —Look at us, Shell. Who can blame him?

—Yeah but why did Jessica step in?

Shrug again, one shoulder. —Just looking out for us, is all. Jerry's probably told her to, yeah?

—Who's Jerry?

—My agent. Got us on the guest list? I told you about him, yeah?

—Oh yes. I remember.

The banging belly. The warm spurts.

—What's he like?

Grace swirls the ice in her drink with a straw and then sucks up some of the drink through the straw. —He's gunner make me famous. And rich. Rich and famous he said.

A cheer goes up from downstairs. Loud and sudden. Shelly and Grace crane their necks to see but the balcony that looks out over the lower dance floor is crowded, crowded with VIPs gawping. The DJ shouts something from his box but his words are distorted and anyway drowned out by the cheering and the chanting that has started up, one name, repeated.

—What's going on?

—Some famous person, yeah? This is Alma, Shell.

—Yeah but who?

—We'll find out in a minute. They'll be coming up here.

—VIP area.

—VIP.

Grace grins. Shelly grins back at her. They met at primary school. Six or seven years of age they were, twelve, thirteen years ago. They both had braces and were wearing the same blue shoes and they noticed that about each other but didn't say anything then but sought each other out during afternoon break. I like your shoes. I like yours. Where'd you get them? They're the same, look. And on their lunchboxes too they both had glittery horse stickers, not exactly the same but similar, and they couldn't believe it. They spoke about horses, that day. Horses and shoes and other things. Many other things. Shell told Grace about her dog and her dad and Grace told Shell that she didn't have a dad any more and asked her why she was called Shell and Shell said it was because she collected shells off the beach. And because her proper name was Michelle. The next day they each brought in sheets of glittery horse stickers and swapped them. Grace got the head of a black shire horse for the head of a brown pony with a white blaze. They wore the same shoes, again. Twelve or thirteen years ago when they were six or seven years old. Five, maybe. When there were colours of an intensity that spurred and flavoured their dreams and when there were things that crawled and flew and fascinated.

The people at the balcony that looks out over the lower dance floor have turned their heads now to look at the top of the stairs that lead up from the lower area. Grace and Shell look with them. A couple of huge men in suits and with shining shaven heads appear first and then three tall and lean men come after and the people in the VIP area cheer and clap and the three tall men do not smile but they do shake the hands of the other men when proffered albeit without enthusiasm. Grace once heard her mother use the phrase 'stinking rich' but she'd never understood it until now. Waves come off the men. The emanate a vinegary reek of wealth, the way they move, their clothes, the way they seem determined not to smile, the way their eyes scan the room, never settling on one face.

The smell of money is a fact in Grace's nostrils. Probably in Shelly's misaligned ones too. Money and something else. A kind of worshippy thing.

—Ohmygod Grace says, like that, one word. And again: —Ohmygod.

—What is it, Grace? Who are they?

—They're the harvesters, Shell. The footballers. Why we're here, yeah?

And there they are, in skin, moving, not like Grace has ever seen them on a football pitch but just as she's seen them in tabloids and magazines and on screens; the tall mixed-race defender with the number one crop and the sneering top lip (result of an accident on his bike when he was small, Grace knows), the shorter and stockier Northern Irish winger, just breaking into the first team, and the midfielder from the Med somewhere with his hair in a sideways fin all greased and the perpetual pout. The harvesters. The women shoal awaiting reaping.

—Ohmygod, Grace says again. —It's them. It's really them.

They stand, tall, casting their expressionless eyes over the faces around them. The big besuited men flank them like faithful mastiffs. Jessica is there now, with them, holding up a tray of drinks; the Northern Irish guy and the mixed-race guy with the funny lip take up flutes of what looks like champagne. The Mediterranean feller accepts an orange juice.

—Look at them.

—I am, Grace, I am. I'm looking. What are they doing?

—They're harvesting.

—So you've said, but what's that mean?

Grace doesn't answer. Just stares. The men sip and look, sip and stand and look. Other men gaze at their faces and the women roundabout now look everywhere but at their faces; at their own nails, their drinks, at the screens of their mobile phones, into the middle distance as they flick their hair and suck through straws. Grace notices this so rips her eyes away to look at her friend and suck at her straw and her heart is thudding through the alcohol buzz and bleariness which a minute ago was threatening to knock her unsteady and maybe nauseous but has cleared now, has been blown like thin smoke

66

away by the appearance of the tall lean men and the abrupt pumping of her blood.

—What's going on, Shell? What are they doing?

Shell peers over Grace's shoulder. —They're just standing there and looking around. One of them's pointing. Oh God she's coming over.

—Who is?

—That Jessica.

—Is she? Over here?

—Yes.

—No way.

—She is.

The long and tapering fingers on Grace's shoulder. The pointed white nails. Jessica leans from her tiny waist until her lips are level with Grace's ear.

—The boys would like very much for you to accompany them to their hotel.

—Me?

Jessica smiles and nods. —Just you.

—Now?

—Yes. Well, very shortly. They'll be sending a car. Be outside the club in two minutes, that okay?

Jessica goes. Grace watches her leaving back and sees, too, the backs of the harvesters descend the stairs, almost obscured by the doorbacks of the men in the suits. Watches their heads vanish below the level of the topmost riser. She turns back to Shelly.

—Oh my God, Grace.

—Oh my God, Shell.

—What are you going to do?

—Go and wait outside the club. Didn't you hear?

Then Grace is in the toilets. She reapplies lipstick. Fixes her hair. Waves away the woman with the atomiser. Returns to her table to fetch her bag.

—Grace.

—Just get a taxi, Shell. To the hotel.

—Grace.

—Don't forget it's paid for. I'll see you later, yeah? I'll text you or something.

67

—Grace.

Then Grace is outside the club, on the pavement, in exhaust fumes, with three other women. The night air pulls her skin into goosebumps, flesh, pimples, a million cold thin threads rooted in her pores and gently tugged by a high and invisible hand. On her pale skin, the reaction in her papillae to the night air. Raising the hairs. Once to trap warmth, in more hirsute days. Horripilation, on her pale skin. An involuntary response to the cold night air or to a strong emotion such as fear or awe. She's drunk, Grace is. Swaying a little. The other women stand and wait and rock a little on their heels and do not speak to or even directly look at each other but smoke and stand and wait and teeter and peripherally assess each other sidelong with slits of eyes between spider-leg lashes. Their bumpy skin. Fight or flight. See it in cats, in chimpanzees. In the pigeons at roost on the roofs above the waiting women, the feather-fluffing, skin contracting to erect the feathers then relaxing so that they fall into alignment and trap air. For the insulation, for the smoother aerodynamics. Or maybe Grace was a marine mammal. Maybe these women here in exhaust fumes once in other forms perched like the birds. Deep history in Grace's pale uneven skin. The people in the queue begging access to the club gawp at the women and the doormen leer and one says something to the other about the Wurzels and they both laugh. Grace has swallowed a flock of starlings. She touches her new nose. An oat she is, swaying in the draught from an open door. Then there is a long white car parked at the kerbside and a uniformed man is holding the back door of it open and Grace is climbing inside the car with the other women, holding the hem of her dress down, careful not to reveal too much of herself as she clambers inside.

★

Huuuuuuuuuuuuuuuuurrrrrrrrrrrrrrrrrrrrrrrrrrrrrrrrrttttttttttttttttttttttttttttttttt

★

Blurred, unreal. Everything blurred and the world unreal. The passing city outside the tinted windows unreal. The other women in the vehicle, talking to each other now, talking faster than Grace has ever heard anyone talk. Incoming texts to her mobile, from Shell; **U ok? Wir r u?** From her mother: **U ok? Wots apnin?** From Damien: **U ok? Wots goin on?** From Jerry Wellin: **Having fun Gracie?** Grace, Gracie. That's her name. She puts the phone back into her bag. Feels like she might vomit. All that vodka, blue label too. She talks with the other women but does not know what she's saying and none of them laugh and then they are in the marbled lobby of a hotel and there are many people there including the three footballers from the club and others like them, tall and lean and unsmiling, and a shorter, much older man with a purple face and a trenchcoat telling the tall mixed-race guy with the funny top lip to keep everything under control, to keep his boys under control. *If I read bad headlines in the morning I'm holding YOU responsible, you hear?* There is champagne and some talk. Blurred and unreal. Then there is a lift that Grace is in with the Mediterranean man with the fin haircut and then there is a room that she is in with him and he is kissing her. He is undressing himself. He is standing above her naked with his hands on his hips and his penis is pointing at her. Squinting at her. He goes into the bathroom and when he comes back out his skin is much shinier and he asks in broken English why Grace still has her clothes on and then she doesn't. Boobs too small and the dressing on her back. *What is this?* A tattoo. *Not disease?* No. There is an urgent pounding on the room door and some male voices shouting. The man cups himself in one hand and opens the door and two more men enter, maybe the same ones from the club, Grace isn't sure, they look kind of alike. They are wearing jeans but no shirts or shoes and as the shiny man climbs on top of Grace the other men turn on the huge wall-mounted plasma TV and flick through the channels and they seem to be arguing over whose credit card to use. *Yes! Jenna!* one of them shouts and the room is filled with yelping and squealing. A mouth is at Grace's ear, she feels hot breath on her face and smells something sweet like chewing gum.

—Jenna Jameson. You know who Jenna Jameson is? Go on, do a Jenna. Do a Jenna for us. Take it all.

Yanking her hands, her ankles.

—Aw fuck man. Aw baby. Aw fuck.

Grace is full to bursting. She can taste herself. She sees one of the men standing at the side of the bed pointing a mobile phone down at her then he's prowling around the bed, assessing angles. Then he's handing the phone to one of the other men who pulls out of Grace and is replaced. Over a male shoulder, the muscles working under the sunbed skin, Grace can see on the TV screen a blonde woman with huge breasts doing just what she's doing. She regards the scene with one eye as blank as a camera's. Suddenly her hearing has been crippled and there is a pressure at each ear and panic rises for a moment but then she realises what has happened; her knees are to blame. She sees her raised feet above her face, the toes spread and flexing under the ceiling light, beams descending separately between them. This reminds her of something but she can't quite remember what. Then she is gagging and she can taste herself again.

She understands, sort of, that these are not just footballers, not merely men. For one thing, she's never seen any one of them kick a ball but she has seen each of their faces on paper and on screens a thousand times each. Not just men, no, but emissaries from a world that has yet to be named. Aliens unbenign, perhaps come to spread an infection here or introduce it at least so as to prepare the ground for the full arrival which must be imminent because Grace can feel her innards beginning to fall. Not just footballers, not merely men, but events, no, a concourse of events; a happening made of several parts that might one day have a name but which exists only in outline as yet. But which inarguably exists and which will require every cell of Grace to complete itself.

This is it, are the words in Grace's head that are trying to come out of her mouth but there is a blockage in there. *This is it. Great, big, and shining. I need it all.*

★

Hurtling is the word they're using and it is the word they always use. Things to them are always *hurtling*. Once it was a meteor or a comet earthbound which happened before in 1908 I think it was Tunguska it was called. In Russia. Many many acres of flattened forest. And which one of a thousand stars was aimed at this planet with massacre on it or if not that then earthquake. Or if not that then plague. Electronic meltdown. God-like weapons to burn us all but first it seems that we will drown. The dinosaurs them terrible lizards we are and Tunguska was a pebble. Now no more or see them still in birds, in birds. An extinction event is coming.

I breathe in. I exhale. A thin wind in my lungs. Each atom of oxygen forged deep inside a star. Carbon in my muscles and calcium in my bones made very far away in a fiery heart. All these heavy elements in me cooked in the distant fiery hearts you see them glow at night. I breathe in. I exhale. There is a winter on and in my skin and it is such a heavy burden. The knowing that I belong to a species the only one capable of enjoying the suffering of another, of creating a weakness to exploit. When leopard eats the antelope it is no more cruel than when the antelope eats grass but I. But I. But I.

It is forming they say off the east coast of Greenland, a huge and angry eye of cloud. The sea heated and causing this. Hurricane, tsunami. It will batter they say the mid north-western bulge of the country which is where I live after its momentum has traversed thousands of miles of open water and by the time it reaches here it will be a wall of furious water bearing ships and oil rigs and whales and islands. It is coming, it is coming. It cannot be prevented now. It cannot be stopped from happening, they say. Unfixable, what we've done. Gone too far we have. Done too much. Take this knowing and blind my eyes and stuff my mouth with sand. These children, too. Make them un-know. Keep them unaware. For what world will we leave them if they survive the fires and floods? Yet waters and flames surround them still. Surround them already. Being eaten they are, the children I see every day. Such things are coming. Famine. Malaria in Norway. People will kill and eat each other. Mass suicides. Berms of human bones at the feet of cliffs. Fires eating forests and cities under brine. Oceans, vast vats of acid. No white bears ever, ever again. Just an eternity of static. What we violate includes time. Extinction is a rape of time. Shit on the sacred, undo the unique. It's gathering in a place where the world is white and ice and where that ice is beginning to crack and it will approach here at a horrendous force with a rage that levels mountains and cities, this is what they say. I breathe in and I exhale and I wish my skin was made of steel I wish my skull was stone. Such a wild wind in my lungs.

So his days go:

The radio alarm wakes him at 6:30. Chris Moyles's voice. He hates that voice but he leaves the radio tuned to it because there are rare occasions when he is coaxed out of sleep by a song that he likes but usually it's only that voice – shouting, hectoring, in hysteria's borderlands. He presses Snooze and sleeps again. Reawakes ten minutes later and turns the radio off and gets out of bed and sometimes showers but always splashes his face and brushes his teeth and uses the toilet. Goes downstairs, dons his overalls, leaves his house the back way, across the small garden and through the iron gate and on to the lower field and across that and up to the school where he enters his hut and takes the ring of many keys from its nail and opens up the school gates and then the school itself, all the doors, deactivating the alarms before he does so. As the first teachers begin to arrive he returns to his house and breakfasts, usually on cereal and tea and toast, then if he hasn't done so already he showers and shaves then puts his overalls back on and leaves the house again. The first trickle of children appearing. This morning he must tighten the bolts of the bicycle rack on the concrete dais next to his hut which is also a boiler room and this he does, aware of the small animals leaching their decay into the soil beneath the concrete beneath his boots. Used to be a pet cemetery, here, for the school's small animals – the fish and the hamsters and guinea pigs and gerbils. When the school was permitted to keep them, before some Health and Safety official decided that they might spread infection. Which they might've done, but all he remembers is the rapt children. And then that same official decided that the cemetery had to be concreted over to prevent the children from digging up the corpses. Which they might've done, but all he remembers are the earnest little funerals, the sobbing children and the sombre teachers and the bunches of daisies and dandelions and the painted shoebox coffins and sometimes the songs and prayers and the lessons in loss. What no school could ever teach, not then nor now. Bolts tightened he walks down to the field's bottom where the digger sits next to its hole, its bucket at rest atop the mound of spoil. A new swimming pool this will be. Outdoor and heated. He peers through the chain-link fence and sees that water has seeped into the hole but he recalls the workers telling him that they would be bringing a pump in today. High water table they said. So close to the sea as it is. The workers have not arrived yet so he returns to the school around the main entrance to which now many children scamper and shout. Their light urgency, their loud and fast and feverish fun. Five of them are gathered around a small bush and are looking into it then turning away all big-eyed. One of them shouts: —GUSTIN! GUSTIN!, then bends to look again.

He approaches. —What's disgusting? What is it?

—It's all spit! Spit an snot! All over the place!

—Where? Let me see.

He bends and a child parts the bush for him and the other children point at wet frothy clumps in the grass and leaves.

—See? GUSTIN!

He laughs. —No, it's not disgusting. Look —I'll show you what it is.

—It's spit!

—It's not spit. Well it is, kind of. But it's not from people.

He plucks a long stem of dry grass and places the end of it very gently into the nearest gobbet. Softly he moves the stem in a circular motion.

—Look, I'll show you. It's a froghopper. A tiny insect.

—A frog?

—No, but it's called that. Because it looks a bit like one. It's called a froghopper but it's not a frog and this stuff around it is called cuckoo spit but it's not from a cuckoo and it isn't spit.

73

The children lean in and watch. He can hear them breathing. The way they stare. Nothing but this interest. This fascination. As he gently brushes the spittle away from the insect he tells the children that the froghopper is related to the aphid and the cicada which some of them may have heard if they've ever been on holiday to Spain or somewhere hot like that. They look a little bit like frogs and can hop for miles if they're disturbed and their lives are divided into three stages: egg, nymph and adult, and because the nymph's skin hasn't hardened yet it needs to protect itself with this soapy stuff, see? The children lean and breathe. There's the little insect. The children lean and breathe. He tells them that the soapy stuff prevents the insect from drying out and keeps it hidden from things that want to eat it and he tells them that the insect sucks in the sap of the plant and turns it into the frothy stuff inside itself which it fluffs up with air bubbles produced through a valve which is like a tiny bellows. Bellows? None of the children nod.

—Like when you blow bubbles, he says, and now they nod.

—I can see its eyes! Look!

The children lean further in.

—No, they look like eyes but really they're its wings. Or what will be its wings.

—Does it have eyes?

—Yes it has eyes but not like yours or mine.

—Can it fly?

—Not yet. But it will be able to fly, soon. Like a kind of beetle it is.

They stare and say nothing. The little creature in its sap. The children enthralled. In him he knows that behind the loneliness of the world lies a thing never told, a thing like a balance or a scales which sits forever in equanimity even though one cup contains the dead of all wars and the other this single clot of froth. But he does not tell them this. And that they all live on a cold sharp rock adrift in a vast and airless nothingness which means that they must every single day look closely and smell and see and admire and touch he does not utter either. Just lets them watch and wonder at the little froghopper in its little frothy nest.

—And what do we have there, Mr Caretaker?

—Cuckoo spit, he tells the headmaster. —Froghoppers. The children thought somebody had been spitting into the bush but I was showing them what it really is.

—Good, good. But it's time to get inside, children. Bell's gone. And it might be best to leave the natural history lessons to their teachers, Mr Caretaker.

The headmaster waves the children away towards the school with his hand. The children turn away from the bush. 'Mr Caretaker'. One snotty bastard that man. Never uses people's names. Says it benefits the children to learn about identity through work. Says a lot of things that make no sense.

So his days go. He works until eleven, smearing anti-climb paint on drainpipes and railings and trees, removing graffiti, the strange codes he'll never break. He clears out drains, he unblocks toilets, aerates the playing fields. Weeds the borders. Observes the men digging the new swimming pool. Is shown the pump at work. Is shown the security fence, reassured that no child is in danger of breaching it and falling into the hole. The swimming pool was scheduled to be built on the other side of the main building but that was halted because it was discovered that the coppice of trees adjacent to the site was sometimes used by breeding dormice. Or dormice that bred, once. He has not seen a dormouse for years. They come out of hibernation too early with the warmer winters when there are no berries on the trees and so they starve. In recent years. He thinks of a future time when he will show his grandchildren pictures of dormice all asleep and curled up like furry commas and the children will look on in joy and marvel and he'll have to say: *These animals used to exist on the earth. Now they are all dead.* And then pictures of white bears and tigers and bumblebees and blue whales and rhinos and gorillas. *These too. All such animals used to be alive on the earth but now they've all gone. All of them. We boiled them all to death.*

At eleven he walks to the corner shop nearby and buys newspapers and tobacco and food. He returns to his house and catches another hour's sleep or so then makes himself something to eat and puts the TV on and reads the newspapers. There's a photograph of some coffins wrapped in union flags being wheeled out of a Hercules. And here's Cheryl, snapped at Heathrow airport heading for departures, looking glum but glam. She's wearing Ray-Ban Aviators, £118; a Balmain grey T-shirt, £1,015 (this season); Balmain leather trousers, £2,902; Giuseppe Zanotti shoes at £500. And the bag she's carrying in the crook of an elbow is an Alexander McQueen, £975 (last season). A close-up shot of her shoes is captioned 'Heels!' and next to it is the face of the cheating footballer husband she's leaving behind captioned 'Heel!' The caretaker eats and reads and watches *A Place in the Sun*. Maybe surfs the net but he prefers to do that at night-time because he knows how easy it is to get lost in that world, how adept it is at stealing time. At two he leaves the house and works for another four hours. Unblocking, painting, weeding, cleaning. Checks the boiler and anything else that might conceivably pose a danger. When he smokes he is very careful not to do so either indoors anywhere nor in possible view of any children. The bottom of the field, by the new hole, has been useful for this in recent days. Peer through the chain-link and light up. I'm just checking on progress, Mr Headmaster. And I'm forty fucking two years old, by the way.

So his days go. When the school's closing for the day he stands by the main gates to oversee the traffic as the parents pick up their children. Each child to him unreachable inside a phial of magic fluid. Their noise and activity. Their speed and shouting. Unsmeared they are as yet and appreciate them for that. Their bodies unmarked, not plastic as yet. Flesh, bone, skin. Muscles and hearts and lungs. And if there is anything on them of the emulatory and the imitative then the parents are at fault not the children. Today he notices one little girl upset, standing at her mother's knee, her tiny fists held in the cups of her eyes. She's complaining that a teacher has been nasty to her. Her mother bends level:

—Why was he nasty?

—She said I wasn't listening.

—Well, listen to *me*. The mother pulls the girl's hands away from her face. —You're gonna be thinner and prettier than she'll ever be. Who was it, anyway?

—Mrs Hughes.

—Ah. Might've known. Take no notice of her. Just jealous, that's all.

The little girl climbs into the back of the car and her mother straps her in and hands her two books: one by Geri Halliwell and *Colleen's Style Queens*. The mother turns and catches the caretaker's eye and sees him looking and her own eyes narrow to slits and her lips tighten thin and bloodless and she looks at her daughter reading in the car then back at the caretaker again and her arms are folded firm and her eyes are lost in narrow slits and the caretaker smiles at her, just a quick upwards lip-flicker, then turns and moves away. He stands at the gate and directs traffic to ease congestion and when most of the cars have gone he enters the school and cleans what needs to be cleaned and throws away what needs to be thrown away and removes any litter from the grounds and turns the computers off and at six he locks up and returns the keys to their nail next to the boiler in the hut then he locks that up too and stands on the field where it begins to slope down towards the back garden of his little house and he rolls a cigarette and regards the reddening sky where the sun is sinking into the sea. Can't see the ocean from here, behind the rows of houses as it is, but he can smell it and hear the calls of the gulls and he knows what it will look like – blazing and incredible, scarlet and saffron. Odd how you know you're by the sea even when you can't see it. All day he has not seen its water, not one sun-sliced glisten or glitter, but he has felt it in his veins, as a fact in his veins. And two crabs, last week, found here on this field. Moving away from the shore they were. He returned them to the beach in a bucket. Never seen such a thing before, crabs this far away from the shore. And all those starfish recently, all washed up on the beach. Tens of thousands of them. The *smell*.

He returns home, runs a bath, cleans himself. Makes food; tonight, a pork chop and mashed potatoes and processed peas. Watches TV, the news; a man pointing at a map of Greenland.

He's talking about 'a number of factors'; how the colossal ice sheet is cracking and how Hurricane Gwen, if she doesn't quickly blow herself out in mid-ocean, will rip loose a chunk of ice the size of Belgium thereby creating a tsunami, the path of which, as traced by CGI arrows, will pass between Ireland and Iceland and, after having picked up massive momentum over thousands of miles of open sea, slam into the country at a place very close to where the caretaker sits, chewing meat. The school will probably go. *Evacuation? Now, there's no need to panic just yet. There is some time to go, yet. And the likeliest scenario is that the ice will hold and the hurricane will exhaust its energy out in the middle of the ocean. We're going to have to be very unlucky. But it could—*

He turns the channel. Anne Robinson. Flick. Kerry Katona. He chews and watches with the tray of food on his knee then he cleans the empty plates and smokes a cigarette in front of David Beckham. The coming World Cup. Someone talking about how *Beckham the brand is all about salvation, redemption, even resurrection.* What? *It is not me that is saying Beckham is a pseudo Christ-like figure, but it is how he is often portrayed, and it is how he portrays himself.* What? Some talk about hoping for miracles in the coming World Cup and then a little chuckle. Dr Brick is this man's name. Picture of Beckham on a white shirt under the word 'redemption' taken after France '98. The *Sun*'s picture of his broken foot and the text asking its readers to put their hands on the picture and pray for healing. The big crucifix tattoo on Beckham's back. His son called Cruz. Madame Tussaud's nativity display; Beckham and his wife as Jesus and Mary, in wax. *This guy can't bring peace and harmony to the world and there's something fundamentally wrong in believing he can.* The voice carries on over a film of Beckham himself. Rapturous people on terraces, many of whom are topless to show the same crucifix tattoo on their backs or shoulders, marks of infection, a popping bubo. Beckham scoring with a free kick. His differing hairstyles. Then speaking. The caretaker watches. Leans back in his armchair and observes, the smoke from his cigarette curling into a question mark in the air between his face and Beckham's. This ventriloquist's dummy squeakily mouthing its pointless junk. Pabulum for the famished. This desert of dignity in the infinite availability of his omnipresent baffled smile. Fuck the World Cup if this is what we'll see. Fuck it anyway. Something wrong with you if you don't support England. The stupid and pointless joy of obedience. Bunch of pampered wankers. Boy-men without accountability and with obscene money. Fuck it all, when it comes. Fuck it before. Fuck it now.

He closes the curtains against full dark and turns his computer on. Fetches a bottle of white wine from the fridge. Drinks and surfs as the faces on the TV burble at his back. Ice cracks. The sound it makes like the rending of fabric that keeps two dimensions separate. He visits memorial websites, reads the new comments on them. Stephen Gately. Patrick Swayze; **I hope you have found peace** they read. Local suicides. A new one, seventeen years old. At any time, at any time. Bottomless darkness on which he surfs. He empties the bottle, opens another. Finds, as he knew he would, lonely man, pornography. Makes sticky his fist. Finishes the second bottle. Tries to persuade himself *not* to call the number but does and she can tell just by the sound of his 'hello'. *You're not talking to Ella if you've been drinking. Or me, for that matter. How many times have I told you? Call when you're sober.* Dial tone. He doesn't ring again. The faces on the telly burble. He surfs more and drinks more and just before midnight goes out into his little garden to smoke a last cigarette before sleep and regard the moon. Steps into the pond and soaks his foot. *Shite.* The pond but a sunken bowl, a hope to attract frogs and newts. He kneels and looks in. The moon in there. Glaucoma'd eye. Eyes all around. Eyes, eyes. Small and silver strings of bubbles rising from the leaves of the water plants. So sunlight, moon-light, starlight converts six molecules of water and six of CO_2 into one molecule of sugar and six of oxygen. So we can breathe. So it began and so it goes on. So it began at first and happens at last. The air that I breathe. The wind in my lungs made here. In this little pond. What gives life life. All that has ever lived and loved and drawn breath on the planet is here in this lifting tinsel of tiny pearls without which my lungs would crumple like used chip wrappers on the promenade. Leave the natural history lessons to the teachers, if you would, Mr Caretaker. Thinner and prettier than she'll ever be. Flesh pounds flesh. Pink and glistening. His body reacts. All we have of Christ. Pack my eyes with vileness. Pack my eyes with excrement. The fall to witness is so fast my face is stripped by windburn. And why did you sow in here the seeds of choke-weed that will shit on your favoured creation which is itself which is itself you fucker why do you let us. That time all those years ago when he was a child returning from Sunday school and he was just a boy and his mother had made him go so that she could have the house to herself and his dad and when he returned she was on the couch crying with her nose all black and twisted up and blood scabbing over and he told her not to cry cos Jesus loved her and the blood crusted and the tears ran. On to her blouse, on to her neck. On to the settee. Ruined the upholstery.

He steps his cigarette butt into the soil of his garden. Flowers will soon be out. Some already are; snowdrops by the gate, look. Little white bells, clusters of little white bells in the moon's fallen blue light. He goes back inside, brushes his teeth, pisses. Locks the door. Sets the alarm and goes to bed and falls asleep. So his days go.

His computer desk faces the wall opposite the television and the main window so that when he surfs, the television and the world outside are both at his back. To the left of the humming screen lies an open pouch of Golden Virginia tobacco and a Bic lighter, red, and an ashtray, clean since he prefers not to smoke in the house and has recently been prohibited from doing so anyway by the school authorities although he lives alone. Moving clockwise around his desk, orbiting his computer, there is a white mug without a handle that contains pens and a book of first-class stamps and a notepad with a tatty and scribbled-on cover. A box of disks, kept primarily because they contain old files, which he hasn't yet transferred to a memory stick. A stack of white envelopes held together by a red elastic band. The lid of his laptop, when open, touches the wall, creating a triangular space between wall and machine that would be a perfect spot for a spider to spin a web although the man is punctilious in his habits, or can be, and is careful to run a feather duster through that space every third day or so. The wall that he faces when surfing is bare, without posters or pictures of any sort. Just Anaglypta painted a light eggshell blue. For the soothing effect. The hoped-for soothing effect. To the right of the computer is a framed photograph of a little girl on a beach. She has brown curls that have been blown away from her high forehead and she is not smiling but she looks sort of happy and she is sitting on the sand and she is holding a small yellow plastic spade. She is wearing a dress with a horse on its bib and leggings underneath that and her feet are bare and caked in wet sand, a smudge of which adorns her left cheek like a birthmark. At her side, and half-buried, can be seen a pair of small pink Crocs. Below this picture is a small stack of folded-up news-papers, the *Daily Mirror* uppermost, and resting on these is a used wine glass, a small puddle of old alcohol in it slowly vinegarising. These objects surround his computer. A laptop, closed for the night, waiting to hum and hum once again come morning.

I can never stop the noise. Always that noise. Not even when I sleep because then I see their faces blown up to monster-size, mountainous, and their words then split my ears. It is hot and heavy and so so fast. I cannot bear it. Their whining never-ending. Shut my ears. Shut my mind. Life has been turned into an audition unending and what the fuck are you rehearsing for? Do you think you'll get a re-call? Yes you will of course you will but not in the form you envisage except what you envisage is to you the sole truth. We have seen the death of metaphor. Gravestone lichened and tangled with ivy and there it lies and there it rots. They wank off pigs so that you'll look. They paw through their own shit in public so that you'll turn your gaze upon them and this is literal I mean precisely this. There's the pig's dick in the woman's fingers. There's the hand dabbling in faeces. And you actually will watch them, you actually will, not with respect or admiration or even liking but you'll look. You'll waste your life in the looking but still you'll look. Short space, short time. And how the world pulses and can spin you delirious and so close it is so close to you but why won't you stop? Stop looking. Tell me why won't you stop? This noise.

The YouTube footage before it is rapidly removed from the site shows a girl on her hands and knees on a big bed. Her body looks young, eighteen maybe, nineteen, although the low resolution and scan-line distortion blurs the skin of her and those around her, makes it furred and downy. There is a white dressing at the small of her back. She is making squealing noises but these are muffled because she is being penetrated at each end by tall lean men who endeavour to keep their faces turned away from the cameraphone. A voice yells: *Get some! Get some!*, which is probably the voice of the man filming the activity. *She wants it! She's getting it! Yes! Yes!* The aggressive thrusting of the men sends one of the girl's legs off the edge of the bed which makes her groan but the man at the back of her hooks a hand behind her knee and drags the leg back on to the bed then slaps her arse several times, loud cracks which, each time, elicit a muffled yelp. The man at her face thrusts at the hips and the girl appears to gag and try to pull away but the man wraps her hair around his fist and forces her face further on to him so that her nose presses into his flat stomach, which sends a deep shudder through her body and limbs which jerks the other man away and out of her, his erection bobbing and shining. *Shit! Bitch gagged me out!* he yells, to laughter, then reinserts himself. The men continue to thrust. They meet each other's eyes over the girl's gleaming and knotted back and clasp each other's right-hand thumbs and then they grab each other's napes and tug each to each until their foreheads touch and they are grinning whitely and widely, looking into each other's eyes. Then they break and the man on the left looks at the camera's eye and says in a half-growl: *Up to my nuts in guts.* Much laughter. Footage ends. Comments arrive: **spitroast chicken yeh** and **oof she won't be sitting down for weeks**

lol. Comments from America, France, Australia, all over the world. Singapore and Ireland and Chile. India. The world over. **Another ho fuckt stupid ha!**

★

Life leaps now, for Grace, jerks, moves in a series of blaring spurts. She watches the footage and watches the footage and watches the footage some more until, on the twelfth viewing and not now eating acid, she thinks: *Those tits are much too small.*

She amasses wattage. She feels it, inside her, making her skin glow. Damien calls her and screams three words before she cuts him off. He emails her; she opens the message and reads three words and then clicks on delete. He texts her and she deletes it completely unread. She calls Jerry Wellin but he's not answering his phone so she emails him and he replies within an hour from a BlackBerry: **you know what to do, Gracie. Must I spell it out? Okay then: D U M P H I M. It's time. He'll only hold you back. I've seen it before. You need freedom. Get rid of the boy and wait for the calls to come in. First one will be from me, in the morning.**

At midnight she asks her mother for a temazepam. Knows she won't sleep. Knows she'll sit at her computer until her eyes feel sore and sandy and the birds are twittering outside behind the yellowing curtains. Her mother stops watching *What Katie Did Next* to ask her daughter if she's okay. Grace says yes. Her mother tells her they're in the bathroom cabinet. Grace swallows a pill and goes to bed and when she wakes up her world which is the world complete has leapt forwards one colossal bound into a place so fast and fevered that it might as well be another dimension so little does it share with her world pre-sleep even though it had been turning in that direction as if programmed, incrementally. Jerry calls her mobile. Damien's been a busy boy, Tweeting through the night. Tabloids are full of the new roasting video. Grace accesses her home page as she talks on the phone and there it is, the questions, the questions: **Who are these footballers? Do you know this girl?** Offers of money for names, information. Some tabloids are using a word like 'disgusting' but all carry a link to the footage nonetheless. Jerry seems happy: *Here we go, Gracie*. But concerned, too: *You sure you're okay? Dealing with this? Absolutely one hundred and ten per cent? They didn't hurt you or make you do anything you didn't want to do? Against your wishes, as it were?* Grace starts to reply but then Jerry goes all serious and tells her to listen to him very, very carefully. Tells her that she'll be identified soon, her name will be known and exposed, probably, no, almost certainly, by Damien, the jealous and disgruntled ex, he's seen it happen before, many times over, so he's made a pre-emptive strike: *Know what that means? No. In your case it means I've contacted* Zoo *and* Nuts *and the* Daily Sport *already,* Animal *magazine and the like, and granted them interviews with you. Exclusive rights. They'll pay, Gracie, pay a lot. You'll be modelling for them by the end of next week. Mark my words. This is going to be big, Gracie, YOU'RE going to be big. And I know what you're thinking – you need more up top for the modelling, am I right? Yes. But Jerry's gone and thought of that. I shan't tell you the details yet because they haven't been finalised but suffice to say that those bumps of yours are soon going to be the size you've always dreamed of them being and it's not going to cost you a penny. Not one. Trust me, Gracie. Trust Jerry. He's going to make you star material. Now go and celebrate and I'll ring you soon. Later.*

Grace closes her phone. Stands in her bedroom in her Silly Moo pyjamas holding the phone and the room and the world beyond it whirls. She sits on the bed in case she falls, in case she's spun out of all control. She scrolls her Contacts list down to 'Day' and is thinking of what words to use but then she reasons that she's already dumped him, really, if his last few messages were anything to go by, he won't be wanting to see her any more. Not after the footage. Her phone bleeps in her hand like a small animal crying to be fed; an incoming text from an unrecognised number. She reads it: **u need tits to make it ha ha fried egg slut u fuckn**. Press Delete. Damien, no doubt, using a borrowed mobile so she wouldn't blank the text. Sneaky bastard. That's him packed. Holding her back. Won't get anywhere with him tagging along the way he behaved that night in the restaurant with Jerry. No ambition in him. All he wanted to do was, was what? Live off her. Live off Grace. A parasite. Good rid.

There's a knock on the bedroom door. Grace hides the home page on her computer screen.

—Grace? You up, love? I've brought you some tea and toast.

—Okay.

Her mother enters, carrying a tray. On it a steaming mug and a plate of toast and three, four glossy magazines. She puts the tray on the bed.

—Did you sleep okay?

—Okay. In the end.

—Good. I've brought you this week's mags n all, look.

—Ta.

—You speaking to Jerry today?

—Probably, yes.

—Seeing Damien?

Grace shrugs. —Dunno.

—Oh. Fallen out?

Another shrug. —Maybe.

—Well this is bound to happen, love, yeah? He's gonna feel left out, end of the day. You're the one who'll be getting all the attention. He'll be jealous, yeah? Does he know what happened the other night?

—What?

—That you met them footballers? Have you spoken to him since?

—Couple of texts, that's all.

—Well, you need to spend some time with him. That's if you want to.

—Maybe.

She bends and puts a quick kiss on top of her daughter's head. —I've got to go to work. Call me later, yeah? Tell me what's going on. I'm so proud of you. My Grace. Gonna be famous.

Grace smiles.

—Oh, yeah; Rachel rang last night.

—Did she?

—Yeah. Seemed very keen to speak to you. Quite late, this

was. You'd gone to bed. Seemed a bit upset about something to be honest. She's coming round tonight.

—Tonight? Ah Mum.

—I know, love, but you've got to see her soon. She's your sister. She hasn't even seen your new nose yet and end of the day she's family. We'll have a chippy tea and you can show her your new nose yeah? The great unveiling.

Grace nods. —Suppose so.

—Right then. And go for a walk or something, yeah? Get out of the house for a bit. Do you good. Go and see Damien. She opens the bedroom door. Turns. —Have you heard what Katie's doing now?

—Katie?

—Price. She's divorcing Alex. It was on the telly last night.

—The tranny?

—And cage-fighter, yes. Already! Can you believe that? She's a one. See you later love.

She leaves. Grace accesses her email, deletes many messages from Damien unread, leaves a couple from Shelly and some of her other friends to read later. Her mobile bleeps. Text from Shell: **tell me thats not u grace. is that u?** Grace knows exactly what she's talking about. Doesn't reply. Her heart seems to skip a little then speed up its beating so Grace turns on the TV at the end of her bed, Jeremy Kyle, and sits cross-legged on her bed and eats toast and sips tea and outside the window the sun climbs up the blue sky and gulls call, wail. The town comes to life. Truck engines rumble. Voices. The beep-beep-beep of a wagon reversing and a distant siren somewhere, not police, fire engine. Her heart, her heart. Swallowing she is. Prickles in her skin, only mild, like she's been on the beach for a few hot hours and is yet to shower. Can be coped with. Summer coming.

Jeremy tells someone to *put something on the end of it,* then and Grace takes the top magazine from the shallow pile on the tray. Jeremy's audience whoop and applaud. *Glamour.* Article: **Cosmetic Surgery Saved My Career**. Tania Christiansen, thirty-nine, had plastic surgery to look like Pamela Anderson. Barbed wire tattooed around her left bicep. Breast enlargement, eyelid reshape. Laser resurfacing, lip fillers and Goretox implants, which are plastic tubes inserted into the lips to give a permanent pout. Cost of all this fifteen grand. Tania's from Finland. She didn't even know who Pamela Anderson was at first but people would often remark on the similarity. *Other people study for degrees for their careers, I decided to qualify with operations . . . I knew that even if I didn't end up looking exactly like Pamela, I'd still be a better version of myself . . . I haven't told my mum. She wouldn't like it, but she lives abroad, so she hasn't seen me since the surgery.*

Grace eats toast. Chews it into a mush then swallows it. Blows on and sips tea and swallows that as well.

The first operation swelled Tania's breasts from 34C to 34DD *which is the size Pamela was in* Baywatch. *I went to New York for the operations because I wanted my new breasts to look American: round and high. This was followed by work on my face — only my nose was left untouched because it's better than Pamela's.*

Opposite to Grace, then; it's only Grace's nose that has been touched up. Yet. Today. At the moment. And she thinks her nose is better than Pamela's? Big-headed bint, arrogant cow. How can she say that? The fuck does she think she is? And what did she look like before? What face was she born with and how was it developing and evolving and what was it becoming? In what ways was her individual and unique life sketching itself on her features so that, snowflake, there would be no other like her on the planet over? Snowflake. Dissolving to nothing but a small wet smear on the open palm of a hand.

I don't feel I've lost my sense of identity, I'm still the same person inside. I know one lookalike who committed suicide; she couldn't reconcile herself with the person she'd become but I know where to draw the line . . . Pamela has had her implants taken out and put in again. But I'm sticking with the blonde-bombshell look, even if she has another reduction, because that's what people expect when they think of Pamela Anderson.

Grace looks at the picture of Tania for eleven seconds then turns the page. There's Jo Hodgkins, thirty-two, an actress from Shropshire, had a breast reduction at a cost of £5,000. Reduction? Grace turns the page. Reduction? Like, she paid all that money to have her tits made smaller? Grace pulls the neck of her PJ top away and looks down it. Turns the page. Toni Mutch, twenty-two, model from Yorkshire. Her 'Before' picture is blonde and baseball-capped; her 'After' is brunette in a floaty dress. And her nose is much, like her name, better. Mutch, much better. The work on it cost £4,100. She's been modelling since she was seventeen for jet-ski, car and boating magazines. Wasn't making much money because she didn't get much work: *I had a bump on my nose and it was slightly hooked. Modelling isn't just about how you look, it's about confidence . . . I withdrew my life's savings and borrowed the rest from my mum. My friends were worried and thought I looked gorgeous as I was, but they understood my determination . . . My boyfriend blacked out when he saw me – I think the bandages and bruises were a shock. My mum and my sister told me I looked awful.*

Jealous bitches, then. Jealous sister. Toni Mutch has had *at least 30% more work, and I'm earning around £17,000 more a year.* See? Ignore nature. Accidents of and at birth. Grace strokes her nose, the nose that she still thinks of as 'new'. Remembers bright lights and pain. Spewing up blood. Then leaps from there to seeing her own feet above her face with the toes spread and slicing bright overhead light between them and feels again hands at her ankles and wrists. The taste of herself. Remembers the taste of herself at the back of her tongue. Full then empty then full again as places were swapped. A tunnel, temporary. Shock of air inside muscle rings agape. Gagging and bursting. Full to bursting. Now the world leaps and takes Grace with it. Some churchbells peal beyond the curtained window. Grace sips tea gone tepid.

Well well well says Jeremy.

Considering Plastic Surgery? asks the *Glamour* panel. *You need to ask yourself some serious questions first . . .*

Around 65,000 people a year have cosmetic surgery in the UK and numbers are rising. Here are some things to think about before going under the knife.

HAVE YOU CONSIDERED THE ADVANTAGES AND DISADVANTAGES?

It's easy to get excited about improving your looks but cosmetic surgery does have a risk attached, not least, the results might not be what you hoped for. 'I would definitely advise people to draw up a pros and cons list,' says body image expert Dr Kerri McPherson.

HAVE YOU THOUGHT ABOUT THE ALTERN-ATIVES?

Dr McPherson: 'There are other much less drastic measures that will have a positive impact on how you feel about yourself. For a fraction of the cost you could employ your own personal trainer or completely overhaul your wardrobe and still have money left over to splurge on new make-up.'

WHAT ARE YOU DOING IT FOR?

Only go under the knife if you're absolutely positive it's the right decision for you . . .

ARE YOUR EXPECTATIONS REALISTIC?

'Plastic surgery cannot halt the ageing process or change your personality,' says Dr McPherson. Many people's anxieties about their looks are a symptom of deeper insecurities.

AND IF YOU STILL WANT TO GO AHEAD?

If you do opt for surgery, ask your GP for a referral to a reputable clinic, or contact the British Association of Aesthetic Plastic Surgeons, www.baaps.org.uk.

A good clinic will want to ensure that you're making the decision for the right reasons. At the Harley Medical Group, for example, patients must be approved for treatment in three separate consultations before they have any cosmetic surgery. A nurse, counsellor and surgeon will ask why patients want surgery, what results they're hoping for, and whether they've ever suffered from depression or anxiety.

Grace closes the magazine. Yawns and stretches. *Get off my stage* says Jeremy Kyle. Baaps will give her bigger baps. Mutch bigger baaps. She gets off her bed and moves to her window and opens the curtains and looks out at the backs of the houses, the slate roofs, the chimneys. Sees a gull on one of the chimney pots. What's it looking at? What's it waiting for? Why that pot and not any other? Behind her, on the bed, her mobile cries with an incoming text. Her PC gently hums on the desk and she knows her inbox will be full to bursting. Full, bursting. She remembers full and bursting. She runs a palm over her chest. Feels the small bumps. Clenches her fist and rubs her tightened knuckles over those small bumps. The gull shifts from pink foot to pink foot. Hoping no doubt for more stranded starfish. Free food.

The day's out there. Grace needs to shower and use the toilet so she sits at her desk and checks her email and sure enough her inbox is bursting but there's one from Jerry so she opens it and he must be back in his office by now or at least was when he sent it because it's headed 'Limelight Management' and Grace opens it and all it says is: **You need to call me when you can. Soon, soon. Speak soon. Jxxx.** Grace exits her email page, jumps back on her bed, calls Jerry's number on her mobile. Straight to voicemail. She leaves a message. Sits back on her bed and waits for the phone to ring. Looks out the window at the gull, sees it flap its wings, open its yellow beak to release a noise which she can't hear across the roofs and through the glass but knows it will be ugly, a squawk, a screech. Suggestive to her of torment. The bird takes off and leaves a white splat on the roof slates. *This Morning* comes on the telly. That Holly Willoughby, she's so pretty. And with such perfect breasts. Ring, mobile phone, ring. Please make a noise.

★

It hurts. His foot, the top of his foot. The top of the foot on his right leg. It's the tendon. Bruised. Probably just bruised after he dropped a paving slab on it a few hours ago. Ordinarily he'd contract out such groundwork but only three slabs needed replacing, at the gates, where a mother had cracked them in her Range Rover, so he thought he'd do it himself and he dropped a stone on his foot. The reinforced steel toe of his boot took most of the force but the edge of the slab caught his tendon. Bruised it. He wiggles his toes. Hurts a little. The tendon is used for disflexion of his big toe, to pull it back when, for instance, walking up stairs so that the toe clears the riser so he expects to wince when he goes up to bed tonight. Look at it, though. He wiggles his toes again, despite the pain, just to see the movement under the skin. The thew and sinew. The system of bone pulleys and cartilage hawsers and cogs of muscle going on under there, across the body, foot to knee to hip and then across and up to the scalp. Toenails need cutting. So does his hair. Wiggle the toes and see the strings move. Like a harp or something. Like a harp.

That girl, that girl. Something about her. What was it about her. He stands up and takes the wine, limping a little, over to his desk and the humming machine. Clicks to YouTube but the footage has been taken down. No matter, no matter; easy to find elsewhere. Four clicks of the mouse later and he's watching it again. When she gags and the convulsion of her body ejects the footballer behind her. The laughter. Me nuts, in guts. What is it about her? Distorted as her face is he sees in it nevertheless an echo, something, a reverberation. Sets off some spark at the back of his brain, even dulled as it is with the wine, a little spark starts to crackle. How many times can he watch this. The footage ends and he is asked if he wants to play it again but he clicks away from it and then stands, unsteady, and moves away, unsteady, from the machine itself. Limps back to his armchair. Pours another glass. His head bathed in a lilac jumping light from before and behind; his screensaver, the stars in space, and the television screen. Katie Price announcing her divorce from the cross-dressing cage-fighter Alex Reid. Her face. Reid's face. Both of their faces. Those eyes never to be lit. That sheen. How many women want to look like that woman and for what? Not even Katie Price looks like Katie Price. Pamela Anderson does not look like Pamela Anderson. But that Katie Price will divorce again is considered newsworthy. This is on the news. Ape an ape. Imitate an imitation. I close my eyes and I see the reflection of a floating and broken cloud in a shard of smashed mirror on a rubbish heap.

Nights such as this. These nights, these nights: we were a botch and a ruin that would devour the world and shit it out the moment we came down from the trees and began walking upright. The instant we learnt how to sharpen a stone, in that moment the whole thing was fucked.

Pain in his foot. He wiggles his toes to feel that pain, to make his foot hurt. He'll have a limp for a couple of days. They're aggressive in structure and in nature, the demands they make on us. The way they confront us. Love me love me. Always there their faces, always there, wherever and whenever you look, homepage TV newspapers magazines in overheard talk even, now, in the faces of others who are not them. In the faces of the childen in the faces of their mothers echoes of these faces all around. Their lips and their eyes. The colours they put on. The identification becomes both adoring and hostile and how can it be anything but? It turns deadly. It has to turn deadly. Aggressive envy. Be like me but you'll never be like me. I'm just a normal person but you'll never be like me not as rich or desired or envied so what does that make you? Seething. Silent screams in the skull and how can it be other? This is what you've made. You wanted this and here it is. My foot my foot. It hurts. There is pain in it. But only when I wiggle the toes.

Nights like this. All nights are like this.

He sits and drinks and watches and an hour or so later he moves towards his computer again but stops himself halfway and stands, just stands, regarding the waiting screen. The stars. Not again, no, not tonight. He will not watch it again tonight. But her face. Her face. Not that the viewer can see much of it on the grainy footage and obscured as it is by hips and by hands but in the rare glimpses allowed – there's something about her face. Sparks in his skull, at the back, at the brainstem. Douse them. Move the toes, pour the wine.

★

—You can't be certain it's me. Not absolutely certain.

—Grace, I'm your sister.

—Not one hundred and ten per cent certain.

—I'm your sister, aren't I? I'm not stupid.

Grace shrugs. —Whatever.

—I know what my own little sister looks like even if there is a wotsit in her mouth.

—Rachel!

—It's true, Mum. You must never, ever watch it. Promise me you'll never watch it, Mum. Promise.

—And anyway, Grace says. —What are you doing on the web looking for porn or roasting vids? Doubt God would like that. Don't think he'd be very pleased with that.

—It's all over the papers, Grace. Stop being so silly. Saw a still from it in the *Star* and I knew straight away it was you. Even with that, that. She points to the centre of her own face. —New nose. And anyway someone Facebooked me and tipped me off.

—Someone? Who, someone?

—You don't need to know.

—Damien, Grace says with a hiss. —That twat.

—Grace!

Grace shrugs. —But he is, Mum. Sooooo is. Best thing I ever did was get rid of him.

—And the worst thing you ever did was give yourself to three footballers on camera. And for what? Cos you want to be famous? You're that desperate, are you?

Grace shrugs yet again and smiles. —Whatever.

—'Whatever'? Is that all you can say? What's happened to you, Grace? What's happening? My little sister.

—Listen, listen. The mother leans fowards in her chair. A triangle of related women, here; the mother at the head of the coffee table in an armchair, Grace to her left in another armchair, hair tied back, pyjama'd legs tucked up beneath her, Rachel to the mother's right and facing Grace on the two-seater settee, wearing black trousers stretched tight on the thighs and a white shirt with a silver crucifix around her neck, pointing to her cleavage and reflecting the light from the sinking sun and reddening sky outside the bay window. On the coffee table some mugs of tea going cold and an open box of Jaffa Cakes. The plan had been to have a chippy tea together and talk but Rachel had brought thunder through the door with her and the row had begun immediately. The TV, for once, off, here, in this three-womened room. Three points of a triangle these three women who share blood. —This is the important thing. It's happened, yeah? We can't turn the clock back. It's happened and Grace has done whatever she's done so end of the day we might as well make the best of it yeah? Make some money from it. Exploit the situation. What's done is done, know what I mean?

Grace nibbles at a Jaffa Cake. She's looking at her sister and there is a spark of something in her eyes and a smile, a smirk, dancing around her lips.

—That's not the point tho, is it, Mum? Rachel says.

—Isn't it?

—No. You know it's not.

—What is the point then? Tell me.

—Yeah, Grace says. —What *is* the point? Of you even being here I mean.

Rachel breathes in. Fills her lungs. Her breasts push at the fabric of her shirt. The action resembles a preparation for a yell but when she speaks her voice is calm: —The point is your soul, Grace. That's what I'm talking about and that's why I'm here. Your soul.

Grace laughs. —Soul? She flaps her hands. —Whatever.

—I'm not talking about heaven or hell or anything, Grace. I'm not talking about God or Jesus or anything.

—Oh aren't you?

—No I'm not.

—Well that must be the first time in ages, then.

—I'm talking about what you do with your life and your body. *This* life, I mean. Here. I'm not talking about what happens to you after you're dead.

—It's my body. No one else's.

—All the more reason for you not to offer it to strangers, then. Even if they *are* famous. Or to change it through plastic surgery or whatever you want to do to it. Because what happens to your body affects you in here. She taps her sternum. —And in here. She taps her skull. —And if you let your body be violated then everything else gets corrupted too.

Grace snorts. —'Violated'? Right, yeah. Whatever. Jog on.

—'Corrupted'? says the mother.

—Is there an echo in here? Does neither of you have the first clue what I'm talking about?

—Soooo chatting crap, Grace says. —Soooo chatting crap, you.

—Grace. The mother leans forwards again, elbows on her knees. —The soul, you say, Rachel. Well answer me this: how

94

will Grace's soul be any better off if she goes into the jobs market? With no qualifications or experience? What's she gonna do, become a lawyer? Church minister? It's either do what she's doing, what she's trying to do, or stacking shelves in Tesco's. That's not enough for her. She wants more, don't you, love?

Grace smiles and nods. —Exactly right, Mum. Bang on.

—So you'd sooner her be like all the other no-marks of her age round here, is that it?, the mother goes on. —Stacking shelves, on the tills, rest of her life? What kind of option is that? She doesn't have much choice.

—But she can *get* qualifications. She can *get* experience. She's young, she's got the rest of her life ahead of her. Why waste it like this?

—'She'?, Grace says. —Erm, like, I'm sitting right here? Who's this 'she'?

—It's not as simple as you think, Rachel continues. —Everyone wants everything to be so easy. That's not what it's about. Having it without working for it.

—Nothing easy about a nose job, Grace says. —*You* try getting one.

—I mean you look at that and them. Rachel points to the TV and a stack of glossy magazines next to the coffee table. —And the people in them and you believe that they're all about happiness, don't you? And why? Because they're famous? Is it that simple, that you just want people to look at you? Is that what you think being happy is?

—But the alternative, Rachel. Think of the—

—That's not the *only* alternative, Mum. That's what I'm saying. Even if you want to be famous, I mean. Even then. There's, there's singing, or playing an instrument. Something. Some hard work and application. You're pretty, Grace. You got the looks. And you're not thick, although I have been wondering about that lately. There are other things you can do.

—And how's she meant to support herself?

—How does anyone? They get a job.

—Time.

—You *make* time. It you really want to do something

you'll do it. You'll work twenty-four hours a day, seven days a week. It's about having the determination. Doing something with your life other than getting roasted on YouTube by footballers.

Grace laughs. The mother shakes her head. —You're not understanding me, Rachel.

—I am, Mum, perfectly. Better than you think. It's about doing something, isn't it? With your life. Making a mark on the world, leaving something behind. Right?

She looks at Grace. Grace reaches for another Jaffa Cake.

—Something you'll leave behind when you're gone, yeah? So that people will know that you were here, that you existed.

—That's exactly what I'm doing.

—What?

—I said that's exactly what I'm doing. Making sure people remember me.

—But remember you for what? For being fucked in public by three strangers?

—Rachel!

—That's what happened, Mum. Face facts. She was fucked by three men because they're famous and she wants to be famous too and now millions of people all over the world have seen her. All over the world, Mum. Should've seen some of the comments that came in. Laughing at her, all over the world.

Splash of colour now to Grace's cheeks. —And who's gonna remember you? What have you ever done?

—I don't *want* to be famous, Grace. I don't care. I don't need anything other than what I've got.

—Nice hubby and nice house with nice kids and a nice garden. Soooo ambitious.

Rachel shrugs, now. —And that's enough. That's more than enough for me. I'm happy with what I've got and what I am.

—Cos you think that you'll live forever in heaven. Grace snorts so hard that a hammock of snot appears at a nostril, a new nostril. She wipes it away with a tissue.

—Here we go. Rachel's eyes roll. —That's not what it's about. I've already said, I'm talking about what happens in the here and now. You're building your life around other people and that's not good. And you so young.

—And that's what someone like Katie's done, has it? Built her life around other people?

Rachel looks at her mum. —Who's Katie?

—Katie Price. Jordan. No one controls *her*.

—Course they do.

—She controls the *press*, Rachel. She's *that* powerful.

—She's a monster.

—What?

—She even looks like a monster. She's unnatural.

—All women want to be her and all men want to have her. And she's worth millions.

—And she treats people like dirt. And her ego's as falsely inflated as her tits.

—She's had a reduction.

Rachel laughs, if laugh it can be called; that humourless bark. —Listen to you two. You've got lives of your own, why are you living through someone else? Some greedy bint who cares only about herself? Are you so miserable and uninterested in anything around you that you've got to take such an interest in the way someone else lives? Why should you care about Jordan's tits?

—Sooooo not a big deal, Grace says.

—I know she's not. But you make it one.

—Not talking about her.

—What?

—I'm talking about boobjobs. Not a big deal any more. People get them done in their lunchbreaks now. Be getting one meself.

—A boobjob?

Grace smiles and nods.

—Which you'll be paying for with what?

Another shrug from Grace. The redness gone out of her face now she carefully peels the layer of orange goo away from the sponge base as she speaks. —Got a call from my agent. A magazine's sponsoring me, gonna pay for them to go bigger. 'Before' and 'After' photographs, yeah? Best surgeon, best hospital, the works. It'll cost them a fortune, Jerry said. Best surgeon in the country.

—Oh Grace, says the mum.

—Oh Grace, says Rachel, but in a different way. —And you're proud of this. You're thinking this is good news, aren't you?

Grace eats the orange goo. —Course I am. End of the day it's what I want. She eats the sponge disc too.

—Which magazine? Rachel asks.

—Not telling you which one. Not telling you which one cos you'll only call up their office and make a scene, yeah?

—I can find out, Grace. I'm online at home.

—Soooooo jealous.

—What did you say?

—You heard me. Soooooo jealous, you.

—Don't be stupid, Grace. Grow up. What if your dad could see you?

The mother shouts one laugh. —He'd do nothing but encourage her. He'd see the pound signs and tell her to fill her boots. You're too young to remember what he was like.

—I remember more than you think I do, Mum. Much more.

The mother leans and pats Rachel's knee three times then sits back. —Rach, love, I'm happy that you're happy. Honest I am. And I don't care what's made you happy, whether it's God or marriage or what. I remember when you were ill—

—Depressed, Mum. I was suffering from depression.

—When you were depressed then and I came to see you in the hospital after you'd had your stomach pumped and my heart broke in two, honest it did. Broke right in two, seeing you like that. But what I'm saying is that I'm happy you're happy and I don't care why you're happy, just that you are, and can't you feel the same way about your sister? Just be happy that she's happy? The reasons why aren't important, end of the day.

Rachel puts her face in a hand. In her right hand. She wipes her face with her palm and her chest heaves once then subsides and she squeezes her nose between thumb and forefinger and then she drops her hand back to her lap and it curls up fisty and without looking at her mother or her sister she raises her voice to the darkening uncurtained window outside of which the first flying flickers of the spring, bats, swallows and martins, all three perhaps, cross-hatch the dusking sky.

—She fucked three strangers at the same time! Because they were famous! Not even twenty years old and she let three strangers fuck her at the same time because she wants to be famous! One at the front and one at the back and then they swapped places and millions of people all over the world saw it happen! She's disgusting! She's repulsive! And now she's gonna get bigger tits so she can be famous! That's her only dream! She's making me sick!

—That's enough! The mother stands up. —You're hysterical, Rachel. Thought we could have a nice little talk but no, you've gone and spoilt it. Don't know why you can't just be happy for her.

Rachel makes a noise in her throat, half-growl half-scream, and grabs a handful of her brown bob in each hand. —You're driving me mad! Both of you!

—Well go and calm down then. Come back when you've calmed down and we can have a proper talk, yeah?

Rachel stands, slings her handbag over her shoulder. —Nothing good will come of this, Grace. It's already obscene.

—Whatever.

—And I'm disappointed in you, Mum. Encouraging her like this. No bloody dignity. No shame.

The mother shoos Rachel in the direction of the front door with her hands. —Enough, now. Ring me when you've calmed down and are ready to have a sensible conversation, yeah? Give my love to the kids.

Rachel leaves the house, again making that growl/scream noise, and the mother closes the door. Stands with her back against it and looks at her youngest daughter.

—Where did I go wrong with that one, eh? What did I do? She shakes her head slowly, without a smile. —But we've got to talk about this, Grace, you know. Just me and you.

Grace reaches for the remote and turns the TV on. *Celebrity*

Fifteen to One. —Yeah, whatever. Starts to dismantle another Jaffa Cake.

★

He sleeps, in this season, with his bedroom window open, and is dragged out of the mad and antic lands to which slumber had carried him by a wind that enters the bedroom with the sound of a distant labouring engine, turning the curtains into panicking ghosts. He lies awake for a minute or two, in the darkness, his head beneath the duvet, listening to the wind, allowing it to transport him back to boyhood, curled up safe beneath the duvet, guarded from the ravening teeth that the darkness has always harboured. Hear the heart beat in this cupped, warm space. Feel the air leave the lungs and enter the lungs. The body tucked around the canals of slow blood. He pushes the duvet away and sits on the edge of his bed and puts his right foot carefully on the floor, gingerly putting his weight on it. Stands and hobbles over to the open window and bends between the flapping phantoms and puts his head out into the black and frantic night. The wind tugs tears, burns his ears. Thrashes his hair and yanks mucus down his nostrils. The limbs of the trees toss in spidery silhouette against the yellow moon and the stars themselves appear to rock and sway against the moleskin sky as if hung up there loosely on threads. Salty, is what the night smells like. Briny. Come off the sea, then, the wind. Bringing with it what? A bite of ice, from a distance where the bears are white? A hint of spume and angered suds? Vanguard, this, opening shot, and the night should be crossed and ticked by bats or at least those trees should be irregularly bumped with roosting birds but nothing there, tonight, in the saline wind. A promise, then, a preview – the annihilating blast to come. Airy scouring of the planet the way a man might blow a greenfly off the newspaper he's reading. Horses, trees, owls; like candles they blow out. Simply snuffed.

He stands and closes the window and redraws the curtains. Limps back to bed and pulls the duvet entirely over himself, only a tuft of hair on the pillow. Within minutes the duvet is rising and falling in rhythm with his sleeping breath.

WE KNOW ROASTED GIRL! the papers scream that day. They don't name her, but they give her initials, and declare that they'll print her full name *as soon as our legal boffins say we can*. GA, GA. The articles are accompanied by facial silhouettes of the footballers rumoured to have been involved with *the incident in a swanky hotel bedroom during one team's infamous 'harvesting' season*. GA, GA. Online. **ROASTED GIRL IDENITFIED.** Click, click. A Tweet from someone who calls himself crazyday and then the name. G for Grace. A for Allcock. Open Google, search that name. Many hits: for Facebook, for Twitter, for Bebo, for Myspace. Something sparks. In the search window, follow the name with the name of the school, *his* school, click on Search and there's a string of hits and click on the top one and load the page and there she is, a photograph, class of sometime in the late 1990s. Smiling children in ranks. Smiling children. Front row, third from left, Grace Allcock. A child. Her hands on her knees, a pretty pink dress, feet together in black pumps and little white socks. Yellow curls. Smiling and the enamel of her teeth just catching a spark of the sun. Something ignites and he leans towards the screen, nose nearly touching and squints. Can just make out the plaster on her knee, *just*, a faint beige smudge on her left knee. Her little fist curled around something. Clutching something tightly she is in that little hand. Look at her smile. Grace Allcock. Little girl, a child. With a grin and a grazed knee and the hand clenched around something. That face aged a little and grown and stuffed with pumping meat. Bitch choked me out. Something ignites.

And once there was no death. People reached their optimum age of late twenties or early thirties and then stayed that way forever and the population ballooned and the earth groaned and people married thousands of times and had thousands of children and then, one day, without warning, they started to age; grey hairs, collapsing joints, decrepitude. And then they started to die, at about the age of 250, they started to die. And

God said: What did you expect? You fuckers were getting nothing done. All's you did was lie around all day and have sex with each other until you got bored with each other then you'd move on to someone else. You got bugger all done. I didn't make you to be lazy. And I've noticed by the way that none of you seems happy. The faces on you – like a wet Sunday in Rhyl. You bicker all the time. All that sex, and all you do is take out your anger at yourselves on someone else's back or breast. You know nothing of joy. So this is it – you've got mortality, now. Your lives will end. Each and every one of you will one day die. Now you've got something to live for.

So people began to do things: write, sing, sit under trees. Walk by rivers and marvel at the dragonflies and the birds because now they knew that there'd come a time when they wouldn't be able to appreciate such things any more. Now they knew they would one day die. They saw it happening to others; one day they'd be upright and breathing and the next they'd be ashes or in the ground. After a few millennia of this they began to smile and enjoy their lives and celebrate the world around them. And then again without warning, they started to die much younger, in their sixties and seventies and eighties, often even earlier, and God spoke again and said: I had to do it. You were living too long. You'd faff and fanny and fart around for a couple of centuries and then in the final few decades you'd start producing poems and paintings and things, by which time all fiery energies had died in you and all's you were doing was moaning and whinging about your rapidly approaching death. So now, if you want to make something of your lives, you've got to start doing so much earlier, because now your lives are so short that the knowledge of their ending will weigh on you throughout, every minute of every day. Actually, I'll go further: I know I said that thing about three score years and ten, but really you now have no given age at which death will occur. You could die tomorrow. You could die now. Cancer, arteriosclerosis, aneurysm, congenital heart disease. Your years are few, so if you don't enjoy them, squeeze every drop out of them, then you'll waste them in anger and self-pity and self-loathing. Know what I mean?

You have to live *now*, today, this second, and relish every short minute of your existence because there will be so few of them. Minutes, I mean. So few minutes. And don't ask me to change this, either, cos I won't. It's this way forever. I allowed the incredible world around you to come about and none of you bastards appreciated it so from now on and forever it's going to be this way. So go on, now – fuck off and live. Hear that clock ticking away? See the evening coming in? You know about such things as wheelchairs and incontinence and dementia because I have shown you such wonders. So I'll say it again, one last time: Go on, fuck off, *live*.

Creosoting the fence at the bottom field he splashes some of the liquid on his forearms and regards the marks as they burn. Like liver spots. I can see in them my future. He takes a damp rag out of the pocket of his overalls and wipes the splashes away and continues to apply the creosote. Guard the wood from weathering. From wind and rain and the heat of the sun. Bury me upright so the sun doesn't blind me. I won't be able to see the stars but the sun won't sear my eyes.

He sits on a stool outside his hut in the spring sunshine and smokes a cigarette and watches the children walk past in single file holding hands in front and behind like the cut-out linked paper families they make in art class and hang in the windows. Sometime in the late 1990s, this is. School-photograph day, and the camera-man has set up benches and his tripod at the bottom of the field to avoid glare and that's where the children are headed, excited and laughing in one long linked line, each holding hands with the child in front and the child behind to make one long child many-legged and many-headed. They're wearing their smartest clothes and have polished their shoes and had their hair fixed; neat combings for the boys, some spikes, and bunches and scrunchies for the girls. He watches them as they pass. Some of them wave to him then grope for the momentarily released hand again and he returns their waves and smiles and smokes his cigarette and enjoys the sunshine, the come-again spring sunshine. Sometime in the late 1990s, this is. In early spring.

The little girl at the very end of the line, tugged by so many children as she is, stumbles and falls, on to her knees. Pretty pink dress and black pumps and little white socks and yellow curls. Trips to her knees on the ground. The teacher bringing up the rear helps her up and she's crying and the teacher looks over at the caretaker.

—It's okay, I'll fix her up. You go and sort out the photo shoot and she'll be with you in two ticks.

—Thank you.

—Tell the camera-man to hang fire.

—Thank you. You okay, Grace?

The little girl gives a tearful nod and gives a tearful look down at her grazed knee.

—The janitor will mend your knee. Don't worry.

The teacher jogs away to catch up with the other children and the caretaker takes Grace's hand and leads her over to the stool and sits her down on it. She sniffles and looks at her knee.

—Let's have a look at this.

A graze, just. On her left knee. A small abrasion on the skin like stippling with a red pen, tiny ruby pinpricks. But this is a special day for her.

—I'll get you good as new. Won't be a mo.

The caretaker fetches from his hut a mug of warm water and two clean cloths and an Elastoplast and a toffee from a bag on his workbench.

—You like toffees?

The little girl looks up from her knee.

—It's a treacle one. I like them best and I thought you might too. My last one but you can have it.

The little girl nods. He unwraps the sweet and gives it to her and she puts it in her mouth and he crouches down at her swinging feet in the new black pumps and the ankle socks.

—Let's have a look. Can you stretch your leg out straight? She does.

—There we go. Not broken, then. I'll just give it a little clean, okay? In case there's a bit of muck in it.

The little girl looks worried. Says in a voice made thick with concern and toffee: —Will it hurt me?

—No, no. But there might be a bit of muck in it you see so we'll just have to give it a bit of a clean. I promise it won't hurt.

He dips one of the cloths in the warm water, wrings it out over the mug and very gently dabs at the little girl's knee, the tiny wound on there. She sucks air in over her teeth.

—That okay?

She nods. Her eyes huge as she watches what he's doing, toffee tucked into her cheek hamsterly.

—Brave girl. Got to look nice for your photograph, eh?

He passes the damp cloth over the scraped skin three times very gently then very gently dabs it with the dry cloth to take the moisture off.

—And we'll put a plaster over it, okay? Only for today, till it heals. You can take it off tonight.

—Okay.

—What's your name?

—Grace Allcock.

—Well, Grace Allcock. He takes the backing film off the Elastoplast and places it across the graze and smooths the sticky edges down across the knee with his thumb. The skin like satin. So young. How he would love a child of his own. Not just an insurance against impermanence but a candle flame in the shadows around. That little flicker. Skin so soft, unmarred and unblemished. Jagged gravel the only safety net and he and his wife will continue to try for a child despite that. Despite everything. —We'd better hurry and get you in that photograph, hadn't we? Can't have a school photograph without the school's bravest girl in it.

He takes her hand and leads her down across the field and halfway across he stops to bend and pluck a daisy and he gives it to the little girl called Grace and she grins and thanks him and clutches it in her wee fist and seems extremely pleased with both the flower and the dressing on her knee and at the bottom of the field all the clean and expectant children are arranged in tiers on the benches and only one space remains free, front row, third from left. The teacher stands.

—Everything okay?

—She'll live. Won't you?

The little girl looks up at the caretaker and smiles.

—Yes, you'll live, he says again.

The teacher shows the little girl to her allotted and waiting seat and retakes his own and the photographer bends to his lens.

—Good, that's it. Big smiles.

The caretaker turns and walks back up the field towards his hut. In the come-again spring sunshine, the early spring sunshine. Skin so soft. The trust and the gratitude and how the world has some things within it that will never die. Or should never die. Sometime in the late 1990s, this was.

Click, click. Class of '97 or thereabouts. Around then. Add to Favourites. Click on Bookmark This Page. Add to My Documents. Front row, third from left. The Elastoplast on the knee. The yellow curls and the smile and the demure hands on the unblemished lap and the nose so small no longer the same nose. Sliced away, now. So that the men can take turns. Up to me nuts in guts. Bitch gagged me out. The hand holding the daisy so tight as if never to let that flower go. Roast chicken oof. Slapping her, choking her, dragging her leg back on to the bed and she so passive, agreeing to this. As if an offering she has made. She won't be sitting down for weeks lol not like the day she sat for the photograph and not like she still sits in that photograph, hand clenched tight, her eyes above her smile squinting up into the sun. You'll live. Something sparks.

Two arms and two legs. A nose, two eyes, two ears. Nipples. Genitals. Two feet and ten toes two hands and ten fingers. A throat. Lungs and a heart and a stomach and an anus and a central nervous system, you are a collection of endless wonders. A universe entire in your skull each moment alive with contacts between ports, neurological ports, a hundred times more of them than there are people on the planet and each of those billions a box for the infinite. Each moment enacts the frenzied glory of creation. You know joy – to recognise it and to create it. Sadness. You can cry for a dead bird. The soul inside you a breath in a vacuum a moth flickering from a dread desert darkness this is how you are made, the million marvels in your make-up. And *this* is what you're doing with them. *This* is all you can think of to do with them. You are told to ignore and reject them and you do it with glee. White blocks of air in your heads. Not a boot on a human face but that face catatonic and expectant below a scalpel and then on YouTube distorted and stuffed with meat. You leap up gladly on to the hooks. Why such glee? Why such eagerness? You do nothing so you mean nothing. You are nothing. Yet you have a legacy and a message and it is for others to follow you, to be like you. As you rip away your clothes for the giant eye so you too divest your flesh. What made you you now swirls down a drain clogged with tangles of hair and skin and that is you and you smile as you watch it wash away. I wish I'd never been born. Not into this. At this moment, in this world. Nothing comes off you but disappointment and disgust and you tendril the planet with that. Such a big web you make. Vile net, see it wrapping the globe, the virtual mega-cities of networking sites. Bombay is a hamlet. Tokyo too. Myspace has over 100,000,000 members and how you can get lost and swamped but that's okay for you. Anonymous and unnoticeable unless you scream or take your clothes off. Take your skin off. Flay yourself as others watch. Your name taken from you, who you are taken from you, the loneliness is bottomless yet that is what you seek. Emptiness, hollowness. Self-promotion. I am great they say I am magnificent I am sexy and that is what they believe. Too much self-esteem or no self-esteem. This is not a good condition. Not a good recipe. But millions no billions believe that it is. I have seen everything that is not you in the antler of a snail.

We came about so that the universe could have contained within it something that could extol its glory if not entirely grasp its immeasurable magnificence. Could feel that rapture without the recognition of which the universe itself would have no point or meaning. It is through you that the universe can worship itself and appreciate itself and know its own immensity. Become self-aware even. The universe whole in each damp and tiny one of us, the wee wet bowls of our skulls. Which means that the spread of your corruption, canker, is nearly complete. If it seeks to see itself through the windows of your eyes then what it sees is a chasm. All that comes back to you through the aperture of the universe is your own gaping and needing husk of a face. What hope. What hope.

Yet there are moments, for him, moments of the world and in this season, little leaps of colour and sound that amass to make a life. The instant when the bumblebee launched itself from out of the flower's chalice into the come-again sunshine, golfball-round with a drone so deep he felt his ribcage rattle. Or the moment when the frogspawn reappeared in his little pond one night when the moon hung high and fat and aubergine and in the morning he studied it and saw the tiny black commas of jerking life and felt the season unwrap itself around him in its green and ferocious insistence on life's return, its keenness to plug the gaps made by winter's dismemberments. He saw and felt the urgency. Heard the robin offer a challenge from the hedgerow. Walked by the river after work that day and watched dragonfly nymphs prepare themselves on the yellowflag iris leaves and knew that they'd been agog for this moment since the eggs were laid on the water's surface three or four years ago. A lifetime for a dragonfly. The patience and the knowing. The trust. He watched one closely, saw the big eyes black and opaque, the head folded around the massive jaw. Knew awe but also utter incomprehension as the nymph's thorax as he watched abruptly split and the adult insect emerged, head first, hoisting itself out, breaking the delicate white threads of the breathing tubes as it detached its body from what it once was. Twice as long as its own nymph. Fit a ship in a paddling pool. A jumbo jet in a garden shed. It dragged itself as he watched to the edge of a leaf and pulsed its wings there, dusk-light in the lacework, twilight in the tracery, the abdomen long and thin and striped yellow and black like a racked wasp. Warmth lifted the wings. He watched them shimmer, then thrum. Eighty million years in this. Nothing in the dry husk of the nymph's exoskeleton to suggest this impossible creature that took itself up into the warm air as he watched and flicked with a low buzz across the rippling shallow river which seemed to chuckle in appreciation. Hunger already piloting the body, an astounding arrow launched into the gorse on the opposite bank.

So yes and yet there are moments. Sudden jumps that make a life. The bee and the dragonfly and the flowers and now, as he sits in his small garden at sundown, smoking, the yellow arm of the digger craning in the haze at the lower end of the sloping field below him, now there are hirundines – swallows and martins – and swifts. Particularly swifts, the sickle-winged screamers, throwing stars, darting blades of birds, come down from the high blueness to gulp the jostling midges at head-height and exult in flight and speed and, when exhausted, to concertina their wide wings into their bodies and vanish into small holes in tree or gable or eave. A miracle, again, almost magical, that such a tiny space can accommodate the bird. Or that such a bird can shrink itself so small. Things fit, now, in this season. Things fit each other, somehow and always.

He sips wine and smokes and his belly gurgles as it digests pasta. Not unsteady on his feet as yet but in his head there is a pleasing note, a hum. The digger away over there, in the haze, the school closed. Alcohol and nicotine and food and the sinking sun. Without such things he'd want just Ella. Want to see just Ella. Head up he watches the birds zip but a burp at his feet draws his eyes down. A toad, squatting at the edge of his little weed-carpeted pond. Small brown toad. Awkwardly he settles to his haunches to observe and at this movement the toad extends its legs and rises to the shape of threat like a miniature wrestler. Out of the dank dark hidden pocket of the world where it had spent the winter it brings that part with it into his garden; the webbed and warty underworld dragged into exposure below the sky slashed scarlet. Where has it been? To where did it retreat from the snow and the ice? Its disappearance, too, a mystery. As is its presence, again. Its burping reappearance. Hid itself inside a rock was once the belief which beat the belief that the world could be altered and changed since that belief or need which became a belief has resulted only in losses irrecoverable, not just of the animals themselves or the plants themselves but that which tied us to them. Geese were born from barnacles, and in that people could grasp a power and a capability. In that, geese were else, but close. Geese were connected. Not from barnacles did geese grow but from the human need to understand and to manage. And this little burping toad at my feet has crawled not from ooze or compost but from some other world under our feet and in its patience there is a wisdom of antiquarian pedigree. Moving between earth and water and air at will it shifts shape around a granite-like repose, little belcher born from petrified mud. Animal of a darkness forever unreachable, your defence in your repellence and nothing but that. You are not beautiful but you are a thing upon which our notions of beauty hinge. And so if I see the world in which I must live bipedal mammal that I am with soul and mind and heart, if I see the world in which I must live adopting the hues of rot and manure, and if I smell it too, and if I hear it seething with myiasis and the hot sizzle of corruption, then, little brown burper from the dark deeps of a filthy earth, I also see you. I also see you.

He stands and groans as his joints complain. Forty-two years old. He toes the stub of his cigarette into the soil, filterless and rottable as it is, and finishes the wine in his glass and watches as the sun sinks below the slate roofs of the town and then he goes back inside his house to where the bottle waits on his desk next to his humming laptop. A life made out of these little leaps. It flows and is formed from a million drips and drops.

*

Grace removes her bikini top and applies barrier cream to her nipples. The buds on these too-small boobs but not too small for long, no. Bigger ones are coming. Heads will turn. She smears the barrier cream on to her hands and knees and elbows too and then piles her hair up on her head with one hand and fits a shower cap over it with the other, tugs it down tight to her ears, arranges the front of it so that it lies flush with her hairline.

—What are we going for? asks the lady with the gun. —What percentage today?

—I'm thinking ten.

—Ten? That's pretty Katie.

—Exactly.

The gun-lady smiles. —See her on the telly last night? Divorcing that Alex one?

—Missed it. Got it online this morning, though.

Grace pads barefoot in to the booth, turns her back to the lady.

—She's mad, isn't she?

—Just knows what she wants, that's all.

—Never knows when to stop.

—And wouldn't it be boring if she did?

The lady pulls a dust mask over her face and steps close to Grace and raises the gun so that the nozzle points at the middle of her back, inches away, and squeezes the trigger. A beige spray hits Grace's bare back and the skin there begins to colour, to darken. Grace releases a whoop.

—Cold!

—Keep your mouth shut, yeah? Don't want to breathe this stuff in.

The woman moves the spray over Grace's body, her back and legs and shoulders, then taps Grace on the arm and she turns to show the front of her. The woman is skilled at her work and the colour goes on Grace's skin evenly, without streaks or patches.

—Close eyes. Hold your breath.

Grace does and the woman sprays her face. Grace in the booth now gone a new colour. With her new nose and her boobs soon to be bigger. Standing in her bikini bottoms, an old pair that she can discard now stained with the spray as they are, sitting high on her hips because she knows how sexy that tan line will look now. On the beach come summer. On YouTube or wherever.

—There y'go. Two weeks of Ibiza sunbathing in ten minutes, yeah?

The woman shuts the gun off and Grace leaves the booth and stands before the full-length mirror. Turns to the left, turns to the right, turns her back on herself and looks over her shoulder.

—Good job.

—Course it is. The woman blows at the nozzle of her gun like a gunslinger in an old western. —I'm the best tanner in town.

—Looks real, doesn't it? As if I've been in the sun. Properly, like.

—Does. And who wants to spend all that time lying sweaty on a beach and reading a book? Boring, end of the day. More time to do other stuff.

—God yeah.

—Give it five minutes to dry then you can put your kit back on. Some mags in the waiting room.

Grace puts her bikini top back on, loosely, and then her robe. Thanks the woman who is now recharging her gun ready for the next customer. —You're welcome, she says, without looking up.

There is a difference between being failed and being a failure and Jade, poor Jade, Jade Goody was failed, by her family, the school system, and then, finally, by the *collective imagination*, writes a contributor to the website. Yes yes – the collective imagination. *Oh very good* comes the response from someone who calls him or herself educatedfan. *You've read Lucy Mangan's article in the* Guardian *as well? Get your own ideas!!!!!*

Grace scrolls through the site and feeds the tiny spider. Explores the site and breathes, pants almost, and sends food into the web of the tiny spider behind Willy Roberts's squinting eye. There's the diagnosis video: Grace clicks on Play. The diary room of the *Big Brother* house in India. Jade's face and the shock in it. How would you feel? Twenty-seven years old. Soon you will die. So brave. So brave. And then the pictures of Jade with her head shaved, one of which Grace recalls showing to Damien when it appeared in a mag and then shouting at him for his insensitivity when he aimed an imaginary pool cue at it. The shiny white dome. He laughed at her upset. Good riddance, yeah?

Failed. Failed finally by her own body. By nature.

The name – Goody. No accident, there. Forces at work. *Jade*

Goody saved my life, one message reads. *Cos of her I got cancer screened and my cervix was pre cancerous and I got it treated and now I've recovered fully. Papilloma virus, HPV, too much sex lol!!! I owe my life to Jade. Far as I'm concerned she's up there with the angels.*

Grace nods. No accident, that name. No coincidence, just. Forces at work.

I'm Indian and I wasn't offended.

And whoever was was stupid and oversensitive. She didn't mean anything. Shilpa Poppadum, Shilpa Fuckawallah. Errr! Sense of humour failure! Nothing racist in those words and anyway she thought she was like some kind of queen, that woman. Snotty. Shetty. Shitty. Swanning around the house like she owned the place. This is Britain, love. No Bollywood royalty here, get real, yeah?

And look, now, look: Jade saves lives. Brave Jade failed by everyone goes on saving lives. Jack's continuing to fuck up but the poor lad's bereaved and he should be left well alone. We deal with grief in different ways and that's his. Leave him alone. His Jade is saving lives.

Carole Malone's *News of the World* piece called **Jade's Dying Wish** is up on the site. Written for the anniversary of brave Jade's death. **Best pal tells of tragic last days.**

At 27, Jade Goody never imagined she'd be writing a list of Things To Do In Case I Die.

But when doctors first told her her cancer had spread and she had just a 40 per cent chance of survival – that's exactly what she did.

Maybe they weren't great odds for anyone else, but for the Bermondsey girl who had beat the bookies to catapult herself out of poverty into the glittering world of celebrity, it was enough.

Brave Jade. Grace reads on. Click, click. Scroll the screen.

Jade knew a 40 per cent chance meant the most precious gift of all. Not fame, not money – but hope.

Such a brave girl. Who, knowing that they would probably soon die, would do what she did? The choice to go public in order to raise money to leave Jack and her sons. To die like that.

With a New Year just days away, her resolution was to take the gift of time she'd been given – and run like the wind with it.

Forty per cent. Less than half. Jennifer Smith, thirty, one of Jade's closest friends who stuck by her through her illness said: *I know those odds would have floored most people but not the Goodster . . . Cancer wasn't going to beat HER and with that in mind she set herself, and us, goals to keep us occupied during her treatment.*

Grace finds herself sniffing. God the sacrifice. Saint is the word. St Goody. Has a ring. There will be appeals and beseechings to this brave young woman. There already are, look: *Bless me, Jade* says the message board. *See me through this illness. Help me to carry on being strong for my little ones. Help me to beat this disease.* Grace blows her nose, her new nose, on a Kleenex and is surprised to find herself dabbing at an eye. Little bit of moisture there. So unfair, life, so unfair. Why did Jade have to get the cancer? Why her? Others deserved it, not her. That Jo O'Meara should've got it. Not Danielle Lloyd cos she's too pretty to have her head shaved but the Goodster was always the better one than Jo O'Meara that much was obvious and still is.

So Jade made a list, it seems, at the top of which she wrote *40% chance to live so live.* One of the things on the list was 'pole dancing' but she'd spelled it 'pool'. Jennifer says: *We all fell about wondering what the hell she wanted to play pool for!* Funny, but then the shock and the heartbreak; a few days after writing the list Jade was told that she didn't have a forty per cent chance at all. The cancer, the evil stinking thing, was terminal. Twenty-seven years of age. Still a girl. Children, she had. Husband. Mother, disabled, who relied on her totally. Such a cruel world.

Give me strength, Jade. Send me some of the strength and braveness that helped you in your time. I don't think I am strong enough to cope.

A picture of Jade with her bridesmaids, all of them wearing caps so that they look bald. Only Jade in the picture really *is* bald. Only she ever kept it real. *Now Jack is just like a lost kid. Loyal Jennifer refuses to say a bad word about Jade's 22-year-old widower Jack Tweed – now awaiting trial on a rape charge . . . If Jade was here he'd never ever leave her. He wanted to be with her. She planned his whole life – even down to the clothes he wore. That's how dependent he was. I used to say Jade was mum AND girlfriend to*

Jack. She was in control of every aspect of his life and he was so laid-back he liked that. He was lost when he didn't have it any more.

Poor boy. Going off the rails. Lost all meaning in his life now that his great love has gone. We deal with grief in different ways. Excuse him. Forgive him. Grace scrolls quickly now, past the pictures, Jade kissing Jack, Jade all tubed up in hospital whites. A man who would need her that much no not one man there'll be thousands of them needing her soon. Millions. The interviewers are coming tomorrow. Coming up from London to speak to Grace, Grace Allcock, to interview her, nobody else. And soon the new boobs and now the new nose and the pictures and every man will need her. Every man in the country. In Europe. The world. Look at her with longing. A time when everything will have been worth it. Grace scrolls: *'Jade: A Year Without Her', a new TV documentary made by another of her closest friends, Kate Johnson, is on LIVING next Saturday, at 9 p.m.* Watch that. Remember. Remember poor Jade. The Goodster. Never let her die in the memory. And if that was the bargain – if that was the offer – global fame for a short life – recognition across the world but you'll die at twenty-seven – of cancer – leave behind sons and a husband and a disabled mother – if that was the offered deal – the exchange –

Back to the message board: *Wasn't fick man! She was worth 4 mil when she died!*

Help me, Jade. I am so scared. I do not want to die.

Grace leaves the site. Glances at her home page, an image of the planet seen from space, a giant cloudy eye swirling slowly across Greenland, turning its gaze to the east. Logs off.

Yes yes yes.

Grace leaves her room and goes downstairs. She can smell onions being fried. Good, she's hungry. Goody.

Grace receives a call on her mobile around midday and answers it. One of those excited and excitable London voices, youngish and female, the kind that would and does pronounce 'girl' as 'gahl' and expresses agreement by saying 'yeah' five times rapidly like a machine gun: yeahyeahyeahyeah*yeah*. She tells Grace that she's parked on the promenade opposite the amusement-arcade-looking-thing and Grace tells her that she'll see her in five and closes the phone and shouts to her mother:

—Mum! Quick! It's them! They're here! Ohmygod ohmygod!

She runs on the spot. She grabs her head in both hands and makes a kind of desperate, frantic noise. Her mother thumps up the stairs and calms her daughter down then whips her up into agitation again when she herself starts to panic, darting between bathroom and bedroom, checking and rechecking her hair, touching up her lippy, ripping off her gold top and replacing it with a plain white shirt no too frumpy where's that orange strappy thing? Only bought it last week.

—Mum! You're getting me all flustered, yeah? I'm gonna look all sweaty and horrible, yeah?

—Okay, okay. Her mother stands still and breathes deeply. In, out. —Calm. Deep breaths. No need for panic.

She pulls the orange strappy thing over her head. —How do I look?

—Fine. What about me?

—Gorgeous, love. Proper special.

The new nose. The hair, washed and styled that morning, piled up in a controlled burst of blonde curls on the head with ringlets down each side of the attractively made-up face. Lots of black eye make-up, bit of a sex panda thing going on. The crop top showing two inches of tanned tummy and, now that the dressing's been removed, the tattoo. Low-slung Miss Sixty jeans. Flowery ballet pumps on the feet.

—You look absolutely gorgeous, love. How you feeling?

Grace pulls a face. —Nervous.

—Yeah?

—Dead, dead nervous. Feel like I'm gonna be sick I'm so nervous.

—Listen. She moves over to Grace, grabs a shoulder in each hand, stares into her eyes. —They've come here for *you*. To see *you*, no one else. All the way from London to see *you*. If anything, they're the ones should be nervous, yeah? Just be yourself. Nobody else. You want to make it in this business then these are the things you have to do, yeah? Deep breaths, c'mon. In and out. Like me.

Inhale, exhale. They breathe together and settle and have a final primp side by side in the bathroom mirror and leave the house and link arms as they step out on to the promenade, both cursing the breeze off the sea as it musses their hair. Some strollers on the prom. Sounds of gulls. Soft collapse of the waves on the shingle beach and there are two people there, at the railings with the sea at their backs, standing next to a people carrier. The woman has dyed red hair the colour of a raw steak and is wearing a thigh-length black coat and jeans tucked into pointy-toed high-heeled boots and the man who is fiddling with a camera and tripod is hiply and gleamingly bald with eyes behind square-lensed spectacles and some geometrically arranged stubble on his face.

The woman says: —Gracie, yeah?

Grace smiles and says yes. The woman takes her hand and pecks her cheek and then takes Grace's mother's hand too.

—I'm Nat. This is Dylan.

Dylan looks up and smiles.

—And you? Should I say Grace or Gracie? Jerry called you Gracie. As in Fields, yeah?

—Gracie, says Grace's mother.

—Gracie it is, then. Either way it's a beautiful name. Gracie Allcock. Such a ring, yeah? Where you thinking, Dyl?

The man looks down into the lens of his mounted camera.

– Right here. Maybe. Got the pier in the background.

—Okay. Before or after?

—After. Hopefully that cloud'll blow over. You do your thing and I'll go and grab a cup of tea or something. Want one?

—No ta.

Nat leads Grace over to a bench and they sit down and Gracie's mother leans back against the railings, her eyes flicking from Nat to her daughter as if watching tennis. Nat holds a small machine to Grace's lips and asks her to say something.

—Like what?

—Anything.

—Yeah but what?

—That'll do.

She checks something on the machine and nods to herself.
—Fine. Oh and before we start.

She digs out of her bag a sheet of typescript. Grace's mother asks what it is.

—It's just a release form. It's a legal requirement? Gives us permission to use Gracie's words and pics in our publication? Yours too. So if you could just sign, yeah?

Grace signs. So does her mother. Nat folds the page neatly in half and tucks it back into her bag.

—Right. Formalities done, let's get started, yeah? Straightforward questions, Gracie, answer them in as few or as many words as you want but do try to keep it snappy because we don't have much time, yeah?

She's got nice eyes, Nat has. They go good with the blue eyeshadow. Skilfully applied lipstick and blusher and those earrings must've cost a fortune. Nice smell coming off her, too. Soapy.

—Gracie?

—Huh?

—Our readers are wanting to know about the girl behind the roasting video. They want to know who she is, what she is, about her life. Right?

Nod.

—So I'm just going to ask you a few questions. Simple stuff, not taxing or anything, yeah? If Mum wants to intervene or add anything at any time she can feel free, alright?

She squints at Grace's mother with the sun on her shoulder and Grace's mother smiles and nods.

—Who are you?

—Grace Allcock.

—Gracie Allcock. Where were you born?

—Here.

—In this town?

—Yes.

—How long ago?

—What?

—How old are you?

Grace tells her.

—Family?

—Hey?

—Do you have a family?

Grace looks at her mother, who says: —Just me. No father any more. Oh and a sister, older.

—Partner?

—What?

—Boyfriend or girlfriend?

Grace shakes her head. —We split up.

—Before or after the video?

—Just after.

—A man, right?

—Hey?

—I'm assuming your ex-partner was a feller.

Grace nods.

—Okay. So tell me what happened that night in the club with the footballers. Did they . . .

—I was drunk.

—Yes, fine, but how did they, erm, *get* you? Y'know, did they chat you up, send a bottle of champagne over, what?

—Can't really remember. Think they sent a feller over.

—A feller? For what?

—Well to tell me that they, the footballers like, wanted me back at their hotel, yeah? She looks at her mother. Her mother looks back.

—Did you know who they were?

—Who?

—The footballers. You recognised them, yeah?

—Knew they were famous. I mean I'd seen them on the telly and stuff.

—Did you know their names?

—No.

—Do you know their names now?

—Grace hasn't been following the story, her mother says.

—Okay. So you'd been drinking. They sent a 'man' over. She puts the word 'man' in finger quotes. —Back at their hotel, what happened? In the room?

—Erm, there was one of them at first. In the lift? The feller, not the, he wasn't British? Think he was from Spain or somewhere?

—Did he speak English?

—Not very well. I mean I had trouble knowing what he was saying.

—What did he do, in the lift?

—Well it was more in the room, really. He went into the bathroom and then the other fellers came in.

—More footballers?

—Yes.

—And then oh hang on. Maybe Mum would like to go for a bit of a walk at this juncture?

The mother says nothing.

—This is important, Mrs Allcock. I need to hear what happened that night and our readers need to know. But I'm thinking that it might be a bit uncomfortable for you to hear, though, yeah?

The mother nods. —I'll wait over there.

—Okay.

Nat smiles and watches the mother walk away, about thirty paces along the promenade. She leans back against the railings, keeps her eyes on her daughter. But she's out of earshot. Folds her arms across her chest.

—Now, Gracie, don't be embarrassed or ashamed. I've seen the video, I know what went on. They're good-looking men and you're a young girl, right? But I'd like to hear from you what happened. Or what you thought about what happened. What you *think* about it, okay?

Grace shrugs. —Just, y'know.

—I *don't* know, Gracie, no. What?

That machine hovering at Grace's lips. Insistent like a fly.

—Well you said you've seen it. They took turns like, know what I mean? One in here. Grace puts a fingertip to her lower lip. —And one, y'know. Then they swapped?

—But there were three of them.

—Yeah, well. Another shrug. —They fitted in.

—Did they hurt you?

—Oh and they put some porn on the telly. I remember that.

120

—And did they hurt you?

—Can't really remember. Suppose they did, sometimes, yes.

—Did you feel violated?

—What?

—Violated. It means, like, used. Like cheap?

—Erm . . .

—I'm looking for the *real* Gracie Allcock here. The girl in the video, the *real* girl. Millions of our readers want to know about her as well. Did you feel cheap? Did they make you feel cheap? Got to be honest with me here, Gracie. We need total honesty, yeah?

A breeze lifts some curls on Grace's head.

—Well, I.

—What?

—I suppose I did, yeah. I was drunk.

—And you were taken advantage of? They took advantage of your vulnerable condition?

Shrug. —Yes.

—You'd say that, would you? That they took advantage of you in your drunken condition.

—Suppose.

—You didn't have much say in the matter. In what went on.

—Not really. Just kind of went along with it yeah? They were famous. I'd seen them on telly.

—They abused you, then.

Grace looks over her shoulder at her mother who gives one firm nod. Turns back to Nat and the machine at her face.

—Yes.

—This is what our readers want to hear, Gracie. Did any of them have any distinguishing marks on their bodies?

—How'd you mean?

—Tattoos, scars. Funny blemishes.

—Funny what?

—Blemishes. Birthmarks, moles, stuff like that.

—One of them, the foreign feller, he had this like kind of shiny skin? And when he came out of the bathroom it was even shinier? Like wood or something?

—Wood.

—Like when it's varnished?

—I get you. Like he'd been polishing himself?

—Sort of, yeah. And one of them had a funny top lip.

—Like this? Nat curls her top lip into a sneer.

—Yeah. He hurt it in a bike accident or something when he was small. Fell off his bike.

—This is what he told you?

—No. I read about it somewhere. They didn't really speak to me in that way.

—The shiny skin and the funny top lip, our readers know about those things already. They've seen those things yeah? I need to know if they had any marks on their backs or thighs or wherever. Places that the general public wouldn't know about but you would.

Grace isn't the general public. She's not in the mass any more. She smiles. Privy to exclusive information as she is, to specialist knowledge, she smiles as the sea breeze gently lifts her hair.

—Gracie?

She shakes her head. —I didn't notice. I was, y'know.

—What? Drunk?

—No, well, I couldn't really see properly.

—Because you were so intoxicated.

—No, because I. I mean *they*. Things were in the way, y'know?

—Ah. I see. I understand what you're saying. And what do you think of them now? What would you like to see happen to them?

—Who, the footballers?

—Who roasted you.

Grace looks at her mother. Nod again. Back to Nat and her machine.

—What d'you mean?

—Well, would you like to see them punished in some way or something?

—Punished?

—For what they did to you.

—Well. I wouldn't like to see it happen to anyone else.

—Another girl you mean? Like yourself?

—Yes.

—So people should be aware.

—Yes.

—So they can watch out for themselves.

A shrug.

—Right then. Nat clicks the machine off. —That's enough of that, I reckon. Thank you for that, Gracie. For reliving that experience. Must've been hard for you and I appreciate it very much as will our readers.

A smile.

—Your mum can come back now.

She beckons Grace's mother over. Tells her: —You've got a co-operative and friendly daughter, Mrs Allcock. She's given me a lot to go on.

—Good.

She exchanges smiles with her daughter.

—And now I'm going to ask just a few general questions, okay? Just so I can fill Gracie out in the article, kind of thing, like make her more of a person? More real?

—Keeping it real, Grace's mother says.

—Too true. So, again, if you want to interject, feel free, yeah?

Grace's mother nods. Up comes the machine again, nudging at Grace's lips, a robot fuelled by spit.

—I'm admiring your nose, Gracie. I saw your Facebook page, where you showed it off. It's a brilliant job. Can you tell our readers about it?

Grace and her mother tell Nat about the hospital and the vomiting and the cost and the pain and that they're delighted with the result. Dylan returns, fiddles with his camera again.

—And Jerry told me about the boobjob for *Animal* magazine, that they'll be sponsoring it. Are you excited about this?

—She's always wanted bigger, Grace's mother says.

—Why's that, Gracie?

—Just do.

The mother says: —Improve on nature, end of the day.

—Want more curves. Grace arches her back so that her breasts push against the fabric of her top.

—And *Animal* are going to run 'Before' and 'After' photographs, is that right?

—That's what Jerry said. And they'll be paying for it, as well, the op.

—Couldn't we all do with an extra couple of inches. Had it done myself.

—Did you?

—Augmentation, yeah. Had it done myself a couple of years back.

—A boobjob?

—Yes.

—Really? Did you?

—I did. Just a cup larger.

—Did it hurt?

—You'll be fine. It was worth it. So where now? What does the future hold for Gracie Allcock?

Grace looks at Nat's chest but can discern no shape beneath the thick black coat. Her mother talks about modelling opportunities and about how hopefully something good can come out of this experience and Grace smiles and nods at Nat's face.

—Right. We're done. Nat clicks the machine off, puts it in her bag. —Thanks very much to both of you. You good to go, Dyl?

—Grace, can I just have you over here, leaning on the railings . . .

He arranges her with her forearms on the top bar, facing the sea, behind her the pier and behind that the church on the small mound with the rotting bodies in it and the carven names fading to blurred nicks with the years' weathering and erasure. He tells her to look at the camera, not directly, just with her eyes. She does.

—Good. That's good. Now let's have your profile. Look at the water.

She does. Dylan clicks away.

—Excellent, excellent. Good-looking girl, Gracie.

She turns to him and smiles and he shouts: —That's it! That's it! Hold it there!

Click click click. —Gorgeous. Click click click. Grace has

never felt so desirable. Her new nose, her soon-to-be-bigger boobs. Her make-up and her hair and her sunbedded skin. She is young and she is sexy. Look at that smile.

—Look at that smile! These'll blow them away.

Grace's mother watches and claps her hands once and then Dylan's putting his equipment away.

—Is that it?

—Got more than enough. We're done.

—Got to shoot off, says Nat. —Bit late as it is.

—For what?

—Got to go back and speak to Jennifer. She's got a new film coming out.

—Jennifer? Jennifer who? Not Lopez.

Nat laughs. —Not Lopez, no. Ellison.

They're loading their gear back into the people carrier. Grace and her mother watching.

—But thanks to you both. You've been very helpful and it's much appreciated. Article will be going out next week and the payment will go through Jerry, yeah?

—Okay.

—Thanks again. Take care.

Nat climbs up into the passenger seat and Dylan slides the door shut after her and smiles and waggles his fingers at Grace and her mum then he jumps into the driver's seat and starts the engine and then they're gone. Grace and her mother watch the van's back window shrink then look at each other. Then they burst out laughing and leap into an embrace.

—Did you hear that? Jennifer Ellison!

—The same people! Grace says into her mother's shoulder.

—You and her Grace! You're both the same!

They squeeze each other tightly then part.

—Ohmygod, says Grace. —Ohmygod ohmygod.

—It's happening, love.

—I know it is.

—I can *feeeel* it.

—So can I. Ohmygod ohmygod.

They hug again. A seagull lands on a litter bin behind them. Glowing wings.

—Was it okay? What did she ask you?

Shrug. —Stuff.

—What kind of stuff?

—Just stuff, yeah?

—I'll read the article, Grace.

Shrug. —Whatever.

The seagull beats its shining wings and rises away. Grace and her mother decide on an ice cream to celebrate. Three scoops with all the sprinkles and stuff. Raspberry sauce and everything.

★

Silicone never rots. They say that silicone implants will never rot. Worms, bacteria and grubs, they do their thing to skin and the flesh and eventually the bone but the jellybags will remain intact and Jordan and Jodie and Pamela and all the others, when you die – which you will – and when you decay – which you will – those bags in your bodies will remain whole in the soil. When your bodies crumble. When you unbuckle, when the bugs disjoin you. All the world's cemeteries and all the jellybags in their dirt. Like that's all there is of your time on the planet, nothing to show for your presence and passing but a bag of unrottable jelly. Everything else to break down into nutrients and soup from which grows grass. Trees. And the creatures that eat that grass and the creatures that eat those creatures and so it all goes on and begins again or just continues because there is no end to this but these pouches of silicone they will remain. They will stay. What a thing to leave behind. What an awful thing to leave behind if that's all there is and nothing else. The stars reclaim you, all your cells but not those sacks of venom that you carry in your breasts.

As vessels I see you. As husks. As shells from which the life has fled.

With tea and toast and eggs and beans from the cafe inside him he takes a tabloid down on to the pebble beach to enjoy the sunshine and there, under the gulls' shrieking and the hiss of the waves, the music of borborygmus begins in his belly; the liquid trills and trickles, the grumbles and mumbles as internal sphincters open and close and juices sluice through. It's a sound he likes. There's a magic in it; the happy little symphony of his organs as they break down and convert the food. He remembers when she was pregnant with Ella and he'd watch her eat and he'd think of what was happening inside her, the human form appearing in the damp darkness inside her, taking a shape from the food she ate, the atoms she consumed. Cornflakes to a human baby but the ungraspable equation of her body between. He'd watch her eat a cheese roll and see the fingernails appear. Yoghurt and then hair. Chocolate and kneecaps, apples and eyes. Each item of food itself extracted from the soil and the sea and before that from the blazing hearts afloat in space. Reached up she did and pulled them into her, absorbed their pale flame. Balls of far fire tucked into her belly and that's what she did and he watched her do it. All of us made from these borrowed things. These atoms and molecules to be one day reclaimed by the living dust and then the bigger things who too will release their constituent parts and out there waiting in the sky are the burning bellies, the hanging banks brightly blazing awaiting the return of their capital. With what accrued interest.

He rolls a cigarette and unfolds the paper. Top right-hand corner the strapline: **WE NAME ROASTED GIRL! Full story pages 4 & 5.** He swallows and turns pages. There she is, smiling at the camera. A big smile. The hair piled up on top of her head. Jutting out from her left shoulder into the sea is the pier, the pier he can see as he looks to his left which he does, twice, at the pier itself then back at the photograph of it. He looks over his shoulder at the railings of the promenade then looks back to his paper. Gracie Allcock they're calling her. The little girl clutching the daisy. Little girl with the scraped knee. Little girl made from pastry and coffee and oranges and star-spore.

Alone, now, this stunning young girl has split up with her long-term boyfriend. The video caused a rift between them that sadly could not be healed. They are no longer together and Gracie is nursing a broken heart.

He inhales smoke. A gull lands nearby, probably suspecting food from the hand-to-mouth movement, and struts on the pebbles in front of him.

Gracie has blocked out memories of that night when, after forcing her to watch vile hardcore porn, three Premiership footballers used her like a piece of meat. It was 'painful', and 'made me feel cheap', Gracie told our reporter, bravely reliving that fateful night.

The gull preens under its wing. Looks out at the sea for a moment then makes a moaning sound and flies away.

This bright, pretty, sharp young girl who.

He looks at her face. Her smiling face. The pier behind her as if growing out of her head. With that smile she does not look distressed but the article tells of her sense of shame. Of violation.

Once again the pampered brats of football, the spoilt boys of the Premiership, have taken cruel advantage of the innocent dreams of young girls. The vanity and arrogance of these men beggars belief. According to Gracie, one of the three – who cannot be named yet due to a court ruling – polished his skin in the hotel bathroom until he 'shone like varnished teak', before the sex took place. What kind of man.

A smile made from milk. Tomatoes in the cheeks.

The unwilling centre of an orgy.

Next to that smile the silhouettes of three heads, three profiles coloured black. Meat in them and potatoes and blood pudding.

Gracie finds forgiveness in her heart. Not bitter, she simply wants the names of these three men and other sexual predators like them to be made public so that other innocent and naive young girls can be careful.

He reads the article twice. *Gracie's proud and protective mother.* Bitch choked me out. The way they scurried around her searching for holes to plug. The way they all laughed. The two of them high-fiving over her back and the grunting, the grunting. Roast chicken. Another ho fucked stupid lol. He looks at the smile once more then turns the page and there's Cheryl and Colleen shopping in somewhere, some city, where is it, Milan it says. Look what they've bought. And how much happier than Cheryl Colleen looks because her Wayne has been phoning her up every day from his training camp in somewhere hot, indiscretions with hookers evidently forgiven. She's grinning, Colleen, and her arms are weighed down with labelled bags. Hermès and Louis Vuitton. In Milan.

He skims the rest of the paper with his mouth dry and a kind of racing at the back of his blood. A warming atmosphere he reads about. The eye over Greenland and the ice cracking and does the satellite imagery show this crack? This great zigzag across the ice sheet, photographed from space? Is that a crack? *Boffins are undecided. But if it is.*

If it is. Come wave and wash it all away.

He folds the paper into four and slots it beneath his head as he lies back on the pebbles and drapes an arm over his eyes. Gulls calling, the sound of the waves, some children playing somewhere. His belly makes a little bloik. All he wants to do is sleep, now, in the sun, just sleep in the come-again sun.

It was a favourite place of his, always, under the pier, as a boy. The salty coolness of it under there and the footfalls on the boardwalk above and down there he was happily removed from them, down there with the barnacled rocks and the smells and the weed-streamered stanchions frilled with mussels blue-lipped. Hours he'd spend under there, as a boy, sometimes entire days, only surfacing into the light to buy food and then return with it under the pier to eat. A troll he was, apart from the lighted herd, happy with the crabs and the shannies and the gobies. Sometimes there would be coins dropped from above, slipped out of the hands of those aimed at the machines in the amusement arcade or at the stalls of ice cream or hamburger. Like rare gifts. Silver flakes through the gaps between the boards. And once, no longer a boy or a boy and a bit, he took Ella down there, about two years old she was, in yellow wellies, showed her the mussel mats at which she cooed and stroked, sat her on the sand and lifted a rock and watched as she stared saucer-eyed at the scuttling life he revealed. He put a pea crab on the palm of his hand and held it out to her. The crab, tiny as it was, raised its pincers in a defensive posture and Ella clapped and burbled in glee and he watched the two, his daughter and the tiny crab, watched the two interact, both obeying ancient instincts, tried to see each through the other's eyes but only summoned shapes in his own, undefined shapes which shifted and moved then blurred and broke even further apart. Under that pier, out of the sun, he and his daughter and the tiny crab. Sounds of others on the wooden slats above and the odd and confusing world they made and inhabited and into which he must return, blinking, reft of a settling, with his baby daughter. The crab back beneath the wet sand in a paring of darkness. Ella cried, he seems to recall. Wriggled in his arms and pointed over his shoulder at the pier as he carried her away and yelled: *Back, Dada, back! Back Dada!*

The radio rouses him from a sleep deep and apparently dreamless yet he feels neither restless nor particularly refreshed. Some voices talking, two voices talking, one he recognises as the half-whine from the Midlands somewhere belonging to that fucker with the perpetual smirk what's his name? Used to be in a boy band but left to go solo. Obsessed with the Loch Ness monster and the yeti and stuff. And his own self of course. Got a new song out. Willy Roberts, that's his name. He presses Snooze but when he's woken up again ten minutes later Willy Roberts is still talking and he says one word – *whatever* – before the caretaker slaps the alarm off and gets out of bed.

The tea bag in the mug, releasing its flavour. *Whatever.* The moment of the shrug, isn't it? What difference does it make because I can have whatever I want. *Whatever.* This incident marks the centre of my ability to move and choose amongst the options. *Whatever.* Shrug. Means nothing. Who cares. I have it all. That is my entitlement. As an actor I can choose from it all but all of it is meaningless to me and as an actor why should I feel shame? All I'm doing is playing a part, reading lines and performing scenes that have been written for me, and so I feel no shame. My every move is not just pre-planned but recorded too. Civilian I am yet eyes I will never see see me move and speak. And so dies shame. Another cough to rack its dying form. There is no shame.

Fuck it. Just woken up. A new day, and me in it. And you. Oh such promise.

He squeezes the tea bag then throws it away then butters some toast and takes his breakfast into the front room. Opens the curtains. The morning is bright. Opens a window. The morning is musical. Turns the TV on and sits and eats toast. Images: the hooded figures on the boxes and those wires that appear to sprout from them like tentacles or antennae. The snarling dog. The grins beneath crew cuts. When something huge is hurtling towards you the sane thing to do is to get out of the way. But in fact we stand before it and watch it come with our arms outspread so as to present a larger target. In a posture of ready embrace. What the fuck is wrong with us. With *you*.

There is this: you are no more than your hunger. That's the sum of it, the totality of it, and that's why everything is so completely without hope. The dreams of your bodies know no joy. What you are defines you and all you are is a howling hole insatiable.

The news ends and he is taken back inside the studio with the two presenters on the sofa and now they have a third with them and it's Willy Roberts who must've helicoptered across London or something because there he is, in the studio, that face of his part 'who me?' and part 'yes *me*'. Answering his own question. Of himself. He his own questioner. The snake that eats its tail. Auto-fellatio. Probably a website for that. Unless the radio studio is in the same building as the TV one because then just an elevator. Or a walk along a corridor, just. Here to talk about his new song.

He turns the TV off and washes his dishes and goes upstairs for a shower. Fences to be painted today. Radiators to be bled. Other such tasks.

★

Pamela Anderson tits. That's the aim. The target. Not Katie's because they're perhaps a bit *too* big and you'd get backache and wouldn't it be a pain trying to find tops that fit you but Pamela's, yes, are perfect. And every woman with a small-frame should not go bigger than a B-cup. But what about Victoria

Beckham? She's small-frame and she's got watermelons. Brown watermelons. The eggs of an insect on a twig and what will hatch or has hatched. Pamela's, though. They're perfect.

The British Association of Aesthetic Plastic Surgeons. BAAPS. Grace looks up from the magazine at her mother who's busy doing something clinky at the sink.

—Mum?

—What, love?

—What's 'aesthetic' mean? Is that like when they put you unconscious for a bit?

—No, love, that's '*anaesthetic*'. 'Aesthetic' is, like, to do with beauty kind of thing? How something looks, yeah?

There are pictures of botched implants. Breasts like crossed and googly eyes. Nipples pointing skywards or down at the person's toes. Bruising. Some open suppuration. The ads online mention *celebrity clientele*. The warnings mention association with Good Medical Practice in Cosmetic Surgery and the Independent Healthcare Authority's Code of Practice which Grace's eyes skim then lock on to the words *augmentation mammoplasty*. It's a simple procedure. Small incision, one of two types: periareolar, surrounding the areola; or axillar, the underarm. The areola, that's the pink and pimply plate surrounding the nip. Small incision in both cases. Almost invisible scar. Or, even, *Minimally Invasive Mastopexy*, the Cup and Up, the bra you wear one centimetre under your skin. So that your bra is *in* your body. Your bra becomes part of you. Sling-shaped silicone cups are inserted through slits beneath each breast and stitched to the upper ribs with titanium screws. This can be performed under local aesthetic, no, *an*aesthetic. Invented by Dr Eyal Gur in Tel Aviv but what does that matter?

Grace skims, flicks, darts her eyes. Slanting sunbeams in the kitchen through which specks, motes, drift and then dash like midges, living things, but they are not. Once were, maybe – flakes of dead skin. Yet they constellate then smithereen with each breath and displacement of air when Grace turns a page or scratches her head or her mother puts a newly sparkling dish or glass on the draining board.

Augmentation Mammoplasty, another site telling of. A

procedure here called *magical* because the effects are immediate and dramatic and generally unobscured by bruising or sutures. Cuts a pocket under chest muscle, palpates the nerve there, fits implants, fills them with silicone. The breasts apparently rise visibly. Must be like pushing a button or working a pump, that simple. Quote Dr Robert Alan Franklyn, 1950s' surgeon who pioneered such surgery: *My goal was to help the embarrassed and self-conscious woman Nature had neglected.*

These words flash a little inside Grace, flash a little like light off steel with an edge or something else dangerous. She closes her eyes and senses that she is blindly butting at something colossal. Like immeasurably big. The size of the planet. Cold and vast and monstrous in that it is capable of wilful neglect and what the fuck does it know of Grace? What could it ever know? And such is the war at the heart of it all the tiny cries at the centre and core. Here I am. You must notice and you must care but you do neither and so I will budge at you and poke at you and continue to cry until you do. I will make you.

Grace rubs her eyes. Looks over at her mother who is facing the window with her rubber-pink hands in suds and humming something to herself, a tune that Grace cannot make out.

Points of data float like and with the motes. 75,000 cosmetic surgery procedures carried out each year in the UK. Why the fuss? Consumer lifestyle choice. Transform Medical Group off Harley Street in London. It's normal, then, it's normal. So many people are doing it. Nothing at all of the unusual or remarkable or freakish about it these days but Grace does want it to be so – remarkable. Wants her bumps to look fake so it's obvious to the watchers that she's had them done. Had the op. Or those who *will* watch and gaze and gawp. Abi Titmuss: *I think I just have a great pair of personalities . . . I didn't make myself famous. Someone else did.* A surgeon: *It's just sculpture. A 21st-century form of sculpture. My patients are artworks in progress.*

Grace looks up from the screen. —Mum?

—What, love?

Grace looks down. —Nothing. It's okay.

Risks of infection and bleeding and asymmetry and leaking of silicone. Visible scarring. Numbness of the nipple. But it's *my* body so it's *my* choice. Kelly Brook. Loads of others. Tiny holes made, pulled apart and jellybags stuffed in. Blood and bruising. Oxygen masks and bleeping machines and people unconscious or drowsy in gowns on gurneys. Don't look at me now but *now* look at me. *Animal* photographers are coming tomorrow. For the 'Before' shots. This will all happen. Is happening.

Grace looks up from the screen. —What are you smiling about, Mum?

—I'm smiling because my youngest daughter is so gorgeous.

—Aw shut *up*.

—It's true. And you're only going to get more lovely.

—Aw shut *up*.

But there are smiles and there are clicks and there is the scrolling and turning of pages. There is the calling up of images.

Jitter and jump of life on the spinning world. Some scenes, some spring scenes, from the story of the earth, here and at this time:

They arrive at mid-morning and set up a makeshift and temporary studio in Grace's bedroom. Two of them, again one male one female, the man with the camera and the woman with what? Reassurance, maybe. Support, for Grace. While the man sets up his equipment the woman drinks tea and talks to Grace and makes her laugh and makes her proud. *You're so lucky*, she says. *So brave. I'd love some augmentation too but I haven't got the money OR the guts and here you are, getting it paid for. We'll make you famous, Gracie.* The man directs Grace to stand before her Willy Roberts poster and he snaps away and the camera chunners and he asks her if she could take her top off, would that be okay, and Grace removes her Kookai zebra-striped strappy top and then her bra and the man doesn't look up from his camera and Grace can see the top of his head, the sideways swoosh there of his fin of hair. She remembers skin dark brown and gleaming like laminated wood. *Brilliant, Gracie, lovely. Now clasp your hands together and raise them up to the ceiling. Perfect. Perfect. Just perfect.* This will be worth it, this exposure. It'll be: Look how I *was* now look how I *am*. Look look look. Look at me. *Right, keep your hands together and bring them down to your belly button. That's it. Squeeze your elbows together. That's it. These are good shots, Gracie.* The woman gives Grace a smile of pearly power. *You're doing great, Gracie.* Grace smiles. The camera chunners. Already Grace is not as she is. Already she has been projected into a futurity in which she is different and improved. She is already, here in her bedroom half-naked with her hands clasped and heating up from the halogen blaze from the light on her left, else and other and new and improved. Grace growing. Her future in her present as she stands half-bared. *Lovely, Gracie, just lovely. Just a few more and then we'll be gone. Hands behind your back, now, if you would.*

Outside, down in the garden below Grace's bedroom window, some wooden shelving slowly rots. Uncollapsed as yet, it continues to hold a few flowerpots in which only soil is and a few garden implements: a trowel, a fork, a dibber. When the mood is on her, Grace's mother likes to potter in the garden but she hasn't done this for a while and the shelves which need replacing continue to buckle in places in the weather. Under the overcast sky today they are faintly lit up vaguely blue with the bright light trickling down from the bedroom window above them and they stand in their crumbling as if illuminated by sustained and distant lightning and at the back of them where they meet the outside skin of kitchen brick and where dampness has gathered and festered and cannot be evaporated by the sun thrive lice, woodlice, not insects but crustacea, akin to crabs and shrimp, tiny armoured creatures feasting on the mouldering and liquefying chips of wood. A voice dribbles down from the window above, a barely audible, encouraging voice: *That's great, Gracie. You're doing great.* The lice chew and trundle. Chew and trundle. Moving in their segments, their blue-grey segments, tiny armadilloes, their antennae waving and touching independently, pilling up when they feel threatened which defence is futile here in this damp and narrow slice of the world given that predators stalk here, woodlouse spiders, maroon thorax and legs, browny abdomen, sharply pronounced chelicerae large enough to pierce the carapace of their favoured prey coeval and co-evolved and human skin, too. Hunting spider, stalking spider. The delicate tread then the touch and the pounce. The crunch and suck.

Tumbledown voice from the lit-up window above: *Brilliant, Gracie. We'll be back in a couple of weeks or so, yeah, when you start healing up.* The bright light behind the window is extinguished. *When your boobs are bigger, yeah?*

Scenes from the life of the world.

And *it's not your body*, Rachel says. A pudgy child on her lap and another just as pudgy but bigger and able to walk with some sticky slick on his face and bringing a toy tractor to show his auntie Grace and his grandmother. In the front room of Rachel's house this is. The husband is in the kitchen, cooking, by the smell of it, onions. *That's what you don't seem able to understand. And it's not all about you. There is a world outside of you.*

Grace takes the tractor from her nephew and runs it along the arm of the settee she's sitting on making *brrrm, brrrm* noises. Her sister asks her if she's even listening and her mother answers for her, something about this being what she wants and it being *her* body and *her* choice and she's thought about it long and hard haven't you love? Grace says *yeah* twice quickly.

First the roasting thing. The disgusting bloody roasting thing, and now this. Where's it going to end?

The baby on Rachel's lap is squirming and grumbling. Rachel unclasps the top two buttons of her shirt and scoops a breast out of her bra and the baby starts to suck. With the movement, the fumbling suction, the jewelled crucifix around Rachel's neck rises and falls with the drawing-in and release of the breast on which it rests, the rhythmic suck and release. Murmurs from the baby and liquid approval.

That Katie Price? Is that what you really want, to be like her? Ow. This last in response to the early and nipping teeth.

Brrrm, brrrm, says Grace and returns the toy to the boy.

Don't you think that there's more to life?

Grace looks around the room, the slightly too-hot room, at the sacred heart and crucifix above the mantelpiece on which family photographs stand and candlesticks and small ceramic animals, at the children's toys stored in the red plastic crate in front of the TV, a Buzz Lightyear waving from the jagged and vivid pool of them as if drowning. At the CD racks, the DVD racks, the toppled video cases of *In the Night Garden* and *Peppa Pig*. The wallpaper. The sheepskin rug abutting the gas fireplace. The mug and newspapers next to the armchair on which Rachel suckles her baby. At the sugar-sticky face of Grace's eldest nephew running his tractor up her denimed leg, the plastic wheels catching on the material. Miss Sixty and everything.

Be careful. That hurts.

The boy steers the tractor on to the floor and begins to plough the carpet.

At the teatime sunshine falling aslant through the window, Grace looks. To face the hours of darkness in this house. To sleep in it or try to. With those eyes on the wall and the expectation that at any moment the night and sleep would be rent by baby screamings and all of it slightly too hot and onion-smelly and tasting of weak sweet tea and plain biscuits.

Why'd you bring her round here, Mum?

She's got a lot on her mind. Haven't you, Gracie?

'Gracie'? Since when did she become 'Gracie'?

Sound of cutlery being laid out in the dining annex in the adjoining room. The Mondeo outside in the drive. The sound of Rachel's husband humming as he prepares the evening meal.

This is what worries me.

The rolling eyes in the mother's face. She nudges her youngest daughter with her elbow. *Here we go.*

Well why the bloody hell d'you ask for my opinion if you're not going to listen to what I've got to say? 'Here we go', is it? Why bloody bother?

Rachel holds the baby out towards her mother who takes the child and cradles him and wipes his plapping mouth with a tissue. *No, you're right, love, go on. Say what you've got to say. I'm sorry.*

Rachel wipes her nipple with a tissue and tucks her breast away and rebuttons her shirt. Crumples the moist tissue in her hand but does not discard it. Keeps it balled up in her fist further wetting it with her own perspiration. Her milk, her sweat, the Kleenex absorbent.

See, what you don't realise. Neither of you. You don't seem to understand.

What, love?

Get on with it, Grace says, and those are the first words she's uttered in several minutes.

God moves entirely through the actions of people.

Grace actually hears the attentive part of her brain shut down: SHOOooom, like when some electrical thing is turned off in space films. She actually hears it. She's aware that her sister's talking and making words and that their mother is too, in response, and that the nephew at her feet with the tractor is still brrrm-ing and that the smaller nephew on her right encribbed by the arms of his granny is mimbling in his sated sleep like an old man but these are just sounds. Meaningless and, in their way, mad. Nothing but background noise to Grace's parade of herself in her forebrain with the new breasts like conkers all shiny-brown and spilling out of a sparkly dress, her self, her new self, or newself, like that, one word, before and after, the Grace that will be.

Scenes from the life of the world.

And outside of this slightly too-warm room in which the distaff digs and discussions go on and next to the crushed gravel drive on which the Mondeo ticks as it cools beneath the pinkening sky as the sun slides out of it and between the gravel drive and the small neat square lawn there is a thin strip of soil in which flowers grow: some daisies, fuchsias, Welsh poppies, dandelions sprouted from unplanned and opportune seeds. Between these flowers drone languid bees, flying upright like angels, weighed down with pollen pantaloons, air-drifting from bright petal to bright petal. Ants are doing a similar thing, three species of beetle too, and earlier in the day there were butter-flies. And too there is a breeze off the sea which disperses the pollen towards which the stigma reach and pluck and draw down to the ovule hidden in the whorl of the blossom which will replace the little flags above when they wither which they will. So it continues. So the inflorescence awaits its own reappearance after the temporary shrivelling, no petal hell in this. Different, vastly, yet each will die without the other. Die and reappear only in guises different. And voices drift through the window, open a crack as it is, muffled voices but noticeably raised, drift through the ajar-ness of the window above the determined bees and the blossoms avid and agog.

—It's not natural, Grace! It's just not natural!

A baby starts to cry. The bees hum and wander. Scenes from the life of the world.

And then there is a waiting room and Grace is in it. Looking through magazines, flicking quickly through the pages as if angered. Fish in a tank. Her mother is there too and there are nurses moving through the room and from one of the antiseptic and gleaming chambers along the adjoining corridor branching perpendicular in the guts of this big building over the border to the east there is the sound of human laughter. Grace hisses.

—It's alright, love, her mother says. —Soon be over. And then . . .

—Then what?

The mother shrugs and smiles. —It's what you've wanted for ages.

There are lights, very bright lights. A supine and gurneyed Grace with patterns, swoops and ticks like hieroglyphs, drawn on to her bared breasts. There is Demerol to relax the mind and Xylocaine to relax the flesh. Grace on a gurney is wheeled down the corridor and past a sign framed and behind glass on the wall which reads:

> MY GOAL WAS TO HELP THE
> EMBARRASSED AND
> SELF-CONSCIOUS WOMAN
> NATURE HAD NEGLECTED.
> – Dr Robert Alan Franklyn

Grace points at this woozily and groans in something like recognition and a rubber-gloved hand softly pats the lolling pointing arm and tucks it back on to the gurney. Drugged Grace, adrift and half-asleep. Clouds in her head not black gravid with rain but ones just temporarily masking the summer sun. Shh, Grace. Sleeeep. But not yet, no, not before she's lifted from the trolley and altar'd beneath a big blaze and machines are activated and fluids set to gurgle and masked faces lean over her, one of which seems to say:

—Hello, Gracie? I'm your surgeon. I'm going to be building the new you today.

The visible eyes crinkle at their outer corners with a smile.

—Yes, yes. I'm a magician, too. You have absolutely nothing to worry about.

He nods to another masked person. There is a needle that winks. *Now* there is sleeeep, yes, now there is sleep. And here there is no assault on the essential self beneath the lights and blades. The essential self is in flux and motion, forever and always open to change, and the razor edges glint. There are corrective obstetrics and cephalometric movements to be steered by and skin and fat to be sliced and pared and holes to be held open but no violence done to identity or self. The magician's mask burgeons and flops with his even-tempered breath as he leans and cuts through skin and fat and muscle. On the breast he forms a mouth, a lipless mouth at first then a smirking one then a smiling one then a yawning one then a screaming one, toothless, revealing the wet red chute of the gullet behind. Blood slicks and is suctioned away. This is not the point at which a future form of the human will see the abnormal become normal but it is one such moment. A needle jabs and rummages between the superficial epidermis and the deeper glossier flesh and at this the skin and muscle jump and twitch and will do for several minutes until the injected chemicals still the nerves. Beneath the skin the fibres are not messy but are in fact ordered and smooth like the grain in wood. Machines monitor. The blades move slickly through the layers of life. Clamps are applied to pull the lips away from the purple yawn. The patient moans and turns her head. The light above could be said to blaze yet the illumination it releases is blue and cold. Machines make bleeping sounds. The pump sucks. The surgeon's mask billows in and out and the breathing in the room is stentorian and wheezing.

—More Xylocaine.

Again the needle sinks in. Skin is pulled with insistence.

Yanked. The body senses, fights against the intruder despite the anaesthetic's sledgehammer soporifia and so the skin must be pulled and yanked. Limbs loll, as does the head. A corpse before the rigid phase. A spatula lifts the pectoral muscle with a slight rip and slobber away from its anchoring matter and the suction tubes gurgle. Passive, passive. Whimper and loll. Gloved hands blood-slurried take from a blue mat a bag of jelly that wobbles and writhes on the red-run rubber and that bag is pressed against the clamped-open wound which pushes against it sphincter-like and more force is applied until the sliced skin and the slopes and bumps of muscle behind it slurp the bag in followed by fingers which rootle and dig and arrange. Up to the knuckles, the rubbered fingers groping, the nipple rippling and bobbing with their movement, the breast itself contorting like a blanket with a kitten underneath. Machines make noises. Cold light falls. Lungs breathe and skin twitches and flickers and a hiss sounds briefly as veins are cauterised. There is a needle, a curved needle, and thread. The gloved hands take up another scalpel and move on to the other breast and create a second howling mouth on the undercurve of it where the arcing flesh of it joins the top of the ribcage under the armpit. This goes on. And when wrenched out of the anaesthetic sleep, Grace, as other patients do, will gasp and shudder, her entire body heaving up off the altar and arching when the ventilator is pulled from the mouth. Born in contorted shock, the new, the after, and a whooping trauma.

Beyond the window of this theatre, only a few feet away from Grace's entubed and flopping head, in the niche where the top of the glass meets the bottom of the guttering, house martins have made their nest of mud and spittle. Blue head and upper parts, pure white rump and underparts, the birds have chosen this spot to take advantage of the available food, the small flying insects that amass and jostle above the pond in the hospital's grounds at dawn and dusk. Their droppings streak the blinded window of the theatre and the brickwork around. Recently arrived from Asia, these birds, to summer in the country as they and other birds like them do each year with the world's eternal turning, the swifts and the swallows and the sand martins too although they are mostly late this year and few. Come through blizzard and sunbake and paths of predators, the hobby foremost amongst them, and blasts of ice and whirlwind and sandstorm and torrent in obeisance to ancient instinct. Downy feathering on the legs. Brown eyes and a tiny black bill which can gape. Pink toes. Wings that beat five times each second. Noisy bird, chittering in communication, a soft trill of melodious chirrups, a hard *chrrrrpp* in contentment and shrill *tseeep* in alarm. Closed convex cup of the nest and with an aperture seemingly too small to admit the bird and made from mud, successive layers of mud, cemented with saliva, collected by both male and female from ponds and streams and puddles and lined with soft grasses and fur and the wool of sheep. Young in this nest now, four in number, two of which will survive, blind still but skin puckered with first plumage, their haemorrhoid-eyed heads craned to the coin of light which when darkened and occluded by the return of the parent will cause them to clamour. Guests of summer and spring, these birds. Indicators of delicate air although they are late this year and few. Knowers of high niche, cornice and eave, gable famil-iars, they mate and feed and die on the wing, they never land, they never land, and the returning parent bird now beak frilled with the legs of midges and gnats, flickers in an instant past the window to the nest and through the shafts of bright light that pass through that glass, too thick to transmit passage of any sound, the noise of the machines or the lurch and fumbling gasp of the awakening patient and the voice of the nurse saying *all finished, you're safe now* and the question asked in an exhausted croak: *Do I have tits?*

Scenes from the life of the world. These birds never land.

And Grace's recovery is quick. The assault on the body, the invasion and insertion, would seem to obviate a long recuperative period but Grace's recovery is quick. Most, after procedures of this kind, are. She lies in bed in the main or sits at her computer and can lift nothing heavier than a mug of tea or plate of food. Seepage, there is, and bruising. The dressings are taken off after a few days and replaced by a special support bra. There is pain and sensitivity. After a week she returns to the hospital in the big city over the border to the east and the stitches are taken out and the wound is swabbed and examined and declared to be fine but *it hurts* she says so she is put on co-codamol. The breasts remain swollen. Grace of course studies them in the mirror. Where are the shiny-brown horse chestnuts she wanted, envisaged? These are pink and explosive. Ugly. One prod and they might burst. And the bruising, the smoggy sunset beneath each armpit. They do not move, even when she jumps or tries to dance in her room. Hurts to move the arms. The breasts do not move as the body does.

Jerk of life, judder and jump of life on the turning earth. The bruises fade. The nipples, to the touch, no longer burn and flinch. Jerry Wellin makes several calls. The first time he talks Grace through the sobbing and the moaning but on the fifth call he's sharing her laughter. Grace's friends text and email but she invites only Shell round to see and they say nothing of the night in the club and the harvesting nor of how Shell fared on her own that night after Grace had gone off with the footballers and even though the bruising is still evident Shell films Grace standing with her back to her bedroom window and they send it to her Facebook page and on that Grace says: *Look at my new boobs! I'm so happy!* and she can't help but laugh and the comments come quickly in, most appreciative, from Ireland and America and Australia and Italy. Grace's mum admires. Wants to touch. Announces that she's jealous and wants hers done too. Rachel declines to comment and will not come round to the house to witness. Shell will text, asking Grace when they can go out clubbing to show off the new boobs, and Jerry Wellin will email reminding Grace that the 'After' photographs are to be taken soon as if she'd ever forget and that an event in some club is coming up soon at which Grace should be, some Willy Roberts promotion thing, he'll keep her informed, but keep this coming Saturday night free. How her heart beats. How her new breasts do not move with such thumping behind them, how they resist the frailties of the body, remain unaffected by this power. She becomes *very* pleased with them. Can't stop looking, stroking, tweaking, posing in front of the mirror in various outfits. Gowns, bikinis, strappy tops. Bit more spray-tan time and they'll be perfect, absolutely perfect.

The photographers return, the same people. *Wow!* says the woman. *Look at you! You look fantastic!*

Grace takes her top off. Lifts her arms. The scars are noticeable, just – pink smirks on the skin – but they can be airbrushed out. Her breasts are now globes. The nipples are proud. The flesh swoops smoothly from the armpit down into the undercurve and downward on a firm gradient and camber of muscle from the collarbones – there is and nor will there be no sag or droop. The camera chunners. Willy Roberts on his poster leers over Grace's shoulder and the powerful light to the side of the poster casts a slice of its blaze into the thin kingdom between paper and wall and burns the money spider, so delicate it is, frazzles and stills it in its tiny web and desiccates it in a second. Dead speck, now, in the thin world between poster and wall. Tiny dead speck. In an instant killed and crisped by the light and its heat, so delicate is, was, the spider. Grace puts her hands behind her back, on her hips. Gives the camera a hard stare, a pout. *Look happy, Gracie! You've got loads to be pleased about! Lots of reasons to smile, yeah?!* The man laughs. *At least two, yeah?* Which makes Grace laugh. *That's it! Perfect! Hold it! Wonderful!* The camera clicks and whirrs.

Light from the halogen lamp beams through the bedroom window and falls, past the kitchen window behind which Grace's mother sits at the table drinking tea and nervously smoking, and on to the patch of garden nearest the house and next to the crumbling wooden shelves, crumbling further now as spring turns into summer and the green things seethe and detonate. In the wilding grass, and tinily, springtails mate, which is to say that the male darts at and headbutts the female, enticing her to take up the packet of sperm he proffers. Pirouette and spin. Take it up. When she does the ventral tube on his belly fills with fluid in preparation for righting himself after his fabulous leap. The female spins with the packet of sperm shuffling underneath her and the male in a nanosecond is airborne, launched beyond the tallest grass-blades and out of the cast rectangle of light into the unilluminated edge of the garden.

He curls and bounces and comes to rest on a stalk. Ancient insects, these, present in the fossil record of 400 million years ago. They bounced off the claws of giant lizards. The earth bubbled and spat and rent and spewed molten rock and flame and then cooled and around this they bounced, these tiny insects, they bounced and spun in the air around canyons of liquid fire and ricocheted off glaciers and through dust-clouds and under a sky that did not brighten for an aeon they spun and butted and leapt.

A voice from the window above: *Sensational, Gracie! You're gonna be a STAR, girl, yeah?!* The word 'star' raised into an almost-shout loud enough for the mother, downstairs in the kitchen, to hear. Behind the glass, beneath the source of the bright and falling light, she drinks tea and clenches her fist triumphantly and smiles.

The life of the world. As it continues. Some scenes from it, as it turns and spins.

*

The footage shows the girl, naked from the waist up, staring at the camera as she clasps her hands together and raises them slowly above her head on which her hair is tied up in a mess of floppy fair spikes. As she executes this movement, the muscles in her shoulders and neck are seen to work and the abdomen skin pulled taut lifts the belly button on the sheet of muscle beneath it and the pectorals drop a little down from the collar-bones and then shift upwards again to hoist the breasts which, themselves, do not move, balls of a thing other than skin and muscle on her body, stuck there, or sprouted from there in some kind of twin tumorous event. The girl smiles. *Look at my new boobs!* she says. *I'm so happy!* With her arms still held over her head she turns to the right, turns to the left, performs an excited little jiggle and bounce during which the breasts remain unmoving as if on gimbals, as if attuned in some vestibular sense to the movement of the human form and even the turn of the world itself and prepared and equipped to resist such rotation. Another female voice, off-camera, says: *You look amazing,*

Grace. New boobs! Grace giggles and jiggles a second time. Brings her hands slowly down in front of her, still clasped, so that the breasts are squeezed together and for a moment bulge out across the upper arms and reveal the scars, the thin and small pink marks of their burgeoning, like lips compressed with displeasure, on their undersides. Footage ends. The comments come in, from Ireland and America and Australia and Italy, India, the comments come in: *Brilliant! Now show us your ass, bitch. More silly-cone. When will you stupid slappers ever learn? Go for it, Gracie! Looking good!*

The postman delivers a bank statement and three bills, fuel and telephone, nothing else, just those four dull envelopes. He takes them with tea into his living room and puts them on the coffee table and turns the television on. Sleep-crust in his eyes. The face of Willy Roberts, wet-eyed and brow-ploughed. *I'm so scared*, he says, and gulps. *This tour, I'm so [bleep] scared.* Back to the studio. *Apologies for any offence caused by bad language there, but as you can see, despite the reported £82 million four-album deal, Willy's problems have not yet gone away.* Then some bloke talking about depression, all earnest: *I would advise Mr Roberts to seek help, yes, most definitely.* The bank statement is torn open. The roof over his head and the walls around him, they're safe. So is his car. For the time being. Broadband, paid. HP on his laptop and other electrical equipment, paid. Allowance for Ella, paid. Loan payments, other things, all direct debited and paid. He opens the bills, skims them, turns on his laptop. Gas and electricity, he pays them online. Takes down other bills from the wall in the kitchen to the right of the cooker where they've been tacked up and blooming grease lichen for a fort-night or so and pays them via automated phone service. He tries to pay his credit card interest the same way but after five options and the same tinny inhuman voice he gives up and pays them online too. Then he showers and dresses and necks a glass of cold cola for the sugar and emits an explosive burp – 'buh-*RAH*!' – before he turns off the TV and computer and leaves the house.

He's a Walking Man. A Man Who Strolls on this sunny

Saturday, sky just one sheet of light blue above, skimmed across by swallows recently returned which, to him, seem to leave sizzling vapour trails behind them, smokey slashes across the blue sheet, rips to reveal the pure whiteness behind. Tears in a veil. As if a covering has been pulled over the world in shameful concealment and only these comet-birds with their sickle-blade wings know how to lift it. He walks away from the school, parallel to the playing field, the yellow neck of the bulldozer rearing up above the chain-link fence and he thinks of the deepening hole that the machine and the men in it have made and which it now appears to guard. He downhills through the housing estate and on to the promenade, fairly empty at this hour, just a few amblers and a couple of dogs on the beach chasing sticks and swimming. He leans on the railings and watches a black Labrador lollop into the surf. Admires the head homing in on the bobbing stick, just in front of the breakers. The wet fur and the ears flat to the sleek skull. Looks at the expanse of the sea beyond the dog's head, steely-blue water fading into something like green towards the blurred black line of the horizon. If the ice. If it should collapse and fall. How the sea will leap. The dog trots out of the surf with the stick in its mouth and drops it on the shingle and shakes its entire body, blurring itself, the shed swarm of droplets refracting the sunlight and making a brief rainbow before the dog's owner, a fat man with a shaven head and long shorts, picks up the stick and retuns it to the sea. The dog barks and bounds back into the water.

He walks on. A truck is delivering barrels to a seafront pub, outside which a blackboard advertises 'MIDMAD! TWO FOR ONE TUESDAYS'. He passes it. Enters a newsagent's. Buys a packet of tobacco and a newspaper and a magazine with Jessica-Jane Clement on the cover in her undies and then goes to the cafe next door where he buys coffee and a Danish pastry and takes them to a table outside where he skims the paper and makes a cigarette and lights it and unrolls the glossy magazine. Dead pretty, Jessica-Jane. He's seen her many times on *The Real Hustle* and knows how easy it would be to believe, instantly and completely, someone who looks like her. And here she's got her knockers hanging halfway out of her bra. And in the bottom left corner of the cover, black lettering in a small yellow box, he reads: **Gracie Allcock's new boobs inside! It's roasting!!!** He swallows and leaks smoke. Opens the magazine to the contents page. Turns to page twenty-nine. Two pictures of her, both from the waist up. On the left her smile is small and so are her breasts, just bumps, above the little belly button. On the right her skin has turned orangey and her grin is big, the teeth white and the lips red and the breasts like overpumped balls, on the verge of explosion, the erect nipples aubergine-hued like valves withstanding tremendous pressure. How happy she looks. He looks up from the page and across the promenade at the pier reaching out to the horizon and then his eyes drop to the breasts again. That body on the left and the one on the right. It's the same person and the same body but is it? What change has been wrought because some must've been. You cannot warp in this way without it. Once warrior-kings would twist their bodies in battle frenzy and this is what we're seeing here so what is the enemy? Only age and death, nothing more. Anonymity. The oblivion that waits and you transmute that into a noth-ingness here, now, in your flesh. A hysterical denial. The daisy in the hand and the scabbed knee and the tears and she wanted to look good for the photographs. That little girl. This is her now. The children he sees every day at school and how the world waits to make them monstrous. The noise, the noise.

He closes his eyes for nineteen seconds. Finishes his coffee and grinds his cigarette out under his foot. When he opens his eyes again she's still there, Grace, two of her, before and after. Staples the threshold between the two states. He reads the text: how this magazine paid for the tits to grow. **See the sacrifices we make for our readers?** And Jessica-Jane Clement, not Gracie Allcock, made the front cover. Does this matter? What does this mean, before the ocean that will pounce? Anything at all? He notices with some heat that his right index fingertip is touching the page, is circling the 'Before' breasts. He yanks his hand away. The daisy. Think of the daisy. It's her choice.

She's made her choice. Not a child any more but yes she is, she really is, and this is no fucking choice at all. Bury it dead beneath the dirt. My eyes are so sore. He rolls the magazine up inside the newspaper and deposits them both in the nearest bin and walks away and then realises that he hadn't looked at the pictures of Jessica-Jane in her bra and knickers. Shite. He considers for a moment retrieving the magazine from the bin but only for a moment. Buy another, then. Or look online. *Animal* it was called. Before and after. The wilted flower, limp with sweat.

The houses that line the prom. The pictures were taken in her bedroom, sure. The Willy Roberts poster behind, over her shoulder. That one, there, the gable end? Does she even still live in this town? He can't recall seeing her after she left the school but then he wouldn't've recognised her until very recently anyway, re-familiar with her changing features he has latterly become like so many, many others. Millions. Australia and France and Japan. That one, painted a shade of peach, with the spider plant in the window? That one with the wheelie bins outside? That one with the drive and the sign that says NO TURNING? Or that house there, behind the others, the smaller one diagonally behind the Chinese takeaway, with the walled yard? Glass shards spiking the wall that borders the ginnel? He stands still and rasps a hand across his cheek. The beef and green peppers in black bean sauce, that's his favourite. Ella liked the prawn crackers. She once made boats out of them, launched them in the bowl of crab-and-sweetcorn soup, each crewed by a pea picked from his plate of special fried. *My navy* she called it, and the word at her age astonished him. So much we take in. And what the fuck does it matter where she lives or where the pictures were taken? It's not the place that's important. Millions of smirks on millions of walls. And millions of bloated breasts, the skin agleam with sunbed tan and pressure. It doesn't matter. The place doesn't matter. A pride of feral cats live in the alleyway behind the takeaway. He's seen them, many times. Sat on a bench with a tray of onion rings or curry and chips and watched their slim and elegant shapes shadow-slip and slink through puddles of street light. What matters is this. The veldt in miniature in this small seaside town at the western windy edge of Europe.

He's the Walking Man. At the prom's end he turns up into the hinterlands of the town, past the dark stone church on the mound surrounded by the palings of carven gravestones. The enemy, there, in those chiselled dates. What they're fighting against, those dates, if there is nothing else. Just that enrichment of the soil. A rhododendron bush hangs itself over the graveyard walls as if in slow escape. As he passes it he hears the hum of the bees inside its vaulted nave, the bell it makes, and catches the flowers' sweetness in his nostrils. They bloom. An invader-plant, this, strangling the native species and so burnt off and hacked out of the hillsides roundabout. But see how this one blooms, and hear its buzz.

The sea is at his back, now. Uphill he walks, through a housing estate and across a junction where lamp posts and road signs carry CCTV cameras like bolls on trees. Thinks of himself reproduced, time and time over. The day is getting warm and he must pull the hem of his T-shirt away from his belly and up to wipe his face with. He climbs. Pebbledash and lawns small and square on which some people squirt water and stubby gravel drives on which some men rub suds into the bonnets of cars. He hears a radio playing MIA's 'Paper Planes'. A good tune. She takes the Clash and does something new and sometimes that is enough, in these times of ruin, and rubble. Past the town's signpost he walks, the name of it up there. He remembers when, for some weeks a couple of years ago, that sign sported a sprayed-on dick and balls with drips shooting from the end. He laughed when he saw it and it makes him smile now, the memory. The spluttering outrage in the local paper. *What is the world coming to?* The letters page: *In my day. When I was a lad. Clip round the ear.* The harrumphing. Such shock but the things were up there in yellow mid-squirt for several weeks before the council sent a clean-up crew, just before spring took hold and enticed the daytrippers. That's what they'd see, as they entered the town: those giant yellow genitals. If he remembers rightly there were even some painted slashes on the bollocks to represent pubes. He climbs.

He's panting when he tops the hill. Stops to rest on the low wall that borders the car park of the Nag's Head pub, or what was once the Nag's Head pub, sad and flaking shell that it is now. He recalls days spent in there, nights. With Ella's mother. Courting, his grandmother would've called it. And with the friends he once had, the days and nights in the pub with them, drinking, pool, the fruit machine flashing, the disco ball on the nicotined ceiling in the back room. Empty shell now. And only the vertical-drinking places on the promenade with the collars on the pillars to rest your drink on and the jostling groups outside smoking and the 4,000 fag ends stamped into the filth. No one knows anyone any more. I am a lonely atom and so are you.

His breath returns to him. Chest ceases pumping and lungs swell and retract as normal. That's a steep hill. He rolls a cigarette and smokes it then swings his legs over the low wall and ambles across the potholed car park, he doesn't know why, except that he is the Walking Man on this sunny spring Saturday and this was the site of the first kiss with the mother of his daughter. Leaning against his car, or was it hers, here, at the lower end of the car park where the vegetation begins to wrestle statically. The fluttering of his heart. I am a lonely atom. He stands and stares and something wriggles, writhes at his feet. He looks down and sees the tubular and golden glory, the singular and marvellous thew, of a slow-worm. He squats for a closer look. The wondrous s-ing of it and the tiny tongue appearing. Something on its flank, its right-sided flank – a frothing bulge, walnut-sized, protruding guts or something. It's been attacked. Cat, bird, stoat, weasel, whatever. Which predator now no doubt lurks in darkness, its teeth and its hunger waiting for him to leave. He scoops the lizard into his hands and instantly at the touch of him it starts to thrash and twist, knotting itself, rolling and unrolling, turning back on itself, all shapes, the pretzeling geometry of terror. If it could it would shriek. At my touch, just my touch. And the tortured movements of it *are* such a scream and he bends and places it softly beneath a bush and it becomes whole with the shadows under there and he stands and wipes his hands on his jeans. Gulps. That mad thrashing. No pain or manner of death is as horrible to an animal as the tactile attention of a human. The trapped fox, the rabbit bloated and blinded, the gull slimy and black with oil – these will snarl and screech and panic and seek desperately to escape if we approach them. They will do anything to get away from the stink of us. The mist of murder we must emanate. If you are to die now, little legless lizard, oozing your innards as you appeared to be, then do it in private and silent shadows, in hush and acceptance, away, away from these eyes like stagnant pools that reflect no sky.

The world, the world. How his days go. His heart's unpartnered waltz amongst the drifting ash.

Downhill, now, back into the town. Tummy rumbling. He walks into a breeze which cools and then dries the sweat on his face and bare arms. He returns to the caff on the prom where earlier he drank coffee and he eats a bacon and cheese panini and looks at the litter bin where Jessica-Jane Clement and Grace Allcock lie creased and crumpled and made soggy now by the grease from discarded fast-food wrappers and cartons and the lees from cans of drink. Those tits, before and after. Airbrushed smiles and invented eyes crushed and bundled in there to rot in some landfill like the first bodies themselves, the original skin and meat. Harm is done to healthy flesh. Knives slice fine skin. For no known remedial reason this fine skin parts under the blade and is torn and blood puddles and runs. The ocean waits to leap.

He leaves a tip. Crosses the road to lean again on the railings. Some sunbathers on the beach and more dogs. Kites in the sky. To still the twitching in his hands he puts them deep into his pockets but there they still jitter. The thump of his heart becomes noticeable, as does the dryness at the back of his throat. That taste returns, kind of metallic, not so much a taste as a sensation; the synaesthesia of need. He could go home and snooze or watch a DVD or read. Have a long bath. Write up an itinerary for next week, tabulate what needs to be done around the school and thereby take back some notion of control. He takes a hand out of his pocket and touches the railing and feels that it is hot and turns and crosses the road and enters a bar. Telly on in the corner, where the wall meets the ceiling. Still a whiff of new paint and varnish. He orders a pint. Would sit if there was anywhere to sit but there isn't so he leans side-on to the bar, his left elbow on the polished counter, watches the TV. Some women. The volume is low so he cannot hear what they're talking about but he has some idea. Sun comes through the window and rests in a slanted oblong on the wooden floor. Particles shoal through it. Pretty shapes they make, like midges they are or flies, moving as if alive. People pass outside. Dogs leap up at their owners in excitement. There are vests and shaven heads and on all the exposed limbs the same tattoos, the pointed tiger stripes, the designs that want to be Celtic or Maori, that need to suggest such things and no one knows why. The stylised crucifixes on the back because Rooney's got one and Beckham's got one and the people must've seen the same tattoos on someone else and thought that looks original and individual so I'm gonna get it done too. You fucking idiots. Cows you are. Carry your slavishness as a banner and a badge throughout your lives until in fact some time after your death when your pointless ink itself will be fertiliser.

Another pint. Sips it first then starts to gulp. He notices a paper-rack on one of the square columns at the end of the bar so he removes from it a tabloid and reveals, beneath it, the cover of the latest *Animal*. Jessica-Jane Clement and her face and her tummy and the valley between her breasts. He lays it flat on the bar, turns to page twenty-nine. I cannot help myself. Something is steering me. It's like my muscles are not my own and sometimes nor my mind.

—*She's* grown up, hasn't she?

He looks up. The barman is there, smiling beneath his fin haircut with the tips dyed yellow.

—Ey?

—Her, there. Gracie. I went to school with her.

—Did you?

—Yeah. Well she was a couple of years below me but we went to the same school.

—Primary or secondary?

—Both. Small town, yeah?

—Do you remember her?

—Nah. Not really. Just kids, y'know. Wouldn't mind getting to know her *now*, tho. She's . . .

Her swivels the mag on the bartop a few degrees so that he's not looking upside down at Grace but kind of diagonally. His fingertips on the 'After' belly.

—She's really grown up.

The barman studies the page for a few seconds and then a thought seems to strike him and he looks up at his customer and his expression has changed a little. His eyes look at the man's greying temples and the deltas around his eyes and the flecks of white in the stubble and then he looks back down at the magazine again and turns it on the bartop back to face the man.

—Anyway. Get you another?

—No thanks. The man gulps his pint. —Got to go.

He leaves. And why should I remember you or you remember me. Just another adult, just another child. His face hot in the sunshine. Twenty steps away from the pub he realises again that he hasn't seen Jessica-Jane in her frillies. Shite. Go back in? The thought of himself opening the magazine under the eyes of the barman makes sweat crawl down his neck so he goes into the Spar on the road behind the prom, running parallel, and he buys a cold fourpack from the fridge and three bottles of wine, a chilled white and two red, and an oven pizza. With these items in his basket he stops before the magazine rack. Rack? No, Christ, it's a library, a small library. All the faces – Roberts Cole two Beckhams Kelly Brook Moss Brand Clancy faces from *Hollyoaks* and Price Price Price Price Price Price Price. Everything we require that is not food or sex or air. The same faces, always. Jessica-Jane, again, but if he gives in and buys it he will hear in his head a sigh and he does not want to hear that. What does he want more? To avoid that sigh or to see Jessica-Jane Clement in her bra and panties? Not food or sex or air or water, the water that waits to stand upright and hurtle towards the shore.

There's always the website, anyway.

He pays for his stuff and bags it and heads home. Uphill.

Through the housing estate, some dumfa dumfa sounds from the open windows. Net curtains ghosting outwards, away from the red brick walls. Past the playing field and the resting yellow arm of the bulldozer and into his cool house where he fridges the lager and white wine and pizza and picks up the phone and dials the number but there is no answer, only the invitation to leave a message. He does: *Ella, it's your dad. Just wanted to say hello, that's all. Hope you're having a good time and being a good girl and looking after your mum. I'll call again soon as I can. Love you, bye.* He returns the cordless phone to its cradle. Sits in his armchair with his face in his hands for a moment then goes upstairs to shower away the accumulated sweat and muck of the day, Willy Roberts's new song on the radio. He lies on his bed and tries to doze with his front window open and the seabreeze stroking his skin with salty fingers. Closes his eyes. The noise. The stroboscopic faces that flicker and loom. The swollen lips and the unlined shining skin. The skulls visible behind the eyes and in the grins. Temazepam? No, fuck it. He'd wake up feeling like he'd been eaten and shat out and feel like that for the rest of the night or he'd sleep right through to around 3 or 4 a.m. and then have nothing to do but sit there in the ruins and look for a pink light coming into the sky. Booze, then. Booze.

Downstairs. Cold can from the fridge. Laptop on. I am a lonely atom. He is the Watching Man. The roasting video. The choke. Her back ripples when she gags. The muscles in it. Her name is on the screen in blue so he clicks on that and then, again, sees the 'Before' and 'After' videos and too the pictures that he's already seen. It's a 'Before' and 'After' gallery. He is the Scrolling Man. Boobjobs, nosejobs. Now you see the dorsal bump and now you don't. The 'Before' pictures, they strike him as elegiac. That's what they are to do with, that's their din and business. And the 'After' pictures represent what the mind alive in the body was growing towards, so the picture itself becomes more important than the face it captures. And is there loss in those faces? Sadness and mourning for the gone parts, the parts that were on them as babies or waiting in the air and the grasses to *be* on them? Is there one pang in the heart like a plucked string overtuned, on the verge of snapping? You'd imagine there'd be a mourning, of some sort. A

more

Click click click and he's in the porniverse. As he knew he would be. I am such a lonely atom. In this world live young and pretty women who do not seem stupid or drugged, who have two arms two legs two eyes a spine and a brain, two arms two legs two eyes a heart and a brain and a spine and a soul, who do not appear to be drugged or stupid, who are bright and articulate. Like Taylor Rain, who squats in a shower while three men piss in her face. *It's warm*, one of the spurting dicks says. *See how nice I am to you? Look in the camera and say, Mom, I'm your little piss whore.* Like Sasha Grey, who is facefucked until she vomits. The camera does not flinch from this. Like Adriana Sage, who is led crawling and blindfolded to a bed where three men lie on their backs with their legs drawn back, strangers to her, waiting for her to worm her tongue up their arseholes. Which she does. This is the porniverse. In this place live women who take three swollen cocks into their bodies at the same time. Who are slapped, punched, spat and pissed on, who lick semen up off floors, who lick the rims of toilets, who kneel with funnels in their mouths. Men, too, who do not appear drugged or stupid, with arms elbow-deep in their arses. All of this from which the camera does not flinch. And after the spending and with the tacky fingers and the crumpled crusting tissues and the shame he can wonder about what he's just seen, about young and beautiful and not-stupid not-drugged women doing in public what they do. The frenzy of it and the accessibility. One click. Choice, choice. My body. Empowerment. And how did we get here, how did we reach such a notion? Look at you, empowered, all holes gaping wide and oozing slime. Your anus yawning open and releasing custard runnels of sperm which a hairy arm catches in a spoon and feeds to you, how empowered you are as you spray spew around the pistoning prick that continues to pump as your entire body heaves and bucks and strains to reject it. Choice, yes. And empowerment. The marvel of you.

He logs off, takes his can to his armchair. Sits in it. Realises with a lurch that his penis is hanging gunkily out so he tucks it back into his shorts and finishes his can and fetches another from the fridge. There's a song in his head, so he returns to his laptop and logs on again and accesses YouTube and finds it – 'Shame, Shame, Shame' by Shirley & Company. He clicks on Play and turns the volume up as high as it will go and the song starts and he does a little dance, can in hand around his living room, weaving between the furniture, and for a moment he's happy, just for a moment, but what more could he expect? Moments are all we have left. And somewhere in such a moment, somewhere in his moving body and behind his contented face, he is wondering if what he's feeling can really be called happiness anyway. If anyone really knows about that any more. Yet it must, it must be. What else could you call it? As he dances. What else could it be called? As he dances, alone. A moment out of grief begins with a fading, a retreat of the lost object from the stage of the heart and the mind. How you fade, retreat behind the drape. You are the 'Before' pictures. And everything we now have is *after*. The world is *after*. What else could it be called?

The Man Who Drifts and Drinks. Drifts around his living room, between fridge and armchair, through cyberspace, through the channels. At play amongst the ashes. He eats his pizza in front of *Mock the Week*. Beer gone, he takes the bottle of chilled white out into his garden to watch the birds and the bats and the sunset and thinks of taking a walk down to the bottom of the field to peer down into the hole in the earth that the yellow digger and the little man inside it have made and he even stands preparatory to doing just that but then he is as if steered back into his house and armchair and the remote is once again in his hand, his right hand, because the bottle's in his left and is cold against his fingers. He presses Menu and scrolls down through the listings, again he is the Scrolling Man, the Watching Man, and what does he see, what do his eyes lock on to like lasers – lips leaking pus. Swollen and burst. The lips of a fish that rummages through slime on the ocean floor. Granulomas, pustulent grape-clusters on the lips, buccal haemorrhoids. Immune systems attacking the invaders that have been invited to invade. Split figs leaching sap, green pus, burst to show maroon matter, crimson strings gleaming red-black. A hideous chimera. A thing unlike itself. What is this? What is this programme and what are these images? Back to Menu. It is *Pete Burns' Cosmetic Surgery Nightmares* and what is being shown is a human face. What is being heard is a voice talking about dysmorphia, about not recognising his own face as a child. First nosejob reduced his nose to a nut, hence the eye-patch, in Dead or Alive – distraction was the aim. As it always is. Lip augmentation, collagen shots. Such is the man's history. His chemical and surgical history. Talks about stuff squirting out of his face. How his body fought an *extreme battle to try and push out the substance*. Again the leaking lips. Doctors discussed amputating his lips but a Genoese doctor stepped in – eighteen months of operations. And then the lips yet again on the screen, the cloven plums and their rotten gleet. *I'm a victim of it and perpetrator of it.*

The Watching Man raises a bottle to his lips and rolls a cigarette and why does he do this? Why does he sit and why does he stare like this? His spine has fused to the chair-back. A moth pinned to a board. I am transfixed utterly. Dissolution before my wide open eyes.

This is a model talking. A woman who says she is a model, first name Toni. Four kids. Wanted breast augmentation. Went to the Czech Republic to have it done. See her there, on home video, in the Czech Republic. She shows pictures of Jordan/Price to a Czech surgeon and she says: *These are the tits I want. Really round.* The surgeon says: *This is horrible. I refuse to do this.* Toni says: *I don't want them to look natural.* Surgeon recommends *teardrop-shaped breasts* and Toni says: *I don't want poxy teardrop. That's what I've got now.* Surgeon refuses to implant anything over 400 ml so she settles for that and, healed, she reveals them – big and round and unmoving they are, even when she jumps. Then she began to feel ill. An abscess developed. Woke up one morning slicked in blood and pus. Infected implant. The NHS will operate, remedially, if health is at risk but will not correct cosmetic surgery so one implant was removed resulting in lopsided breasts, one big one small. Unbalanced she was and side-heavy. A clinic in India replaced both implants free of charge in exchange for publicity and she went from B-cup to E-cup and now she wants to be a glamour model. What it was all for, to display the basketballs on her chest, the things of her that are not flesh. *I felt a lot of guilt towards my children because I'm in hospital all the time.* She is now due to return to India to have her breasts swollen by a further sixty per cent. To have her nose done too.

Voice of Burns: *Ultimately nature does win and does fight against foreign things in the body.*

Back to Menu. *Pete Burns' Cosmetic Surgery Nightmares*, it says again, ITV1, first shown in 2006. Repeat, then. Repeat repeat. Repeat after me. Click buttons and sip. Scroll. Something about St Kilda. A place he's always wanted to go. The Yearning Man. A giant fin of green rock, fog-topped, surging out of the sea. Some fiddle music. Monochrome photographs of people in shawls and hats and boots. Click.

Katrina Taylor is pretty. Broke her nose at twelve and, at twenty-one, wanted it corrected. Met a surgeon. Ten per cent of nosejobs have complications. Surgeon said her operation went well but her nose had collapsed. Eh? How is that going well? Cartilage was sticking out of her right eye. She saw a third surgeon but couldn't face a third op. NHS helped at her local clinic. Voice of Burns: *I am a nosejob survivor.*

Click. Island abandoned in the 1930s. Stone tools found on the main island of Hirta suggest that Bronze Age travellers from the Western Isles colonised the islands 5,000 years ago. In the 1830s the Revd Mackenzie found burial cists in Village Bay. In 1844 a souterrain, an earth house, possibly a store, roughly 2,000 years old, was discovered. Goblinish hole in the ground between stone lintel and jambs. Records of early chapels. Two incised stone crosses found. Norse occupation confirmed through discoveries of brooches and steatite vessels, and through place names such as Oiseval, east hill, and Ruaival, red hill. What must it have been like. How hard. The scything wind and the waves and the cold stone underfoot.

Click. Clicking through the images at which he stares. Willy Roberts singing his new song. Winking at the camera. Scattered buildings and bloated floating bodies could be New Orleans Haiti or somewhere in Asia. Australia. Angry water. Click. He is stuck to his chair. Only his fingers move and the eyes in his head, they dart and zip and spin in their sockets. Katie Price and that thing she's marrying, married, is divorcing. Reid. Monstrous two-headed hydra they form with their teeth and hunger. Click. Coffins swathed in the Union flag. Football. John Terry looking furtive, Rooney furiously flushed. Earliest dwellings stone-built corbelled structures and black houses and in 1697 someone called Martin Martin wrote that the houses were 'low-built, of stone, and a cement of dry earth; they have couples and ribs of Wood covered with this earthen turf . . . Their beds are commonly made in the Wall of their houses to make room for their cows which they take in during the winter and spring.' Click. Reid is telling Alan Carr that Katie likes to stick needles in his balls. Click. Roberts, sobbing. Has he seen this before? *I'm so fucking scared.* Yes, this morning. In the before-times. In the long long ago. Was it £82 million? Thereabouts. And here he is talking of how hateful his life is. The press, the commitments, the pressure. St Kilda would be the place. Nothing but your own heart and the wind in your lungs and whatever the world wants to give you of itself. Stay over the waves. Get away from me, miles and miles away from me. If I had that money then that is what I'd sing. Do. Escape the angry water.

Linda Allison had implants and Botox and *treated* herself to a tummy tuck on her fortieth. Private clinic. After surgery, a nurse dressed the wound three times and six weeks later she saw another surgeon who shoved a huge syringe repeatedly in her open and rancid wound to suck out the pus. Her husband: *Linda hit the roof.* She was given antibiotics and sent home. Her hubby Jack took her dressing off and said he could see into her stomach. The organ itself. A hole went straight in. *All this green and yellow and red stuff was pouring out.* Linda went to see a consultant and one night felt a sudden agony so she dialled 999. Ambulance came and took her into hospital. *I was screaming.* She'd developed an abscess and was rushed into theatre and six months on from the emergency operation has needed daily care. She lies back, a middle-aged woman. Breasts in perfect semi-spherical shapes above the scab-ridged and weeping hole in her belly. The goo visible beneath the cracked black crust.

Burns talks with a 'celebrity consultant' named Alex some-thing. Toni says she's never felt such pain, such horrible pain, and *I've had four kids*. Alex talks about people who take extreme-makeover programmes seriously and think they can be changed and improved in half an hour. *People will go for surgery to countries where they wouldn't take a holiday.* But if the improvement is small then the operation isn't worth it and he couldn't do it, says Alex. What? What? What did you just say?

Click. Away from everything I would be there. At the foot of that steep green hill. Untouched I would be. This fucking noise. A school on the islands from 1884. Gaelic-speaking St Kildans. Martin Martin, Martin Twice, said that they loved music and games but the narrator states that by the late nineteenth century their adherence to the Free Church of Scotland led to a less joyful life. As it would: the promise of eternal scorch. Being born itself a sin. Born into this, born into this. This stink. Image of women against a stone wall, their scarves and shawls all black, as are the bare soles of their feet. Their faces in shapes made by the pounding of brine and the chiselling wind. Contact with the 'outside world' increased and the SS *Dunara Castle* in 1877 began regular summer cruises to the islands. SS *Hebrides* followed. Gawping from the gangways. Whalers and fishing fleets brought supplies. John Ross, schoolmaster, noted in 1889 that islanders now spent much of their time producing goods to sell to tourists – sheepskins and tweeds and knitted gloves and scarves and eggs and other bird-begat items. Feathery frip-peries, the like. Did the waves then start to look alluring? Did the thought of land masses over them now steal their sleep and discover their dreams? Goodbye dearest Annie for I am called and cannot resist.

The Clicking Man. He rises and goes to the kitchen and returns with a bottle of red wine and retakes his armchair, contoured to his body, its curves and points. Rolls a cigarette, pours a glass of wine, clicks. The world at his fingertips or what of it the skin he knows allows to be seen. Mites in the carpet and motes in the air but what he can see is what's on the screen. There it is, there, easy and accessible. God I am a lonely atom.

Discolouration and slime. The facelift was too tight and a nerve was severed which has left one side of her face partially paralysed. It droops a bit. Other parts of it as still as stone, even in laughter, even in pain. Looks better now she says that there is a strange stiffness to her features. Burns talks about the 'serves you right' attitude that prevails in Britain. Cites Leslie Ash receiving death threats when her lip operation left her looking like a what? A parrot fish upright. How we revert. To some, what, thing. Not itself. A thing projecting its own nightmare. And oh the gleeful vengeance, a vengeance without initial insult. How it surrounds us and waits, lurks in the outer dark. Home movie of Sue with a normal face. *This is why I want a facelift. If you want to grow old gracefully − why?* This is a question that she asks. With half her face as if made out of concrete this is a question that she asks. Grace! She talks about the media. *We're not allowed to grow old or have wrinkles.* Burns: *the images we see aren't real. This is a digitally altered age.* Might as well tell me I have knees and elbows and that one day I will die. Fuck you. No one to blame but you. A hairshirt labelled 'victim'. Well, fuck you. It's coming. Burns tells Sue that many celebrities need make-up to cover their surgery scars and Sue is shocked. *But I see it working for all of them and I want a piece of that.* Open your eyes.

The daisy clutched in the hand and the smart, pretty dress. Here is a world that the little girl will soon be a part of. Of hidden scars and fine skin sliced. Where does the human end and the machine begin? Tell me I'm immortal. Tell me I'm star-born. And more little girls following her and wanting not to be *like* her but actually *be* her and now she's, she's, what did he say? That barman. *All grown up.* Barely alive in the 'After' world. To the right of the crease and the staples is where you barely exist and to where you are dragging the unmarked and pristine pages and skins of the billion stories. Australia and France and Japan. Sewage.

The knife works better than anything. If it's sagging, bagging or wagging − cut the thing off.

Sue nods at Burns and part of her face is immovable. *I agree. Yeah. If I won the lottery I think I'd spend the first three years in hospital.*

Oh Christ. Gravity, my enemy. Age and death. More images of Sue's face, in mid-mutilation. If I won the lottery. If I had all that money and all that freedom that goes with it. Why are you so afraid. Why are you not permanently vomiting up whatever it is that has latched on to your soul. Hookworm, parasite. Stuff my eyes with the waiting clay.

Cosmetic surgery can change your life but it can be really hard to change it back again.

One solution, then. There can be only one solution because this is a problem and this is a question and this is a clue. Wash us in blood.

Gradually they lost their self-sufficiency and came to rely on imports of food, fuel, and building materials. Some left for Australia in 1852, most dying on the way but some settling in what is now the St Kilda area of Melbourne. Despite the contact, the islanders grew to feel increasingly isolated from the wider world and disliked especially the lack of regular communication. Snared in the paradox of dependence. A food shortage in 1876 saw the first St Kildan mailboat sent out as a distress signal with a letter sealed in a wooden container and with an inflated sheep's bladder acting as a float. Little boats, shoebox-sized, making landfall in mainland Scotland or Scandinavia. Famine, then, in 1912. 1913, influenza. War in 1914 brought gunships to Hirta and hence regular deliveries of mail and food but with the armistice in 1918 the isolation intensified. We are all lonely atoms. Adrift on a sharp rock. More emigration. Complete breakdown of island society and economy. In 1930 the remaining thirty-six islanders requested evacuation. St Kilda itself sold to the Marquess of Bute in 1931. Keen ornithologist. Bequeathed the islands to the National Trust for Scotland in 1957. Back a bit, though, back a bit. Always a seabird breeding ground. Still are, the islands. The islanders took gannets and fulmars and puffins for food and feathers and oil, some of which they used themselves, the rest going to pay the rent. The birds were caught by hand or with a fowling rod and a snare, long nets to scoop and snatch the birds out of the sky. And on the islands died the last great auk. About two centuries ago. The islanders apparently thought that it was a witch and so they killed it. A white stag will command a high price for the right to kill it. No; the owner of the land on which the white stag lives will. Unlucky the unique thing. The rarer the animal the more we will want it. The blade through the fine skin. The damage done to healthy flesh. The need and the hunger. Look at me. Look at *me*. And I wonder, what did they use to kill that final bird? A spear? Stones? Did they kick it to death? By what method did they draw the life of it out, and was it harder than usual to extract that last speck of life from an entire species, so to usher in an eternity of static? And did the bird fight with unprecedented strength and were its wails all the louder and more desperate, being the very last of its kind? Or was your determination all the greater, the stink off you all the stronger during this act of extinction? This ultimate event?

An extinction event is coming. There have been many such before. The sea will leap up and hurtle towards you and if you see it coming it will be only in the mirror and over your shoulder and fuck you forever, can you not see? The world you want and have made is never-ending white noise. Can you not see? See the lad pissing on the woman who he thought was drunk but was in fact dying and as he shakes the drips off his dick he shouts *This is YouTube material!* This is the world of 'After'. The children at the school. Their faces with the frog-hopper. Your world awaits them. Fuck you forever you will not see. Your field of vision is full of reflections of yourself. Always I will wish that I could simply turn my back.

Click the TV off. Click click click like a fucking deathwatch beetle. So long since the postman came. Let us be the Sleeping Man. Always be the Sleeping Man. I am drunk and I am tired and I am ever exhausted by your emptiness.

★

A sea fog has crept greasily inland overnight and dragged itself up the low hills that back-border the town and it now rests in rolls on the hills' ridges like a massive muffler or as if the sky itself has folded its forearms and is resting on them to peer down at the tiny human traffic of the small town by the sea. The sky, or a titanic being of foam that dwells within it and which has caught an intrigue for the scurryings that occur and never cease below.

Grace's mum brings into the kitchen a folded tabloid and a worried frown. Grace is in her PJs at the table eating Marmite on toast with her top buttons undone to show the new depth of her cleavage, even here, in the house, the only audience her mother and her own lowering eyes in the mirror which if a gaze could wear it out would have been scoured to the mercury backing long since.

—Have you seen this, love?

—Hundreds of times, Mum. You have too, yeah?

—Eh? She looks at her daughter. Smear of black goo at the corner of her mouth. —No, it's not the one with you in it. This is today's. It's. You'd better take a look.

She drops the tabloid on to the table, beneath her daughter's newish face. Grace pushes her plate of nibbled crusts aside and looks. Gasps; actually gasps.

—That fucking little shit.

—Oi! Language!

—But he *is*, tho, yeah? I mean he *must* be.

—I know what he is love but don't swear like that. Got responsibilities now yeah? Role model, yeah?

—There's only you here.

—Yeah but it's like anything – you've got to practise. Got to work at it. Anyway shut up and just read the fucking thing.

It's Damien. Damien's in the paper. He's sitting on a bench on the promenade and looking all serious and showing off the tiger-stripe tattoo on his upper arm and he's had some shapes slashed into his hair, some swirls, and a nick put in his eyebrow. **GRACELESS**, the strapline reads, and beneath: **ex tells truth about roasted girl**. *She dumped me by text. All she wants is fame.* Grace's eyes dart and jitter and a hotness comes into the skin of her face and her nearly new nose starts to throb. Her mouth is dry.

—What. *What.*

—He's just jealous, love. Just cashing in, end of the day. He's the shameless one, not you, yeah?

She makes out that she's the victim but she's the one went looking for footballers that night. They're just young healthy lads, what does anyone expect them to do? She's a sexy young woman. She knew what she was doing, alright.

Grace tries to read on but the words have become blurred and swirling and there is a pounding in her chest and what is this it is like panic. She shouts a nonsense word and runs upstairs to the sound of her name being called and locks herself in the bathroom and sits on the toilet seat with her arms folded and resting on her thighs and leaning like that she releases sounds, hisses and growls, a kind of restrained scream. Puts her face in her hands. Waits for the outrage to become a simple sadness and prompt tears but it doesn't and when it has reduced itself to a manageable simmer she stands and looks at herself in the mirror, her profile, twists her head to the left and the right, hoists her new breasts in both hands and then goes back downstairs. Her mother is at the table, smoking. The paper folded in front of her, an ashtray on it, as if to weigh it down.

—You okay, love?

Grace says nothing.

—Want me to throw it away? I'll burn it if you like, out in the garden.

—No.

—Let's burn it.

—No. Wanna read it, yeah? Properly like.

She sits. Lifts up the ashtray, takes the paper, unfolds it. Anger is at her teeth, in her jawbone, but now it is an anger that does not beg and which has a strength that propels her blood and sets a tingle in each knuckle. She reads. Looks at the picture. Remembers warm come spattering on her face like oily rain. The grunts of Damien somewhere beyond her eyelids. That dirty bastard. Him and his bukkake sites. Only thing he ever liked to do. Got his kicks that way. And look at him with that stupid 'do, what *does* he think he looks like. *Broken-hearted* says

166

the paper. That's what it says he is, *broken-hearted*. Grace's eyes dart across the text, and lock on to words like *lonely* and *sad* and, again, *broken-hearted*. The article ends with the words *see Comment, page 33*. Fingertips flick the pages. Eyes read words about *girls, hungry for fame and money* and *WAG wannabes* and *exploitation* and how, with the World Cup coming up, *our lads need no distractions of this kind* and how *we've seen it all before. At the end of the day these boys are young and virile and who can blame them for accepting what is offered to them on a plate?* Grace gulps, and remembers gulping. And gagging, too, she remembers that, and also the feeling of being filled, stuffed, crammed, the sensation of being stretched, close to splitting. *They have nothing to be ashamed of and nor, readers, do you. Let them know we're behind them all the way, and that what they do in their private lives is THEIR business. Come on, lads. You'll do us all proud.*

Grace looks up at her mother.

—You okay, love?

Grace says nothing.

—It's nothing to worry about, love, honest. Just a bit of a backlash, that's all. End of the day all he's doing is cashing in and *that*. She flicks a cigaretted hand at the editorial page and ash flakes across it. —Tomorrow's fish and chip paper. Don't worry.

—Fish and chip paper?

Grace's mum leaks smoke through a smile. —Figure of speech. They used to wrap fish and chips in newspaper. Just means that people will have forgotten it by tomorrow, that's all.

She sees her daughter's eyes widen and her lower lip wobble. A rising horror in the dark irises. That word 'forgotten'; wrong one to use.

—I mean they'll just forget that, that, article. They won't be forgetting *you*, tho. No way. You'll see.

No good. Grace's eyes have fallen again, to the newspaper. Top of her head, her hair hanging and in need of a shampoo, fallen into a centre parting that reveals a thin line of bare blue-white scalp. Oh God. Think before you speak.

—I mean—

Grace's mobile trills on the windowsill. Grace puts it to her ear and her mother whispers 'Loudspeaker, love' and Grace presses a button and puts the phone on the open tabloid and Jerry Wellin's voice comes out of it.

—I'm assuming you've seen the paper.

Grace nods.

—Gracie? You there, kid? I'm assuming you've seen the paper.

—Yes.

—First thing to know is this: It. Does. Not. Matter. That's of paramount importance, okay? Gracie?

—Yes.

—You don't sound convinced. I was waiting for this to happen, for the worms to crawl out from under their stones. He's cashing in, Gracie, pure and simple. Nothing more, nothing less. Making a fast one.

—Told you!

—That you, Mrs Allcock?

—Sorry.

—No need. Absolutely no need. And I'm glad you're there because you need to hear this too. The fact that the inevitable backlash has come early can be turned to our advantage. Know how? Well, the public are just getting to know you, Gracie, and they're still intrigued. The honeymoon period is still here. Had you been in the public eye for a few years or so then yes they'd be getting a mite tired maybe but this, at this time . . . All it does is enhance the mystique. Makes you more interesting, in their eyes. And I can't find anything to be upset about in that. Yuh *get* me, yeah?

The last four words delivered in a rude-bwoy voice which makes Grace smile.

—Yes.

—Sure? Positive?

—Yes.

—Okay, then. Repeat these words: It. Does. Not. Matter.

—It does not matter.

—Once more with feeling.

—It does not matter!

—Now you, Mrs Allcock.

—It does not matter!

—And now both together.

—IT DOES NOT MATTER!

—Lovely. We're all in this together. All you have to do is trust me. Understand?

—Yes.

—You *do*, don't you? Both of you?

—Yes.

—We can benefit from this. They're hungry for you, Gracie. For *you*, I mean, you yourself, not some opportunistic little turd's opinion of you. So we'll give them what they want, right? To which end, kid, I'm taking you, this coming Saturday night, to the pre-tour launch party of a certain Mr William Roberts.

Gasp. Two gasps.

—We spoke about this, remember? Or I mentioned it at least. Two tickets, me and thee just, which means you can't bring any friends. I'll be your chaperone, okay? Just old me. Old Jerry.

Nod.

—If you're nodding, Gracie, then I can't see you. You need to speak.

—Yes.

—Good. Thought it would be. I'll clarify the details in an email but all you need to do is be in the hotel lobby at 7 p.m. this coming Saturday evening.

—Hotel?

—Same one as last time. You remember? And don't nod, speak.

—I remember.

—Good. Great. The staff will be expecting you. Don't worry about a thing. Just be in the lobby at seven this Saturday night looking as beautiful as you always do and I'll come and whisk you away into the night. Next week the papers will be begging you to be in them. Believe me. Have I ever let you down?

—No, never.

But I know that your spunk tastes a bit like cigars.

—Well, then. Till Saturday.

The phone goes silent. Grace clicks it off loudspeaker and replaces it on the windowsill, next to the spider plant and between two dead flies, on their backs, their legs stiffly in the air like bristles. She shakes her head as if to rid it of a voice. Looks up to give her mother a big, big smile and accept another one straight back.

Big girl, woman, grown-up woman, grown-up Grace on her own in the hotel lobby all tasteful lighting and marble surfaces and gleaming wood and big green ferns. Pink Star Gazer glitter on her eyes although they're hidden behind Giant Vintage sunnies. A bustier kind of top thing, white to show off her spray-tan and undone at the top to show off her new cleavage. Denim shorts and gladiator sandals, outfit suggested by Louise Redknapp's holiday wardrobe. Plum lipstick. Hair Alice-banded back into a styled blonde wave that laps below her clavicles. She's getting looks. She sits in a large armchair and crosses one leg over the other and studies her feet, the white pedicured nails and the toe-ring. Glad of the 2 mg of diazepam she swallowed earlier and the two vodkas she took in her room as she was getting ready. Glad of the tan and the tits and the knobble-free nose and glad, just, to be Grace. Should see the looks she's getting.

—Can I get you anything? A drink while you wait?

A choice-bald black guy in a black jacket and white shirt and black dickie bow. Carrying a tray he is. Grace orders a vodka and Coke with loads of ice and he comes back with it just seconds later, it seems, places it with a big grin on the small circular metal table at her side.

—On Mr Wellin's bill.

Grace nods. —Thank you.

—You're very welcome.

She sips the drink. It is cold and there is fruit in it, a half-moon of lime and a wedge of lemon that has been jammed on to the rim of the glass. Stuffed with crushed ice, the drink, so that she must sort of slurp it through the mini Arctic. The iciness of it hurts her teeth. Sets up a small and even throb in the bridge of her nose, the place they smashed with a chisel. And God wasn't it worth it. Hasn't it been worth every pain and penny. Look where she is and what she's about to do.

—Miss Allcock? Your car is here.

The same black guy. She puts her drink on the side table and follows him across the lobby and through the door he holds open for her and she allows him to usher her into the back of the limo that waits pulsing at the kerb. The door shuts behind her. She's sitting opposite Jerry Wellin and God how he grins at her, all teeth and wrinkled eyes, pink scalp showing through the bristles of the grey crew cut, spotlit by the car's overhead illumination, close as it is to his cranium. The car makes no noise as it pulls away from the hotel and starts to move, ghost, through the city.

—My God Gracie but you look stunning. May I? He leans forwards in his seat and hoists, one in each hand, Grace's new breasts. She feels muscle tug at her ribs. This is uninvasive. No violation here. Partly belonging to Jerry and she's just carrying them for him. —A fine, fine job. Tremendous skill. Your surgeon, he's a sculptor. I know his work. A Michelangelo whose medium is flesh and bone, believe me.

He gives each breast a little jiggle then releases them and sits back. —You're happy with them, yes?

Grace nods.

—As you should be. Superb work. Drink?

He extends a miniature bar from the middle of the bench seat he's on. Glasses, bottles, a small and sweating silver bucket of ice. He shoots his cuffs before he delves into the bucket so as to keep dry the sleeves of his brown leather jacket.

—Vodka and Coke, right?

Grace nods.

—Ah, I know you too well, Gracie Allcock. I'll have the same I think.

He pours Finlandia over ice into two glasses. Shares between them a tiny bottle of cola. Grace has never seen cola in glass bottles before. Plastic bottles, maybe cans, but glass? Yet another thing that only the initiated are privy to. There are so many.

Jerry adds lemon slices. Hands her a fizzing glass whose sound makes her think of frying rice.

—Cheers. Here's to new, and magnificent, boobage. And to what I trust will be a very enjoyable and profitable night.

They clink glasses and drink. Jerry sits back in his seat, the glass leaving a ring of moisture on the thigh of the stretched-tight material of his trousers and held in a fist chunky and agleam with rings.

—Speak to me, kid. Tell me how you've been.

I've sucked your cock are the words that spring to Grace's tongue but the ones that actually do exit her mouth are different. The vodka helps her form the words and she talks about operations and friends and a sister and a mother and they discuss a certain ex-boyfriend and internet footage and 'Before' and 'After' photographs and lots of other things. Stuck in traffic in the centre of the city they drink more vodka and talk and at one point Grace is made, by Jerry, to laugh, happily and long. Jerry cracks the smoked-glass window a little then lights a cigar and some of the city's sounds come in, music and shouting, singing, screaming, abandon. Car horns. A siren. *It tasted of cigar smoke.* Slap slap. Each slap pushing shards through her healing nose.

—And so now I'm going to meet Willy Roberts. Am I?

—Assuredly. Not even a man as unpredictable as Mr Roberts will miss his own pre-tour launch party. I'll introduce you, of course.

—Will you?

—Of course. I've never let you down yet, Gracie. I'm hoping he'll already be there. He's about to be swept off his feet when he meets you, Gracie. He won't know what's hit him. Trust me.

Grace smiles behind her raised glass and sunglasses. Shades she's glad of when she steps out of the car into a blizzard of flashes and hot gazes, cameras popping up into her face, a queue of people shouting and seeming to wrestle with each other that she's peripherally aware of and Jerry has taken her elbow in his hand to steer her and a big man in black with a clipboard beneath a moth-bothered white neon sign above the club's doorway. Big moths and little moths wrenching themselves from the outer night to flit frantic and velvety and bump and spin against and around the white and humming light.

—Mr Wellin, the big man says. —And plus one. Welcome, sir. He scans the clipboarded list. Smiles and nods his head backwards. —In you go. Enjoy.

Into music Grace is led. 'I Kissed a Girl'. Plus one, he said. She's only a plus one. He didn't know who she is. Yet her nerves are filamenting out of her skin, one to each pore, extruding, waving like the tentacles of an anemone, reaching into the surrounding air to snatch colour and sound. She sees darkened eyes looking at her, made-up eyes, long lashes and orange skin and thick lipstick and too the eyes of men gone big like hungry mouths for she and those like her are here the pabulum. The music is very loud. She sees faces that she recognises, from page and screen, now made real as soft dolls here in this club and of whom she also is one. She feels her legs move. Is led by the figureheads of her new breasts and Jerry's guiding hand on her bare shoulder. A heated whisper in her ear:

—Turn right, Gracie. That stairway? See it? We need to go up there.

Up, up. Aware of her arse and hips swaying in Jerry's vision. Up out of the immediate volume of the music and past another big man who lifts a red rope to admit her entrance. Softer, the music, up here. A lit bar at the far end of the room. A balcony. Tables. Eyes looking at her. And then a person no longer a shadow she has seen on film or leaning out from her bedroom wall or on a glossy page with a staple in his face, no longer that, no longer a phantom she has theorised and supposed and fantasised about. A thing now with skin and hair and teeth and eyes and a voice.

—Jerry! You terrible cunt!

—My boy, my boy.

Seated eyes look up, standing heads swivel.

—More like Uncle Monty every time I see you. Getting the same size as well.

The man pokes a finger into Jerry's belly. Looks at Grace. Her feet, her legs, her tummy, her chest, her face.

—And this must be the Sunday roast, right? The great British Sunday roast.

The people seated close by laugh, too loud.

—I recognise you. His gaze drops for an instant. —Recognise *both* of you.

Again the laughter, too loud, too long. Louder this time as Grace is laughing too. So's Jerry.

—I'm Willy.

—I know who you are.

—Course. The man grins. —Join us. Fetch a chair up, Jerry.

Grace takes the only free chair at the table and takes her company amongst the beanie hats and checked shirts and fin haircuts and tattoos and bared thighs and belly buttons and teeth and cosmetics. Jerry pulls a chair up next to her. Grace feels a trembling, in her extremities, set in. Willy Roberts to her right like a cartoon he is, unreal, too much colour in him, the ankle of one leg resting on the knee of the other, pouring himself a drink from a bottle of champagne.

—More Cristal. More Stolly, he says in a cartoon voice, unreal, and holds the bottle he's just emptied aloft. Within seconds that bottle has been replaced with a full one which a waitress takes up and uses to fill proffered glasses. She has straight black hair tied back in a ponytail which points to the top of her arsecrack almost bared by the halter top. The antler design drilled in. Black trousers. Very, very brown skin.

—Gracie? Bolly or Stolly?

—Erm. Champagne.

Roberts clicks his fingers in the air then points sideways, across his own chest, at Grace. Peculiar animation to his movements. He ruffles his own hair. —What the fuck was I talking about?

—Waves, Will, a young woman in white says.

—Yeah! yells a man in a baseball cap. —Waves of *destruction* . . . This last word said in a voice deep and made doomy.

—Ey, don't joke. Nothing to laugh about.

—Waves?

—What?

—You mean like that one gonna come out of Greenland? Grace realises she is talking so she shuts herself up with a swig of her drink. Bubbles tingle her nose but she manages to keep

174

captured the cough or the sneeze or whatever it was that wanted to burst out of her face.

Willy's looking at her. Eyes both real and unreal. His face and his features bigger in her vision, bigger, and moving as if assembling themselves. She sees a tiny yellowhead zit in the hair at his temple, a child's ball caught in bracken. —Greenland? What?

Jerry's knee nudges Grace's beneath the table in warning or encouragement she's not sure. She doesn't know. Sorry she spoke. Swallowing swelling regret with each fizzy swig.

—Don't know anything about Greenland. Don't know for *shit* about Greenland. Haven't the first clue what you're talking about, sweetheart.

—Mindwaves, a man on Grace's left says. —Like radio waves, yeah? But for the mind. From alien intelligences.

Willy nods. —*Hostile* intelligences. He pronounces the word in the American way, like 'hostel'. —Bigger than we could ever imagine, just waiting for their moment. Know where I've been for the last six months? He turns to face Grace. —The Nevada fuckin desert, yeah? Binoculars stuck to my face. Watching the skies man. And I've seen things you people wouldn't believe.

Jerry groans. —And all these memories will be lost in time . . .

—Like tears in rain, Jez, yeah?

Willy laughs. Others follow him. Why is he looking at Grace? He's talking at the table in general but largely he's looking at Grace. Why?

—And we're *all* gonna be crying, Jerry son. They're already here. They walk among us, man, yeah?

More laughter. Grace looks into her glass and sees that it is empty.

★

She shits and pisses and sneezes and breathes and does things like menstruate and eat and digest food and sleep and dream yet the world is watching her becoming less and less. Reduced to a blurred outline with tits on the web or down into two dimensions on a glossy page. I know she's real, I know she's a person, a living thing, yet before my eyes and the eyes of the other millions she's being reduced to a shadow. What she was with the flower and the dress and the scabbed knee is more real to me than what she is now. See her fade. I see a world in which people do not want to be themselves. White kids talk in patois. Middle-class people believe that they are poor, that they possess a kind of raw emotional authenticity when they were brought up in some semi-detached in some lawned and pebbledashed suburb. You can become Other. Pete Burns. Michael Jackson. What's her name, that gargoyle who fucks footballers . . . Could be one of millions.

He clicks a few links on his laptop, finds a name, returns to his armchair in front of the TV.

Alicia Douvall. Do not accept what you were born with. You have vitiligo. You need remedial surgery and it went wrong. Rip away the features with which you were born, shed your skin like a snake you snakes.

He drops his cigarette butt into his empty can, hears a hiss from within the tin. What's she doing now. Where is she. In an operating theatre, in a club, what, in bed dreaming. Dreaming of a dead little girl who cried because she wanted to look pretty for a photograph and a bump of the earth took her footing and bloodied and bruised her knee.

He opens another can. Loss has a mass, a volume and a mass and I feel it on me like a terrible weight. The yoke you hang around my neck and every day you add to the void. The awful burden of that void.

Light from the television greying his hands and face.

*

It's when she's in the toilets that the enormity of what she's doing and who she's doing it with hits Grace in the belly. In the gleaming toilets, all marble and mirrors with a vase of real red roses next to the sinks and an African-looking lady standing by a tray of sprays, a full appreciation punches Grace in the taut tanned tummy and she ducks into a cubicle and sits on the toilet saying to herself *ohmygod ohmygod*. She takes her mobile out of her handbag but the emotions are too big to text so she replaces it, whiffles air out through her lips and fans her face with her fingers. Thinks she might cry. Or scream with laughter. She doesn't know. She fishes a blister pack out of her bag, pops a pill, snaps it in two and dry-swallows one half. Low dose. Shouldn't drink with diazepam but the bit she swallowed earlier has long left her system and with such a low dose she'll be okay. Can continue on the champagne. The Bolly. *Ohmygod* she says to herself in this place of running water. *Ohmygod ohmygod*. If they could see her. Everybody. Well, see her they will, next week, in the papers and magazines. They see her all the time.

She leaves the cubicle and moves over to the mirrors. The African lady approaches her with an atomiser in her hand as if she's about to Mace her. Grace waves her away. Didn't Cheryl Cole when she was Tweedy which she might yet be again punch someone like her? In this very club? No, that was in London. Maybe. But similar nuisance. Grace takes a lipstick from her bag and leans in towards her reflection to touch up her lips. Unflattering in here the light but she reckons that she looks okay. The nose is perfect, the make-up's good. Tops of her boobs bulge umberly out of her chest, slight sheen of sweat on them. Deep cleavage, now. She touches the corners of her lips with the tip of her little finger, right then the left. Does the same to the eyelashes of her right eye. Puckers her plum lips towards her reflection which does exactly the same towards her.

There's a face at her shoulder, her right shoulder, a face Grace recognises from the table. Overstated make-up and too much, too high black hair and centipede eyelashes and lips that yell Botox. This face has been sitting all night diagonally behind the shoulder – from Grace's viewpoint at the head of the table – of the flamboyantly gay lad with the fringe and the cold sores and the blusher. It glowers, this face, at Grace's face in the mirror. Grace smiles at it. —Hello.

—Who are you? The face sneers. —Who the fuck *are* you?
—What?

—With your stupid tits like balloons. Who the fuck *are* you and what are you doing here?

The African-looking lady swoops in with the atomiser. The snarl is turned briefly on her, one dark flash of quick teeth, then back to Grace again.

—And who the fuck do you *think* you are swanning in here like you own the fucking place? Jog on, bitch. Get back to your fucking footballers, yeah? Slapper. He's mine.

Grace gets it, then, instantly and in full – jealousy. The green eyes, again. This is how ugly it is. It comes from many quarters like she'd been told it would and she finds herself half-barking, half-yelling a laugh. A kind of sudden and growling laugh that leaps out of her. It is a brilliant noise and it comes from a chamber inside Grace that she didn't know existed and which could perhaps be called A Future, days ahead waiting inside her, days of doing and of never-lonely nights and of no more empty dawns witnessed alone. Of days and nights without end. It is a brilliant sound. Grace does it again.

—Laughing at me, bitch? Fucking laughing at me?

Grace shakes her head and delicately touches her lips again, the corner of her plum-coloured lips. Leaning in towards herself with her eyelids lowered and her cleavage deepening and her top riding up a little at the back to show her tattoo.

—Fuck's sake, the other face says after a swift downward glance. —Slag antlers n all. Class act, you, girl, yeah? Fucking tramp-stamps.

Grace blows a purple kiss at herself in the mirror. Knows that she doesn't need to say anything and that in fact everything would be best if she didn't but knows, too, that if she does say something, if she does open her mouth and emit sounds, then those that will escape will be perfect and true and born in the same laboratory as the excellent, spotless laugh. All of this she knows, Grace does. With absolute certainty.

—Just fuck off, yeah? The snarling face goes on. —Nobody wants you here. *He* doesn't. He's told me. Just do one and take that fat cunt Jerry with you as well. Just fuck off, the pair of yeh.

Grace turns away from the glass to face the flesh. Smiling

as she unclasps her bag and drops the lipstick tube inside and snaps it shut again. Somewhere in this place she's in there is the sound of running water and indeed the air itself is slightly moist as if in the process of being cleansed. The woman opposite Grace has fists and sharply pointed boots and white teeth in her snarl, her sneer, which has pulled her top lip up and out to reveal the naked pink skin beneath the cosmetic. Eyelashes clogged with mascara. A scabby red rim to one of her nostrils which flares with its twin with each heavy exertion. This is how ugly jealousy is. Grace looks at this face. *At* it.

—You smell nice, she says.

—What?

—Didn't you hear me? I said you *smell* nice.

Why these particular words, Grace doesn't know. They've just silvered out of her chest and up her gullet and out of her mouth and she feels that no others could've been better. The snarl vanishes and the eyes lose their light and then the African lady swoops in again with her spray.

—You again! Fuck off out of my face! I've *told* yeh!

The woman swings a fist. It hits the African lady's face with a meaty dullness and she goes sprawling in her colourful muumuu over her tray of sprays and lotions and potions and Grace flees giggling from the toilets and runs into a lady bouncer with a sharp face and a severe ponytail and a black padded jacket.

—It's kicking off in there, she says. —Some nutter's attacking the attendant, yeah?

The bouncer thunders into the toilet. Grace swallows giggles and returns to the table where she retakes her seat between Willy Roberts and Jerry Wellin and sucks at her drink through a straw. See that? He saved her seat. He saved her seat for her while she was gone. How mad is this?

★

I'm not even entertained. None of this even entertains me. All I am is distracted like a dog at a window watching passing traffic or gazing at the porthole of a working washing machine. Is this all your lives are? Is this all you do with the miracle of your eyes? Someone's sleeping on the TV screen. He presses buttons on the remote control. Where's St Kilda? There's Jeremy Clarkson in a car. Fucking Jeremy Clarkson in a fucking car. There's footage of Willy Roberts on stage. There's a chef doing something to a melon and there's a surgeon cutting into lopsided and gozzy tits. None of this entertains. I do not ask for constant education but for Christ's sakes you must feel the pull of something else at your skin and at your hair.

He sighs out smoke. Blue light flickers on his face and he drops the butt of his cigarette into the empty lager can he's been using for an ashtray. Drinks from another can. Nearly empty bag of Doritos on his lap crumpled like shed skin. This is what Ella is growing into, this is the world that waits for her. As we wait in rain for the thunderbolt. Fall, flame. Let it be utter and let's start again. Burn everything away. Burn it off as farmers scorch crop stubble from their fields and plough it under for fertiliser or come flood and rinse it clean. I wait for the wave but I cannot wait for the wave. So I will light the fire.

Something about the Clifton suspension bridge. About Brunel. Yet his eyes are slowly closing or if not that then taking on that granular feeling that tells him he's succeeded, or will have very soon, in drinking himself to sleep again. Almost. Do you really enjoy watching a stranger sleep? For hours? There he is, look. In night-vision so that he is a phantom or ash-man. Drool on your chin, there must be, and nothing reflected in the pupils of your eyes. I am not even entertained.

I've given you the line. Don't disappoint me even further by using it against me.

★

—This is possibly the worst thing ever to happen to the planet. And I mean *ever*. It just, it just fucking *amazes* me that people aren't as interested as I am in this stuff.

But they *look* interested, here at the table, rapt even, each keenly leaning in towards Willy and his words. Every eye big and underlip hammock-slack. Willy's hands gesticulate as if he sows seed, a medieval land-worker, and only Jerry Wellin leans back in his chair, hands laced across his paunch, face booze-red and damp.

—And you know what? I'm, I get as star-struck around UFO experts in the way that other people feel star-struck around pop stars.

—Like you, Will?

—You said it, Bruce. Not me.

Bruce, shaven-headed and with a goatee between black tie and square spectacles, smiles and sips his drink. —Can't deny it, tho, bruv.

—Wasn't going to. Cos it, it just proves what I'm saying, yeah? That there are more important things happening in the world than fame, than, than, fucking celebrity worship. Get me?

A man in a grey suit appears and taps Willy's shoulder. Willy swivels.

—What do you want? I'm talking here, yeah?

—Sorry to interrupt Mr Roberts but one of your, ah, entourage is being ejected from the club. Just thought you should know. I'm afraid she assaulted one of our toilet attendants, sir.

Jerry grunts mirth. A kerfuffle draws gazes and Grace sees the jealous snarler from the toilets being bundled towards the exit door by two bouncers, one male one female, each clasping an arm. The jealous woman is screeching and the pointy toes of her boots hover and kick above the floor.

—Laurie! Oi, leave her alone! the gay lad shouts and springs from his seat and runs across the room. He hips a chair aside and it spins on one leg before it falls over.

—And what business is this of mine? What d'you expect me to do about it?

—Well she was with your party sir. I thought that—

Willy waves a hand. —Some cokehead bint wants to give one of your lackeys a good Cheryling, that's no concern of mine. Do what you have to do. I don't care. Fuck all to do with me.

He turns that famous smirk across the chuckling table and the suited man goes away.

—Christ, that Laurie. He faces Jerry. —Always like this. Has she always been this way, Jez?

Jerry nods. —Ever since she lost the eyeliner gig, yes. Too much. And here he closes a nostril with one finger and sniffs loudly through the other.

Willy nods. —Thought as much. Waste of time. All you need is Adderall.

Jerry and a couple of the others laugh but most just look puzzled. Someone yells 'Fizz!' and a bottle of champagne is hoisted from an ice bucket and passed dripping around the table. Grace studies Willy over the rim of her glass. The bubbles popping like breakfast bacon but only when she drinks from the glass because then the liquid is close to her ear. Or like a faint snake. There are wrinkles around Willy's eyes like tiny lines, a net of tiny lines. And that zit at the hairline. His eyebrows appear to meet in the middle and the brim of bone on which they sprout appears too, what, sticky-outy. Like an awning for the eyes. There is a pudginess to his neck, especially at the back where the collar of his shirt has ruckled it up. The eyes seem to be set too deep in the face and where his nostril curves back to meet the cheek, in the little dark crescent there, black-heads form a cluster of full stops. What's going on? Grace has seen this face in close-up, extreme close-up, many many many times over and never before has she seen wrinkle or pimple or misgrown hair. What is this? Maybe it's just the way skin and flesh lie. How our bodies lie. One of the *Animal* photographers mentioned the strange word 'air-brushing' to her but she doesn't think that applies here. She is witnessing two worlds. Two worlds that coexist and this one she's in at the moment is the darker one, the one that lies, the one in which there is crumbling and pus.

That impure face swivels to regard her and the slightly flaky lips open to ask something of her but then the first bars of a familiar song come up from downstairs and the people at the table cheer as one and a roar from below follows the known drumbeat up and Willy leaps and darts over to the balcony and the roar from below suddenly swells, a jet engine, a rending howl. Roberts holds his arms out and akimbo and stands there like a cross with his head nodding but not small as-if-in-agreement nods, no, rather it's as if he's repeatedly heading a football, each nod powered by the pudgy pillar of his neck. Grace can't see his face but she knows what expression it will bear. Nodding to his own sound. Arms pinned spreadeagled by his own sound. The roar does not diminish in fact it climbs.

The people around the table stand and clap and whoop, all eyes on Willy's back. Before she joins in Grace glances once at Jerry who's already looking at her and he smiles at her and winks.

★

He wakes from a half-sleep with a start, a lurch of his whole body in the armchair. Groans and rubs his eyes. A trick developed when we slept in trees, such lurching, is a theory he once read about. That in sleep when our muscles relax a movement too much one way would announce a perilous fall so the body would jerk into alertness and that is a physical memory we retain. Still we do it. The ape in us. That's what he read, once.

He rises and washes his face in cold water at the kitchen sink and parts the curtains above it to see the moon but covered by cloud it is, a vague and blurred small brightness hidden behind wire wool. Still, it's there. He knows it's there. He returns to his armchair and considers trying for sleep but he's awake again, now. Eyes open. From a dream of slicing. Of blades that gleamed and sliced. Blood pumping to his hands and head and feet and the television burbling, something about hospitals with a small feller doing sign language in the lower right-hand corner. A tiny person. Another person, bigger, on a gurney behind him. An operating theatre. He changes the channel. Foreign football. Plaps his lips to rid them of a scum and then returns to the kitchen to drink more water and fetch another cold can of beer from the fridge.

Sunday tomorrow. He can sleep late. The night alive beyond his walls.

★

She's clapping, Grace is, clapping and whooping like all the others around the table are doing. The roar is still going and the music too and Roberts still stands there, at the balcony, his head going, his arms still akimbo. When she'd dreamed such moments as this in the days before, Grace always imagined that she'd be able to see herself, observe herself, mark her own movements and expressions; but she sees nothing now. Now that it's actually happening she sees nothing but flashing lights and a moving head.

★

And I wonder how you can stand and watch your children do this to themselves. I wonder how you can let them hack hack away. Not an option but a must-have. Bump in the nose? Give me that hammer. Wrinkles? A syringe full of fat. Roll of flab, a saw a knife a scalpel an axe. At their own bodies. At their own muscle. At their own skin, bone, and then you will come and you will take up that hacken flesh. Then you will come and take up those bared bones and parade the clanking skeletons and clog their crying mouths with filth.

★

—I'm going down, Willy says. —I want to go down, yeah?

Jerry shakes his head. —Down there? Into that bearpit? They'll tear you limb from limb, William.

—Yeah but I want to go down.

—Then what can I do? You have minders, yes?

—Course. Willy raises a hand and two big blokes appear from nowhere to flank him. He talks to them but Grace cannot hear what he's saying but his gestures – nodding at the balcony, pointing with his finger at the floor – are readable. Each big

184

man puts a hand on Willy's shoulder and like that they steer
him towards the stairs and Willy's head takes up its nodding
thing again as they descend.

Jerry rolls his eyes. He and Grace and everyone else at the
table dash to the balcony.

★

If we take—

See, if we take – I mean—

– if we—

And how much must you hate. How much must you hate.

There are such things as blackmail sites. Voluntary blackmail. What it is you email a young woman pictures of yourself
in, what, women's underwear, make-up, stockings and
suspenders, whatever, and you also email her your wife's
mobile number and/or her email address and thereby set
yourself up to be blackmailed. So the young woman in
cyberspace then has control over you for as long as you live
and this is what, a turn-on? What is it?

How much must you hate.

Your wife your kids yourself your life

★

At the epicentre of the surge Willy removes his white shirt and
whirls it around his head. There are screams and whoops
and wordless hollering mixing with the music. The big minders
are the boulders on which the human waves break but hands
and faces yearn for Roberts, reach for him, hands in his hair,
on his shoulders, on his back. Just one touch. Just one touch.
The lights flicker and the waves of meat and hair threaten to
engulf Willy and his white shirt continues to whirl. No
surrender here, no truce, Willy's arm moves as if he's turning
a crank, frantically turning an overhead crank. There are tattoos
on his bare torso, Grace can now see, from above, where she
stands. A lion or a tiger on one deltoid. Lots of tribal designs
from a tribe that has had their name ripped away and glued

to something that they never used in the first place and would not recognise now. Some crucifixes and words, text, lots of words everywhere, drilled into the skin, none of which Grace can read, high as she is, and because of the grabbing and grasping hands slapped away and replaced in a moment.

How mad is this? Look where she is and what she's doing. Ohmygod ohmygod how mad is this?

—Enjoying yourself, Gracie? Jerry is at her side. —You're having a good time I trust, yes?

Grace nods her head vigorously. How mad. —It's brilliant, yeah? It's brilliant. Bit smaller than I expected, though.

—What?

Grace glances once at Jerry. I've tasted your spunk and it didn't taste very nice. —Thought there'd be more people? Like not so small?

Jerry laughs. —This is just a warm-up, for invited special guests. The real party is yet to come, back at the hotel. William's rented out an entire floor. Or his record company has.

—Oh shut *up*. Honest?

—To God. This is just the warm-up, my lovely Gracie.

Grace looks down. Willy, still topless, is aloft, on people's shoulders. His minders are scowling and reaching up to hold him steady and secure and his torso shines with sweat and still he twirls his white shirt over his head which now hangs back on his neck which bears a series of tattooed stars and his mouth is wide open. Could be pain or could be pleasure. Difficult to tell in the bludgeoning noise.

Invitation only. Special guests. How fucking mad is this?

★

Flick, flick. Raise can to lip and thumbtip a button. Not a dance no but a slither.

+1°C, and the Arctic sea ice will be gone, entirely, in the summer months. Heatwaves and forest fires. The Med and southern Africa and Australia and south-west USA will bake and burn. Most coral reefs will be dead. Twisted growths of lifeless leprous undersea forms surrounded by drifting fish all floating belly up. This includes the Great Barrier Reef. Colours gone. Just white and grey and necrotic. High glaciers that supply meltwater to irrigate the land of mountain farmers will begin to thaw and the crops will wither. Malaria, diarrhoea. Dysentery. People shitting their own innards out.

+2°C. Each year European heatwaves of the severity we saw in 2003 will happen and many tens of thousands will die. Parching. Dehydration. Browning and barrening land. The American basin becomes pampas and desert. Increasing CO_2 levels will turn the seas to acid and all remaining corals will die along with scores of thousands of other marine species. More colours gone. Our eyes will evolve to recognise only brown and black and grey. Ice sheet will collapse in the west Antarctic. The entire Greenland cap will melt and the planet's ocean will start to rise. At this point we will see the beginning of the end of a third of the planet's life forms.

Flick, flick, twitch of the thumbtip. How much must you hate, loathe, abhor, despise, detest. Adverts: get celebs get real life get *Closer*. Some boxing. He watches this for a while but it's a dull fight, too much ropework, too many clinches. Sip at the can. If we take –

+3°C.

*

The corridor to the smoking area of the club is low lit by pinlights in both floor and ceiling which give off a maroon half-light and the hue of the walls and carpet, purple and red, add to the sense of fleshiness, of internal meat. Only one of his minders accompanies Willy who has his shirt back on now but is sweating and panting and pink with eyes of high wattage, as if his real eyes have been scooped out and replaced with flashlights. Others of his pack are with them, laughing a lot, rolling cigarettes or removing them from boxes as they walk, in the corridor, in the half-light. The minder opens a door and they all step out on to a grilled iron balcony, a hooded iron-grill balcony. Slap of the night air on overheated skin. A roof-scape under a blue half-moon and chimneys and drifting silver clouds. The music and ruckus of the club all of a sudden gone background.

Grace feels eyes on her. Is not herself looking but knows that eyes are on her. On her face, on her chest. Oh yes you've seen these things before, on pages and screens. But look at them now and here they are.

A hand on fire touches the cigarette in Willy's mouth. He inhales deeply and blows out little smoke.

★

And at that point any efforts to alleviate the rising damage will be in vain, useless, a penknife against a two-ton bomb. Millions of miles of rainforest will be aflame and the released carbon from the burning wood and leaves and soil will further fuel the furnace, that's all. Deserts will eat cities in southern Africa and Australia and the western USA. Refugees in the billions as people flee their traditional agricultural lands in search of scarcer food and water. The Mediterranean lands will be parched, arid. Half the amount of water that there is there now.

And +4°C. At just +4°C. Arctic permafrost nearly thawed. Methane and carbon dioxide in the soil released into the atmosphere. Arctic ice permanently gone, so too polar bears and beluga whales and many other native species and riotous, calamitous superabundance of their prey. Antarctic ice sheets melting. Many island nations Atlantis-ised. Those towers under the sea. Italy, Spain, Greece, Turkey – all vast deserts. Vast deserts. Southern England's summer climate will be baking. All scorched.

Flick, flick. Here I am and I have no shame. My wife and children exist only as adjuncts to my need. How much must you hate. Flick, flick. A satellite image of Greenland. The camera from space closes in. *Scientists believe that this line, highlighted here, is a deepening crack. Operatives on the ground, on the ice sheet itself, are*

and if this section of the ice should break off
if it

Yes but this will not be it. This will happen to a world already dead. Rearrange the rubble, set fire to the ash. Nothing of any use will be left to burn away. How many more humans could be constitued from the flesh, the fine flesh and muscle, that is incinerated in hospitals every day? Stitch the bits, harness the storm to jolt them, and still they'd be prettier than you. How much. How much.

Because if we take—

★

The gaze intensifies as Roberts leans back against the wall next to her. She can feel it, the gaze, on them, the eyes, discern their colour and hear it, even, crackling in the air. The people round-about on the balcony are laughing together and talking loud to each other and calling each other 'blud' and 'bruv' but their eyes are scurrying all over her and her new nose and boobs.

—So Jerry didn't tell you, then?

—Tell me what?

Talking to Willy Roberts she is. He asked her a question. *He* asked *her*. How fucking mad is this.

—That I wanted to meet you?

She just smiles and shrugs. Like she knows exactly what to do in this situation.

Willy turns away and holds his temples and groans.

—What's up?

—You. You're so sexy, yeah? Driving me mad to look at you, Gracie. I can see now what—

Her head hums.

★

Because it all points to a self-loathing of proportions gargantuan. The urge to uglify catastrophically misunderstood and confused as the desire to improve. The collapse when it comes which it will because it has momentum now will be both utter and very soon. Or no fuck that because happened it has already and this is the aftermath. So shattered, fallen so fucking far that it is all irreparable. How to reverse atomisation? With Sellotape? With glue? We're not a fucking nose. This is the aftermath, these are the ruins. The fall has happened and the impact the cataclysm occurred with very little sound and most of you did not notice so stolen had you been of sense. All eyes turned inwards. This littered and plastic plane of shrieking need and you don't even know what it is you need, what you're crying for. All you know is that you want to scream about it.

Once on YouPorn he'd watched a skinny young man give himself a blowjob. On his back on a bed he flung his scrawny legs back over his head and fellated himself. The straining sinews and the twitching arsehole in its hoop of hair like an old mouth with dentures removed. The guy came in his own mouth and gulped and turned to the camera and grinned. On YouPorn this was. Posted three months ago. 1,222,846 views. Rate this.

*

Willy is saying something about a rival team. That they, them footballers, play for a team who beat *his* team three times last season, twice in the league and once in the FA Cup to knock them out of the quarter-finals. Doesn't like them, he's saying. No surprise to him that they used her in the way they did. Horrible bunch. No respect. None. Absolutely no respect. Spoilt, y'see. No accountability.

A light breeze has sprung up and is blowing two seagulls reeling above the nearest roof which, with the trail of the blue-ish moon down its slates like a ladder of light, resembles a sloping lake. The gulls shriek and spin. The balcony sags a little with the amount of smoking people on it one of whom, a lad with big teeth and white hair who, Grace has noticed, speaks a little like Jonathan Ross, simperingly approaches her and Willy. He's even clasping his hands, kind of wringing them, in front of his chest. He even has a kiss curl on his high pale forehead.

—Can I bum a Marlbowo, please, Willy? I've wun out.

Willy takes a packet out of his breast pocket and hands it to the boy then waves him away. Glares at his back then re-faces

Grace. Says something about wanting to be where *they've* been. About wanting to do like a gent and a role model what they did like chavs and overpaid spoilt brats.

—Without the cameras, of course. He smiles at Grace. She's not entirely sure what he's talking about but she smiles back.

★

Not *too* drunk but sleepy. That heaviness in his limbs and grittiness in his eyes. Not drunk enough to have knocked himself out but he thinks, feels, that he'll sleep anyway. One more can and one more smoke. The room will stink tomorrow but the forecast is for fine so he can air it with the windows open and squirt a bit of Oust around. Stupid rule, anyway. It might be their house and yes they own it but he lives in it alone. Who the fuck else is he harming? Who is he harming but himself?

★

Tinted windows in the long white car. Jerry is next to Grace and he has his big arm around her shoulders but protectively, that's all. Willy is standing before them but he has his head and torso out of the sunroof and Grace can hear him roaring at the passing city and she can see the people of that city through the tinted glass windows, their pointing, their quick recognition, the immediacy of their hysteria outside pub and club and kebab shop and chicken joint as they dash out automatically into the road towards the car which sails past. Jerry is laughing. Grace can see a belt-buckle and a bulge and jeans with a neat hole at one knee and desert boots. Moving through the city behind darkened and strengthened glass.

★

Flick, flick. Press thumb down on button and telly goes dead. Blank screen. He leaves his armchair and goes to his desk. Turns his computer on. One last surf. Just one last swift surf before bed and sleep. What for? Who knows. Let's see.

A slight hum. And if it is true that when you commit a hurt, when you do harm, there is something in you that hurts too then the entire planet is in pain, constant pain. Is howling in agony. Because everything you do, every fucking thing you do is I mean. I mean self-regard of such depth and size can only result in—

Screensaver, home page. Thumping heart.

*

It is a storm, a blinding storm that sets searing kaleidoscopes in Grace's sight and buffets her about across the pavement. There'd been none outside the club because they'd used the secret back exit into the ginnel where the cars were waiting but here at the hotel, in the few feet between leaving the car and getting through the revolving door, is a meteor storm, flashing and fervid, hysterical.

She's clutched between Jerry and a minder. The minder is forearming people with cameras out of her way and she can glimpse Willy ahead of her, also with a minder but not held by him, his hands clasped above his head.

—Over here, Gracie! a voice yells and she cannot help but look. Flash, in her eyes. A white detonation. She stumbles and would fall were it not for a big supportive hand in her armpit.

—Fuck off! a voice shouts. —Get that fucking camera away or I'll smash it! Fucking paps. Scum of the earth. Just trying to have a good time here!

A camera is held in front of and below Grace's face, viewfinder pointing up. This time she closes her eyes but the flash still explodes behind the lids and again she needs the supporting hand. Then she is on carpet and it is quiet and the hands release her although she can sense a crush at the doors behind her, hear banging on glass, see more flashes, bursts of light, reflected off the polished wood and marble of her surrounds.

—YEAH!!

She looks up. Sees Willy, his arms outspread, amongst tall greenery. Ember eyes.

—YEEEEAAAHHH!!!!!!!

*

Where to go. Where to go. Christ it's a mad world.

*

Jerry is laughing into Grace's ear. —This is the dream, kid, he is saying, and she can feel warm breath and droplets on her lobe. —And you, dear Gracie, are living it. Oh yes you are. This is everything you ever dreamed of.

*

I mean it's not even in the frenzy or passion of war. It's just a steady and sneaky erosion. A constant chipping away. A never-ending abrasion into nothingness which you let them do, invite them to do, until you start doing it to yourself. That's how far you've let them destroy you. That's how far—

*

A lift, then another corridor, in which people mill and dance and talk and drink and there is a lot of laughter and shouting and Willy vanishes beneath a roaring scrum, is engulfed. Then there is a room with a great big window looking out over the city and lots of white flowers in vases and jugs and more people. Bottles everywhere. Girls in dresses and high heels and so much gleaming skin. How mad is this, how mad.

Jerry says: —See. And it is only half a question, not even that. And Grace sees herself the last time she was in a hotel room. The fuzzy footage of herself, her skin furred, and the men scurrying around her and she sees glimpses of her own

193

pinned limbs between the muscled and pressing limbs of others, the last time she was in a hotel room, up fuzzily on YouTube.

—See, Gracie?

*

Why lie to himself? Why put it off? He knows what he wants, what he dearly wants and at the same time is too terrified to see. The tears and the box and the little girl. What he's seen before, many times over. Appalled by his own need he is for the little girl and the tears and the box. His thumping heart.

*

At some point Grace snorts a bump of clogged white powder off the back of someone's fist that she is told is cocaine but if it has any effect on her behind the foggy delirium of the drink and diazepam she cannot tell. There are bottles and people everywhere, some of whose faces she recognises from page or screen or both. Some of these familiar faces nod to her as if they in turn recognise her own features and maybe that is what is making her float so. That and everything else. The spread glimmer of the city behind the windows high and wide.

*

The cursor blinks in the Google search box. It throbs with impatience. His fingers hover above the keyboard. In his ears his blood booms. The little girl. The crying. In the search box appear the words *toy story 2 when she loved me* and click and then click and then it begins, the box and the tears and the little girl. And the doll. And the loss. And the weight. The unbearable weight. Like an excision, an amputation. Lost forever. Look at me. Fucking half-drunk and blubbing over *Toy Story 2*. But it's that bit when Jessie's gazing out of the slit in the box at the end and the car is driving away and it's all abandonment and pain. What am I doing? I'm forty-two years old. What am I—

The weight, oh, the—

★

—Willy! It's you, bruv!

—Turn it up!

The room is filled with a hush that dribbles into it and spreads. The real Willy Roberts stands up on the bed to see over the heads of the silent huddle of people and the TV Willy talks. *This tour . . . I'm so fucking scared.* A sigh softens the crowd in the room as one. Heads turn to look at the real Willy, the meat Willy, standing on the bed at the back of the room.

—Aw Jesus Willy man.

The lips tremble. The hands come up to cup the face and the shoulders tense and flex. People, young women mainly, surge up on to the bed and Willy is softly engulfed, again.

Grace looks around for Jerry but can't see him. She sees the toe of a desert boot extruding from the maul of legs on the bed so she takes it and holds it in her hand. God how mad is this.

★

They sat through the credits so they could see the out-takes, Jessie and the dinosaur and the cowboy one – Woody? – and Buzz Lightyear, and still he laughed. Even though his entire body wanted to shriek some laughter leapt from his lips. He led Ella out of the cinema by the right hand because in her left she clutched the Buzz doll that he'd bought for her after the first one and he bought ice creams for them both in the foyer and they sat on a bench outside and ate them and Ella was too young to ask him why he was sad or even really notice and nor could he tell her, too old was he, why so immeasurable and many were the reasons and long-rooted inside him. Like his mind was vomiting. As if inside his skull uncontrollable spewing was occurring and it had been that way for years since, before, even,

Ella was born. For years. Since he himself was a child. Since sunlight. Since the first sparrow fell, a bundle, from the nest in the eaves. After they'd eaten their ice creams they returned to the car and he lifted little Ella into the front seat and strapped her in and she fell quickly asleep and he picked up a length of hose from Homebase on the way home and, in the garage at his house, slipped one end of the hose into the exhaust pipe and fed the other end of it into the car through a crack in the driver's window and then he got back in the car and turned the ignition and watched Ella sleep. The car engine thumped. He watched Ella sleep and waited for sleep.

★

The minder stands big in front of the TV. A little electric Willy talks and gesticulates between his legs.

—Mr Roberts would like to sleep now. You can continue the fun in other suites but Mr Roberts would like some time to himself now. So if you could all . . .

He makes scooping movements with his hands, towards the door. Some people file out of that door which another minder holds open, waving them through with a hand. Others, mainly young women, clutch Willy on the bed.

—Shouldn't be on your own, now, Willy.

—I'll stay with you. Let me stay, yeah?

—You need looking after. Tonight of all nights.

—Come on, now, ladies. Mr Roberts needs to sleep. Don't want him knackered for his tour, do you?

Grace releases the desert-booted toe. Willy looks up at her and wiggles, worms his foot back into her hand. A big *please* in his eyes. Grace holds tight.

★

Yes well the meds worked. And the therapy, kind of, to an extent. As they did for his soon-to-be-ex-wife but live she will forever with what she found, the two blue faces in her nightmares and memory and the stink the reek of emission.

Log off. Turn off. Standby. Move towards the stairs and the bathroom and the bed.

★

—This one. Willy points at a small young woman, lots of curly black hair, false eyelashes like implements to clean with. Lips too full to be untampered with behind raspberry lipstick. —And this one. He points at Grace.

—That all?

Willy nods. The minders nod in return and begin steering, hands on, the other women from the room. There are snarls and sneers and gazes that scorch and even some thin spittle that misses Grace but spatters the counterpane which the small dark-haired woman then kicks off the bed with a diamanté heel. Willy puts an arm around the nape of each woman, Grace and the other, and gathers them to him and hydra'd they huddle on the bed and the minder quietly closes the bedroom door and the party noises fade out into the hotel corridor and other nearby rooms. Three-headed on the bed, the intertwining arms all squiddy.

—I'm sorry, Willy mutters. —Much as I'd love to I just know I won't perform tonight. So much pressure. My head is too full. Can't relax. Nerves, y'get me?

He breaks the clinch to look into the women's eyes, Grace's first, then the other's. They nod.

—But I need you both here, yeah?

Nod again.

—We can sleep together. I mean *sleep*. Don't leave me alone, yeah? *Please* don't leave me alone.

—We won't, Willy. We're here for you.

Is this Grace speaking? She doesn't know but she thinks it probably is. Unless the other woman, the small one with all the hair, has a voice very much like her own.

★

Must've been bad. Horrible. To find us like that – to find *her* like that—

Christ I am so fucking sorry. I've always been so fucking sorry.

Feet a bit unstable he pisses down into the pan. Watches the greenish stream and its meeting with other waters in ripples and in foam. Spindrift bubbling up the porcelain, so powerful is his leaking. Feels his stomach muscles harden as he strains to eject the toxins.

And thankfully there was no brain damage. To either, although that's what the hospital said and he's only really certain about Ella and even then—

— even then—

If killing myself would rebuild it all then that's exactly what I'd do. If to cease to breathe would be to stop the horror then my breast would rise no more. Even if Inca-wise the devils would only be assuaged in their rage by pain then I'd drink battery acid, I'd take an electric carving knife to my fingers and toes and hands and feet until one-handed I'd be a flopping torso putting the blade to my final vein. All of this I would do. I'd end myself so that it all could re-begin. I'd take out my eyes with a spoon, pour salt into the holes. I'd—

He shakes off, tucks away, zips up. Squeezes paste on to the bristles of his electric toothbrush. Presses a button. Buzzzzzzzz.

★

—There, Gracie. See that little brown bottle by the mirror? Fetch it here, yeah?

Grace leaves the bed and brings the bottle back to it. Sits back on the mattress with her legs curled beneath her, conscious of how the skin on her thigh glows with light reflected. She uncoils herself, sits on her arse and begins to pick at the straps of her sandals to remove them.

—Aw Gracie. What are you doing?

Willy's eyes big. Something of the insulted in them and something of the reprimand in the other woman's.

—I'm taking my shoes off. To go to sleep?

—Do it where I can't see. Go to the bathroom or something.

—Oh. Okay. Sorry.

Willy shakes his head and shakes three pills out of the little brown bottle into his palm. —One each. Open wide.

The other woman lets her mouth hang open. Willy drops a pill in there and she chases it with water from a bottle.

—You too, Gracie. Just a sleeping pill. Grown-up's Horlicks, yeah?

Grace tilts her head. Must squint against the overhead light as her mouth falls open to accept.

★

He turns the bedside light on then turns the overhead light off then checks that the window is open, which it is. Undresses. Stumbles a little as he's dragging his jeans off his feet and has to right himself, steady himself, with one hand against the built-in wardrobe. Needs the breeze through that window. Needs to feel the night breeze on his skin as he sleeps. If he sleeps. Which he thinks he will because the booze, the booze. And the sandy stuff in his eyes.

Clambers into bed and turns the sidelight off. Lies in the darkness. One blessing: that I never saw Ella's face in blue. Because I was unconscious. Because if I had've. If I had've seen her face as if in death. If that. If I.

★

Willy between them, the duvet up to their chins. Under which they wriggle out of their clothes.

—Gracie. I need to ask you something.

—Okay.

—Your boobs. Them new boobs. The fingers of Willy's right hand flutter an inch or so above his own chest. —Is there still some, like, swelling and stuff? Bruises and that?

Grace pulls the duvet up a bit, then the neck of her top, and looks down. —A tiny bit, yes.

—Then leave your top on, yeah? I don't think I could stand to see that. And his entire body shudders.

199

—Oh. Okay. But they're—

—They look dead nice and all that but let's wait until they're proper healed, yeah?

He holds Grace's face in his hands and pecks her on the nose. On the end of her new nose.

—No offence, Gracie. But I'm squeamish, yeah?

Over Willy's prone body the other woman, supported on her elbow, sends Grace a smirk. The duvet has slipped from her and she is topless and her breasts should be pulled by gravity to the dexter armpit but they aren't. They sit high on her chest, still. There are two tiny pink sickles on their sides where the scar tissue has resisted the sunbed's rays and the nipples are blackberry eyes.

Soon. Soon you fucking bitch. The healing will be quick.

Willy points a remote control and presses a button and the lights begin to dim.

—Goodnight, ladies.

*

And there is one truth yet that cannot be destroyed. You give your lives to denial. Of age, of connectivity. Of fucking dignity but especially of age. But bared and fleshless your bones one day will be and under the dirt too, the dirt that you've spent all your life pretending isn't there yet you've eaten it by the mound and force-fed it to others too. Shovelling it in. Mud-feeding fish you gulp the slime and there it is around you. Bared your bones will be, will be. This can never be denied. Like a—

*

Powerful pill to bring on tiredness so quickly. Two chests rise and fall beside Grace and she can hear the sounds of celebration faintly elsewhere in the hotel and outside it, too, in the city. A distant siren. Somewhere a dog barks four times. A helicopter whutters between the stars. How mad. How fucking mad. Glass breaks. If you could see what I'm doing. If you could only see what I'm doing and where I am and who I'm doing it with. Feels like that up until now—

★

long and lonely and from which you will not wake at least in any form known to you or those you love or who love you. But maybe in doing it and the new forms of life that will come from it the harm will be healed. Maybe. Or arrested. Maybe. But it is a chance if only a very very slim one, tiny, microscopic. Yet what else could we do could *I* do but accept the vileness so fall into it, fall into it, fall into the—

★

I've been waiting to awake, living in a not very nice dream. Wanting to wake up. From a—

★

easy sleeeeeeeeeeeee

★

long long sleeeeeeeeeee

★

eeeeeeeeeeeeeeeeeeeeeeeeeeeeeeeeeeeeeeee

★

eeeeeeeeeeeeeeeeeeeeeeeeeeeeeeeeeeeeeeeeeeep.

SUMMER

RAINY DAYS, CLOSE air, sticky and heavy. Warm nights. The planet turns, far away from heat-death, it hangs and spins slowly and clouds move low and sluggish, made gravid with sweat. Below them and their drifting and breaking skin knits to skin and implants are accepted, the flesh is fooled and drugged into acceptance. Not recognised as alien any more. On some days the clouds dissipate and the sunshine falls freely and some sort of healing happens.

Willy Roberts goes away on tour. Grace follows his movements online, through his Twitter feed, a tourblog, watches the broadcast of one of his gigs far away in Italy. At one moment his face lurches towards the camera and her heart does the same, recalling the kiss, the quick peck on the end of the nose before sleep and the same lurch that came with the recognition that she was alone in the big hotel bed on waking and this is what she'd dreamed of, dreamed of so many times, and always they were dreams of fulfilment and so from where comes this loneliness? As if she's lived through an experience no others can share. A journey underwater perhaps, a trek taken across desert or ice sheet alone to preclude any camaraderie. The people she sees on the street, passing her mother's house, from the front window – they know nothing of her and what she's done. They walk in bags of ignorance and mediocrity. There is no one to share this with. Alone on the earth again she is. Back to sitting on the sofa in her Silly Moo pyjamas and eating toast and watching Jeremy Kyle. To reading the magazines that her mother, before she left for work, left in a little stack on the coffee table along with a handwritten note that Grace doesn't read, only glances at long enough to see that it ends with some 'x's and lots of '!'s.

She turns the TV on and sits on the couch. Tucks her legs beneath her. Eamonn Holmes oozes smugness like moisture. Fat prick he is. Look at the size of him. How did a damp lump like him ever get a job on telly? Grace takes the top magazine and looks at the cover and instantly there is a thumping. Willy, there, on the shining cover. In the shirt he wore that night and kept taking off and who is that behind his shoulder? A woman with piled-up blonde hair but a blurred face. **THE PRE-TOUR LAUNCH PARTY – WE WERE THERE!!!** Pages flutter like wings. Ohmygodohmygod. It's herself, taken from below, her eyes closed as if in thought, her nose perfect. She looks unhappy in the picture, and she remembers the blizzard of flashes, the crush of people, the forearming minders and the stumbling. That is me. That is me, there, in the magazine. **A worse-for-wear guest**, the caption says. Pictures of Willy and – was his name Bruce? – and the other woman, her with the black curly hair, who slept in the bed. Mentions of a fracas in the nightclub and how the toilet attendant will be pressing charges. **It's Cheryl all over again!** Talk of a floor booked, an entire hotel floor. A breakdown of the estimated cost, many zeroes, and Christ who the fuck cares. That's me. There I am. And there she is again in two tabloids this time with her name, the same picture in each as in the glossy but with different captions: one calls her **star of roasting vid Gracie Allcock** and the other just calls her **Gracie Allcock**. Just her name. As if she's, as if.

Grace dumps the mags and papers back on to the coffee table and puts her face in her hands. Kicks her legs a little. Ohmygodohmygod she says to herself. When she drops her hands she's smiling and she runs upstairs and turns her laptop on and as it hums and boots she sits in the chair with her heels on the edge of the seat and her knees drawn up to her chest and her arms wrapped around her shins. Grinning. The pressing of her hugged thighs against her breasts produces no pain of pressure but she does not notice this, the happened healing, nor the rays that fall aslant in through her bedroom window and obliquely on to the wall above her laptop, casting shapes of shadow and light, the window's negative, on to Willy Roberts's frozen face. Some sort of healing has happened.

★

He resets his alarm to Radio 2, unable to bear the voice any more, but the first morning after doing so he is awoken by the Beautiful South so he resets it to Radio 1. And is yanked from sleep by that voice bellowing about how he wants to have sex with Marina Diamandis. To Marina Diamandis. Fuck's sakes. What can you do? If you're ignorant and thick, don't broadcast it. Don't scream about it. And don't make ditties about being average either. Just, just fucking shut up.

God, God. This world.

Summer holidays. Childless, the school is quiet. Some teachers can be seen behind the windows of the main blocks doing whatever it is that teachers do in the school holidays and he himself has painting to do, drains to unblock, other chores. Plus there are men working at the swimming-pool excavations yet this morning they stand at the lip of the dug hole and lean on shovels and the digger is quiet and unmanned and there is another one with them, an important-looking man in white short-sleeved shirt and tie and yellow hard hat. Their faces are serious, they do not smile. They greet the caretaker as he approaches them across the playing field, slides sideways through the gap in the chain-link.

—Something's been found.

—Has it?

A nod.

—What kind of thing?

One of the men points with a finger at the hole. The foreman narrows his eyes at the caretaker as he leans and stares down at brown bones, a jumble of brown bones in mud, a smashed cranium and half a ribcage, a fibula, a lower jaw long-toothed. Some slabs of stone, too, sandstone, their straight edges made by a man's hand.

—Ancient grave, the foreman says. —Unearthed it this morning.

—Jesus Christ.

—You said it. Viking or something, I reckon, by the looks.

—How can you tell?

—I mean it's old. Very, very old. Not a crime scene is what I'm getting at.

They stare down at the old brown bones. Celt or Viking or Saxon or Roman or whatever the old brown bones moulder in the mud. Their ends are splintered or rubbed shiny on the ball sockets. The long teeth grit up from the mire.

—Cover it up, lads. We're running late as it is.

—What?

The foreman shrugs. —Just cover it up. This gets known and they'll move the site or suspend the job while they flock here with their tiny little brushes. Fucking *Time Team* will be on this by tomorrow. Bury it, tamp it down, let's get that liner installed. This has got to be ready for when the kids come back to school. And where's your hard hats?

—No one's working overhead.

—Doesn't matter. I'm wearing mine. Health and Safety. Get em on.

The men go into the prefab hut nearby to fetch their head protection. The foreman looks at the caretaker.

—Okay with this?

Grimace. —I have to be, don't I? You're the boss. No choice in the matter.

Nod. —Don't worry about it. Not the first time this has happened in this area. Hundreds of these things around here. Burial mounds or whatever they are. Ten a penny. But we've got to make a living, aye? Got a car park after this.

He pats the caretaker on the shoulder then follows his workers into the hut. And there amongst the smells of the living men, their sweat and smoke and the foreman's Lynx, and the reek rising from the charnel pit below he knows that at its very core the world knows, too. That the hot heart of it is aware of every scratch and scurry that occurs on its skin. How did you come to be bones, you people? How did you die? How did you live? What colour were your eyes? And did you in visions visit the future world the one in which the world you'd made would be stamped down into dirt? Maybe you did. So the slabs and the sarcophagi and the tumuli of earth. Keep me safe from what will come, bury my name with my body, and would there were a tongue still vocal in the clay. If only one muscle could vibrate with news still new but neglected nonetheless and not just of blind despair. If there was an earthquake that rent the ball in two. If there was a destruction that cracked the big ball. That holed the globe.

A worker comes back out of the hut wearing a white hard hat with TOMMO marker-penned on it and climbs into the cab of the digger and starts the engine. Big blue exhaust farts. The arm reaches out and scoops up earth and swings out over the hole and releases it on to the bared brown bones and the caretaker returns to his house to put his overalls on. There is a drain to unblock. Girls' toilets.

This is not hate, although it shares some characteristics with that. Nor is it disgust or depression or anxiety or nausea or fury, yet it shares some characteristics with those things. What it is is a thing that to label it would be to render it inaccurate. Because it is new. It has never been seen before. Born in blood and bile it is like nothing else that the world has ever known.

He squats and lifts the grid with its clogged thatch of lique-fying leaves and other detritus and the action disturbs the foul water beneath and vile gas rises, sulphurous and salty. He heaves and swallows spit and breathes only through his mouth. He rolls the sleeve on his right arm up to his elbow and supports himself with his left palm flat to the tarmac and he sinks his right hand into the wet filth in the clogged drain which clings and drags on his skin. He scoops out horrible mulch, vile dirt, an empty packet of pickled-onion flavour Monster Munch and drops it all into a stinking mound on the tarmac floor at his side. The stench confuses his senses and he can taste it in his nose and smell it in his mouth, behind his compressed and bloodless lips. Rotting food matter, sludge khaki-coloured. His hand goes in deeper, into the water, if water such ordure can be termed. Into the pipe. His fingers touch and loosely close on a ball of what feels like matted hair and he withdraws his hand with the clump tight in it and the brown liquid bubbles and hisses in a great gurgle and stink erupts and the liquid vanishes, sucked into the sewage pipes beneath the school. He does not look too closely at what he has removed, foul as it was to his touch, but the side of his eye tells him that it might be a dead rat as he drops it atop the pile of shite already extracted. A hint of yellow buck teeth and veiny ear and bones just breaking through. Wrapped in other things, grass, human hair, unnameable stringy stuff. He washes his hands and forearms at the standpipe nearby then with a short-handled shovel scoops the extracted sludge into a plastic bag and then takes it to and deposits it in the general waste wheelie bin, bound for the incinerator. Seemed organic except for the crisp bag but God it was rank. Toxic. The stink of the stuff still sticks to the skin of his right hand so he goes into the school building and enters the girls' toilets and washes his hands again, this time with soap. Then he opens the doors of the cubicles one by one and peers down separately into the pans. He flushes one and the water returns transparent, clean. He nods.

If you Google 'shaved heads' you get many hits two of which are Nazi collaborators and Britney. Eyes like mineshafts. Stares that gulp a thousand yards. **This crazy bitch rules!!!**, Perez Hilton posts. And under each leaf there are things that you will never understand, collisions and overlaps of lives incomprehensible yet indispensable to that isolate spinning in space and any other way would just not do.

And still it draws him back. Last night he watched a short film of a woman anally penetrated to the extent that her rectum prolapsed and protruded, a red-black head of broccoli, from between the cheeks of her arse. She did not seem bothered by this, especially; seemed amused by it, in fact. She gave a giggle. The three men or four men or five men standing around her looked down at her as she fingered and toyed with the hanging bag of her own guts, her long and prettily-painted fingernails, each one sporting a tiny sunset and palm-tree silhouette tickling the mucus-gleaming muscle, maroon sea-cucumber with a gummy slit for a mouth. The woman gave a giggle. This page offered links to other, similar pages; prolapses, it appeared to him, are now apparently a popular category of pornography. Swinging sacks of innards to entertain and thrill.

And even in that goo that he pulled from the drain, even in that the quick does leap and it does flicker. In the rat's decomposition it seethes and engenders itself and will not be burnt by the acids turned amniotic so great is the will to be and continue. Under every leaf, under every blade of grass. Crab spiders rustle in the petals. The toads are in the pond.

And still it draws him back. This morning he saw photographs of the girl who fell and held the daisy taken outside some hotel or club or something somewhere during the night of a pre-tour launch party for the fucker with the permanent smirk, what's his name, gets his arse out at every possible opportunity if there happens to be a camera around, Roberts, Willy Roberts, smirks in your face shoves his arse in your face and you act like a cat with cream. Taken from below the photos were as if the pap had thrust his camera under her face which had been lowered to avoid that camera she, the girl who fell and held the flower, whose knee he swabbed clean, Grace, looked sad and scared. **Star of roasting video** said the caption. **Star**. Another ho fucked stupid lol. Bitch choked me out. Yet sad and scared was surely accidental. Just an expression of an instant removed from context and anyone could look anything when captured like that. Same pictures online, link to Willy Roberts, click, click. Quote from a newspaper article: *he has overcome the limits of his voice to become what this country does best: a personality-driven cabaret turn with a comforting touch of mediocrity to make us feel they're just like us.*

What this country does best. Smirk and show the pimples on your arse. And then he watched a girl hold her passport up to the webcam, just above the pulsing details of time and date, to prove that she'd been eighteen for just a few hours before she took two dicks inside her, one in vagina and one in anus, at the same time as another in her mouth. Her passport picture showed her as unmistakably a child, five years or so ago. Why does this draw him back? Yet still it draws him back. And there was a cranefly spread on the wall next to the lamp on the kitchen worktop before he went to bed last night. Thing of thread, cotton and lace. He trapped it beneath a pint glass carefully to avoid catching its legs and wings and he slid a slip of paper beneath it and he held it up before his red-rimmed eyes and he watched it whirr and dangle inside the glass. Saw the pinhead moustache and the jointed legs and the wing's fretwork, filligree. Opened the back door and let it go out into the still night and caught a silvery glimpse of it as the outer darkness enveloped it and there was this and there will be more of this yet still he is drawn back, back. Almost as if in hypnosis, or mesmerised by those depths. Blank-eyed in headlights or with the glitterdust wings of a moth sizzling, crisping in a flame. Sick it is sick and I am sick and yet it draws me back. Come water, come wave. A bald and serious man on the TV says that it *will* happen, but we don't know precisely when. Ice cracking. That crack deepening every day.

★

Jerry says, on the telephone, his voice coming out of the mobile switched on to loudspeaker on the kitchen table between Grace and her leaning mother:

—They've all done it, Gracie. Aisleyne Horgan-Wallace, Grace Adams-Short, Jennie Corner, Sam Heuston. Imogen Thomas too, and she's a natural beauty. You yourself, Gracie.

—Me? Grace looks up at her mother and then back down to the telephone. —When?

—Last month. The 'Before' and 'After' shots. Or was that an invisible brassiere you were wearing?

—That was different.

—How was it different? End result was the same.

—Which was?

—You showed your assets. I won't quite say 'natural' because after all they're not what you were born with but regardless of that they're you, now, Gracie. A part of you. And you have every right to put your trophies on display.

The edition will be a special one in the series of Boob

Bonanzas that *Animal* sometimes runs and it is to be called Silicone Happy Valley. The email had been in her inbox that morning, the request for her to appear. **We'd love to feature you**. Really it's already been agreed to. Grace's bedroom itself gave a big nod to the request and then the telephone trilled to the tune, this week, of Rhianna's 'S&M' and Grace answered it and why Jerry apparently believes that persuasion is required is a wonder. But there is one thing.

—No one's forcing you, Gracie, you understand that, don't you? You too, Mrs Allcock. No one is forcing your daughter into this, it's vital that you understand that. This matter is and always has been one of personal choice. Allow me to quote my good friend Phil Hilton, esteemed editor: 'This raucous fun-loving working-class culture, this take-me-or-leave-me attitude, it's really taken off. It's the women who are doing this. That's their choice.' End of quote. Pithy chap, Phil. Couldn't've put it better myself. I have his words here, right in front of me. I'll send you the link if you like.

Both Grace and her mother cover their little laughs with hands. They regard each other with bright eyes above folded fingers.

—Gracie? If you're nodding then remember that I can't see you.

Grace puts her palms flat on the table and takes a deep breath. There is one thing.

—I'm a bit worried, end of the day, she says.

—About what?

—Well, I'm thinking. What will Willy think, yeah?

—Willy?

—Yeah. What will he think of me if I do this?

—Willy's in Belgium. Why would he think anything? And more to the point why are you worried about what he might think? What's it got to do with him?

—I thought . . . but . . .

—What? Gracie?

She shakes her head.

—Gracie? You thought what?

She shakes her head again. Does not meet the gaze from her mother that she can feel on her face. —Nothing. Whatever. Tell them yes.

*

Amongst the spam and crap in his inbox is a message from a name he hasn't seen or heard in a while: Pete Franks. He opens it, reads it. Small smile. Let's meet for a bevvy, it says, along those lines. Me and Matt have been given the night off and it's been too long and we were talking about you the other day and it says other stuff, other words, of that sort. He clicks Reply. Writes an agreement with a time and suggested place that night. The response comes back in a couple of minutes: **sound see you there.**

It's been a long, long time. Since before the thing with Ella and the exhaust, in fact. That long? Yes, that long. Already he can picture Pete and Matt across a pub table from him, the search-lights of their eyes on his face, seeking a trace of the one who tried to kill himself and his daughter and wondering if the meds are working still and if he's just generally *better now*. They'll be serious at first and unsmiling or they'll be chucking too big and false smiles all over the place and they won't ask him about The Thing. That'll be avoided yet will all night buzz between them like bees about to swarm. Yet he was asked. Pete's asked him, and that's something, a thing unlike a hanging lower intestine. Alright, then. Beneath every leaf.

He gives his house a perfunctory clean in the morning then walks into the town and eats a panini outside a cafe on the promenade and watches the people pass then he walks back home and stops at the bottom of the lower field by the exca-vation for the swimming pool, the digger there, the arm at rest. The torn earth and the bones, the old brown bones, stamped back into the mud. It was an old burial mound of some sort. Like the pet cemetery that now lies beneath concrete, that he himself concreted over. All those little bones and what they meant, what the flesh and muscle and fur around them meant to others and the rents their dissolution caused. He stares at the churned earth for a while then returns to his house and naps for an hour or so then takes a bath and stands in his bedroom by the open window to dry himself. The breeze on his back. It's been a long time and he's forgotten what to do, how to prepare. There was a time when he'd play some music or something and maybe snort a small line of speed and open a cold bottle of cider or something but now he's a grown man on the edge of middle age if not dipping his toe in that condition and it's been a long long time and he doesn't know what to do. Digits pulse pink on the radio alarm clock at the side of his bed. He puts on deodorant and aftershave and runs a thin slick of Dax through his hair, feeling the scalp beginning to appear through the crown, sensitive to the touch because of the sunburn. Working outside unhatted. Naked he looks at his face in the mirror then stands back. The shoulders aren't bad, chest a bit flabby, spread beginning to appear below it. The genitals loose and in folds. Two onions in a carrier bag. No, not yet. He's not old. And it's a body that I've written on, that the world is telling some tales on.

He dresses slowly. Boots and jeans and a grey shirt with a thin blue pinstripe. Thin black jacket because of the sun. Prefers his winter coats, his bulky and fur-lined winter coats, but the sun, the sun, the season. Goes downstairs and microwaves some leftover pasta which he eats in front of the evening news which he barely acknowledges. War. Some same faces rapacious. Then he puts his bowl in the sink and gathers wallet and tobacco and lighter and keys and mobile phone and turns the television off and leaves the house. Walks back into the town, towards the sea, past the digger, past the hole.

Saturday, 7 p.m. A summer Saturday at 7 p.m. The sun still hanging high over the ocean and the beach still occupied as it will be for some hours yet, dogs and people in the surf, bathers and kite flyers on the shingle. A few footballs. Last games of the season and outside those bars which receive signals from Spain or wherever crowds of people mill with drinks in their hands and there is a lot of pink skin. People at tables, on benches. He walks among them and whilst they baffle him he harbours no malice yet he is anticipating already the sense of remove from them that alcohol will put in him, that alcohol has always put in him. They do not disturb or disgust him, nor do they frighten. They are things seen under a microscope or he is like that to them. There is something in them that is not in him, this is what he knows, this is what all of his senses and experience announce. I feel what I feel and I believe what I believe. There is a thing that should be in them but is not and so there is an emptiness and it is not a thing that has been robbed from them or if it is they have waved it away with glee and relief but rather it has the nature of a jettison, a willing unburdening, a shrugging off of weight which has taken something with it and so light these people are despite their muscle and their flab. The vacuum inside them that should not be there. They are balloons. Just air inside their own air and exhalations with their own poisons. I am not afraid or disgusted. I feel what I feel.

This is his town, the town where he lives. Cafe, bar, shop, boarded-up window, tattooist's, cafe, amusement arcade. All open and season-busy. Souvenir shop, sweet shop, cafe, bar. Public shelter in which a family sits and eats chips. Some expectant gulls at their feet. Video rental, Chinese takeaway, bar, boarded-up window. Above some of the shops are living quarters, flats, some permanent, others holiday rentals. All of it facing the sea.

At the end of the promenade just before the hill begins that leads up above and back out of the town and at the foot of which the old stone church squats on its mound he enters the pub, one of the few drinking places left in the town in which you can sit, that has not been either shut into an empty shell or converted into private accommodation or into a vertical drinking establishment. No two-for-one offers, no drink all you can for a tenner. I am forty-two years old. And I am very fucking thirsty. The pub is busy and there is a big screen on in the corner but the bar is not crammed and he orders a pint of lager which he intends to sip but when the bubbly coldness of it hits his throat it is as if it is all of a single piece and he gulps it back and gasp/ sighs and orders another. Wipes his lips with the back of his hand and bites back a burp.

—Jesus, says the barman. —Thirsty man.

He nods. —*Dead* thirsty.

—There's plenty more in the cellar, man. No need to rush.

—I'm not. This is my normal speed.

The barman places a new pint on the bar. Takes the money and turns to the till. That smell, that smell. The cool yeastiness in here.

Someone calls his name:

—Kurt. Over here, mate.

He turns. Pete and Matt at a table in the bay window. The sash window is open a few inches and a light sea breeze ruffles the half-empty packets of peanuts on the tabletop and the slowly sinking sun has them in a goblet of grey light, white flecks drifting aslant through it, a recollection of a curl of smoke coiling upwards through that beam trawled up from before the smoking ban. Like a folk memory, a thing once seen, falling from knowledge and experience. They'd probably seen him come in and observed him down the pint in one go and that has worried them that his hinges might have flapped loose once again because they do not smile at him as he approaches them and their eyes carry out a quick inspection of his face yet they do stand to hug him and clap him on the back twice and ask how he's been and how work has been going and all of that stuff. The Thing waits to plummet or pounce above them, guillotine blade, so he takes its power by asking them how their wives and children are.

—Fine, Matt says. —Getting some size now.

—The missus or the kid?

—Both. Sept one's growing *up* and the other's growing *out.* Told her, said she's just throwing money away on the Pilates classes if she's still gonna eat takeaways every night. Wonders why she can't shift the flab and she's sitting there with pie and chips.

He shakes his head and drinks. Pete says:

—Mine's the other way. Disappearing before me eyes. Has to run around in the shower to get wet. Addicted to the gym, she is. Little boy's about to start school. How's your Ella, Kurt?

Kurt gives a nod. —Fine. Doing well, so her mother says. Good man, Pete. The question's been asked, the blade's been dulled. It will not fall, now. Under every leaf. And so early in the evening, too.

They sit and drink and talk. Framed in the bay window is the sea and the sky and the pier and the sun sliding down that sky like a slug on a pane of glass and turning it alight, casting scarlet scoring down to the horizon which bleeds up to meet it, rises like fire to meet it. The light on their faces moves from blue-grey to off-white and slowly into peach then orange, a kind of faded orange like the fur of a ginger cat, on the planes of their cheeks and their eyes are pulled into shadows as are the corners of their lips and the cleft in Pete's chin and the wrinkles at their temples, early in their fifth decades as they are. A window is cast in miniature on to Matt's shaven head and the stubble there, where there is stubble, seems to prickle as if a magnet has been passed over iron filings. The grease in Kurt's hair appears like slashes of silver, a purer, cleaner silver than the depigmenting hair that ribbons his head and which in recent years has also discovered his chest. As if the black contains within it more silver than does the grey. The life of the pub goes on around them, people leaving and arriving, young groups in for a few before they crawl the prom bars and then double back on themselves to end the night at the club on the pier, couples after meals or before meals or during strolls, groups from the cinema around the corner, groups doing nothing but drinking and talking. The big screen burbles on but nobody watches it. The fruit machine chirrups. The promenade itself beyond the window for a brief time empties of people and is then populated by a different crowd, louder and livelier than the first, coloured brighter. Just before it sinks the sun seethes and the low sky and sea become one steel-blue sheet overhung by a large and curving cloud, florets of it still lit up red and lilac as the planet rumbles and rolls.

They talk of many things. There is oil and dirt beneath Pete's fingernails and when asked about his job as a mechanic he shrugs and says: —Pays the mortgage. Matt expresses worry that his position as a fitter and maintainer of burglar alarms will not see out the recession: —People don't have much left to steal. Kurt talks about the swimming pool being dug at the school, the find of the bones and the slabs. Matt nods and tells him that the same thing happened when the footings were being dug for his kitchen extension; unearthed a slab of sandstone, the builders did, called him out to look at it. —They put a bar under it to shift it and Christ! The stink! Told them to cover it up again.

—Why? Might've been treasure. Like that feller in where was it? Leicestershire?

—Staffordshire, says Pete.

—Staffordshire. Set up for life, now, him.

Matt shrugs. —If it's down there it can stay down there. Just wanted the extension finished, that's all.

—There's a lot of them around here, Pete says. —Burial mounds and stuff. Should get a metal detector. That's what that bloke in Leicester did.

—Staffordshire.

—I meant Staffordshire. Metal detector. You never know.

They drink. Just pints, no nips, although even only a few years ago they'd have made a big dent by now in a bottle of whisky or vodka. But children take the stamina and age takes the stamina and suddenly intoxication seems not as important as once it was although Kurt himself cannot see how that could possibly be, the buzz in him now, the wings bearing him away from the people's heat around him to a soft and cushioned place of removal. Almost ecstatic, it is. It almost always is.

—So what did they do?

—Who?

—About the bones. What did they do?

—Covered them up again. Said they were behind schedule as it was. Foreman asked me if I was okay with it and what could I do? Just said yes.

Pete nods. Matt says: —I don't even know if that's legal. Think you're supposed to report that kind of find.

—To who?

Pete shakes his head. —Not worth it. Foremen are all funny handshakes around here. Wouldn't be worth losing your job over. Whose round is it?

It's Kurt's. He fetches three more pints from the bar. Pete gulps a couple of inches of his but Matt's looking a bit green.

—Out of practice, I am. Glass or two of wine with the missus on a Friday and that's me, these days.

—And so the last shred of youth slips away unmourned and unmissed, Pete says. Kurt laughs, Matt doesn't.

—Shite. Getting bladdered, that's staying young?

—No. But you'll be puffing on a pipe soon. Bet you've already got slippers.

Matt nods. —Tartan ones. Prezzie last Christmas. He looks genuinely saddened and does not join in the laughter. —Didn't it go fast?

—What?

—Y'know. Matt gives a backwards nod of his shaven head. —Being young n stuff. It's just all gone. I mean I'm happy with my life and everything but I just wonder where everything went. And how come it went so fast.

—Bit early in the night for this, Mattie. The misery usually doesn't kick in till around the tenth pint. You've got a few more to go yet.

Matt doesn't look at Pete. Doesn't look at Kurt, either.

—I'm not miserable. Who's coming for a fag?

They slide beer mats on to their drinks and leave the pub and stand outside the window so that they can keep an eye on their table with the drinks and the jackets there. Other people are outside, smoking, collars pulled up, some wearing hoods or hats, a slight bite to the air although it feels warm to Kurt, heavy yet, of a piece with the ozoney and briny whiff in and of the air. Mediterranean, kind of. And the cries of the gulls and the thick stink of seaweed rotting on the foreshore.

Kurt and Pete roll cigarettes, Matt removes a Benson from its packet. A guttering flame is passed from face to face. Kurt inhales deeply and looks over the road at a group of young women, loud and colourful, laughing, a hen night or something as some of them are in nurse's uniforms and one or two have small wings stuck to their backs and others have deely boppers bouncing like antennae on their heads. Like an alien species, come to observe. Bare legs can be seen, between heels and hems both high. Kurt sees these young women with bags of their own guts swaying purple below the hems of their tiny skirts and he really wishes he didn't.

Matt examines the end of his cigarette. —Got to give these fuckers up, he says, as he always does.

—Do it, then, Pete says. —It's easy. I've done it nineteen times.

—It's the cost, man. So fucking expensive.

—Straights are, says Kurt, who knows, truly, that having something to look forward to is essential to the well-being of those with an innately melancholic disposition, even if that thing is only the temporary relief and cessation of a physical need. —Go on to the loose baccy. Half the price. Less.

—Wife won't let. Says it'd remind her too much of her grandad.

—Her grandad?

—Aye. Smoked half an ounce a day.

—Yeah but. You're not him, tho, are you? I mean you're not old. What's she talking about?

Matt blows smoke. —Stopped trying to work that out years ago, mate. Just let her get on with it, now.

The wind off the sea picks up a bit of speed. Dark as it is out there the horizon cannot be seen but Kurt wonders if it has risen at all, if it has stood up, if it is rushing yet to meet the land and the soft bodies on it. A dropped kebab lies on the floor next to an overflowing litter bin on the ocean side of the promenade and as Kurt watches a piece of shadow breaks off from the pit of shadow beneath a waiting taxi and becomes a black and white cat which slinks over to the food and crouches and begins to eat.

Pete catches Kurt's gaze and follows it. —Stray moggie. Family of them live behind the Chinese.

—Oof, Matt says. —Thought that sweet and sour pork tasted off. Bit Whiskas-y.

—They live like lions, Pete says. —In a pride, like. And the females go out to hunt while the toms sit around and sleep all day. What a life, man. Fanny on tap. Bringing you food and everything.

The crouching cat chews. Falling street light highlights the white patches, deepens the black on the curve of its back cast almost blue.

Kurt says: —I like cats.

—So do I, says Pete. —Little lions amongst us, man. One of mine brought a rabbit back the other day. Full-grown rabbit like, dragged it in by its ear. Still alive. Thing's screaming, the little girl starts screaming, the wife. Chaos. Fucking cat near opened a vein when I took the thing off him. He pulls the cuff of his shirt back on his right arm to show a healing, scabbed gash. —See that? If cats were twice the size. He shakes his head as he studies the wound in something like admiration.

—Can't stand the little bastards meself, says Matt. —Just selfish. Expecting a tickle behind the ear and some food without giving anything in return. Give me a dog any day. They're proper companions, them.

Pete drops his butt down a drain. —Take a young and healthy dog up into the mountains and leave it there. In ten days that dog will be a whimpering bag of bones. Do the same with a young and healthy cat and in ten *years* that cat will still be young and healthy.

Words come out from under Matt's frown: —And? So what?

—Just saying. Cats are cool. Dogs are pathetic. Can't respect something that eats its own shite. Cats are *dead* cool. You just need imagination. You don't like them cos they won't do what you want them to do.

One of a group of young men in various pastel-shaded shirts takes a running kick at the cat but the animal bolts over the road, a strip of meat hanging from its jaws. The man nevertheless executes his kick and sends the kebab debris flying. His mates laugh. The cat sprints into the slim shadow of an alleyway.

—Dickhead, Kurt says.

Pete nods. —Pissed dickhead. We all done?

They go back inside the pub and drink more. They talk but Kurt keeps an eye on *Match of the Day* to see how his team did. Scoreless draw. Around their table is a contented cloud but elsewhere in the pub and on the prom outside too the air has somewhat thickened, been charged. Expressions have become contorted. There are sneers and scowls. Shoulders spread and palms turned outwards and chests puffed out and scuffles break out alongside the sea. Everyone seems of a sudden to hate everyone else or if not that then to mistrust them. To suspect them. Eyes are slitted, lips set and bloodless if not smirking or sneering. This is an angry place. A police car blasts past the pub in a blare of lilac lightning. This is such an angry place. From where Kurt sits, he can trace the movements of a CCTV box as it swivels on a lamp post opposite to track some movements and manifestations of this anger. He sees a group of young men shout something at two young women who look and scurry away. One of the men chases them and reaches around them to grab breasts, one in each hand. One of the women spins on her heels to slap him but misses and loses her footing and reaches out and takes her friend over a bench with her in a sprawl of panties and white thigh. The men are laughing, two or three of them doubled over, holding their bellies, so hard do they laugh.

This is such an angry place. Humiliation is an element. It clings to lamp posts and declares itself in public signage. It moves blood, keeps it pumping. I see nothing but this. I am a lonely atom but I think I know what I must do. The country is crammed, stuffed full with waiting rage. Lurking fury. And you tell me to mistrust revelation and to regard it with questioning suspicion and so you prove that you have never experienced revelation. Might as well deny the shark that eats you from the feet up.

—Anyone want to go on?

Kurt and Matt look across the table at Pete, who repeats the question.

—Where to?

—Dunno. Anywhere. Bit of a crawl, change of scenery.

Inside Kurt the booze is buzzing. Thinks he could do with lights and music. —Alright then.

Matt shakes his head. —You two go on. I'm gonna crash. Told the missus I'd be back early, got her folks coming round tomorrow for the dinner. You two go on, tho.

They drink up. Both know that it'd be futile to attempt to change Matt's mind and besides in the past hour or so his drinking has slowed and he has become taciturn and sullen so they see him into a taxi outside and move down the promenade past four men fighting with each other outside a chippy, blood on one shirt, some women screaming, two coppers in yellow high-visibility jerkins running and huffing towards them. Past a billboard advertising a range of underwear or something on which a model poses with inflated tits in a lacy bra, across which someone has spray-painted the words BEACHBALL BOOBS SO MUCH MORE EXCITING THAN EQUAL PAY. Past a riot van and a copper with a straining Alsatian on a leash. Past a man dressed as Batman and other men wearing dresses and some carrying a blow-up doll, students by the looks of them and the sound of their accents all the same and without apparent origin. Past some women wearing angel wings and tutus. Through a lens, Kurt looks. Through a long lens and at a long distance and squinting through a gauze of alcohol as he is he is just detached, even, in a way, interested. Because of the booze. He wants to drink more.

It's a dreamtime that the evening has moved into. Pepper in the air, and everything in a hover. All objects suspended in a curious haze.

Kurt and Pete enter a bar, through the crush of smokers at the door and past the bouncer who stares at their faces for an assessing second or two then looks away again. La Roux is loud, 'In for the Kill'. The air is hot and close and redolent of farts. Perfume and aftershave in a constant cloy. A crowd at the bar. Pete makes to shoulder his way through but there is a sudden commotion at the door, a kerfuffle, some abrupt excitement, and heads go up on craning necks like gazelles scenting cheetah.

—Aw fuck man, a nearby voice says. —It's Gracie fucking Allcock, yeah?, and in a second the bar is clear as the crowd surges away from it towards the door.

Kurt trembles as if Taser'd. She's there, she's there. Arms are raised around her in celebration or something like that and sleeves roll down to reveal the same tattoos or similar, pointy tiger stripes, designs that someone somewhere once thought were Maori or Celt. So the meme grows in the mass mind stunted and slowed. Between those raised arms and necks and heads Kurt gets glimpses, a sunbed-tanned cheek, a sunbed-tanned neck and jawline, an ear, blonde hair piled up in pineapple spikes. His feet are moving him over there. No, they're not, but momentum amasses in the muscles of his calves and the bones of his hips. Like a magnet. A chant begins: —Gray-*see*! Gray-*see*! The crowd surges and jostles. Big men are shielding Grace and one of them pushes out with an arm and the crowd collapses into itself for a moment and in that moment Kurt gets a hectic second of brown cleavage, a white lace-up top pressing the breasts together, inflated, flanking the deep valley. Kurt breathes in and the air is aflame. Help me here. What do I do. This gift this gift. Oh my lungs and oh my heart. The petals wilted in the clutching palm. *Fuck*.

—Local girl makes good, Pete says at Kurt's side, passing him a pint. He takes a sip of his. —Or bad. I mean for fuck's sake. You'd swear she'd found a cure for cancer or something, not just got fucked by some footballers and got her tits out for a lad's mag. Jesus Christ.

Kurt douses fire with cold lager. Hears a hiss and sizzle inside him somewhere. —You know about her, then?

—How can I not? I read the papers. Go on the internet. Her face is fucking everywhere. Well, no. Not her face.

—She went to my school, Kurt says. —When she was little.

—Did she?

—Yes. And she.

Pete's eyes are scanning the room. The activity at the door has lessened in frenzy but some are still chanting and the jostling and shoving is still going on. Some are drifting back to the bar, smiling, talking, shaking or nodding their heads. One young man looks to his mate, his face set in that Christ-I'd-fuck-that look; the eyes narrowed, cheeks slightly puffed. His hands cup large invisible breasts at his own chest, at the checked shirt he wears beneath the beanie hat.

—And she.

Kurt and Pete drink. Pete scans. Turns back to Kurt and

without looking at him nudges his arm with his elbow and says in a low voice: —Ayup. Two o'clock. Looks promising.

Kurt looks, a couple of degrees to his right. In a corner seat there are two women, their backs to the wall on which a film poster and a NO SMOKING sign hang. Kind of blonde hair, kind of red hair. They're both looking and smiling at him, one leaning in to whisper in the ear of the other, her eyes not leaving Kurt. The blonde one laughs and shakes her head and her ponytail frisks up on to her shoulder like a squirrel nibbling at her lobe.

—See them?

Kurt nods. Not young, these women, and evidently uninterested in the presence of Grace Allcock because they kept their seats. Did not rush to look. The scrum at the door has dissipated and the bar is re-crammed but Kurt can see no sign of Grace. He hears, behind the music, faint sounds of angered shouting behind the bar and he sees the bouncer dart outside into the night. Some drunk fuckers arguing. Just another Saturday ruckus no doubt. No not young these women, his own age maybe, but they look clean and happy and pretty too. He gulps down the memories of the glimpses of Grace. The neck and jaw and cleavage. Swamps them with lager.

—We've pulled, Pete says.

—Looks like it, Kurt says. —Come on. And he walks over to the table and takes the stool opposite the women.

And then things move fast in a blur and only moments will be recalled with any clarity on the hungover morrow. Talking with the blonde woman, drinking vodka shots with her. Pete and the sort-of-redhead vanishing. Finding out her name: Marie. Nice name. Dancing with her downstairs, feeling self-conscious and foolish despite the drink, then necking with her in the taxi back to her place on the hill above the town. Photographs of children on a sideboard. A story of divorce. An old Dobermann in a basket in the kitchen which growls when Kurt scratches its head. Taking his clothes off in the bedroom as she takes off hers, the nightlight orange-ing even further her sunbed sheen, all over except for the little pink smiles beneath each breast. The cicatrice never tans. Licking her toned tummy, down past the Brazilian, the landing-strip of fur. Enough light to see her by; nothing like the usual thing he remembers, the coral curls and folds, just a thin slit like a bloodless razor-slice. She writhes when he licks her, grabs his head, pants, lets out a tiny cry. *You okay?* She nods. He'll remember clearly her nodding. *I had a labial reduction not long ago. Still a bit tender.*

—Want me to stop?

He'll remember her nodding.

—Will it be okay if we have sex? I mean it won't hurt?

He'll remember her nodding.

—But don't press against me.

The condom rolling on. Not hard enough, he's not hard enough. Shite. The booze. Quick, quick. Just don't press against me. Sitting on the edge of the bed with his back to this Marie all supine and expectant he tugs at himself, tries to coax some resilience in to the floppiness. Closes his eyes. Dredges up a memory of a girl he once knew now not a girl but not much more than one on all fours on a hotel bed and the glimpses of her soft skin between muscular legs and buttocks and that dressing in the small of her back. Here we go. Up she rises. That's working yes that's working. She choked me out. The laughter. Another ho fucked stupid lol God help me fuck God help me this is working. Oh what am I. What have I become.

He'll remember propping himself up, away from her, on his locked arms, so that his pubis does not rub against her. She'll groan and clutch and scratch his back and appear to come and he'll have one face and one body in his head when he comes too, a body with staples in it, the arms behind the head, and that mouth stretched around meat which he's not sure whether he has actually witnessed or has just many times imagined. Could you see that, in the footage? That detail? She choked me out. She choked me out. He'll recall Marie falling asleep and starting to snore, filled with vodka, and he'll remember sitting upright on the edge of the bed, his penis slack and rubber-smelling between his white legs. If there were wishes, he'll think, but not remember thinking that. If there were such a thing as wishes I would wish for. I would crave. If there were such a thing.

He won't remember getting home, which method he took. Walk, taxi, what? But home he'll get.

★

—How mad was that? How mad was that? Grace fans her face with her fingers and capers across the pavement in her ballet pumps outside the bar, under the street light. Faces are pressed against the bar's windows, blinkered by hands, straining for a further glimpse of her. Just one more. She fans her face with her fingers and smiles hugely at Shell who returns the smile.

—You're a star, Grace!

—Did you see them? Ohmygodohmygod.

Grace's little dance takes her towards the road and a big hand takes her upper arm and pulls her gently away from possible danger. One of the two minders that Jerry told her would be a good idea when she told him she was going out on the town with Shelly. *They'll make a good impression*, he said, and hired them. Grace didn't need persuading. The volume of air displaced as they all four of them move through the bars. The looks they draw, the heads they make swivel.

—Did you see them Shell? Ohmygod I'm famous!

Or if not a good impression specifically then at least an impression, Jerry said. *Which is what all of this is about, dear Gracie.*

—You're doing it, Grace! You're living it! You're the shit!

Grace and Shelly hug and squeal. The minders watch the promenade, the doorway of the pub, the loud crowds passing, but evidently not well enough because across the road towards them comes a white face screaming *SLAAAAAAAAAGGGG* with a young man's body behind it.

—Fuck!

Grace and Shelly tighten their embrace as they turn to face the scream and the hurtling figure. The young man cometing over the road towards them, leaning at the waist, fists clenched at his sides, the mouth wide open and releasing that screech.

—Fuck! Damien!

226

Shelly grips Grace tighter. Like two fledgelings in a nest they are. A big fist meets at speed that rushing face and Damien is jerked back across the bonnet of a car as if on hawsers. The minder is across him, his hamhock fist raised again. People have stopped to stare. Many are laughing, grinning. The bouncer from the bar has appeared too and is holding Damien down on the car bonnet with one arm across his chest while the other arm is against the minder's chest, big fist raised, keeping him away.

—You'll kill him, man!

A glimpse of Damien's face, the blood in a black splash across it, stunned eyes on Grace. The nose appears to be flatter than it should be.

—Come on, ladies.

The other minder ushers Grace and Shelly away. They break their hold and allow him to lead them, looking back over their shoulders at Damien.

—Vin! the minder yells, and holds an invisible phone against his ear. —When you're finished here, yeah?

Vin nods. Looks down at Damien on the bonnet of the car, over the shoulder of the bouncer from the pub.

—Come on girls. We need to get away from here.

He leads them away. A wail follows them, a broken sound from a broken mouth: —Grrrrrraaaaaaacccccccee!

Fuck. How mad is this. How mad is this? It's awesome. It's the *shit*.

★

The hangover lasts for more than one day and makes his sleep shallow and disrupted and he lies awake in bed, memories of Marie creeping out of the darkness. Holding himself away from her on his locked arms. *Ow.* The pink scars and the too-neat slit. Nothing of the human should be that neat. After a couple of sweaty and restless hours he accepts wakefulness just past dawn and showers in a spray as hot as he can stand then dresses and drinks some tea and tries to eat some toast but it turns to ashes in his mouth and he can only manage a few tentative bites, even with Vegemite on, his favourite. Takes more tea and a cigarette out into the garden to watch the sky brighten above the sloping field, the digger's yellow arm at rest at its foot, the slates of the low close roofs catching a gleam of the rising sun. Some early swallows flitting and feeding across the grass, darting low. He goes to his pond, his small pond, lifts the surrounding leaves to look. No toad. The hot wet summer has caused his little garden to burst in colour and he stands among it for a moment, its silent blare, the obvious innocence of the ox-eye daisies. He remembers her nodding. No words, really, just a series of nods. Don't press against me. In truth it had been a long time, for him. And he held himself away from her on his locked arms. *Ow.*

Back inside his house he opens his laptop and turns it on. The tea and tiny toast-bits in him like concrete, something else heavy in there too. Into Google he types the name of his nearest city, the big one over the border to the east, plus the word 'escorts'. Has many hits. Looks at a few. O and A and OA and VVWE and CIF and CIM and CIH and BDSM and COB and DATY and DFK and PSE and then he finds the three letters he's looking for: GFE. There's a picture of her, the face smudged and pixellated and the body in black underwear, one spike-heeled foot up on a chair, hands on hips. A fine body, but he's not particularly searching for a fine body. The text tells him that same-day appointments can be made with one hour's notice but he must not ring before 10 a.m. so he writes the contact number down on a Post-it and stows it in his wallet, next to the picture of Ella, tatty and creased. Logs off. Turns the TV on. Stares at it and listens to nothing and sees only a moving wallpaper. Turns the TV off. Gets wallet and keys and mobile and tobacco and leaves and locks the house and moves around the house to the driveway and gets in his car. Days since he's driven it, maybe over a week. Closer to two. He has no real need for it, pretty much confined to the town as he is. Turns the key and reverses out of the drive and heads for the big city, over the border to the east. Puts the radio on. Breakfast show. The shouting. Too early for that shouting. Turns it off. Coasts up the slip road on to the motorway, into the thinning end of rush hour. Double-headed lamp posts on the central reservation like plume moths at rest.

And I *do* get it. I *do* understand. How it's taken many years, decades, to strip away any sense of connectedness or responsibility and how what should be models of accountability are paragons of nothing but greed. And I understand alienation. I understand worthlessness. I see dead children either drowned in floods or crushed in earthquakes or burnt and blown to bits by bombs dropped from the edge of space. He's fucking dead *now*. Sawing off the head of a kneeling woman weeping. I get it, yes. And decency is a long fucking struggle because there are forces out there, voices out there, that in persuasive whispers talk of belonging and being like us and how that is the only thing worth pursuing because in that identity lies a sense of self-esteem which the fuckers behind the voices have themselves constructed and I will have nothing to do with your painless and petty and stupid joys, the in-this-together, in-the-same-boat, the herd-like obedience selfish and swinish. I *do* see this. And too I see the hanging guts and the displayed birth certificate proving nothing but innocence in shit and I see Ella beneath the pier and I see the wilted flower. And I see you acting and behaving like some smug and ugly cunt with power wants to, needs to, see you act and behave, to point and say see? I told you so. And so I see all of this but I do not understand. Two eyes four limbs a brain and a soul. I do not understand. Come quickly wave. Scour it. To point and say see? So why should we care? And no one cares about anything but drawing the fucking gaze and there is something in the fundamental urge of renown but can you not hear the whispering? True it is low and true it is soft but you must learn to listen. Unstop your ears. Remove the dirt from them the time for that has not yet come and come it will soon enough and do you not feel this? Fuck you forever. I am so lonely. A jerking puppet in an endless darkness and so are you and yet you make the silent vacuum. Nothing there is nothing. The world is filled with faces and voices my head is filled with faces and voices of imbecile rapacity I cannot escape they are everywhere and hollering and when the noise becomes too much and I turn my eyes to look and open my ears to hear I hear a roaring silence of no eloquence and see just an endless emptiness. Yes I understand and yes I know and yes there are some things that I see. But you – you see nothing. Nothing behind your own snapping face. Just a jabbering mouth in starless blackness, perpetually gibbering. Break in the dirt till the earth breaks down. These are my bones. This was once me and here I am.

He turns the radio back on. External voices, that's what he needs, inanely bellowing or not, just external voices. But there are no voices, just the opening bars of that Helping Haiti song, the cover of REM's 'Everybody Hurts'. Oh Jesus Christ. The groaning, the oh-so-sincere groaning. It's a charity single, Leona, not a fucking orgasm. And no doubt this makes you all feel so much better about yourselves. Give because of the corpses, the people crushed and drowned, because of them. Nothing else. Mariah Carey and Kylie Minogue and JLS – fucking JLS! – and Rod Stewart and James Blunt oh God how much you care. And if he was to crash now, on this motorway, lose control, skid, run in to the back of another car. He'd be here dying with his ribs crushed and hot oil sizzling on his face and the engine block on his mangled legs and the last sounds he'd hear before he left this life would be these voices, this warbling and straining self-delusion. The soulful gestures and the faces all serious. And he'd know, for sure, then, that the universe is one gigantic sick joke. External voices. He needs external voices. And I know it is the sickest joke ever anyway because of the continued existence of certain people. And the eyes watch. The million eyes watch. The hands applaud. All the eyes watch and the world is not right.

If we take. See, if we take—

External voices. Fuck it all.

Like Jeremy Morlock. In the face of that man as he holds the dead child's head up by the hair for the camera to gawp at, in that face, in that grin, there is nothing but pure evil. True evil. Because in it there is nothing of the blankness and anhedonic unreadability of the empathic lack. No, in the face of Jeremy Morlock is knowledge of the suffering of others, an understanding of the suffering of others, and an absolute delight in that. In that face—

– in that face—

External voices. Fuck it all. He turns the dial and gets a local radio station from the approaching city which is playing Pam Dickinson's 'Bad Boy' which he hasn't heard for years and that will do. That and the white lines. Just watch the lines and listen to the song and let it all leak out of your ears. Trance. Don't think, don't think.

Soon he leaves the motorway on to the ring road which he follows towards the docks until an arrow guides him to the city centre which he drives into, heading for the multistorey car park but he finds a smaller car park by one of the city's main railway stations and he parks up in there. Buys a ticket from the machine, sticks it to the inside of his windshield. Heart a bit harder now, the beat of it and pulse. Checks the time on his phone. Goes into a nearby caff and buys some coffee and takes it to a table outside where he drinks it and smokes then walks some way away from the cafe and takes the Post-it out of his wallet and unfolds it and after checking the time again he taps the scribbled number into the phone. The beat of his heart a throb in his ears and his neck. A hawk in his stomach, beginning to thrash. He hears a ringing.

—Hello?

Swallow. —Is that Chloe?

—Speaking.

Swallow. —Erm, I'd like to come and see you. Today, if that's okay.

—That's fine, hun. Where did you find out about me?

—Internet.

—And what are your interests, hun?

—GFE.

—Nothing else?

—Just GFE.

—What time were you thinking of?

Swallow. —Soon as possible.

A little laugh. —You're keen. Are you local?

—I'm in the city, yes.

—Okay. Give me half an hour to get myself ready and come round.

—That soon?

—We can make it later this morning if that's better for you. But I'm all booked up this afternoon.

—No, half an hour's fine. Swallow. —Where are you?

She gives him an address and tells him she'll see him soon and he hangs up and walks for a few hundred yards then realises he has no idea where he is going. The skin of his face has heated up. He retraces his steps and goes back into the cafe and asks the woman behind the counter for directions which she supplies him with. Head towards the docks, she says. Pub on the corner called the Beehive. That's the road you want.

He walks. He passes the railway station, a soaring vaulted structure like the breaching back of a glass leviathan. Past the hotel once grand when this city was in its maritime boom years. Past Burger King, Yates's wine bar, Schuh, TK Maxx, Tesco Express, Top Shop. Still quite early and the city centre does not as yet teem. Sun not high as yet but strong, strong, and people wear shades and hats and shorts. Gulls call above the buildings and behind the noise of the traffic. His mouth is dry. A memory: being called to see the headmaster at school. Feels a bit like this. The tummy all aflutter, the wet palms, the arid throat. The heat in the face. He goes into a newsagent's and buys a bottle of water which he drinks as he walks down to the pedestrianised central street, drinks thirstily, and puts the empty bottle in a litter bin at the foot of a statue. An iron man, arrested in mid-stride. As the flesh crumbles the form takes on permanence. As long as you. That is, if you—

WHSmith, Boots the Chemist. Jigsaw. Monsoon. A couple of designer shops. McDonald's on the corner, Greggs the Bakers, Waterstones. A jeweller's. Kentucky Fried Chicken. Cranes above the buildings like the reaching necks of giant creatures that graze on cloud. Noise of a nearby jackhammer and the sound of a piledriver, the metronome boom that he feels in his feet along with his thumping heart. Smells in the air; concrete, ozone from the sea, the sweet and manurey tang of ancient earth disturbed. The clang of barrels; he looks and sees a man rolling steel kegs down into the cellar of a pub called the Beehive.

Swallow.

He sits on a bench at the corner of the street and checks, again, the time on his mobile and rolls a cigarette leaning forwards with his elbows on his knees and his left foot twitches and there is a rubescence to his face that has nothing to do with the strong early sun and he keeps his eyes downcast and licks his lips nervously and looks entirely like a man at some contraband practice. Swallow. Remember to breathe. Scratch the side of your nose. Feels like your scalp is crawling and why should that be? Do this, *do* this. To feel better. Maybe. *Do* this. He grinds his cigarette out underfoot and takes a mint out of his pocket and sucks it for a minute then crunches it to grit between his teeth and swallows. Wishes he'd saved some water. Just a swig. So dry, so dry. He stands and walks and finds the door, the green door she told him to look out for. Top bell, she said. He presses the button. Waits. A voice fuzzes from the intercom grille on the wall:

—Yes?

He leans in. —Chloe? I called earlier.

—I'll buzz you in. Top floor, flat nine.

Bzzz. He opens the door and walks in. Clean foyer, tiled. A large fern. His footsteps scrape and echo as he climbs. So dry. On autopilot, almost. He reaches the top floor and she's standing there smiling in the open door. White blouse and tight black skirt and black stockings and heels and black straight hair and red lipstick and white teeth shown in a small tight smile.

—Hiya, hon.

—Hiya.

—Come in.

He smiles at her as he passes her in the doorway. Older than he thought she'd be, a few years younger than himself. Some lines around the eyes. Bit of a cleft to the chin. She points with a pink manicure.

—Front room, there, love.

Closes the door behind her. CD racks, a bookcase. Big window, uncurtained at this height, view of cranes and spires and a tall thin tower like a mushroom and beyond that the sea. Large TV. Cushions and lamps. A coffee table and rugs, one of which he stands on.

—Right. Shall we do the money thing first? Get it out of the way?

He digs a rolled wad out of his pocket. She takes it. —Have a seat, hon. Make yourself comfortable.

She takes the money out of the room somewhere and Kurt sits on the sofa. Takes his jacket off. Squeezes the bridge of his nose between forefinger and thumb. Swallow, swallow. Remember to breathe. Ow. I am a lonely atom.

★

Here she is again, here *it* is again, the scene of Grace's mother coming into the kitchen carrying a tabloid with a serious look on her face. Grace is at the table with a bowl of Coco Pops and she's in her PJs and sleep is still smudging her features and as she looks up at her mother some brown milk from her raised spoon falls and lands with a cold splash in her newly deep cleavage.

—You'd better have a look at this, love.

—What is it *this* time?

—Best if you just read it, yeah?

She puts the folded paper down on the table. A picture of Damien, recognisable as him even behind the big splint across his nose and the blackened eyes and the swollen lips, the lower one sprouting stitches like hairs. The caption underneath says:
HEARTBROKEN AND BRUISED: Damien after the beating.

—What happened the other night, love?

Grace reads.

★

—I'm lonely, he says into her breast, the grassy smell of her shirt's washing powder in his nostrils.

—I know you are, sweetheart.

234

—And I'm unhappy.

—Ssshh. She strokes his hair. —You can talk to me, hun. What's making you sad?

—Everything. Everything.

—Such as? Give me an example.

—I once tried to kill myself and my daughter. She was only a child.

—How?

—Car exhaust.

—How long ago was this?

He shrugs.

—Do you remember why?

—I was depressed.

—Obviously, sweetheart. But what about?

—Everything. Everything. The waste.

—Don't cry, honey. The nylon of her stockings makes a swishing sound as she moves her legs. —It'll be fine.

—But it won't, though, will it? It'll never be fine again. It never really *was*, was it?

—Wasn't it? Not even when you were a boy, a child? Wasn't it fine then?

—But *this* was waiting. *This* shit.

—You didn't know that, though, did you? That's only what you know *now*. You weren't aware of it then, were you.

—You're nice.

—Well, you're paying me to be nice, hun. It's part of my job.

—Yeah but you're nice anyway, though. I can tell.

She releases a little laugh and presses his head to her bosom. He can feel the woven lacy edge of her bra against the skin of his cheek, imagines the interesting crenellations that will be left in the skin there when he disengages.

—She's okay now?

—Who?

—Your daughter.

—She's fine. They were worried about brain damage but she's absolutely fine. Smashing little girl she is. They got us out in time, before any real damage was done.

—Good. Do you still see her?

—Her mother won't let. It's up to her, y'see.

—And you.

—What?

—How about yourself? You're not the cheeriest feller I've ever met but you're getting better, yeah?

—There's medication.

—And that's helping?

—Kind of. Just gives you a distance. Kind of a cushion. Know what I mean?

He feels her nod.

—You got any kids yourself?

—No, she says, with an abruptness that startles him slightly. Strokes his hair again. —No kids.

★

Damien was interviewed whilst in hospital, according to the article, *having his extensive wounds patched up*. Those wounds are listed: broken nose, cracked ribs, loosened teeth, black eyes, *a cheekbone that doctors were worried was fractured*. He is referred to as *victim* several times.

I'm so unhappy without her. I see her giving herself up to those footballers and it just breaks my heart. She's worth so much more than that.

Smoke from her mother's cigarette tendrils across the table into Grace's nose. She sneezes and that reawakens a twinge, only small, of pain in her newish nose. —Ow.

Once again we see how one person's desire for fame destroys those who care about them. Proof, if more were needed, that we are breeding a generation of young people who care about nothing but themselves.

Grace looks up at her mother.

—This isn't true. Damien was going to attack me, yeah? Ask Shelly. I was just being protected, yeah? I swear down. And why are they being like this? They loved me last month, didn't they?

—I think it's called a backlash, love. I think you'd better phone Jerry.

I'm so unhappy without her. She's worth so much more than that.

★

Not by nature a garrulous man the words gush now clutched in the skilled and rented arms. Close to a torrent, by his lights.

—I remember it when I was a kid, when we'd find videos in mates' dads' bedrooms, or borrow them off big brothers and that. I remember that anal sex was hardly ever seen, and if it was, it was kind of extreme and taboo. Transgressive, like. Now, though? Have you *seen* what's out there? Most of what is offered as porn these days is criminal activity or a medical emergency.

She laughs.

—It's true.

—I know it is, love. But you don't have to watch it.

—I do, though. Cos I mean it's out there and I'm interested in what goes on in the world and it kind of sucks you in. It's just a couple of clicks away. What's happening to us? It doesn't turn me on. It frightens me. An an an an anyway, even if I don't watch it, I still know it's there, out there, and it's about real people. It has real people in it. And anyone can watch it and it's becoming normal and I can't imagine where it's going to go. What's happening to us? And there's this girl.

Swallow.

—A girl? A specific girl, you mean?

—Yes.

—Who is she?

—I'm a caretaker at a school. I mean that's my job. And ages ago there was a little girl late for her school photograph and she was running and she fell over and grazed her knee and I had to dress it, y'know clean it and stuff? And she was upset so I gave her a flower. A daisy I think it was.

—And why does this make you sad? It's a sweet story.

—Because the same girl is now a young woman and she's *out* there, doing things, that she shouldn't be. Doing things.

—What kind of things, love?

—She's been roasted by footballers. I've seen the clip, it was up on the web for a while. Still is. And she's in magazines and stuff showing off her boobjob and her nosejob and all I can remember or think about is that little girl with the daisy and how everything's gone to shit. I can't stop thinking about her.

—That's what it's like these days, honey. Everyone wants to be famous and they don't care what for.

—Doesn't make it okay, though, does it?

—What doesn't?

—That everyone's doing it. Doesn't make it better. Just makes it worse.

She strokes his hair.

—It feels like I'm in mourning. All the time it feels like I'm in mourning.

She strokes his hair. —Sssshh. Sssshh.

*

I was waiting for this, Gracie, Jerry's voice says. Something like this was going to happen sooner rather than later. The thing with Willy forestalled it for a bit but only for a bit. But listen to me — it's fine. I'm going to make it fine and that's something I'm very good at doing and if I wasn't then people wouldn't pay me to make it so, would they? Leave it with me. Give me some mulling time. Jerry's going to make it all better. But you must be prepared for it to get worse, for a wee while. Be prepared for it to get worse before it starts getting better. But you can deal with that. I know you can. And never forget that I'm here for you.

*

—There used to be a little fairground there and every Saturday my granny would take me. In the summer months, cos it was closed in the winter time. I was close to my granny. She kind of brought me up, really. My dad's mum. And I'd go on the carousel, y'know the bobbing horses that go round? And my granny would stand there and watch me and every time I'd go past her she'd be holding something more, treats like for when I got off. Candyfloss and ice creams and toys and once a goldfish in a bag that I called Jaws. I'd never see her go and get these things, I mean she'd always just be standing there whenever I went past on the horse, holding more treats for me, and God knows how she did it. She was a little old woman. It was like magic. I used to love those times with my granny.

★

Just trust me, Jerry said. *You've just got to trust me. Have I ever let you down, dear Gracie?*

Instructions: *DON'T* go online. Leave it be. Let the fuss die down. Don't surf, don't check emails, don't Tweet, don't even log on for God's sakes. Leave it for a few days. Let it die down. The *Animal* wet T-shirt thing is in London, a venue in Hammersmith, in two days' time. Jerry won't be there, no, but it'll be straightforward, you won't need a hand to hold or anything, you're a big girl, Gracie, take a friend if you want, a car will be supplied to take you there, and then when that's all done get yourself to this address, Jerry's house, where there'll be a biiiiig party. Lots of special people for you to meet. Take a taxi there from Hammersmith, get a receipt, Jerry'll reimburse. You'll have a great time. Don't worry about a thing. Only thing to remember is this: let all this die down. People will soon forget Damien and his problems in a few days and then you'll be in the news again with the *Animal* thing and they'll all start to like you again and before long they'll be pure bloody *loving* you if Jerry has anything to do with it which he will. Trust him, just trust him. Leave it all be for a few days. Get out of the house. Go somewhere. Don't watch TV, don't read the papers, and for Christ's sake don't log on. Got to protect yourself, here, cushion yourself. It'll just upset you. Withdraw for a while. See some friends. Go on a short holiday or something. Let it all die down. Haven't we been here before?

★

—Let me take it away, for a minute or two. This is what I'm good at. Lie flat on your back.

239

She slides off the sofa and kneels at the side of it and Kurt lies supine. She smiles at him and unbuttons his fly.

—Oh.

—Part of the service, love. Let me take it away for a minute. Just relax.

She wanks his penis to hardness then rolls a condom down it and sucks it until he comes, which he does with a yelp and a grabbing of a cushion in his two fists and a few seconds of no-time bliss. She stands and smiles then leaves the room and he can hear a glass filling in the kitchen, water running up the scales. He removes the condom and sits up, smearing some semen on the hem of his shirt. Chloe returns with a big bundle of tissues and he wipes off and buttons up and wraps the condom in the tissue.

—There's a bin in the kitchen, she says. —The red one.

Wobbly legs. Adductor muscles a bit achey. Two bins in the kitchen, one blue, one red. He drops the tissue in the red one and returns to the sitting room. Chloe's back on the couch. He sits next to her and puts his head on her shoulder.

—Hit the spot, honey?

—Yes. God yes. And now I want to sleep. Can I sleep for a bit?

—Course you can. You've still got fifteen minutes.

—Wake me up then, then.

—Okay. Close your eyes.

He does. With the muscle of her shoulder as a pillow, the grapefruit deltoid, he closes his eyes and falls, slips, into a light half-sleep, a silvery fog through which long-limbed hominids drift stately and funereal and silent, some seemingly bearing wreaths at their narrow and long and slat-ribbed chests. It is a sleep, kind of, and a dream, kind of, in which a knowledge revisits him that a moment of grief begins with a fading, a retreat of the lost one from the stage of the heart and mind, except that now they do *not* retreat and they forever remain, lit up, loud and invasive mementoes of what has been lost and loved and will be always now missed, terribly and achingly missed. And what is better? What is to be preferred or striven for? The long erasure of the loved or the constant reminder of their absence? Your heart, there, on a cold white slab, under a searing light. Every time you close your eyes. See it bleed. See it pump. Ripped from the breast as it is it continues still to pump on that ice-cold slab under the light that scalds.

It is a sleep, and it is a dream. When she wakes him by gently shaking his shoulder he feels refreshed and renewed. Uses her toilet to pee in and then before he leaves he thanks her, Chloe, thanks her.

★

It is her eyes, though, in these last photographs, the ones taken at Willy's party. Looking at them again, her eyes, and her forehead and her lips too, there's a pallor and a purulence, a slight hooding going on, the skin starting to sag or if not that then at least not look as healthy as it could or should. What did Jerry say? *We need you to look innocent.*

Grace digs through the piles of magazines at the side of her bed. Many of them, most of them, have Katie Price on the cover but there's one in particular that Grace is looking for and she can remember it because in the picture you can see Katie's shoulders, her bare shoulders, she's wearing a strapless gown. There it is. Grace extracts it, flicks through it. Finds the article, the words she recalls and reads again: *People are scared of Botox as they think their face is going to end up frozen and blank-looking but I don't have a very expressive face anyway so I don't worry about not being able to show emotion. It's not like I'm an actor and I need to have that ability.*

Two times, Grace reads these words. She eats the peanut butter sarnie that her mother has made for her and sits back on her bed and reads the words again, again. Imperfect is not good enough.

Without TV or internet or even current newspapers what the *fuck* do you do. Grace rereads the magazines at the side of the bed, all of them, and listens to Radio 1 but Willy's latest song comes on as she feared it would and she wants to turn it off but she doesn't turn it off. She fans her face with her fingers and then laces her fingers at the nape of her neck with her elbows squeezed in towards each other and she releases a strange noise, kind of a whine, a straining whine. Her bare feet drum on the bed and this sound brings her mother upstairs.

—You okay love? What's the – ah love.

She sits on the bed and hugs her daughter. Feels the buoyant breasts unyielding and falsely firm against her own and a stab of something stings through her stomach. Of what? She doesn't know. Or care: her youngest daughter's upset.

—Tell you what, she says into the needing-a-wash-hair at the crown of Grace's skull. —You're gonna need some new underwear, yeah? For the *Animal* photos, like. So what say I drive us to La Senza and you can pick some out? Yeah? Sound good?

No word from her daughter. But her head nods and for a second her arms squeeze tighter around her mother's waist.

*

Bright morning, big sun. Promenade, coffee, scone with jam, tabloid newspaper. So his days go. Less of the acid in him now, the burning in the belly, after Chloe, less too of the weight in his head, after her. So his days go. But he'd noticed that the hole at the bottom of the field had been lined at some point in the past few days and three sides of it had been tiled and it was looking like a swimming pool, just awaiting water. A clean and smooth hole with a steep camber. The steps for the diving board beginning to appear, just a few of them – the board will not be high. Open-air swimming pool for the children.

Summer holidays coming to an end. Beach busy, promenade busy, a bouncy castle on it and music and electronic chirps from the arcades. On the *Daily Mirror* letters page, a photograph of Cheryl Cole in shades. There's always a photograph of Cheryl Cole in shades. This one's captioned: **BRIGHTER FUTURE: Solo star Cheryl**, and it accompanies a letter: **SO GLAD CHERYL IS RID OF ASHLEY**. *I'm sure the nation has breathed a huge sigh of relief now Cheryl Cole's divorce has been finalised. I'm so glad Cheryl can look to the future without having love-rat Ashley in her shadow. She has had the worst luck* *but always manages to come back fighting! Marie Gosney, Billingham, Cleveland.*

Fight this. The sun is shining. There is Chloe, *was* Chloe. You have health and coffee and tobacco and food. Look around you. Breathe.

But you are cattle, around me. You are apathetic herd animals. Cudding on distraction, grazing on whatever has no meaning as your only lives are chipped, chipped away at. Eroded away, your freedoms robbed. And what happens to cattle, in the end? They are bolted in the head and disembowelled kicking and skinned and hacked into chunks. You are letting this happen to you. You are letting them wreck you, wreck you. Cattle you are. At every turn they watch you. Every breath is regulated. Every—

No. Fight this.

He sips the coffee, eats half the scone in one bite, flicks through the paper. Hums to himself which draws a glance from an older-than-him couple passing by but he doesn't notice and if he did wouldn't care. Sees a picture of a young man badly beaten up, black eyes, swollen lips, one ragged with stitches, an H-shaped splint across his face. **HEARTBROKEN**, the caption says. **Damien after the beating**. His eyes dart and flicker across the text and then lock on to one word: *Gracie*. And then another word: *Allcock*.

He reads. The world around him shrinks and shrivels. He recalls spiked blonde hair, a glimpse of that, between crowding shoulders and he hears chanting. He sees and hears these things in his memory. They re-live for him. As the planet turns, they are coming together. And something new is happening: a new language is being born. A new way of speaking, a new lexicon, new words: celebutante. Sublebrity. Popwreck. These and the carrion-concepts they carry are entering the world through the cracks, the rents made as the people come apart. A fifth horseman, see him riding, eyes on long wavering stalks like a lobster and bearing a copy of *Heat* in a hand mottled by bulimia.

Fight. Fight. Boy's been beaten up and so what? Paper says it was her fault and so what? Does any of this matter?

Marie Gosney, does she matter? Look at the seagull. See his lizard eyes. His feathers. The way the light pulses in his primaries.

And with it comes a new form of illness. This he has long known. It is a thing, a sickness, that we do not have a name for yet. Maybe in a thousand years, the last minds amongst the ash will be able to name that which did the burning, that which set the flame, the flame that gave no light, that transmitted no heat. Choose to watch *Big Brother* or *I'm a Celebrity* or read *Heat* or getcelebsgetreallifeget*Closer.*

Fuck it. *Fight* this. You are—

You are—

Watch the trees and the birds in them and lift the leaves to peer underneath and you've volunteered for the bolt-gun and you wait in line with either a vacant greedy grin or an acceptance more bovine than a cow is bovine and that is not sane. What name for this. No name for this.

Oh my heart. In my age, this middle age, my heart is becoming as imperious and uncontrollable as my dick once was. Get me out of here.

Fuck it fuck it. Move. Breathe. There's work to be done back at the school. He finishes his coffee and eats the last bit of the jammy scone and bins the tabloid and returns home and changes into his overalls and watches for a bit the men erecting the steps for the diving-board platform and he studies the empty pool, the geometry of expectation, smooth and blank and sloping. Water coming in a week or two, the men tell him. Just after the kids come back. Water over the bones and lost lives, past lives. Children swimming over those bones. The daisy. I'm so unhappy without her. She's worth so much more than this.

He kills the day in work and when he's back in his house, tired and dirty, needing a rest and food and a drink, there is a message on his answerphone. The blinking light. It's from the woman he once copulated with to produce Ella:

Your turn this weekend. It's been six months nearly. Be here at ten on Saturday morning to pick her up.

There in his overalls, smelly and dirty, his hair matted and spotted with white paint and his face roseate from the sun, he listens to the message again:

Your turn this weekend. It's been six months nearly. Be here at ten on Saturday morning to pick her up.

With the whirlwind inside him, the whooshing faces blurring past, the glimpse of blonde spikey hair and the deltas of lines around Chloe's eyes and the colour of those eyes, the unique print of them, there in his overalls stiff with muck he listens to the voice of the mother of his child.

He showers and shaves and shits and eats. Tells himself, over and over, not to but he does walk to the Spar in the town for alcohol, wine and beer, and when he's on his final glass of booze that night he composes a text to Ella's mother: **am away this wknd. Tell ella sorry. i'll call wen back.** He thumbs the Send key. Sits in his armchair with his head in his hands, his fingers in his just-washed hair.

★

Jerry advises her not to travel to London alone but she tells him that there's no one she feels she can take with her to a Miss Wet T-shirt thing so he books and sends a car. Grace and her mother imagine, what, a limo or something, long and white with dark windows, but the car that turns up early in the morning is just a normal saloon. Coloured green. But the driver is wearing a uniform of some sort and the back seat of the car is spacious and comfortable and Grace settles in it in her black lacy La Senza bra and her pointy boots and tight Bench jeans tucked in and her jacket with the fake fur collar, the Diesel one, and her sunnies on. It's an early start and mist is hanging in a layer head-height above the fields and Grace sees and is slightly dazzled by a low sun through the branches of a tree and by the time the silent driver, whose taciturnity Grace is grateful for, turns the car on to the motorway at the outskirts of the big city just over the border to the east Grace is asleep and remains asleep for some hours and when she awakes, scum in her mouth, tearducts blocked with mucus dried to a crust, the car is surrounded by London.

—Where are we? she says, which, apart from 'hello', are the only words she has spoken to the driver. Same with his reply:

—Hammersmith. Well, almost. You slept all the way.

—Wow.

She looks out of the window at the passing city and takes a wet wipe from her bag and opens the sachet with her teeth and dabs delicately at her eyes, careful not to smudge her make-up. She takes a little mirror out of her bag and studies her own face in it then replaces it in the bag and takes a bottle of water out and drinks half in one go and she is driven through narrow streets for a while and many moving people and then the driver pulls up at a building, a warehouse kind of structure, and Grace gets out of the car and the driver says goodbye and drives away and she enters the building and a man with a fin haircut and pointy tiger stripes tattooed on to his exposed arms smiles at her and asks her her name and ticks something off on a clip-board and then gives her a sheet to sign which she does and then he directs her into a room where there are a lot of women Grace's age or a wee bit older all shrieking and laughing but their eyes are wide and dark and darting and a blonde woman gives Grace a T-shirt to wear, a white T-shirt with the word *Animal* on it. There is flesh exposed around Grace as other women take off their tops and bras in order to don the T-shirts and most of the bared breasts do not bounce but stare like bulging eyes from the top rungs of ribcages. *THROUGH HERE LADIES* shouts a man's voice and the women all made similar by the T-shirts and indeed by what those T-shirts just cover skip and scurry into the warehouse proper, the cavernous room, riveted steel girders supporting the vaulted roof high above. The crash of their combined voices hollows out, echoing, their unserious screams and serious giggles. The young women huddle like prey creatures on the concrete floor beneath the high and girdered roof and Grace feels the press of flesh on each side of her, cool and goosebumped arms on her cool and goose-bumped arms and all the women are same'd by the T-shirts and Grace sees men and other women with cameras circling the huddled and excited group as jackals might circle antelopes and there are some people too in uniforms outside a tent-like structure with St John written on it above a red cross and the uniforms are those of medics. Somewhere a generator rumbles and begins to thump and two men appear with hoses and a voice amplified by a megaphone shouts *READY LADIES* and a collective yell rises in response and then water falls and it is not as shocking as Grace thought it would be when it hits her, not as shocking, no, the pressed and close skin, the tightly mingled bodies, but her skin rises and her nipples pull away from the stuffed flesh of her breasts and there is shrieking and loud laughter from her own throat too and behind this noise she can hear music, Katy B, other dubstep, and some soaked women are dancing and smiling and their hair crosses their faces in wet slashes and some of them rub their faces and their eyes are lost in dark pools of melted mascara. Like skulls, like the empty sockets of skulls. A memory flashes through Grace's mind of something once seen on TV, a riot somewhere in the world dispersed by a water cannon mounted on an armoured van kind of thing but that is gone when a man with a camera appears in front of her and points it at her and she raises her arms to lace her fingers in her hair, her saturated hair. *WE ENJOYING OURSELVES LADIES?* asks the amplified voice and another shout goes up to bounce back off the high roof and Grace is dancing and she notices a girl close by with two patches of watery blood on her T-shirt and she is dancing too but one of the medic-looking people takes her by the arm and leads her over to the tent and as Grace watches the girl's T-shirt is rolled up, like a pelt, wet as it is, and there are two sneering mouths on the undersides of the girl's breasts, sneering and dribbling thinly red. One of the *Animal* people, could be the one with the clipboard, Grace isn't sure, approaches the girl looking annoyed and he takes her into the tent and is followed by one of the medics. The water has ceased to fall yet the wet women dance, they whirl and shimmy and shake their arses and snake their bodies with their hands above their heads to thrust out their breasts and the circling cameras pounce and snap and now Grace notices that there are some video cameras about too, and mobile phones held out towards the women who, drenched, dance and dance. The music thumps. All noise bounces back from the hard walls and the high vaulted roof and all the women made similar wetly dance and scream and laugh.

★

There is a smudge in his vision, a blur in the world as he works with the sun sinking before him, scarlet, orange. He removes his sunglasses and squints and sees a blackfly on the lens; speck with flexing wings, a miniature fallen rainbow caught in each. Violet sheen, light-trapping, shading to blue and to green run through with the tracery of vein, a winter tree made minuscule. Velvet sunset captured here, so small, so small. Squint. He blows gently on the lens and puts his shades back on and returns to his work: mowing the small patch of grass in front of the school gates. In the fading light. Metal blades whirr and severed green blades leap. Sinking sun heavy. Tiny flying thing.

★

It's when the women are drying themselves, half-naked in the warehouse anteroom, the wet T-shirts shed and dumped in a cart, putting back on their bras and tops and jackets, that their mobiles begin to trill. The varying ringtones leaping into the breathlessly excited eddy of their voices. Grace puts hers to her ear.

—All done, Gracie? Jerry's voice.

—Just, yeah.

—Enjoy yourself?

She laughs and before she can speak Jerry says: —Knew you would. You need anything?

—Yes! More jeans! Mine are soaked! Why didn't you tell me to bring a spare pair?

—Because I intended, fully, to supply you with such. There's a car waiting for you outside the warehouse soon as you're ready and on the back seat is a pristine pair of VBs that will fit you perfectly. Every curve will be hugged. Towel in the car, smellies, everything you need. The driver will bring you here. Okay?

Grace ruffles her hair into damp spikes with the towel. —Yeah.

—And you signed the release form?

—What?

—Did they give you a release form to sign?

Her tits look great. Compared to the other ones bared around her her tits, she knows, look just fucking great. —They gave me something. A piece of paper, yeah?

—And you signed it?

—Yes.

—Good girl. See you very soon.

★

The man who shared my name blew his own brains out. Blew his own head away with a shotgun at the age of twenty-seven and I was about that age when he did that and I remember hearing the news. The news. Where was and *what* was I, at that time? Sometimes I feel that I was nowhere and nothing. That I was born the way I am now, at this age, just a few years ago, with the grey hair at the temples and the thinning crown and everything, born from a car that spat me out in an afterbirth of toxic fumes, a poison placenta. Exhaust I am. Exhaust I will. A belch of pollution and there I was.

Ah, there are some good things, maybe. Falling through a blue sky, seeing the dinosaur in the bird. Voles and explosions. But there is a new realm in which we are at home and it is not the world.

Beauty lives in harmony, he has heard it said. Marilyn Monroe, Jessica Alba, someone; her forehead is precisely as high as her nose is long; the space between her nostrils and her upper lip is one third the length of her nose or so he has heard it said and seen it written and believed it. Like I heard and believed that my name was a combination of Lancaster's and Douglas's. Or did I believe that? I don't know. Or care. Yet the promises of goodness and of truth can be heard in the music, this too

I think I have believed. And so have and so do you, and so we are dazzled to blindness. Light bounced back off a scalpel. At home here, not in the world. So beauty's music is now the sound that the earth makes as its last hope flees. The creaking of a car door as it was wrenched open, the thump of an engine as it beat itself dead.

I can't go on I cannot go on but go on I will cos you *make* me go on. Kicking through the ashes, and everything is ashes, the dust from the flames that give no light or offer no heat these clinkers just about. And these are the endtimes. Not to come, here they are. You are in them. They are in you. Not by bomb and not by virus, not in flame and not in plague. Ashes in your nostrils, how they clog.

To live as much in the bombardment as without. The world is words and they are sounds only. From every direction and in every register they batter like hail but carry no weight of import cos what they bear is only you and what you want to portray which can be spun on the head of a six-inch nail because your world is you and that is all. Swarms of words and they shriek and clamour in a billion voices that speak, each to each and outwards, only one word, only one word. You blind fucking locusts. Cover your eyes so you can scream. Just one hollow hunger making bare bones of the world.

He floats on two words. Two words he hears that leap out colourful from the babble, the static, the endless fucking noise:

Gracie.

Allcock.

Gracie.

Allcock.

Two of the footballers who roasted her it seems are back in the news again because two of their recent sexual partners have blabbed to the press. One a prostitute, possibly trafficked, and the other a prostitute, possibly underaged. Sold their stories and there they are, young and dark, front page. The footballers' wives are quoted: *I'll stand by my man. No slapper will ever come between us.* And it seems that their football is suffering because their manager is making public complaints. *The boys cannot cope with the media pressure. It puts them off their game.* These words are quoted and they are in Kurt's eyes as they are in his ears, coming out of the lipless mouth in the purple face on the TV screen: *These are young men. They may be in the public eye but they also have a job to do and the media should just leave them alone to get on with that job.*

Yes but she choked them out. They touched foreheads together and looked into each other's eyes above her stretched and straining back agleam with sweat and semen and one of the girls says she was fifteen when she had sex with him and the other says she was trafficked from Lithuania and not only was he aware of that he specifically requested a trafficked girl. *Leave my man alone!* The jilted wife. Suspension from the game, maybe, what?

No because that would be an admission of guilt. We all know the dangers out there for wealthy and famous young men. My boys will be playing on Saturday, make no mistake about that. Get your head-lines elsewhere.

One shot, the man who shared his name. One twitch of the finger and it was all gone yet you *make* me go on. A storm of excrement. The eye widens and watches and it sees everything. All of your scurrying and squeaking is seen and is known. The swirling eye at the top of the planet in a place of ice and blueness and you call them *my boys* and you have no clue how true that is. You in your fucking laboratory. Ash in my shoes and in my mouth my eyes I choke in blindness deaf and dumb.

Gracie Allcock.

These words leap out of the TV screen.

Can you repeat that? The purple face leans. Hue of a mandrill's proffered arse.

I'm wondering, why do you think no charges were brought on your players regarding the Gracie Allcock matter?

Right, that's it. The purple old man in the tracksuit stands up and turns purpler and moves away from the microphoned desk shaking his head and leaves the room. Press conference over.

I will sit in darkness.

He folds the paper and drops it to the side of his chair and presses a button on the remote and extinguishes the television.

Sits there in the silence. Tastes dust and hears a ringing and knows it will not last, that these things will not last. How much does he loathe you. I will count the ways.

Here is my mouth. Stuff it with meat.
   Here is my anus, take it and tear it.
   Here is my skin – slice it rip it and rend.
   My eyes – fill them with filth.
   My ears – attune them only to howling.
   My wife and my children – destroy their lives too as you destroy your own.
   Here is my sky – scorch it black.
   Here is my water – make it acid, make it burn.
   Here is my soil. Salt it. And my totems; pound them to dust.
   My world, burn it.
   My future, drown it.
   My grave, dig it, long before I am dead.
   My neck and my back, stretch them out till you hear the bones crack.
   My lungs, my lungs, sear them with fumes.
   Here are my veins, fill them with raw sewage.
   Everything's negotiable. Everything's for sale.

*

She expected, what, a mansion, a *big* house, or if not that then a penthouse flat on the top floor of a high-rise with a view over the spread city all a-glitter, not this ordinary two-storey townhouse in a terrace down a backstreet just off a main road. Yet inside it is all music and babble and faces formed from television and pages, *her*, look, and *him*, too, *Big Brother* people, each face bigger and solider and more *there* in Grace's eyes. Some of these faces smile at her and one even leans in abruptly and kisses her on the cheek and asks her how she's doing but one with lips like burst figs and eyes like tarmac leans in at her ear when she's standing unsteady and wavering before the thick red drapes of the window and looking hungry and avid across the milling room:

—You're fucking nothing, girl, this face says. Hisses through a snarl. —Think you're all that juskers you fucked a few footballers? Anyone can do that, bitch. Anyone. Put you in that house and you wouldn't last five minutes, yeah? I was there five weeks. Five fucking weeks, yeah? Least I've done something I can be proud of, slaaag.

A long and leopard-patterned fingernail pecks the flesh of Grace's bared cleavage. It's not that so much as the snarl, and the glimpse of nostrils piglike, that startles Grace; this anger, genuine anger. Bits of warm spittle on Grace's face and those eyes all hard and gritty and a dark, dark grey. Storm clouds. Yet a laugh jumps out of Grace, a small yelp of a laugh from her lungs, and those dark eyes widen and the top lip curls back from the bleached teeth but then Jerry is back, with the drinks he'd gone to fetch.

—Ah. I see you're getting the pleasure of Bobbi's acquaintance, Gracie. How are you two getting on?

—Just putting her straight, Jel.

—Yes, well, you've done that, no doubt. Now toddle off and get yourself a drink. And this caution comes rather too late I'm sure but lay off the marching powder, Roberta. You know it doesn't agree with you. And you've to be in the studio tomorrow morning at ten sharp. Don't let me down, yes? Not again.

Jerry hands Grace a glass of something clear and sparkling. The snarling woman sneers at Grace and then takes her rage elsewhere and Jerry rolls his eyes all theatric.

—Good God. That woman. Why she hates the world so I simply do not know. Probably because she herself is in it.

Jerry's scalp can be seen pink and damp through the thin silver spikes of his crew cut. He is wearing a lemon-yellow polo-neck sweater which clings too tight to his nascent manboobs and has rubbed a raw rash on his thrapple. He is all, to Grace, tightness and discomfort and prickly heat. And he's in his own house, as well.

—So, Gracie, yes, as I was saying. We need you to look innocent, again.

He's said this before. Grace has been at the party for fifteen minutes, no more, and that's the third time he's used that phrase. And he has mentioned *Botox*. And he has mentioned *dermal peel*. He's asked her which school she went to and she told him and he nodded as if storing the information away in a mental filing system but he did not say anything more and Grace wondered then and is wondering now at the relevance of that. She's explored, quickly, the house; seen the upright piano, the artworks. Been bewildered and jostled and kissed and assailed by these too-big and fleshy faces, possessed of more dimensions and animation than she's accustomed to. The presence of them, when off the page or the flat screen. Noise. A lot of noise. And preen and approach, here, actions both rapt and slammerkin, all skin-tones variegated and exposed.

A young man, fin haircut, some swirly words tattooed on his neck, below his ear, appears at Jerry's shoulder.

—Fuck me. Gracie Allcock, yeah?

He takes the limp tips of Grace's non-glass-holding-hand in his.

—Fucking legend, girl. Way you took those dudes, yeah? *Free* of em. Oof. He shakes his head in admiration. —Pure star, you, end of the day. I'm not even lying. Great to see you here, yeah? Saw you chatting to Bobbi earlier. Giving you a hard time yeah? Was she?

Grace sips at her drink. Bubbles crackle and burst in her mouth.

—Course she was, says Jerry. —Someone sexier and more famous than her, of *course* she was giving her a hard time.

—Dog-rough, that one, the young man says. —Dog fucking rough. I'd still do her, tho, yeah? End of the day. I'd still do her.

—Yes, says Jerry. —You would. Now run along so I can talk to Miss Allcock, there's a good lad.

—Just want to talk to Gracie, yeah? Gracie *Allcock*, man. He snaps his fingers. —Proper special, man, yeah?

—You can. Later. But for now there are important things we need to discuss.

Jerry takes Grace's arm and leads her a few feet away from the young man, into a corner occupied by a spider plant on a tall tripod table and a sepia photograph of an old woman with

254

a basket and without a smile. The word *innocent* yet again leaves his lips. Grace swallows her drink, swirls the ice in the clear lees.

—Have you heard from Willy?

—What?

—Willy. Have you heard from him recently?

—He's in the States. But that's of no relevance. I need your attention, Gracie. Listen to me now.

She crunches ice. Another time he uses the word *innocent* and the word *Botox* and too the words *dermal peel*. He talks about the paps, about how they'll soon be after her again, following her around, maybe setting up camp outside her mother's house and so she needs to look good, needs to look clean, blameless, like butter wouldn't melt, like a sweet little girl.

—We need them back on our side, Gracie. Need to get them to fall in love with you again and to that end do you know what we need to do? We need to *woo* them, Gracie. *Woo* them. Lovely old-fashioned word, that; woo. Know what it means?

Grace just looks at him. A bedsheet ghost in her head. He shakes his head.

—Doesn't really matter. But you get my drift? And you're up for it, yes?

—Up for what?

—The, you know. The big-ringed fingers of his right hand flutter an inch or so before the features of his own face. —The improvements.

Bright light. Unconsciousness. A while of certain pain. But then the rebirth. —Suppose, yeah. Whatever.

—Right. Good girl. Leave it to me. Good girl. I'll sort it out. Now go on and mingle. He waves at a passing young woman in a black trouser suit carrying an empty tray and points at Grace. —Large vodka and Coke, ice and a slice. The girl nods and goes and he turns back to Grace. —Ask Melody there for whatever you need. What school did you say you went to again?

Grace tells him and he repeats the words with his eyes closed.

—Why, anyway?

—What?

—Why d'you want to know which school I went to?

He gives a little smile. —No reason. Or at least not one that you need to know quite yet so keep *this* little thing out. He softly touches the tip of an index finger to the tip of Grace's nose. Recent learnt reaction, from the time spent healing, she cannot help but slightly flinch. —I'm working on something. And my that's a wonderful job, that nose. Superb work. Now go and mingle and enjoy yourself. Any trouble from Roberta and let me know.

He's gone. Melody in the trouser suit returns and hands Grace a glass and smiles at her a bit shy. Too fat, she is. Grace sees the loose chin on her, the chubby cheeks, the epicanthic folds at the eyes. A proper chubster. Eat some salad, girl, yeah?

—There you are, Gracie.

Grace nods at her and does not say what she wants to say and sucks vodka and Coke through a straw. Melody makes a kind of nervous sound and scurries away and is replaced by the boy from earlier, him with the fin and the swirly stuff on his neck.

—Can't fucking believe it, man. Gracie Allcock, yeah? He snaps his fingers again. —Proper, man, quality. Fucking *free* of em. Pure trooper, you, yeah? The *shit*, man. Saw your vid and then saw that Dani Lloyd dissing it on telly and I thought beat *that*, bitch, yeah? I'm not even lying.

He has big eyes, brown and bloodshot. Grace hears her mobile trill with an incoming text in her handbag but she ignores it. It'll be her mother. Or Shelly. Probably her mother. She can wait. Grace is wearing her La Senza bra beneath her tight white lacy top and pointy boots with her VB jeans (the fit of which Jerry got soooooo right) tucked in and a Diesel jacket with a fake-fur collar pulled up around her ears and her hair is all spiked up and she knows it, she looks cool as fuck and that her nose is perfect and her tits are perfect. Botox and a peel, right, yes. Jerry's got a point. The innocent look. But fuck not now. Not required *now*.

—One pure fucking star, you, the young man is saying.

256

—Great big shining star, you, yeah? I'm not even lying. Comen have a toot with me, yeah?

—A toot?

—Yeah, a toot. You know. And he closes one nostril with a finger and loudly sniffs with the other. —A toot. Cocaine. Charlie.

—Oh. Okay.

He turns and waves an arm at Jerry, who is at the patio doors, open on to the garden. A light outside has spilled an orange wash through the black hair of the woman he is talking to and has made the canker on his Adam's apple appear more raw.

—Jel! Oi, Jel!

Jerry's head swivels.

—Okay to use the den, bruv, yeah?

—The den?

—Yeah. Just me and Gracie, yeah?

Jerry considers for a moment then nods. —Just you two, no one else. And lock it after you. That's if I don't come and join you shortly.

—Quality, blud.

Jerry turns his focus back on the tiger-headed woman and the swirly-necked man takes Grace's wrist and leads her across the room and up the stairs on which people sit and do not talk or if they do then they talk quietly, very quietly, eyes darting across other faces, fingers playing with strands of hair, their own and others'. Up on to the landing and along that and to a door which bears a small keypad. The man stabs four buttons and Grace hears a click somewhere inside the workings of the door and the young man pushes it open and takes her by the wrist into the room beyond. Closes the door firmly behind.

It's like a study. Big desk with a computer on it and a large leather sofa, green, arms and back crazed with craquelure. Three walls lined with shelves. Hundreds, no, thousands, of DVDs. Huge TV in one corner, various slim flashing silver boxes stacked on top of each other beneath it.

—What's this?

—It's his secret room. Jerry's boo-*dwah*.

—*You* know about it, tho.

—Yeah. Not who you know but who you blow, knowmean?

He sits at the desk and takes a DVD from the shelf behind him and takes a little packet out of his pocket and taps whiteish powder from it on to the DVD case. Chops at the little mound with the edge of a bank card.

—What does he do in here, Jerry?

—Works and wanks.

—Wanks?

Laughter. —Yeah. Look at the DVDs, girl. What else d'you think he does, with all this good stuff in here?

Muted music from downstairs: Sugababes, 'Push the Button'. Grace scans the shelves. It's all pornography in neat alphabetical order: *Anal Debutantes Volume 1* to *Volume 27* next to *Ass Blasters* volumes 1 to 14 and on to *Breast Obsessed* volumes 1 to 38 and so on. Hundreds, no, thousands of them. Grace takes down *Best Bi Far* and looks at the cover: a cock disappearing into a stubbly face, a heavily made-up woman looking on. She holds it up.

—Let's watch this.

The boy looks up and squints. —Batty shit? Not my thing, y'get me? Give it a swerve. Me do what me has to do and me don't have to watch that shit, y'get me?

He moves from around the desk and takes the DVD from Grace and replaces it on the shelf in its correct place and takes down a different one which he gives to Grace and then he returns to the big swivel chair at the desk and the powder which now slashes the plastic box in four white lines.

—That's the good stuff, yeah?

Grace looks at it: *Bukkake Babes Vol 6*. Grey syrup rain. She puts it back.

—What're you doing?

—Don't wanna watch it.

—Don't wanna watch it? That's the best one in the series, yeah? It's the shit. Taylor Rain, man, yeah?

Rain. Grey syrup rain. Some other day. Snorting noises, two of them, from the desk, then a big phlegmy sigh.

—Do your thang, Gracie Allcock.

He holds a little steel tube out to her and Grace goes to the desk and puts the end of the tube up a nostril and bends and sniffs. She can't see the title of the DVD but as the powder disappears up her nose it reveals a gaping hairless hole, blue-pink and gleaming. A noose of hair falls around her face and the boy gently fingertips it away. Then gives a little gasp and says:

—Aw man.

—What's up? Grace swallows slime, burning slime. The numb face.

—A thing on your neck, girl, yeah? On the back of it, yeah?

—What is it?

—All red and pussy, yeah?

His face, the curling mouth. Shock in the eyes. Grace slaps her hand to her neck and stands as if shocked. —It's just a boil, yeah? Just a fucking boil. Comes and goes, yeah? Don't wet yourself or anything. God. Just a fucking boil, end of the day. Get over it.

She moves to stand in front of a mirror, a big mirror on the wall above the mantelpiece. Turns her head this way, that way. Fucking *boil*. Pimple. Zit. Fucking boil. Bet Katie doesn't get boils. Bet Jodie doesn't. Bet none of them do. Botox, dermal peel. The pain of the nosejob and the titjob and look at this, this fucking horrible thing on her neck. Behind her, reflected, she can see the boy pouring vodka from a bottle into tiny glasses. Behind her, reflected, she can see the big wooden door slowly swing inwards and Jerry come in, with a grin and a girl, not the girl he was talking to earlier, another one, with hair dyed bright red and cut in a scruffy bob.

—Well. This is cosy. Room for two more little uns?

The girl looks self-conscious, weakly smiling, twiddling a tress of her hair around an index finger. Jerry gently steers her towards the big cracked couch.

—Admiring yourself, Gracie? As well you should, as well you should. A line, if you please, Sylvester.

Grace spins. —Sylvester?

—It's Silver. The young man's eyes are hard. From Grace to

the grinning Jerry, his eyes are flinty. —Silver, Jerry, yeah? You
know it is, man. That's my name, yeah?

—Well. Jerry hitches his trousers up to his waist. —A line,
Silver, if you please. A loooong one.

Grumbling. Grace doesn't think that she's ever heard anyone
grumble before, not properly, with no words, just unspellable
noises. She stands by the mirror with her back turned to it
and watches Silver/Sylvester chop out lines and she swallows
bitter mucus and her face is numb and quickly, very quickly,
she wants to go and sit by the red-haired girl so she does.

—I'm Grace, yeah?

—I know. I know who you are.

—Do you?

—Oh yes, Jerry says from the desk. —Belinda is a fan, aren't
you, love?

A *fan*? Fuck. There is a fan. Grace has fans and here is one.
Ohmygod ohmygod ohmygod.

Vodka, powder. Things fly. Everything hovers in a lilac light
and seems to give off a low hum. It is as if a glorious and
magnificent thing is waiting to happen. At one point Jerry
stands in the middle of the room, talking loudly and rapidly
about the freedom of speech whilst holding up a copy of *Throat
Gaggers 9*. Grace finds this hysterically funny and tries to hold
the laughter in because of the seriousness in Jerry's declaiming
face but it erupts out of her and then Silver joins in and then
so does Belinda and then so does Jerry himself. Vodka, powder.
A swimming haze. The room swirling like the ink drilled into
the skin on Sylvester's neck. Feeling triumphant about something at some point Grace does what she always does when
she feels this way: she reaches up and grabs something invisible
in a fist and pulls it down into her ribs. Vodka, powder. Thick
and shuddering haze. Jerry is sitting in the big swivel chair
behind the desk and Belinda is sitting on his knee. He is smiling
and whispering in her ear. Grace is regarding the ceiling rose,
the intricate patterns of it, and she wonders momentarily how
this could be but then realises that she is supine, on the thick
rug, and Silver/Sylvester is propped up on his left elbow alongside her and the index finger of his right hand is gently toying

with her navel ring, her new navel ring. Grace looks up and down at herself, sees that her white lacy top has been rolled up to just under the wired cups of her La Senza bra. Muted music from downstairs: Willy Roberts, one of his old songs, from his first solo album, 'Heaven', it's called. Grace can hear many voices singing along to it. She notices that the waistband of her panties floats a centimetre or so above the skin of her tummy, a span linking the stanchions of her hipbones, and she likes to see that. Notices and likes also that Belinda is watching her from behind the desk, from her perch; Jerry now has his pink face buried in her red hair and the two look conjoined, Jerry sprouting raw-neck first from Belinda's head. Colours that make Grace think of a butcher's window.

She slaps Silver's hand away. —Gerroff. She stands up and rolls her top down to her belt.

—What? Aw Gracie. Wanna get with, get with, have a thing, yeah?

She fixes her hair in the mirror. Behind her, Silver/Sylvester is mewling from the floor and she leaves the room, closing the door on his sounds and Belinda's stare. Willy's voice, buried in a hundred other voices, is calling her downstairs so she scampers towards that sound and she is grinning, on her numb face there is a huge grin. Nothing, any more; she does not need to do anything, any more, that she doesn't want to do. Nothing. A *fan*. How mad is this.

★

When people wake from nightmares in the films they sit suddenly upright in bed, eyes wide and wild, panting and sweating, hair in spikes, but that's not what happens in real life. In real life, you just lie there, curled, your face flat to the pillow, eyes open, and there may be panting and too there may be sweating but you'll just lie there, in the darkness, alone. In real life, there may be whimpering, and even there may be weeping, but you'll lie flat, alone in the darkness. You do not sit bolt upright in bed. There is no drama. It is not cinematic.

I cannot think of any other response. There can be no other sane response to an insanity such as this. When everything is demented and deranged whatever you do that is not normal must be in some way sane.

*

There is a car on the motorway heading north. Only two people in it – a driver, and, foetal on the back seat, Grace, catching up on the sleep she missed during the night. Her new VB jeans and her fur-collared coat have taken on a grubbiness although that is probably due more to her unwashed body and hair than to any real dirt in the garments themselves although they have absorbed some spillage and some fumes. Strands of hair lie like fair ferns on her sleeping cheek; one, loosely curled before her cracked lips, trembles softly like weed in a current with each gentle exhalation of breath. If she dreams, there is no sign. Peacefully, she seems to sleep. When she awakes, she will be close to home and London will be miles behind her, London and Jerry and Silver/Sylvester and the fan and the water, the falling water, miles behind her, miles away.

*

Not bomb nor plague nor invasion nor wave, just a gradual erosion until there's nothing left for death to take. No ash clouds or giant black skeletons of torched cathedrals and skyscrapers, no convoys of tumbrils laden with the stinking and jostled dead, no fresh mass graves in which the human forms combine to dissolve and end and re-begin in ooze. No skies black with bombers. No red 'x's painted on doors. No bodies hung from lamp posts on the motorways like he always imagined it would be. It has not happened in the ways everyone thought it would. But what you once loved is dead now and decaying with no chance of resurrection and what you love yet is sliding rot-wards with no chance at all of help or reprieve.

This I see and this I know. And if you cannot touch it or taste it it is not true yet I am *not* you. I am *not* you.

He reads his emails at the kitchen table, drinking tea, dunking digestives, the world outside shifting to light. The radio is on; the usual shouting. His home page yet again carries a satellite image of a vast swirling white eye and some stuff about the final series of *Big Brother*. Pete has emailed him: **Great to see you, mate. It's been too long. How did you get on with your one? Mine was wild, mate. Louise. Seeing her this weekend. All four of us together, curry and ale? Fancy it?** Kurt does not answer but he does not delete. Remembers Pete is married. Kurt returns to his home page and clicks on the *BB* tag. There's a quote from Julie Burchill: *Why do people hate reality TV, and* Big Brother *in particular? I believe it is mainly because they hate the human race in general and the working class specifically.* Kurt sniggers. He rolls a cigarette. Lights it. Looks out the window at the brightening, blue-ing sky as he inhales, back at the screen as he blows out. Is that what you believe, Julie? Really? Is it? If it's not, then why did you say it? And if it is, then why did you say it? Christ, Christ. In how many million forms does this sickness manifest itself.

Not in bomb and not in plague. No mounds of earth in the forest glades. What has been killed cannot be buried, has left no corpse. No bones to inter. This I see and this I know.

He reads some football news as he smokes then he turns his computer off and dons his overalls and leaves the house. Nearing the end of the summer holidays, now. No children here. The school is quiet, quiet. Birds sing. A blackbird; such a beautiful sound. No workers at the pool as yet, the hole in the earth that will become the outdoor pool, but they've sunk the railings in the concrete, the stanchions, whatever they're called, the elongated 'n's which will support the diving board two metres or so above the water and the seven or eight or nine steps that will lead up to that board. He can see them from up here, Kurt can; see them erected, sunk in the concrete, wrapped still in thick polythene, awaiting the steps, the seven or eight or nine steps that will lead up to the diving board. The parallel tall thin 'n's. And the hole awaiting water. The liner's installed, it just needs water to turn it into a swimming pool. He cannot see the lined hole from up here, sunk in the earth as it is, but he knows it's there. The empty hole and the seething bones in the dirt beneath.

You all want the drama. That's what you want, the ending in flame, in hurricane, because otherwise what meaning have you? No orchestra, no thundering crescendo to soundtrack a dribble. No touch of the hand of God in the sputtering, nothing of the epic in a damp fizzle. And even in your ending you want it to be else. Even in this, even in this you cannot accept. The sky will not crack. The globe will not split. The end has come already and still the planet turns. This I see and this I know and you see fuck all and know even less. I am *not* you.

The child-less silence is loud. There is the background roar of the motorway not too far away and some hubbub and burble from the prom and faint music from somewhere but the child-less silence is loud in Kurt's ears. A kind of pang in it, a twinge. It's a sound he likes, and misses when it's gone. A plane pulses above and he raises his eyes to the blue and sees sunlight glint silver off a moving speck with a swirling wake of white contrail. I am *not* you. I am not *you*. Beneath that plane the planet turns and also it shrivels, it shrinks. He could be on that plane to Peru. He could be on it to a tiny island off Scotland's far north, a scab of rock above the cold waves and that is where he would live. Build a hut. Drink rainwater. Eat seaweed. Watch the cold waves rise, alone he would be, away.

He follows the footpath around to the bike sheds. A sheet of corrugated iron on the sloping roof has rusted away from the rivet and begun to peel away at one corner and this must be replaced with the new one propped up against the bike-shed wall. Entire shed needs replacing, really, demolished, and a new one put in its place, but the budget won't allow. The spare sheet was delivered yesterday and painted yesterday, too, with anti-rust bitumen, now dry so it can be hauled up on to the roof and nailed in place, after the old one has of course been removed. Kurt takes the stepladders out of the bike shed where he'd stored them yesterday evening and erects them. Stands and looks up at the bike-shed roof, the sheet curling back like a fungal toenail. Then he pulls the new sheet towards him away from the wall and looks down behind it at the scurrying life;

the tiny tanks of woodlice, the red monobrow of a centipede. A cluster of red lentils and empty black triangles breaks apart into several scuttling harvestmen. Corrugated sheet leaning against his braced thighs, Kurt looks down at the quick and slim little world behind it for quite some time, in the child-less quiet.

He took the sleeping infant gently up from the mother's sleeping breast and held her dry and wrinkled skin to his face and so old it felt, wizened, the magnificent tiny sack of her against his hammering heart and he put his face into that skin and inhaled. So small she was, so small. *Ella*, he said. *My Ella*. He never imagined that her skin, newborn, not long from the fluid, would be so dry to the touch, as if the world had already begun to suck, and drain. And how something so delicate, so fragile and small, could be capable of such violence as the heart was ripped from his chest. He said to himself that you are me and I am you and every time this happens on the earth and a father holds his first child above the spent exhausted mother it is God's roar of infinite insistence and if I do not hear that now when it is so eloquent then I never will. And his heart became hers in all its bruising and desiccation and *now*, he thought, *now* – the healing of it can perhaps begin. Take my heart and return it sutured, my one hope, my only hope.

I am not you I am something else, and the heart may be burst into a billion bits but each bit contains a rage and a sadness. The heart is yet a well in which everything else that makes me me has sunk to the very bottom.

★

—There's so many of them. What do they want?
   —They want you, love.
   —Why though?
   —Cos of the Damien shit probably. And cos you're beautiful, yeah? End of the day. And famous. Or getting there.

Grace's mother puts an arm around her daughter's waist and hugs her to her side. Pecks her on the cheek.

—Where've they all come from?

—Newspapers and magazines.

—Yeah but where, though? All from London?

—Dunno. All over the place I suppose. I mean they're probably mostly freelance, yeah?

There are twelve of them, although it's difficult to keep a precise count, what with the milling of them and the blurring of their shapes behind the mesh of the net curtains. Some of them smoke and some of them talk and laugh and all of them hold cameras, in their hands at their sides like weapons or strapped to their chests like armour. They centre on the gate, the garden gate; at times they will singly or in pairs drift along the pavement for a few yards but always and soon they return to the gate, drawn.

—Oh my God look at *him*. That one there in the brown. He's got a bald head and a ponytail. The shame.

Grace twitches the net and will draw it back the better to see but her mother snatches her hand away.

—Don't, love!

Cameras are brandished and click. Voices, small behind the double glazing:

—Just one snap, Gracie!

—Over here Gracie love!

Grace giggles. —God. They're like robots or something.

—Yeah well I hope they sod off by the time I've got to go to work. Don't want to have to walk through them. And I don't want to leave you on your own, either.

—Why?

—With them outside? They're like a pack of bloody wolves.

—What can we do?

—To get rid of them, you mean? God knows. Can't you give Jerry a bell?

Grace just looks, carries on gazing through the gauze.

—Well?

—What?

—Can you?

—Can I what?

—Give Jerry a bell. Ask him what we should do.

—Okay. Grace digs in the pocket of her dressing gown and takes out her phone.

—Not yet, love. I've got an idea.

—What?

—I want to give them a piece of my mind first. Bloody vultures they are.

—What're you gonna do?

—Tell them where to go. Stay here. And don't show yourself to them, yeah? Leave the curtains as they are. They've picked on the wrong bloody person *this* time.

She leaves the room. Grace gazes. Sees, beyond the cluster of cameras and the people that bear them, where the road joins the promenade, a lone man stop and stare. He stands with his hands in his pockets and his back to the sea and he stares at the gathering of cameras. Something about him, his bearing, his carriage, flicks a thing like a memory in Grace but it is soon gone as indeed is the man himself, out of sight behind the seafront buildings the backs of which face Grace, their fire escapes and windows and guttering, features she knows very well having stared at them for close to two decades. The way the fire escapes zigzag, she knows. The ways in which the drainpipes sport strings of icicles in the winter. The feral cats that haunt the walls and the flaking metal walkways and steps.

In the bathroom Grace's mother applies make-up to the eyes and cheeks and lips, quickly and expertly. She ties her hair back but leaves a tress free on either side of her face to curl down on to each cheek and she applies hairspray to each of those to hold them in place. Her face in the mirror: Cher. No, not her; too old and haggard. Demi Moore, then. Yes, Demi Moore. She wants her once-black denim jacket now faded and frayed to a cool grey but she remembers that she put it in the wash yesterday so she digs it out of the ottoman and puts it on, buttons it up, then takes it off again and removes her hoodie too and picks a scrunchie up off the cistern and reaches behind herself to squeeze her bra straps together with one hand and tie them in place with the scrunchie. There; instant Wonderbra.

She regards her cleavage in the mirror. Glad of the sunbed sesh two days ago. Look at that; a vertical shadow. Looks good. She puts the jacket back on again and buttons it up, leaving some of that shadow visible, and then she goes downstairs and opens the front door. Cameras shoot up and click and whirr and thumbs flick and fingers twitch.

—What do you want?

—Just a quick word with Gracie, Mrs Allcock.

—She doing okay? We're worried about her.

—Like hell you are. And she's not in.

—Where is she?

—That's a fib, love, isn't it? We saw her at the window.

—How is she going to respond to the recent allegations?

Grace's mum stands in the doorway, leaning a forearm on the jamb, jutting her hip to one side. Cameras click and whirr.

—I want you to leave her alone. She'll make a statement when she's good and ready and probably through her agent, yeah? This is a private house. Leave us both alone. I'm asking nicely.

—It's for your daughter's own good, Mrs Allcock.

—We want to give her a chance to defend herself, that's all.

—And she'll do that when the time's right, not before. Now if you don't mind you are encroaching on a private dwelling and I'd appreciate it if you left us alone before I call the police. You're not wanted here. Go away.

She stands for a few seconds more, in that pose, the propping forearm, the jutting hip, the cleavage, and a few more shots are taken and then she spins and slams the door and goes back upstairs. Her daughter is pointing at her and laughing.

—What's so bloody funny?

—You. Encroaching on a private dwelling?

—What's wrong with that? They are.

Grace points and laughs. Her mother joins in.

—You've got to be proper, haven't you? Can't just tell them to fuck off and do one, can I? End of the day.

—No but. Big grin on Grace. —Just funny, that's all. You being all posh.

The cameras remain. Some of the men are studying their

stored images, sharing them with others, heads leaning down into viewfinders.

—It's nice, that jacket. You look proper special in it.

—Thanks love.

—Suits you.

—Ta.

—It's sexy.

—Dirty, though. Had to dig it out of the wash.

—You didn't.

—I did, yeah. So what? Nobody came up to sniff it, did they?

They gaze out of the window.

—Did you speak to Jerry?

—Yeah. Well not *speak* to him like.

She shows her mother the screen of her mobile and the message displayed there: **ok will call police in half hour meantime do not speak to them and stay inside jx Sent from my iPhone.**

—He's calling the police?

—Soon, yeah. In half an hour he said.

—What're they doing that's illegal?

Grace shrugs. —Dunno. Private property innit? Like you said. I like looking at them though.

—They're funny, aren't they?

—*Well* funny. Can't get over that 'do. Proper bad.

—When he turns around he looks like the arse-end of a horse.

Grace laughs. —You're not even lying.

—Shall I make us some tea? Might as well settle in, eh? Enjoy the free show.

When she returns with the tea and Kit Kats the group of cameras is half in number and they continue to drift away, on foot, in vehicles. When a squad car arrives an hour later there are only two of them left and a policeman talks to them and they move off, quietly and without any fuss.

—You've got to keep still, love.

—It hurts!

—I know it does but you've got to keep still so I can get all the gunk out.

Grace sits on the edge of the bath, head bent between her knees, hair piled up and clipped to the top of her skull to reveal the nape of her neck. Her mother hunches over her, over her bowed head, both thumbs pressed to her daughter's nape, squeezing the angry purple boil there. As she presses, the neck skin beneath her thumbtips turns white while the head of the boil deepens to ruby, the white head itself becoming shot with blood.

—OW!

—Just one more squeeze.

—OWWW!

Crunch.

—*OWWWW!*

Pus leaps. Some drops spatter wet and warm on Grace's mother's face. She's her daughter, this doesn't matter. Changed her nappy. Mopped up her sick. What's a drop more fluid? The liquid runs yellow and is wet-wiped away, clear and is wiped. A further squeeze and the liquid runs red.

—There. All out. We're down to the blood now so all the pus is out.

Grace sucks air in over her teeth. —It'll be back by next week, bet yeh. It always is.

—Well it's a furuncle. They never go away. Just got to give them a bit of a squeeze every now and again. Drain them, yeah? Grace's mother wipes a wet flannel over her daughter's nape. —Or an infected hair follicle. She dabs TCP on with a ball of cotton wool, three dabs, gentle. —There y'go. All done.

—Does it need a plaster?

—No. Best let the air get to it. Let it scab up and don't pick.

Grace stands, looks at herself in the mirror, turns her head to the left, to the right.

—How does it look?

—Better. It'll lose the colour and the swelling, soon. With your hair down no one'll be able to see it.

Grace unclips her hair, lets it fall. Turns her head to the left, to the right. That Sylvester; the prick. Sylvester: stupid name.

Click:

Botulinum toxin. Botox, Dyspart, NeuroBloc. Muscle relaxant drug group. Overdose danger rating: HIGH. Dependence rating: LOW.

A neurotoxin or nerve poison (?!) that is produced naturally by the bacterium *Clostridium botulinum*. The toxin causes botulism, a rare but serious form of food poisoning. Several different components in this toxin and two are used medically: botulinum A and botulinum B. Used to treat conditions in which there are painful muscle spasms such as hemifacial spasm and spasmodic torticollis. Also used to treat very resistant and distressing cases of hyperhidrosis, or excessive sweating. *Ewww.* Effects produced by the toxins may last three months until nerve endings are formed. Also used cosmetically to remove facial wrinkles by paralysing the muscles under the skin. Given under medical supervision by subcutaneous injection. Every two to three months. Number of injection sites varies. Specialist judgement necessary. Can cause dry eyes and painful swelling and paralysis of unintended muscle groups which are likely to be long-lasting and can cause glaucoma and weakness of the neck and head tremors. Weakness of the neck? Head tremors?

What did Katie say? *I don't need an expressionful face*, or something. And what did Jerry say? *Don't worry about it, I know a man*, or something. *A doctor. Or was a doctor, once.*

Everyone gets it done. Dannii Minogue, probably Kylie, too. Simon Cowell. Everyone. Women *and* men. It's no big deal.

Click:

Acts by blocking acetylcholine, the chemical responsible for transmitting the electrical impulses that cause muscle contraction. Skim this, skim this. Means nothing to me. A more relaxed and smoother appearance. Make-up can be worn immediately after the injection. Effects last for three to four months other site said two to three. This one's better. Headaches, eyelid droop, swelling, bruising. Trout-pout, what was her name? Ash. Leslie Ash. Looked mad. Like a fish. *Nobody minds losing the odd frown, but be wary of removing all expression . . . In other words, pick the expressions that you want to take out, carefully and sparingly.*

I'm not an actress.

In the UK it is only licensed to treat squints and other stuff and injections for cosmetic use are considered 'off-label' and a doctor must tell a patient this and take responsibility for the drug administered. Costs from £250 per area treated. Preventive and corrective.

Click:

There's Katie's face. Katie's face. I'm not an actress and I do not need expressions.

I know a man. A doctor.

Click:

Dermal peel or derma peel without the 'l'. Alternative to chemical peel which sounds horrible, dermabrasion which sounds sore. It's easy, it's easy:

Sun damage and wrinkles and scars can all be treated successfully with derma peel. Derma peel is a revolutionary new skin restoration process, often referred to as 'the lunchtime peel' because it takes only minutes to do and most people can return to work immediately after it. Lunchtime peel: an orange, then. Or a banana. Unique skin rejuvenation technique. Alternative to chemical and laser peels. Because no harsh chemicals or lasers are used to etch the skin there is no pain or needles or anaesthesia or recup, recupa, *recuperative* period or sunburnt look. Highly controlled vacuum and pressure moves microscopically abrasive crystals over the surface of the skin. Little or no discomfort. Outer layer of the skin gently removed. By repeating this process over the course of several weeks or, better, months, the younger, softer skin moves to the surface, revealing significant textural and colour changes.

Several weeks or months? *Several?*

Can treat:

sun-damaged skin
enlarged pores
oily and acne prone skin
acne scars
blackheads and whiteheads
age spots and brown spots
fine wrinkles
post laser enhancements – neck and décolleté

Neck and what? And no boils or not looking innocent enough, that word that Jerry is so fond of. Need to look it again, he said, keeps saying. Many times. Treatment time varies from fifteen to forty-five minutes, depending on the severity of the problem. Most patients require three to ten treatments.

Several weeks or months? Three to ten treatments?

Non-invasive, non-surgical. Softer, smoother, younger-looking. Immediate results.

Click. Teri Hatcher. A desperate housewife. Dannii Minogue, again. So many faces flat and bright on the screen.

Click. Click.

realitytvacademy.co.uk. Runs an intensive half-day workshop in London led by a Reality TV Casting Producer. *Being on a Reality TV show can open up many opportunities for you, from fame and fortune – (who doesn't want some of that!) or simply to boost your existing profile or business.*

Scroll.

Many people who have been televised on Reality shows tell us how much they have loved the experience. The phrase we often hear from people is **'This has been one of the best experiences of my life!'** *If you do get cast on a show you'll be looked after and pampered, you'll be the centre of attention, everyone will take an interest in your life and want to hear about it. Not only that, you'll learn lots from being with fellow contestants, experts and presenters as well as learning about yourself. It doesn't get much better than that!*

But let's not get carried away. It's very difficult to
Scroll.

At **Reality TV Academy** *– through practical and interactive exercises you'll be taught:*

1. How to find casting opportunities and target the right show for you.

2. How to create an attention-grabbing application.

3. The secrets of skip

4. Casting tips – how to avoid skip

5. How to make your own 'slice of life' video to catch the producer's eye

6. How to shine at the audition? (You will be filmed in a mock audition and have the footage analysed by a TV Casting Producer on the day) and . . .

You'll meet an Ex-Reality TV contestant for a Q and A session where they'll tell you how they were skip

Scroll. Click.

At Grace's back her bedroom window turns dark, cools as the planet turns to moonlight and the night presses itself against the glass. Beyond that glass and loose on the darkening world a cat stalks a rat through the alleyway, unseen, the focus of its green eyes fixed and unmoving as it lifts its paws silently and places them soundlessly on the mossy cobbles, aeons of care in that delicate deathbent tread. The sea's waves collapse sluggish on to the anti-erosion boulders on the beach at the foot of the promenade wall and, warm as this late summer night is, people walk the promenade. The high half-moon hangs yellow, highlighting in silver the cotton wisps that float across it and beneath. The bright salt of a few sparse stars. The solemn puzzle of this revolving.

Grace opens another window and checks her Facebook page. A message from Shell: **OMFG! UR ON WIKIPEDIA!!!!!**

Speeding heart. Click. Speeding heart. Fingernails scattergun the keyboard. Racing racing heart.

Gracie Allcock. Born. On, in. 'Roasting' video. Celebrity culture. Fame for. Model.

Fame. Model.

Fame. Model.

Grace bursts out of her chair, runs out of her bedroom and on to the landing. Leans over the banister. Shouts:

—Muuuuum! Come here! You've got to see this!

—What is it love? I'm on the phone!

—I'm on Wikipedia!

—What?

—I'm on Wikipedia! Ohmygod ohmygod!

★

What are they doing? That group of men outside that house. Looks like they've got cameras.

Kurt stops on the promenade, turns his back to the sea he'd been watching, watches something else. Between two buildings he can see the street that runs parallel to the prom and outside one of the houses on that street there is a group of men, about ten in number, milling, chatting, smoking, and yes they're holding cameras. Each one of them is holding a camera. What are they doing? A shadow, a shape, moves behind the net curtains at the upstairs window directly above the front door. Wedding or something? What's going on? Like a ghost or something, behind the net curtains.

He stands and watches for a minute or two but nothing happens beyond more milling so he resumes his walk, along the seafront to the pub at the end of the promenade by the church. He has a paper and a thirst and an afternoon off. Men with cameras. There are always men with cameras. What do they want. They mean nothing to him.

★

Grace's tearful anger has now become a sobbing, a bowed-head sobbing as she sits on the edge of the bed. Her mother sits next to her, one hand flat on her periodically jerking back.

—It's Wikipedia, love. Any arsehole or idiot can write what they want on it. Make alterations, like. Just wankers in their bedrooms, end of the day. Nothing better to do with their lives, that's all.

Grace sniffs snot. **Useless slag**. Some of the comments . . . **Pointless slapper**. The cruelty out there. The cowardice.

—Fuck em, love. They're just jealous. They don't know you, yeah?

Grace sniffs more snot.

—They don't know you, sweetheart. Just wankers with nothing better to do. Remember that, yeah?

Grace remains bowed. Her mother rests her cheek on her daughter's bent back, hears and feels the foreign heartbeat in the plumbing of her face, the life that came from her and is now hers to protect. It's happened before, this pose, this almost pietà, Grace bent crying, her mother holding her, face to shuddering back. After she'd lost her virginity to Robbie Rossiter and it hurt and it, the act, was cold. Five years ago, was it? Six? *It was horrible, Mum. It hurt. And he* . . . Something seemed to snap in the house, that night, in the mother's life, snap and lie in two broken parts. Never to be reclaimed, she thought. Never to be mended. Gone forever, now, is what she thought, that night.

And how to protect in a world of sharks? How to do that in a world of ravening beasts that you cannot even see?

—Don't worry, love. She whispers the words into the dressing gown stretched across her youngest daughter's back which has begun to buckle again. —Don't worry. Sshh. Sshh.

The humming machine and the sniffling and the boom of a heartbeat felt in a face.

★

The YouTube footage shows a large building, cavernous, a warehouse or something, with girders and high skylights, and huddled together on the concrete floor of it is a big group of girls or young women all made similar by T-shirts, each one the same fit and colour with the word *Animal* stencilled across it. Many of the women have their hair tied up on their heads though the footage is grainy, mobile-phone grainy, so each appears to sport a gorgon tangle of snakes or horripilating mane. They mill and huddle and laugh and whoop. On gantries running around the building behind the women appear men with hoses; big, powerful, firefighting hoses. Many of the women spot them and cheer. One or two shout *bring it on*. They appear to be waiting for something. A mechanically amplified voice starts to count down from ten and the massed female voices rise and then the hoses brace then buck in the men's hands and spurt water into the air and it seems to hang there for some seconds, a suspended wave, and then as it falls and smacks into the huddled women there is a collective instant of shocked silence and then one combined scream erupts and there is running and careering and hands sweeping drenched cables away from faces panda'd by melted mascara and the outlines of breasts and nipples and ribs and rolls appear too, of navel rings and muscles as the cloth of the T-shirts clings saturated to the rushing bodies. One woman sees the camera and runs towards it. Leans into the lens, her head to one side, opens her eyes wide and sticks her tongue out then stands so that the screen is filled with nothing but her torso outlined under the wet cloth, the twin swoop and curve of her breasts, her abdominal muscles, the nipples extruding darkly like switches. The screaming goes on, behind this trunk. Hands start to roll the T-shirt up over the flat tummy and then as they reach the undercurve of the breasts the footage stops frozen and is replaced by words: ANIMAL WET TEE! SEE MORE IN THE LATEST ISH! animal.co.uk.

Click.

God. Imagine it as acid. As falling acid. Or try, *try*, to see it as rain, a nurturing rain. No. None of that. Neither. It is neither of those things. But what it is is the plot of a story and that story is wholly new yet it carries the power of ancient pedigree and prophecy and if I have not heard it then I was born without ears. Deluge. Drench. Here we fucking go again.

He walks to the promenade for breakfast. Overcast day, the sun behind a thick hanging bank of gunmetal cloud. Swallows gathering on the wires overhead. If he could be sure. If he knew that they would come again. Newsagent's: newspaper, tobacco, *Animal* magazine. Drawn. On the cover; mainly Lucy Pinder's tits, but there are three small photographs beneath them of young women soaked, hair across their faces, smiles, all wearing the same T-shirts. One of them is Grace. It even bears her name: **GRACIE ALLCOCK IN WET TEE RAMPAGE!!!** Hair in her face but he recognises her smile, her new nose, the drenched pneumatic heft of her augmented breasts. Café: tea and fried egg on toast. He opens the magazine. Grace. Once that little girl. And there you are now, you, another photo of you inside, at the middle pages, how huge and lovely your smile is and you are rolling up the hem of your T-shirt above the chain in your navel and your tummy is flat and the wet material clings to, clutches, your gleaming skin. And the other women flanking you have smiles and tummies too and how made alike you three are with the T-shirts and the water. Making all things the same. The three faces of you, the three wet and beaming faces, so pretty and catastrophic. And there's another picture of another wet young woman with her head thrown back and there are two red sickle-shapes on her T-shirt, two small smirks of watery scarlet. **Oops!** says the caption. **Who couldn't wait for their boobjob to heal, then?**

The tea arrives, and the egg on toast. He blows on and sips the tea. Salts and peppers the egg and puts a forkful of it into his mouth and chews it and it is like dust in the way it draws all of the moisture out of his mouth. He forces himself to swallow and hears his own throat make an exaggerated cartoon gulping sound. His eyes water. There is a noise in his ears like that of a nearby but unseen motorway. Grace, Grace. Soaked to the bone. How you smile, still.

★

Grace is laughing, as is her mother. Grace is laughing more, though; she's covering her mouth with her hand. The magazine is open on her lap and she's looking and laughing at a picture of herself, herself all wet, a wet woman on either side of her too but she can see only her own flat tummy and smile and, wetly outlined, the arcs of her own breasts. Perfect, the shape. Her mother says it again:

—That's a brilliant picture, love. You look absolutely gorgeous.

—I do, don't I?

—Proper special. Lush.

—I do, don't I? Lush.

—Told you, didn't I?

—Told me what?

—That them arseholes on Wikipedia don't know what they're

talking about. What'll they say now, ey? Bet they feel stupid.

Grace gazes at herself again. —Can't believe it. Just can't believe it.

—Jerry's right, isn't he? Trust that man, love.

They are surrounded by designs: Celtic-style swirls and knots and bands on the walls, kind-of-Maori webworks and lacings. Birds of paradise, lions' faces, colourful fish. An octopus. Alphabets in varying fonts. Other shapes, many of them, on sheets up on the walls and photographs of some freshly etched into skin, the skin bloody and purulent in the camera's catching light.

—I'm gonna cut it out, yeah? Put it up on my wall.

—You should do. Tell you what: after this we'll go and get it framed, yeah?

Grace looks at her mum and smiles.

—And then I'll take you out for a bite to eat, yeah?

Grace beams.

—You seen Shelly?

—On Facebook, yeah. Loads of times. Why?

—Has she seen these?

—Dunno. Haven't spoken to her today.

—She'll be dead jel.

—Pleased as well, tho.

Grace's mother spins the magazine on her daughter's lap so that the flatter version of her daughter grins gleaming up at her. Thrusts her tits up at her.

—Wonder if Damien's seen these. He'll be well gutted when he does.

Grace smiles again. —Willy as well.

—Willy?

The tattooist comes out of his booth at the back of the studio. —Ready for you now.

Grace gets a peck on the cheek from her mum and takes the magazine into the booth. Sits in the big black seat.

—That you?

—Yes.

The tattooist picks up the magazine, holds it under the bright overhead light, narrows his eyes at it. Looks to Grace then back at the magazine again.

—You look good.

—Thanks.

He drops the magazine back into Grace's lap. Busies himself with inks and needle-guns. The seahorse on his bicep appears to swim as he does so, and the wolf on his neck to lope.

—I did your navel ring recently, didn't I? And put something on your back a few months back.

—You did, yeah.

—Happy with'm?

—Yeah.

—So what's going on you today?

Grace reaches two fingers into the arm pocket of her jacket and takes out a creased picture, cut from a magazine. She unfolds it and gives it to the tattooist. It's Cheryl Cole, touching one hand to the side of her face, the ink-squiggle on the side of that hand plainly visible.

—This what you want? The Cheryl squiggle?

—Yes.

—That's all?

—Yes.

—Same hand?

—Yes.

The tattooist sits on a stool at Grace's side. A sigh is released, two sighs, one from him and the other from the padded seat of the stool under his weight. He takes the needle-gun up in his right hand and rubs his bearded face with his left.

—Alright. Only take a few minutes. Give me your hand.

—Don't you need the picture?

The tattooist shakes his head. —No, I don't need the picture. Just give me your hand.

Grace does.

★

I am a lonely atom.

He is a man adrift.

★

280

Grace looks at Grace. She sits on her bed with her legs folded beneath her and her mobile pressed to her ear by the hand with the new dressing on the side of it and she looks up at herself on the wall, her drenched self, in a frame, behind glass. The bedroom light has put a small sun in that glass so she must cock her head to look around this mirrored bulb and see herself. Twice-flat and wet and smiling so big and God how good does she look? Grace looks at Grace. Smiles at her own smile. That is me, that is me. Made the cover and everything. My name on the cover. My name. *Me.* On the *cover.*

—I've put it up on my wall, she says into the phone. —In a frame and everything.

—As well you might, Gracie, Jerry's voice says in her ear. —You look stunning on it. I'm so very proud of you, kid.

—I'm looking at it now.

—You made the *cover.*

—I did, didn't I? It said my name.

—And only the centre spread! Couldn't ask for more, Gracie. What's the chatter been like?

—The what?

—The online chatter. Facebook, Bebo. What are the posts saying?

—Haven't looked yet. Don't know.

Her computer hums on the desk as it always does beneath the poster of Willy Roberts who now has TOSSER inked across his forehead. She'd checked the chatter earlier that day and had found no new mentions of her name, not even on the *Animal* website. But maybe it had been too soon.

—I do. It's glowing, Gracie. Fantastically positive. I'm right now looking at the feedback on *Animal* dot com and it's glowing. Log on.

—Is it? Okay.

—Not just yet. Finish talking to me first.

—Okay.

—Botox. Have you given it some thought?

—Yes.

—And?

—Not a problem, yeah? I'll do it.

—No need.

—What?

—Well there might *not* be a need. Yet. Hold off on it for the time being.

—Give it a swerve?

—That's what I said.

—Why?

—I have a cunning plan. I'm working on something.

—What is it?

He uses the word *innocent* again. Grace hears him say it. – Without chemicals, Gracie. Without any operation of any kind this time.

—Yeah but what is it? I mean what's the plan?

—I've been in touch with your old school.

—My school? *That* place?

—Yes.

—What for?

—All will become clear, Gracie. Just a few more tweaks to make, that's all. We're on a road that will lead to your becoming the Nation's Sweetheart, mark my words. Forget Cheryl. Forget Christine. It's you, kid. Or will be soon.

The N, and the S; she can hear him speak them big. —I don't get it.

—Get what?

—I mean all this shit with Damien.

—But that's exactly what I'm for. This is why I take my twenty per cent, sweetheart. I told you, didn't I, we can turn all of this to our advantage. It's a blessing in disguise. Don't worry about a thing. Oh and by the way, there's some wonga coming to you from *Animal*. It'll be in your account in a few days' time.

—Okay. But.

—But what?

—Well I mean what's happening? What do I need to do?

—Nothing, yet. Just enjoy yourself and sit tight and wait for me to call or e. Leave it all to me. It'll all come good. And check the *Animal* feedback now. Speak soon, kid.

End of call. Grace closes her mouth and drops the phone to the bed. Looks up at herself again, the image of her, under glass, on paper and under glass. Smiles at herself smiling at herself and then, for a second, remembers Damien once showing her footage of a skinny lad fellating himself, making a twisted 0 of his own body, a memory unwilled which she doesn't want and which she shakes her head to be rid of. She moves to her desk and sits at her computer. Click, click. Reads. More smiles on her face, her flesh face, not what it once was. Bigger smiles and growing as she reads. They love her, out there. She whoops and wishes her mother was in so she could call her upstairs to share this but she isn't so she texts Shelly instead. Facebooks, Tweets.

*

The headmaster is the kind of man, the kind of early-middle-aged man, who drives a Mondeo and refers to it in the feminine. He's the kind of man whose neighbour's garden fence is encroaching an inch on to his property and he lies awake in bed at nights fretting about it. He's the kind of man who listens to the Arctic Monkeys and calls them 'the Arctics'. Kurt knows what kind of man the headmaster is. He's wearing pristine white trainers and grey jogging trousers elasticated at the ankle and a brown leather jacket and he has his arms folded across his chest and he's leaning back against the workbench in Kurt's shed, the web-draped window behind him, dusty sunlight in a corona around his gelled head.

—So what's your opinion? What do *you* think? After some, it must be said, persuasion, everyone has come round to this bar Alison Hughes who continues to disagree and nothing will change her mind about this. I know her. She won't budge. But hey, this is a democracy, right? And I need to know what *you* think about this, Kurt. You okay?

He reels a bit, Kurt does, drunkenly yet he has taken on no drink. He presses a palm flat against the wooden wall of the shed for support.

—You feeling okay?

—Yes. I've been having these dizzy spells recently. Nothing to worry about. Just low blood sugars, the doctor said. Nothing to worry about.

—Can I get you anything? Some water?

—I'll be fine.

Kurt sits on a green plastic bag stuffed with grass clippings and bush trimmings, other brash. This will be taken to the local tip later on in the day, on this day which has changed utterly in the past few seconds. Composted it will be but for now it is a sofa, a cushion that Kurt sits on and wipes the sweat from his face and waits for the spinning in his guts to cease.

—Don't worry, he says, looking up at the headmaster. —I usually have some Lucozade tablets or sweets around but I've run out. It'll pass.

The headmaster gives a nod. He waits a few seconds, then reads an unspoken question in the caretaker's eyes and offers an answer:

—Well, we're a bit worried about security, I can't deny that. She's in the public eye of course and, erm, the nature of her renown is the kind of thing that might attract nutters, no question. There's the ex-boyfriend for one, what's his name? Local lad. He was in the paper. And the kind of 'fans' that she no doubt has . . .

He did it; when he said 'fans' he twitched his index fingers in the air to indicate quotation marks. He actually did this. The leather of his jacket creaks as he re-folds his arms across his chest.

Kurt rubs his face again. Needs a shave; the rasping sound. —I don't know anyone.

—I'm thinking of *you*, Kurt. I know you're not trained in that kind of thing or anything but all we'll need is a presence, really. And a keen eye, of course. But that's all. We can't hire an outside agency what with the cuts but we can offer you time-and-a-half.

Dust drifts through the space between the two men. On the slant, the drifting dust, each speck twisting as it floats and catching the weak sunlight in the oblique beam until that shaft has been traversed and the far left shadows inside the hut reached.

—We've thought long and hard about it, Kurt. Many of the teachers were of the opinion that she's an unsuitable role model for the young but when all's said and done she *is* an ex-pupil. And whether we like it or not fame counts, these days. It's not *why* you're on the red carpet but just the fact that you *are*. It's the way it is. Don't have to like it, it's just the way it is.

The headmaster gives a shrug. Another creak of leather. The silence of the school grounds outside the shed is loud, only the noise of work from the pool at the bottom of the field is a background thump and clank and groan of a labouring engine. Water soon. Next week, just before the children return. Five steps this morning, five steps up into the space, the empty air, where the diving board will be.

—I don't like it any more than you do. Any more than any of the other staff do.

—Except for Alison.

—Ha. Yes, except for her. But as I say, this is a democracy. And the agent was very persuasive. And to be honest with you it will go ahead whether you agree with it or not but I'm here as a courtesy.

—And because you need security.

—And that, yes. But mainly because I don't want to see you excluded. You're good at your job and you're essential to the smooth running of the school so of course you should be involved. Of *course* you should. Everyone else feels that way too. We spoke about this yesterday, for a long time. Couple of hours.

—Me?

—Pardon?

—You discussed my involvement for a couple of hours?

—No, that was taken pretty much as a given. I mean her coming here. Opening the pool. It'll receive a lot of media attention, not just locally but probably nationwide, considering the fuss. Eyes will be on the school. Might go some way towards fending off the worst of the cuts, you never know. Or at least stand us in good stead for the grant applications which we're going to have to make, now, no question.

Another shrug and creak. The headmaster looks at Kurt. As if awaiting an answer, as if now is the proper time to proffer a response. In Kurt's head there is a web, a vast web that forms a connecting lace across not just space but time too and in that lace are snared many things, many struggling things, and one of them is a little girl clutching a flower and her kicking movements send shivers across each of the million strands of the web on one of which is Kurt himself with his broken heart and stuffed head and on many others are other children with terrified eyes and looking so breakable at the hollow void and endless beneath the precariously hanging web. And a cracking iceberg somewhere. And other things, many other things, that the world has flicked off itself.

There is a faint buzzing from behind the headmaster. Kurt looks up and sees, in the window over the headmaster's shoulder, a fly caught in the sheet-web of a spider. Grey sunlight snared there, too. Kurt squints a little, sees the small panicked blob of the captured fly, sees the spider appear from a crack in the window frame and scuttle so quick across the web to crouch and hunch over the fly. The cage of the legs. The sucking sounds that Kurt hears, in his wide ears, the actual sounds of slurping that come to him through the mote-thick space. The giant house spider, give it its name. A male because the female is more reclusive and spins funnel-shaped webs behind doors and such, not these suspended silken hammocks. Buzz, slurp. Name it. That's what their legs are for, to catch your flailing dreams. Give these things their proper names.

Kurt looks up at the headmaster. Now is the time to give a response and that response can be nothing but one small nod, just one small nod.

—Good man.

The headmaster comes out of his lean, stands upright and pats Kurt's sitting shoulder with a hand. This is the first time that the two men have ever touched. Not even a handshake when first they met. Oh well. Buzz and suck except the buzzing has stopped, now, and the spider's legs are busy about the empty sack of the fly.

—I'll keep you informed of developments. And thank you.

He leaves the shed. The shed is brighter now; there is more light in it. Kurt sits on the bag of dying grass.

It's meant, then. Everything has spun itself and meshed itself all down to this. The story has an ending. Young Hot Hollywood, the website is called, and there is Lindsay Lohan, her face puffed with weeping although it looks like a severe allergic reaction to something. Hot, it says, Young and Hot. Yet Kurt's skin tingles with permanent winter. She's coming home. She's being sent. Salvation is too long to wait and everyone is bored. Ghosts whilst still living, quick on the earth and spectral. Phantoms with pulses and heartbeats. They have nothing to do so they spend vast amounts of money and use drugs to numb and drive fast and go in and out of rehab and marry each other briefly and what they once were has shrivelled and shrunk. What *we* once were. Young Hot Hollywood. What is out there. On the turning world. Online voices scream that Britney is a **skanky whore**. She breaks down and the billions watch. **Don't you just love seeing someone self-destruct in the fast lane? MWAHAHAHA!** Britney's words are *family* and *virgin* and *schoolgirl*, these words she owns now as she publicly crumbles. **Unfitney**. Her hair falling to the floor. **Britney's Beaver Goes Free Range**. And she wanted to look like Britney so her hair went white and she saw the ambulance and the crowd outside the house far away in California and she saw the glimpse of bare thigh on the stretcher as the blanket slipped and the frenzy in the eyes, such eyes, the frenzy and the hunger in all the staring eyes. She wants lips like Angelina's. Wants arms like Alesha's. An invented forehead, invented everything. In the humid brewery of her there occurred swift and unnoticed miracles: the apple she ate on her last day, the Botox pumped into her face, such things transmuted into muscle and fat, energy, the swelling of skin. Real time can never be fled from because it is always there in the biology and you will age and you will die and so she, like many others, hung herself from the banisters in her parents' house. In a hill town not far away. **MISSING YOU** it says on the website gonetoosoon.com. **MISSING YOU BABES**. Young and Hot and Hollywood. She is coming home. Back to the school, the little girl with the dress and the daisy and the scraped knee. Lives shrunk and shrivelled down and down into a full stop. Compressed into this. And this is what their legs are for, their many legs, to catch your flailing, fleeing dreams.

I see you cry and I see your mascara run. What do you weep, you weep black streaks down your face. What do you weep, you weep coal dust, ink. You weep ink.

★

—I emailed Rachel the other day.

—What for?

—She's your sister, Grace. She has a right to know what's going on in your life.

—A *right?*

Grace's mother nods.

—How d'you work that one out?

—Didn't have to. She just does. She's family.

—Yeah. Grace does an exaggerated shrug. —Whatever. Did she reply?

—Just now, yes.

—And?

—And what?

—What'd she say, *duh.*

Grace's mother spins the laptop on the table through 180 degrees so that its screen faces her daughter. Grace leans in to read. Six seconds or so later she turns the laptop back to face her mother. Drops her eyes again to *Heat.*

—Grace?

—What?

—You got anything to say?

—No. She can do what she wants, end of the day. Wants to disown me, I don't care. Don't give a *shit*, yeah? Calls herself a Christian. She gives a little snort, a wee derisive nasal noise, and turns a page.

Her mother sighs. —I just wish she could be happy for you, that's all. I really do.

—Yeah, well. End of the day. Sooooo don't care.

Grace turns another page, and then another.

★

There are voicemails, two of them. One says:

Mate, it's Pete. Haven't heard from you and I'm a bit worried. Get back.

He presses Delete. The other says:

Where are you? You're not returning my calls. Your daughter needs to see you, remember her? Eleanor? Your child? You tried to gas her, one time. Contact me as soon as you get this.

He presses Delete, then immediately wishes he hadn't.

The end of a hot and sticky summer in which the rhododendrons have grown wildly, explosively. Rose tree, the name. The tree of roses. And they scorch the earth beneath the bell of their blooms and if not controlled will spread in a riot, destructively, but pretty are their purple bursts, the scutellate lilac petals. He's trimming a bush back with secateurs; at the school gates this is so as to look welcoming and alluring but the bush has tentacled some of its branches out over the tarmac drive. How fast they grow. Like the one in the graveyard at the end of the promenade, yet there it has such rich fertiliser. Here, no such nutrients; but how it madly grows.

He must squeeze the secateurs hard because the tendrils are tough. He is reminded of potatoes, here, when the blades meet and a limb falls and he can see the moist and creamy flesh. Wonders if it harms the plant, or rather if it hurts. He is wearing thick gardening gloves and he gathers the brash by hand, scoops it up into a wheelbarrow. Tiny specks of life rise out of the tangle on wings or scurry on lanky legs or, grubs, roll on their bellies yet which is belly and which is back to a body that is but tubular. Which is arse and which is head. Aware that crab spiders often use rhododendron blooms for their hunting grounds he peers closely into a severed calyx, looks for a camouflaged movement. Twitch of a leg or palp.

It does not have to happen. Nothing is written in iron or in stone. It does not have to happen. The world will not crack if it does not happen no because it has cracked already yet nothing will be mended or repaired by such an action is what I mean. What I mean. The crack will stay. But nothing in steel and nothing in stone.

His shirtsleeves are rolled up to his elbows against the heat of the day. Sweat from beneath his baseball cap rivulets his forehead and face and he licks his lips and tastes his own brine. The new and fevered heat of the sea. Boiling point. More crabs found on the lower field last week and more starfish and jelly-fish, many hundreds of each, washed up on the beach and reports of a sperm whale washed up at a coastal town further south around a few headlands around which people have gathered to gawp and praise and worship or to do something else and the authorities now have no option but to blow it up, or so it said on the news last night. Leviathan not dwarfed by the cliff it lay at the foot of and scurried over by all the little people, all the little people made mite-like by their need. Blow it to bits for the scavenger birds and gulls clouds of which each night come calling from out to sea, come crying, the desolate and haunted sounds they make. And even apparently the salt-marsh lamb, those put to graze the littoral to sweeten their flesh, they too are moving inland, away from the sea, in raggedly bleating ranks. Boiling point. The heat, new and feverish. If there was ever once a watcher and we the objects of their scrutiny then they long ago turned their eyes away. Yet what is in you is not in me; something there is in you that is not in me or is in me that is not in you and in whose lights am I polluted? When you act like you do you lessen me too but who can judge this mix, unfathomably odd, endlessly strange, unutterably sad? And yet we need to feel that gaze upon us. We need at least to suspect that it might be there. By a prick-ling, perhaps. Or by an itching. By a scampering in my slow blood. And so they bought something that Britney had pissed on for $5,000. Because this is what you do. And I am *not* you yet when I bathe the filth I slough is yours.

Spider, crab spider. Ambush predator you marvellous thing. The unknowable patience of you. All your legs to catch us. Kurt raises a severed cerise calyx up to his face, gently blows on the petals so that they lift and allow him visual access to their undersides. No tiny shifting, no minuscule movement, just a released waft of rose-scent, sweet, sugaring the insides of his nostrils. He swallows to taste and closes his eyes then hears and senses movement and looks up.

—Hello there.

He returns Alison's greeting. Alison Hughes, with a little girl. Both are wearing floppy-brimmed hats against the late summer sun and both are wearing loose dresses of some thin material and Alison's is the colour of a ripe lemon. She is wearing flip-flops and her nails are painted plum.

—How are you?

Kurt nods. —Fine. Getting ready for opening day. This your daughter?

—My only one, yes. From my ex-partner.

—How old is she? Kurt looks down at the girl. —How old are you, honey?

The girl doesn't answer. Alison answers for her: —She's five. First day at big school soon, isn't it?

The girl doesn't answer. But she looks at the bloom in Kurt's gloved hand and then at the pile of brash in the wheelbarrow and asks him what he's doing.

Alison laughs. —She's curious, this one.

—It's okay. I'm trimming the bushes so that they don't get in anybody's way.

—Why? asks the little girl.

—So cars and people can get through into the school. Can't have the driveway all blocked up with branches, can we?

—I think it hurts them.

Alison laughs.

—What does, hun? Kurt drops into a squat so that his eyes are level with the girl's. Some sunburn has lifted a few flakes of skin on her nose and brought a constellation of freckles to her cheeks. Her eyes are deep green, the irises black-rimmed, like her mother's.

—When you cut them.

—You think it hurts when I cut them?

The little girl nods. Such seriousness in her face; the set eyes, the mouth like a shallow n.

—I don't think it does. I've been doing this for a long long time and I've never heard a plant say 'ow'. What's your name?

Alison answers for her, above Kurt's head: —Sally.

—Well, Sally, tell you what. You listen very closely to this and if you hear it crying you let me know and I promise you, promise, that I'll never cut any plant ever, ever again. Not even a blade of grass. Okay?

He hands her the severed calyx. Sally takes it by the stem and holds it close to her face. Kurt stands with a groan of muscle in his thighs and lower back. He's forty-two, not far off forty-three. The body ages.

—I didn't know you had a daughter.

—From my first marriage, Alison says. —She lives with me, though.

Kurt does not ask her where Sally's father is. He does not ask her what happened to him, to them.

—You're good with her.

—I've got one of my own, he says. —About the same age. She's with my ex. Bit like you. Your situation, I mean.

They stand and breathe for a moment. Kurt realises that he's still holding the secateurs in his right hand so he places them atop the pile of brash in the wheelbarrow.

—What you doing here, anyway? On a day off.

—Just out for a walk, really, with Sally. Going to show her the new swimming pool. Is the water in it yet?

—Not yet. Couple of days, I think.

—Oh. Don't think I'll bother, then. She looks down at Sally for a moment then back up at Kurt again. —You know what's happening, don't you?

Kurt removes his gloves and places them next to the secateurs and wipes his palms on the stained bib of his overalls. —What about?

—Who they're getting to open the pool?

—Oh. Yes, I know about that.

—They've spoken to you about it, have they?

Kurt nods.

—Then you'll no doubt be aware of how I feel about it.

Kurt nods again. Alison is looking at him, into his face, waiting for more of a response. Her eyes are so green.

—They mentioned something. But there's not really much we can do about it. I don't like it either. But—

—It's shameful. It's disgusting. I think that what that girl does for a living . . . What kind of role model is she? For *these*. Alison touches Sally on the shoulder and the little girl looks up for a moment from her flower and her eyes narrow against the sun and then she looks back down at her bloom again. —I don't see why. I mean, surely they could've gotten somebody else.

—Fame speaks, though, Kurt says. —Doesn't matter what it's about. It's the only thing that matters.

—Famous for being eff-you-see-kay'd. Her eyes slip sideways in Sally's direction. —By footballers and that's it. And for having plastic surgery. She shakes her head. —I don't understand it.

I do Kurt thinks but does not say. *I do. More and more and worse and worse with every single click.* —It matters, is the only thing he can say.

—I won't be going. I don't have to be there.

—It matters.

—What about you?

—What?

—You going to boycott it too?

—I can't. I've been asked to provide security.

—Security?

Kurt nods. —Keep out any mad fans or something. I'm kind of stuck. There's not much I can do. I can't really say no.

The faint twist of Alison's upper lip is like the kink in the blade of a scimitar. The green of her eyes transmutes from the colour of grass to the colour of flint as Kurt watches and he feels suddenly like he needs to pee. Like there are insects in his skin, swarming. Like his scalp is too small for his skull and might at this moment rip.

—Well. You won't be seeing me there. That's for certain. I think it's disgusting, what she's done. Alison takes Sally's hand in one of hers. —Come on. Let's go and see the sea. You want to keep that?

Sally nods.

—Thank the kind man, then.

—Thank you, the little girl says, looking up at Kurt's face. The tip of her nose gleams with pollen, dust, yellowly catches the late summer sun, the calyx almost as big as her head even with the floppy-brimmed hat. Kurt smiles down at her.

—You're very welcome.

—Good girl. I'll see you in a couple of weeks or so, Alison says. She does not look back at the caretaker as she leads the little girl away. Kurt watches them go, as he must, here, amid lopped limbs and flowers, motes and specks of pollen and fly aswirl around his sweaty head. He knows that he must do this, here and now and hot in his overalls, before he re-dons his gloves and takes up again his secateurs – watch the two of them go.

Alright, alright. It does not have to happen. Nothing in steel and nothing in stone.

He sits in his armchair with tobacco and wine. Before him the TV burbles and behind him, on the desk, the laptop hums. Not a purr, not a purr, nothing in its sound of any contentment, lowly shrill as it is. A whine. An insect that bites.

This person, here, advertising what is it? Some kind of celebrity gossip magazine: *get celebs get real life get* Closer, he says. Quickly he says these words. He won *Big Brother* a few years back; Kurt recognises his voice. Interesting social experiment. A parade of shattered dreams and failure, horrible failure. Like the Jade Goody memorial website which he hasn't visited for a couple of weeks, but if you're involved in the world. In its turning. If people fascinate and appal you. And the need in them, in those who post on the site, the naked screaming need of them and the billion others like them – how they diet and dress up and expose themselves and have bits of themselves chopped off and other bits grafted to parts where they shouldn't be. The endless dependence. If you're involved in the world.

And Jade remains dead. Returned to the inorganic condition from which she once emerged. Salvaged from the void of unbeing and *this* is what you do? *This* is how you spend your days? Oh the powerful and untroubled and formless nothingness from which the beat of your heart with its bothersome stink and stimuli dragged you. That cataclysmic interruption. Yet I am not you and I turn as the planet turns.

Alison's eyes are so amazingly green. And her daughter's too. Alison's feet in the flip-flops and the nail polish the colour of plums.

Let me take it away, for a minute or two. This is what I'm good at.

Kurt sips the wine. Red wine. Not going down so well tonight and it's making his stomach feel sour and slightly sore. Still he drinks it. Circumstances – if they had've been different. Alison Hughes. It's not too late. Not in steel and not in stone.

Lie flat on your back.

The machine behind him hums.

Chloe, again. Maybe. Maybe to see her again would, would what? A stay. A brake. A reprieve even, total. *Let me take it away, for a minute or two.* But time was up, the minutes calibrated in notes. It's her job; nothing but. And scratch a sex worker and you find damage. Always and without exception. Which means, which means, so if you—

Unexamined, leave it that way. Desperation makes us do things that we might not normally—

There are scratches on Kurt's forearms from the rhododendron branches and in the low light they appear black, black slashes, scrawls of ink. Shallow, just scratches, yet hieroglyphic for all that. He studies them, in the flicking light, turns his arm this way and that to examine. Strange writing. An alien lexicon. Words undecipherable scribbled on his skin by the tree of roses. As if to tell him something. As if to communicate yet what has he, what cognitive equipment, with which to read?

He sips the wine. Red, red wine. The TV burbles and the laptop whines. Alison, Chloe. Ella. Grace. The little girl Sally with the bell-shaped bloom as big as her head. Marie: was that her name? Don't touch me she said. I know this; that every one of the billions of grains of sand on the beach is glued to its neighbour by an infinitesimal film of seawater and in that film there is life so small that to it it is a vast ocean. It contains prey-creatures which shoal for protection and move and flicker and shimmy as one to evade predators because yes there are things like sharks in that film of water, so small that millions of them could fit into a fullstop. Between every two grains of sand on every beach. This minuscule life around us. Tiny, tiny. The mind cannot comprehend. Our big minds are set to spinning at such smallness.

He drops more wine into the sour pool inside him. Feels, hears maybe, a gurgle and a fizz. Raises one cheek to fart but decides against it in case he follows through. Feels like he might. Sitting here in a puddle of my own sour shite watching heads mumble on the television. Get celebs get real life get *Closer*.

The machine hums behind him. It's okay, it's okay. Nothing in steel and nothing in stone. Let me take it away from you. His heart accelerates. The whining of the machine behind him. He puts his glass down on the side table and moves himself upstairs into the bathroom where he rummages in the cabinet, past roll-on deodorant, razor blades, a bottle of aftershave. His face in the mirror; don't look. Close your eyes if you have to. He takes out the box of temazepam and pops two from the blister pack and bends at the sink to fill his mouth with water from the tap then he stands and throws the pills into his face and gulps. Shouldn't really, on top of booze. Can be dangerous. But he has. Fuck it.

He returns downstairs. Sits back in his armchair. Flicks through the TV channels and finds a programme about deep-sea fishing or something to do with trawlers and nets and bearded men and odd-faced underwater creatures. See it, there, flapping desperate and panicked on the slimed decking. The eyes and teeth of it. Throw it back, throw it back. It's not for us to see.

Let me take it away from you. Before he has finished his next glass of wine the machine behind him has stopped whining or at least he has ceased to hear it. In no time at all after that realisation he wakes up in bed. Daylight outside. Little idea or memory of how he got there.

It's the access. If you're curious, if you harbour an interest, this is what you see. From the insides of people's colons to the surface of the moon. A rectal prolapse to the Marsh of Decay. Cocks in mouths to the whorls of tornadoes, seen whitely and eye-like from above. This eye of ours, now. Our one enormous eye. Like God we are in what we can see. We have a monster vision. Only the fact of our dying remains.

And then you begin with the one word 'legs'. You Google-image 'legs' and you get spiders and crabs and solifugids and things which may be interesting but are not sexy and sexy is what you want right now so you return to the search box and type in the word 'sexy' before the 'legs' and click the Safe Mode off and for a while that's all you need, the tanned and muscular thighs and calves, the smoothness of the skin, the shapes like visual songs, something wondrously rhyming in the curves and contours. Click, though, and you see those legs spread. Click and they're *being* spread by strange and hard hands. Click and there are ropes. Click and there are slaps. Click and click and click and click and click and click and click.

Blunting is what they call it. Another new word for the language. Boys use it to describe how they switch off the analytical part of their brains when they are watching something specifically for arousal. Blunting. We know we are enjoying – the sweaty palms, the dry mouth, the racing pulse, the facial blaze – something that on another level we know is bad and by which our usual selves in the world would be appalled and ashamed. It's an altered state. A term to describe an altered state. Blunting. Click and click and click and click and click and click. This site here where American soldiers post pictures of dead Iraqis in exchange for photos of other site-members' girlfriends unclothed. A torn-off face in a bowl earns a **dude! that is some fucked up shit** and a sharp-focus image of a naked female torso. The navel chain, the ribs, the flat tummy, the augmented tits. The mask of the face with its empty eyes and bushy moustache still intact on the lip. Click and click and click.

And this is what you yearn for. You need to be told what to do. You don't know what to do unless someone else tells you what to do. What music to listen to, what designs to have drilled into your skin, what to wear, what to think. Cattle, cudding. Squeaking in ignorance you are, flopping and floundering, mewling, puking for guidance. So watch *me*. Watch what I do. This is what you're asking for. I am not you so watch what I do.

And, this night, the clicking does not cease with ejaculation. Drying to crust, to scale, the clicking still goes on. Click and click and click. *Blunting*. Let me take it away from you.

Click to My Documents. Double click on My Pictures. Front row, third from left. Squint and see the Elastoplast on the knee.

The yellow curls and the smile and the hands on the lap in little fists and the nose so small no longer that nose. Sliced away and burnt somewhere in a hospital incinerator. Hazardous material you made your own nose. So that the men could take turns. The rich men, the famous men. Up to me nuts in guts. Bitch gagged me out. The hand clutching the flower so tight as if never to let that flower go. Oof, slapping her, choking her, and she so agreeable. The falling water. The clinging cloth. Look what I've done to my body and my face. This offering. She won't be sitting down for weeks lol not like she sat then and still sits now for the photograph stored here in the whining machine two clicks away from the moment. Squinting a little, up at the sun. You'll live. A spark, again, a spark that flashes and catches flame. A flame that starts to roar although in truth the furnace began some time ago.

What is that noise. That rumble and thump. Coming through the open bedroom window a rumble and then a rhythmic thumping that drags Kurt out of sleep.

Naked he gets out of bed and crosses the room to the window and peels back the curtains. Scum in his eyes, his mouth. Crust on his lips. He looks out, over his garden, over the sloping field, takes quickly in the telephone wires with their bumps of birds, the swallows and swifts, the ancient trackways in their minds and blood reopening again, prior to their leaving. If I could be *sure* of their return. If I could be *certain*. In front of the roofscape of the town at the bottom of the playing field are three tankers, trucks bearing cylindrical steel tanks that gleam silver in the late summer sun. Thick tubes run from each of them, anacondas from their sides which disappear into the earth as if burrowing. Thump, a rhythmic thump. Kurt sniffs and can smell water, chemically treated water. No longer chlorine but what do they use? No matter. If you're involved. If you are curious. At the bottom of the field the water is pumped into the swimming pool, too far away to smother any flame.

AUTUMN

Move away from the sun. The planet turns, grinds on its axis, one blue-and-green speck in space. The light shrivels. There is a wizening of the hours of light. A metallic tint to the air now as if the heavy-bellied clouds above have imparted to it the nickel of their colour, the nickel and zinc and aluminium. Soon the leaves will fall and the grasses will recoil back into the earth but for now they take on the shades of blood and flame. Some kind of healing happens, somewhere.

Grace's mother appears, a small picture of her, in the gossip pages of a tabloid newspaper and on various sites online. At the house door in the denim jacket, the cleavage, the propped hip. Photoshopped, she insists; look at that double chin. They wanted to make her look rough. The hair like straw, black straw. The words **OLD SLAPPER** leap out at her from page and screen and she turns away and then it is Grace's turn to do the comforting, to rub and pat her mother's back, tell her of the sad and lonely arseholes and no-marks who sit in their bedrooms posting snide comments because they've got nothing better to do with their lives. Cowards, they are, all of them. Ignore it all. Think what *I've* had to go through recently.

Water appears, in the hole at the bottom of the sloping school field, making of the hole at last an outdoor swimming pool. Functional, with water; more than a hole now it is. Covered, on the evening that Kurt sits alone on the concrete terracing that surrounds it, but water slides from beneath the cover on to the flat tiled edge and moves in pulsing flat scallops across the flagstones, as if in the act of breathing. The diving board, two metres high, nine steps between it and the tiling. Brown slabs for the surrounds, the edges. The concrete terracing for spectators to sit at. A large stopclock mounted atop a pole at the deep end. The sun sets as Kurt sits and looks. Liquid fire above the roofscape. He hears the soft lapping of the water in the liner beneath the stretched covering as it settles, continues to settle. I breathe in. I exhale. Beneath the cover is the water and beneath the water is the liner and beneath the liner is the concrete and beneath the concrete is the earth and in the earth are the boiling bones. And soon that diving board will bear a girl. On it soon will stand a woman who is not the girl that she once was and around her will be the watching children, all eager to be other than what they are. That's where she will stand. Two metres or so above the water. Nine steps, nine steps.

Moving always away from the sun. Grind and creak as the planet turns and what is aflame goes on burning and what is drowning continues to drown.

★

—Ease off on the diving lessons, Gracie, Jerry's voice says from the mobile phone turned to loudspeaker.

—Ease off?

—Yes. Don't bother with them. Give it a swerve, right? Isn't that what you young ones say?

—Why?

—I don't know. You just do. One of those expressions that catches on.

—Ey? No, I mean why should I stop the lessons?

—Because Health and Safety won't allow it. They're saying it'd be too dangerous. You know what they're like. Won't let you dive in case you injure yourself. Nanny state, it really is. As if you're still a child.

—Oh.

—Yes. But it's okay; the shots will still look amazing. This will boost your profile, Gracie, into outer space. National press as well as local, they're all going to be there. TV news, even.

—The telly?

—Local, yes.

—You just said national.

—That's press. National newspapers, Gracie. TV coverage will just be local but that's good, that's good. That's more than good. Your star is rising again, kid.

Jerry's voice, in the handset, tinny and echoey on loudspeaker, somewhere in the humped and rumpled duvet. Grace sits on her bed in bra and panties, pink, matching, white lace edging and little ribbons, left leg folded beneath her and the sole of her right foot resting on the knee of her left leg so she can paint her toenails, glittery pink like the underwear. Toe dividers like abscesses or growths between her toes. Delicately she works with the little brush, slow vertical strokes on the nail of the big toe. Three spots of glittery pink on the white sheet by her left knee but she does not see them, focused as her vision is.

—Oh they're going to love you, Gracie. Love you again I should say. We'll make you look innocent as a newborn babe. You'll see.

—What's the set-up?

—Set-up? What d'you mean?

—What will I have to do?

—Hardly anything. I've already told you. You *were* going to dive in the pool from the diving board but as I say the Health and Safety bods have put the kibosh on that. There'll be schoolkids in the pool with armbands on and things and the press and the teachers etceter-*ah* standing around watching and all you have to do is stand on the diving board and pose as if you're about to take a swan dive, nothing more. They'll snap and film away at you looking gorgeous and that'll be it. All you have to do is stand and look stunning in your Shell Belle swimsuit.

—I don't have a Shell Belle swimsuit.

—Tomorrow you will. I'm having one couriered over.

—Oh shut *up*.

—I am. I've got us sponsorship. Shell Belle are donating the swimwear.

Grace squeals and wants to kick her feet but can't. —Bikini?

—Oh Lord no, not a bikini. How would that look, you nearly baring all in front of all the children? Press would have a field day. No, it'll be a one-piece. Beautiful garment, though. You'll be pleased, I guarantee it. I know you will.

—And when's this coming?

—Tomorrow. By courier. Sometime in the morning so be in to sign for it. You or your mum. How is she by the way?

—Fine. Great. And that's all I have to do?

—What?

—Just stand on the diving board in the Shell Belle?

—That's all you have to do. Smile at the kiddies and the cameras and look gorgeous. That's it. Simples.

—How will I get there? I mean, can't exactly walk down the street in the Shell Belle, can I?

—Up to you. You can change into the swimsuit at the school in the changing rooms or you can go down there wearing it. Put an overcoat on top or something. Get a lift off your mother. There's going to be security, too.

—That same feller?

—What feller?

—Him who mashed up Damien that time?

—Oof, no. I was going to use that firm but the school said they couldn't afford it so they're supplying their own security. Don't worry about anything on that score, Gracie. You'll be fine.

Grace slips the little brush back into the little bottle and screws it shut and leans forwards and blows on her toes.

—What's that noise? Like a wind. You outside?

Grace laughs. —No. I'm blowing on me toes. Just painted them.

—Ah. Good girl.

—Will you be there?

—At the pool? Alas, no. I'm to chaperone Aisleyne to a function here in London on that day. But I'll have my iPhone with me, of course. And I'll call you afterwards to see how you got on. Don't worry about anything, Gracie. Just be your usual super self. You'll wow them, kid. Nation's sweetheart by next week, you'll see. Shining star. Great big shining star, kid. I have every faith in you, Gracie.

She hears a fuzzy click in the duvet which tells her that Jerry has hung up. Shell Belle. She'll look lush in a Shell Belle. She removes the toe dividers and drops them on the bed and rolls on to her back and lifts her knees to her chest so that her feet are close to her face and she can examine the paint job. Nice. Pink and glittery. The ceiling light is sliced by her toes and she remembers feeling popping-full and rough hands and heated meat in her mouth so she rolls forwards to sit on her arse cross-legged. Stares at the crumpled duvet for a minute or two then digs the mobile out of it and holds it in her hand and stares at it for a similar amount of time. The computer hums on her desk, makes the little two-tone trill that tells her that mail has arrived in her inbox. Shelly, probably. Shelly Belly. Grace sits on her bed and looks up at the picture of herself on her wall. Behind glass. In the clinging cloth. Looks for a minute or two at herself regarding herself then moves off the bed towards her desk and the machine on there that always hums.

★

Rehab redemption. Public apologies from your public sinners and that is what you clamour for. Make such a fuss about. Humiliation is what you demand. Grovelling. Crawling. Mewling. Look at the redemption you demand and there is no surrender here.

Oh my brethren. My brothers and my sisters. The one family we are. Nature's pride, God's sweetest creation. That which all other life aspires towards. How proud of you I am, my brothers, my sisters. How pleased with you and the fuss you make. The universe itself swells with pride. Okay, okay.

★

As *if* she could sleep. As if she'd be relaxed enough in her bed with the images in her head like Xbox graphics speeded up, the resolution, crystalline and frantic. Herself in the Shell Belle. Herself on the diving board and herself in the newspapers and on the telly. *Local* telly. But still. They'll all be there, watching, all of them, the million faces she won't see looking at the newspapers and magazines and at the TV screens. The computer screens. Everywhere. All over the country. The world. Nation's Sweetheart. Into outer space. As *if* she could sleep.

Roundabout 3 a.m. she takes a temazepam, only half, doesn't want to be bleary and red-eyed up on that stage, and this knocks her out until daylight when her eyelids ping open as if starving for input. At some point in the night she must've looked out of the window and forgotten to close the curtains because they're open now, wide open, and a weak and slanting sunbeam has come to rest on her bed, its foot a lopsided rectangle. One thought enters Grace's head: *It's today.* She grins wide up at the ceiling and calls out loud for her mother to come.

★

As *if* he could sleep. As if he'd be relaxed enough in his bed and his head with the images hurtling across, her on the diving board and her in the newspapers and on the screens of computer and TV. He'd taken a temazepam with his wine last night, his lot of wine, and this had knocked him out for a couple of hours but as his curtains lightened he lay awake in the tangle of his sweated sheets and duvet and watched the images jerk and flicker on his ceiling. Sometimes the wind blows and the world turns with it and things get pushed together, driven towards each other, and if there is no message in such concatenations to be read and understood then the minerals of the planet itself are nothing but muck and no hand has ever reached pleading out in darkness. I am forty-two years old nearly forty-three and I am a caretaker at a school and I am *not* anybody else.

He gets out of bed. Moves into the bathroom to throw cold water on his face then returns to his bedroom and puts on clothes, boots and jeans and a black fleece and a black woolly hat. Takes up his tobacco and leaves the house and heads for the beach, the sea, walking the pavements he's walked ten thousand times before, hat pulled low on his brow so that there is no choice but to cast his eyes downwards. He does not see the school. He does not see the pool. He does not see the houses nor the promenade but he sees the shingle, the pebbles of the beach and the sand closer to the tideline where the pebbles have been pulverised over great gulfs of time. All that time to lead to this. This is what you've done, what you do. Did we deserve this ending? Have we not earned something better? But we made it. It was us. And what if there is something else and it is worse yet and she is there, what then. What then. He sits on the sand and pushes the woolly hat back on his head and looks out at the sea and to his left and to his right at the dawn-deserted beach and it is as if all the people have gone from the world. The sea lags and rocks before him, heavy, turning over itself in great greasy rolls. Birds in the sky, gulls, flying silently inland. Weak sunlight comes to the shore and allows him to discern individual items in the high-water scurf of weed and driftwood and plastic bottles: dead crabs, many of them, whitening starfish, small and button-eyed fish once silver turning now to colourless crepe. The birds fly behind him, over the town, like the dreams of its still-sleeping denizens or their souls released.

Rise, then. If you should rise, now. If I see the horizon lift and start to roll and rush then I would not move from this patch of sand. I would sit and wait and welcome the wet end brought. Last chance, this. Rise, rise. Send it to me and come to me and make me be no more because that's the only way to stop this and stop it you would unless innocence is an offence. An insult. Between each grain of sand is. Is. And this we know and have discovered so surely even that means that we deserve, have earned, more, better. But between each grain of sand is nothing, all joy gone and I would like to have been born wrong, like everyone else I see. To have been born with nothing but need. Not from that exhaust-belch and not before that from a woman's womb and not before that in a furnace far away. No point in asking why.

Sunlight comes to the beach. He watches the horizon and weeps for a little while. Sees shapes further down the beach: a large man and a lolloping black dog. The man is throwing a stick into the shallows and the dog is bounding in to fetch it. Heading his way they are. Kurt stands and wipes his face with his hands and feels the straggly stubble against his palms. Hears the rasp of it. Pulls the woolly hat back down on to his brow and leaves the beach and heads back to his house.

*

Grace leaves her toenails sparkly pink and as soon as it is open she's in the beautician's on the promenade. Spray-tan-tartrazine, waxed Brazilian, waxed legs and armpits and a tiny red diamond on a black background on each fingernail. The beautician suggests a vajazzle but Grace declines – the tight swimsuit and that. Make-up is applied, raspberry on the lips, smokey blue around the eyes. Her mother sits and watches and proffers advice. Grace's hair is curled and primped and left to fall in loose curls on to her upper back. You look gorgeous, love. On the way home they stop at a cafe for tea and a doughnut but Grace cannot eat with the nerves, the nerves writhing in her belly. Into outer space. Nation's Sweetheart. She hurries her mother up because she doesn't want to miss the courier and back at home Grace studies her face in the bathroom mirror. The perfect nose. The perfect make-up, hair. The perfect tits. The *perfect* tits. She's showered already but again she soaps and rinses her armpits and legs and between the legs. Applies deodorant, body spray, Britney's perfume in dabs to her throat and behind her ears. Hears the doorbell go, hears her mother speaking to someone, thanking them, then calling her name. She runs downstairs. Her mother grins and offers her a parcel. Grace takes it running back upstairs and rips the wrapping open and lays the garment out on her bed and looks at it then undresses and puts it on, steps into it, one glittery foot, two, pulls it up over her torso and shoulders, releases it to snap back tight and clinging to her body. The *perfect* tits. In the mirror: the halter neck, the underwired cups and spotted tulle detail at the chest. How *good* does she look. Because there is nothing else. There *is* nothing else. A whirling enters her head and she must quickly sit while it passes so she does, on the bed, hunched forwards with her face just an inch or so from her bare knees and when her vision has cleared, has calmed, she sees, on a knee, a small sickle-shaped cicatrice, little pale-pink scar that the spray-tan cannot conceal. Where did that come from? Flash in her head of a fall and a kind man and what, a flower or something, but then that flash over and gone, quickly gone, that flash, because there is nothing else. There *is* nothing else. Tiny scar, tiny; the cameras will not pick it up. Nail paring. Tiny. There is *nothing* else.

Head resettled Grace stands again, before the mirror. If they could see this, her in the black Shell Belle; Damien, Willy, Silver even. Them footballers. All of them. They will, they will.

A knock on the door and a voice from behind it: —Grace, love? Have you got it on? Can I see?

—Okay.

The door opens and her mother enters the room. Stands with one hand on the doorknob, the other to her chest.

—Oh, love. You look . . . I don't know what to say. You'll have them drooling all over themselves, yeah? Swear down. My little girl. I'm *so* proud of you. My little girl.

★

And what did you expect, at this last? A frenzy? What? A storm? Fine gush of words, a destiny-headed wall of hurtling water on which I would be flung? Roaring? What? I want to know because I have tried and I have tried and I have tried. And all there is is dullness. A numbness, deep and anhedonic. Weariness. Colossal tiredness. A thing once intricate and finely landscaped abraded down now to smoothness, flatness. Even now the words when there is very little left of anything. All burnt, burnt away. A numbness, just. Immense fatigue. Gone wonder is all there is. My absence.

He enters his hut. The shadows inside. The spider in its web in the window, waiting. There is a printed note on his workbench headed by his name with what look like instructions underneath and a padded black jacket in a plastic wrapper hanging over the back of a chair. He ignores the note. Removes the jacket from its caul. SECURITY in yellow letters on the back of it. He puts it on. Takes the secateurs up from the workbench and holds them in his hand. Leaves the shed, squinting into the sunlight.

★

Grace with her mother, in the car, finding a space in the lower car park, the newer one built to service the pool and the many new visitors it will attract. The bones of dead animals beneath the tarmac. Space for a score or more of vehicles in the car park but this morning it holds more than that, cars parked three deep, two coaches, some news vans. Minibuses, bicycles crammed on top of each other in the racks. A police van. A St John ambulance. Grace in her Balmain cotton parka, black, and her Love Label 'Katie'-style platform court shoes with the four-inch heels, black too. How lush does she look. She *feels* lush. And the Shell Belle swimsuit underneath. How lush.

—How you feeling? You nervous?

—*Course* I am. How could I *not* be, yeah?

—You look stunning, tho.

Grace lets out a little hiccupy-burp thing – the nerves – and pulls a face. —Ew God. I can taste treacle.

—Treacle?

—Yeah. Ick.

—Just blood sugars, that's all, love. Must be running high, yeah? Nerves can do that, yeah?

Grace gets out of the car and then her mother does too. A warm day, it is; Grace does not feel cold. The warm air itself seems to shift as 200 or so heads gathered around the nearby pool swivel as one in her direction.

—God look at all the people, Grace says and then wraps her arms around herself as if freezing. —Ohmygod ohmygod. All of them for me? Just to see me?

★

He moves down the sloping field towards the massed heads and the sunken surface of the treated water and the steps and the

308

diving board and the cameras. It's a warm day. He's hot inside the padded jacket but he does not take it off. One foot in front of the other. Silent seagulls in the sky above his head but he does not heed them. One foot in front of the other. Easy. The plastic grips of the secateurs a little slippery in his palm.

★

—Over here, Gracie love!

—Smile, Gracie!

Click and shunt of cameras. All the faces turned her way, the mobile phones held aloft. The massed murmuring.

—Hello, Gracie.

There are people around her, people with faces seriously smiling. Solicitous of her welfare and comfort, her warmth, asking her if there's anything she needs. Her mother takes her coat. With one hand on her mother's shoulder for support she removes one shoe and then the other and these her mother holds too. A man is talking to her, thanking her very much for coming. Grace can see over this man's shoulder the diving board, a flat plank above a pool filled with the bobbing heads of children agog, all eyes on her. Smell of the chemicals in the water. Into outer space.

★

One foot in front of the other. Down the sloping field. The crowd of people increasing in his vision as always they have done. For Ella. For everyone. My heart, my heart. Details of faces begin to emerge.

★

A man is standing on the diving board and speaking into a microphone which squeals and distorts his voice but Grace can hear her name and the words *welcome* and *privileged* and then the man is not on the diving board and there are cheers and whoops, lots of them and loud, for her just for her and her name is chanted a few times and then she is being guided, hand on her elbow, up the steps. Seven, eight, nine. She's on the stage. Above water and the floating heads of little children.

★

No eyes turn towards him, transfixed as they are. The pool surrounded by standing people and blinding from him the sight of the children's heads bobbing and rapt but he can sense on his skin their presence. The newness of their souls. He looks up from his boots, once and quickly, sees the top half of her above the pressed and watching heads. Sees her tumbling hair. Sees her arms outstretched. Hears the snap and whirr of cameras, her name being chanted, whoops, feels the heat from the lifted phones.

★

The children's faces below her, in the water. She sees them. Sees their waiting eyes. Flash of a boat trip with her grandfather when she was a child and the seals they saw, flash once and gone. Sees the cameras and the phones raised. Remembers the words 'pose' and 'as if you're about to dive in' and feels her arms lift up from her sides. The T-shape of her, now. Her left hand, the tattooed squiggle on it is not visible so she pivots that hand on her wrist to display the mark. Look; I've got it too. She closes her eyes. Knows that she is smiling, between light and water and amid all the many staring eyes.

★

One foot in front of the other. That's all. One foot in front of the other. Ignore the voices if voices there are. One step, two. Seven eight nine. Go up, go up.

★

The footage, mobile-phone blurry, scumbled, furs the skin of the girl on the diving board raising her arms. Her head tilts back a little, as if to look into the sun or to feel its rays on her face. As her left hand twists on the end of her arm a figure appears behind her, a figure in a woolly hat pulled low and a padded black jacket. The girl looks good in her swimsuit and she appears to know this; there is a confidence in her bearing. There are children's heads in the water of the pool below her, bobbing heads and little water-winged arms, some of which raise and point at the extra figure on the diving board, the man in the hat and jacket, behind the girl. The soundtrack of cheering on the footage falls silent as the figure looms behind the standing girl. It happens in seconds, three maybe four; one hand reaches from behind and takes the girl's chin and pulls it back to expose the tanned throat. The man's face moves close to the girl's, seems to whisper something in her ear or smell her hair. The figure's other hand makes two quick and sharp movements, two sudden punches into the stretched-back throat. These are the only sounds, at this point on the footage; the two rapid thumps. The girl appears unaware of what has happened and stands still with her arms raised as a hole appears in her exposed throat and in an instant dark fluid jets from that hole as if from a powerhose on pulse, strong spurts, four of them, five, catching the heads of the floating children below in an abrupt red drench. As the girl's hands start to claw at her opened throat the screaming begins, and the thrashing, the pool, streaked, boiling with the panicking little bodies and the heaving of the water as the adults leap in. The girl on the board falls to her knees then topples sideways into the water and above the shrieking and shouting a word can be made out, a woman's voice screaming one word: *GRAAAAAAAAAAACCCCEEE!* over and over. On the diving board, above the chaos in the pink-tinged froth, the man in the woolly hat and black padded jacket sits down, his legs dangling over the edge. It is a calm move-ment, slow and unworried, but then he raises whatever blade he is holding in his hand and starts to hack at his own neck and chest and face, frenziedly stabbing again and again. The screaming continues. *GRAAAAAAAAAACCCCEEE!* People appear behind the hacking man, his arm pistoning into his own face, madly scrambling to climb the steps and reach him and he falls backwards on to the board so that he is lying supine, his still-dangling feet in their boots kicking and twitching in the heated air. A crazed and screaming face fills the screen. Footage ends. Comments arrive: **best slasher movie of the decade lol!!!** and **OMG!** and **holy shit! see the way it shoots!!!** Comments from America, France, Australia. **mwaha-hahaha!** All over the world. Singapore and Ireland and Chile. **one way to get a facelift gracie!!** India, Norway. The whole world over.

LAST

Fame is a vapor; popularity is an accident; the only earthly certainty is oblivion.

Mark Twain

THE WORLD TURNS away from the sun and the light and up at its northern curve where it is all blue and white the crack widens and becomes a chasm. There is a huge calving. The generated wave throbs and pulses in the ocean and gains mass and speed. Satellite images show the trajectory of this energy and prompt a recommendation of evacuation from the town and others coastal and nearby or if not that then precautionary advice; sandbags, Scotch-taped 'x's on windows, movement to the upper floors of dwellings. But the destruction is less than feared and the wave hits and churns only the beach-side graveyard of the dark-stone church at the end of the promenade by the pier, which itself escapes undamaged. The water slams into the low cliff there, the very tip of the small headland on which the town is built, turns the red clay and sandstone of it into mud which collapses on to the beach taking with it a score or so of the stones with the chiselled names and dates and also the bones of those who once bore the names announced on those once-standing slabs. Makes of the beach a nightmare littoral.

Firefighter Rossiter, at dawn, stands on this beach, his mask making his breath loud in his ears along with the gusting howls of the wind and the surge and crash of the still-restless sea. A rage winding down, spending itself. The beach is visual aftershock around him, ransack, a demon scene: splats of jellyfish, a whitening scurf of crabs and sprats, driftwood, plastic in many forms, spread in a wet matted fringe worming to the lateral horizon. And what look like sticks, some of them, are not sticks. And what looks like jellyfish, some of it, is not jellyfish. Firefighter Rossiter sees the bleached dome of a skull extruding from the rug of seaweed; the cracked box of a ribcage half-buried in sand and mud, the pointed ribs a cage for a plastic bottle. Washed and cleaned by the sea these bones on the beach appear to glow in the half-light of the dawn yet others remain

315

red, brown, yellow, grey, such colours. Any remains more wet, fresher and more fleshy, have been largely taken by the sea or covered by the roiled earth and sand or have dissolved into nameless slime and this he is glad of yet he knows that the body bags in the Land Rover will later be filled with eyes closed or narrowed or averted from whatever might be on the blade of the shovel.

It whips, the wind. Wails and whistles around the peaks of his helmet, slaps his lifejacket and gauntlets against the skin of his neck and wrists. His exposed eyes water and, inside his mask, his nose runs with clear mucus. Nothing, nothing. He is thinking of nothing, or trying to; willing a white block of unmoving air into his head. The wind is carrying any stench away from him, further down the beach, and probably the bugs from any diseases too so he pulls his mask down to his chin and blows his nose out on to the sand. One nostril, two. Who would notice. Chaos, this is. This is horrible.

Movement up above; Firefighter Rossiter looks up at the frayed edge of the low cliff, the point at which the crumbling was arrested. Figures are gathering up there, hazy shapes in the spindrift, in the sheeting drizzle: policemen, hazmat officers. Someone from the coastguard. Environment agency, the vicar of the church up there, his white hair lifted up into shock-spikes by sleep and wind. Recognised, his face, from the recent funeral. Three weeks or so ago. All the people. Entire town almost. And the paps at the edges, that day, furtive and stoatlike, with their cameras and questions. Most shameless thing he'd ever seen. Or nearly. Awful day it was, and now here's another. Fuck it all. That twig, there at his boot. It glistens. It's a finger with a wedding ring. This is horrible.

He hears a voice shouting, almost buried in the low roar of the wind. It's his Crew Manager, standing further up the beach, ankle-deep in debris. He's beckoning with a gauntlet. Firefighter Rossiter moves over to him. Not wanting to look down at what his boots step and squelch in. The man mumbles behind his mask.

—What?

The mask is tugged down to his chin. —Ever seen anything like it?

—No. And I never want to again, either. The engine?

—Cavalry's on its way. Ten minutes, tops. Might as well go and get a brew.

They do not move. There in the bones disinterred and the uprooted stones and the dead sea creatures baring their bleached bellies and the plastic bottles and bags. In the anger of water and air.

—Guess what I just heard.

—What?

—On the radio in the Lanny. On the news. He's tried to top himself again.

—Who has?

—Whatsisname. That Curtis feller. Him who murdered Gracie. Tried to top himself again, in prison. Shame he didn't succeed.

—What was it this time? Another bleach cocktail?

—Smashed his head against the wall of his cell or something. Brain damage, said on the news. Shame he didn't succeed. Should've hung the bastard anyway, you want my opinion.

The Crew Manager spits a foul taste out of his mouth and looks at his expectorate on the sand. Toes something with his boot. —Christ. What a fucking mess.

—She's buried here, Firefighter Rossiter says but his words are yanked away by a blast of wind.

—What did you say?

—I said she's buried here. Or was.

—Who? Gracie Allcock?

—Yes. I went to the funeral. Firefighter Rossiter looks out at the fuming sea then back down to his hands again, his hands big in the gauntlets. —I knew her, ages ago. She was with me when I sprayed the dick and balls on the town sign.

The Crew Manager yells a laugh. —That was you, was it? Nod.

—I remember that. It was in the local paper, remember? Made front page.

—Long time ago now.

—Did you go out with her? A relationship?

—Not really. We were just kids. Long time ago.

—Says the fucking twenty-one-year-old.

Firefighter Rossiter does not smile. Cannot, could not, through the memory of skin and union and disappointment. A crackling comes from a pocket somewhere on the Crew Manager and he pulls a handset from it and shouts something into it and is answered by static.

—Say again!

More static. —Fuck. Can't hear a thing. WAIT! he shouts into the handset and moves closer to what's left of the sea-cliff and the meagre shelter that might be found there.

Firefighter Rossiter stands. Stays standing. Sees the churning of the grey sea to his left and the halted landslide to his right, large caramel ridges and runnels reset and half-protruding stone slabs and points and curves of strewn bone. Redder, softer bits frozen to the surface clay. The figures on top of the cliff have gone now but there'll be more, many more, soon, all over the cliff and beach. Such a mess. Such a hideous, horrible mess. Something moves, in the still havoc at his feet; a small movement amongst the carnage. A suggestion of jointed legs. Firefighter Rossiter squats and looks. A small crab. Greenish crab, scuttling towards the sea. Shell the size of the head of a tablespoon. It raises its pincers at the towering figure and Firefighter Rossiter looks down at the face between the claws, the stalked eyes, the small shifting plates of its mouth. Never to be known. Such a face. He watches it watching him as it scurries, pincers raised and outspread, across a gravestone half-concealed by ripped bladderwrack, a new stone, clean, marble. Some words can be read on it, gold lettering, clearly carven still, not blurred as yet by the weather's erasure:

IN LOVING MEM
GRACE ALL
BORN 3rd MAR
DIED 11th OCTO
WE WILL NEV
YOU BROU
EVERLAS
TIL WE
IN GOD

With a gauntleted hand Firefighter Rossiter brushes the weed away from the stone, reads the rest of the inscription and the faded marker-pen comments scrawled next to and in between the lines of it: *our Gracie* and *missing you* and *stay gorgoes in heavin*. He reveals another jellyfish except it's not a jellyfish, no markings, no tentacles. He picks it up, holds it in his palm. Regards it. Shifts from his squat into a kneeling position. Feels soft pops of seaweed bladders under and against his knees and it is a bladder of sorts that he holds in his hand, his hand in the heavy glove, a bag of clear fluid it is, a kind of muscular heft to it, meatily resilient. It clings to the contours of his armoured glove, yields slowly to pressure.

—What on earth's that?

Firefighter Rossiter does not look up at his Crew Manager. Kneeling there in the dead and dying things, the wet and battered things, angry air howling in his ears and slapping his damp and stinging face.

—What is it? Horrible bloody thing.

—It's silicone.

—What?

—It's a bag of silicone. It never rots. I've read about it.

—What's it doing here?

Firefighter Rossiter now looks up at his Crew Manager. The jelly-like thing squidged in his glove. —Don't you know?

—Should I?

—It's from someone's boobjob. There'll be another one around somewhere. They'll never rot.

—Oh bloody hell. Jesus Christ. The Crew Manager shakes his head. —Can this day get any worse? Chuck the bloody thing away before it gives you a disease. And what are you doing on your knees? You feeling okay?

—Yes. Just came over a bit faint, that's all. It'll pass.

—Alright. Well get a move on cos the engine's here.

—Okay. I'll see you up there.

The wind dies. Firefighter Rossiter, in the hiatus, listens to the crunch and squish of the Crew Manager's boots as he walks away. Hears, almost lost in the thick and agitated air, an engine somewhere nearby chug into life and thump and strain. Feels

319

the smart of flung brine on his face, his cheeks and eyelids and forehead. Looks at the thing he holds in his hand. Skin and union. Disappointing for them both. EVERLAS TIL IN GOD.

He lets the jellybag slide from his fingers. —Fuck it, he says in a voice so small that it is lost utterly in this dark morning, this strange and terrible dark morning of awful proofs and reappearances. —Fuck everything.

ACKNOWLEDGMENTS

Big thanks to:

My brother, for allowing me to endlessly bend his ear about this book while stuck in a van on the Nullarboor Plain (but not for repeatedly stinking the van out):
Jay Griffiths: Penny Rimbaud: Jim Perrin: Paul Evans, whose writing, especially on toads, was inspiring:
in Portland, Sexbomb Dave Parry, Ceri Shaw, Gaabi Becket, and her wonderful folks; Willy Vlautin and Lee in Portland and Scapoose:
in Chicago, Dave Parry, Jon Langford, Irvine and Beth:
Lisa Blower and Dave:
the Royal Society of Authors and the Royal Literary Fund, without whose generosity the writing of this book would've left me a sad and hopeless husk:
Viv and Richard Greaves:
aunties Jackie and Val, uncle Lee:
and the inventors of Citalopram (I'd never suspected feeling normal could feel so good).

Be happy.

www.vintage-books.co.uk